MW00474740

PRAISE FOR
PATRICIA RAYBON

"History and mystery come together with heart-gripping perfection in Patricia Raybon's *Truth Be Told*. While heroine Annalee Spain seeks justice for a young murder victim, she herself must navigate a segregated and dangerous world. Yet through Raybon's skillful storytelling, we are reminded that with faith, truth, and courage, even the darkest shadows can be overcome with Light."

MICHELLE SHOCKLEE, *Christianity Today* Book Award–winning author of *Count the Nights by Stars*

"This story grabs you right at the beginning and takes you on a ride full of plot twists and turns, keeping Annalee Spain—and readers—constantly wading through waist-high trouble that's 'determined,' 'insistent,' and 'insidious.' Yet Raybon makes it clear that all the answers can be found by seeking Jesus, a search that mirrors our own need for ultimate Truth and a deeper relationship with the One who knows and loves us best."

ROBIN W. PEARSON, Christy Award–winning author of *Walking in Tall Weeds*, on *Double the Lies*

"In Annalee Spain, Patricia Raybon has given us not only an unflinching perspective of reality for many African Americans in the 1920s but also a self-determined heroine intent on fulfilling the role to which God has called her—regardless of the social landscape. This richly layered mystery set against the backdrop of Klan-run Colorado will leave readers breathless, guessing, and desperately awaiting the next installment. A truly magnificent read."

JENNIFER L. WRIGHT, author of *Come Down Somewhere*, on *Double the Lies*

"Patricia Raybon's second adventure for her intrepid sleuth, Annalee Spain, is historical mystery at its finest. Annalee's unique voice propels us through her Sherlockian detective work, the mysteries of her past, and her place in a hostile world of racial injustice. *Double the Lies* is double the action, double the intrigue, and double the insight into the human heart. A must-read!"

STEPHANIE LANDSEM, author of *In a Far-Off Land*

"Inside masterful storytelling, Patricia Raybon conveys a critical lesson of what transpired when the KKK used its powerful influence to sew racial hatred and segregation throughout Colorado's very fabric. A suspenseful and enlightening read about dangerous and ignorant times. Annalee Spain is an unforgettable protagonist."

DONNELL ANN BELL, award-winning author of *Until Dead*, on *Double the Lies*

"This story of Professor Annalee Spain seeking to solve her father's cold case murder is one you won't want to put down."

STEPHEN CURRY on *All That Is Secret*

"This fast-paced mystery beautifully evokes life in 1920s Denver. Spunky Annalee proves a resourceful and intrepid heroine and her allies are fully fleshed individuals. Raybon's lively style keeps the novel moving while shining a light on a sad epoch in American life that still reverberates a century later. I'll look forward to Annalee's next case!"

HISTORICAL NOVEL SOCIETY on *All That Is Secret*

"Patricia Raybon's first novel was created for those who crave nuggets of history."

BTS CELEBS on *All That Is Secret*

"A fast-moving story that's rich with romance and spiritual searching and sumptuous descriptions of 1920s fashion, buildings, and culture."

SUJATA MASSEY, award-winning author of *The Bombay Prince*, on *All That Is Secret*

"An engrossing, thrilling 1920s murder mystery. Patricia Raybon's novel races across its Denver landscape at an exhilarating pace with an unforgettable protagonist, Professor Annalee Spain, at the wheel. The story of Annalee's murder mystery is captivating, the history of the western city's racial divide enlightening. This intrepid sleuth would certainly give Sherlock Holmes a run for his money."

SOPHFRONIA SCOTT, author of *Unforgivable Love*, on *All That Is Secret*

"In Professor Annalee Spain, Patricia Raybon has created a real, rounded, and very human character. . . . Not only a good mystery, but a realistic insight into the African American experience in the 1920s."

RHYS BOWEN, *New York Times* bestselling author of the Molly Murphy and Royal Spyness mysteries, on *All That Is Secret*

"Readers will be hooked from the first line of Patricia Raybon's captivating debut novel, *All That Is Secret*. This well-respected nonfiction author proves her worth with fiction as she delivers rich characters and a page-turning mystery set in the beautiful wilds of Colorado."

JULIE CANTRELL, *New York Times* and *USA Today* bestselling author of *Perennials*

"A winner. Patricia Raybon's *All That Is Secret* is a fast-paced, intriguing mystery that grabs and holds the reader from the opening."

MANUEL RAMOS, author of *Angels in the Wind*

"It's the rare journalist who can succeed at also crafting compelling fiction. But that's what Raybon has done here with *All That Is Secret*, an engaging, evocative period piece as timely as tomorrow's news. Brava, Patricia, for weaving a tale as instructive as it is captivating."

JERRY B. JENKINS, *New York Times* bestselling author

"Patricia Raybon is a masterful storyteller. She is a standard-bearer for honesty as she takes her readers on a journey with an amateur sleuth who has the potential to change our perspectives and help us solve the mystery of how to come together and heal. I highly recommend it!"

DR. BRENDA SALTER McNEIL, author of *Becoming Brave: Finding the Courage to Pursue Racial Justice Now*, on *All That Is Secret*

TRUTH BE TOLD

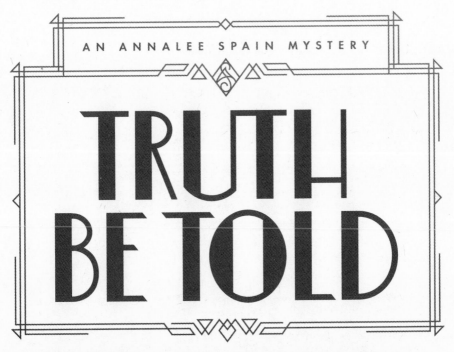

AN ANNALEE SPAIN MYSTERY

TRUTH BE TOLD

PATRICIA RAYBON

Tyndale House Publishers
Carol Stream, Illinois

Visit Tyndale online at tyndale.com.

Visit Patricia Raybon's website at patriciaraybon.com.

Tyndale and Tyndale's quill logo are registered trademarks of Tyndale House Ministries.

Truth Be Told

Designed by Lindsey Bergsma

Edited by Sarah Mason Rische

Published in association with the literary agency of WordServe Literary Group, www.wordserveliterary.com.

Scripture quotations are taken from the *Holy Bible*, King James Version.

Truth Be Told is a work of fiction. Where real people, events, establishments, organizations, or locales appear, they are used fictitiously. All other elements of the novel are drawn from the author's imagination.

For information about special discounts for bulk purchases, please contact Tyndale House Publishers at csresponse@tyndale.com, or call 1-855-277-9400.

Library of Congress Cataloging-in-Publication Data

A catalog record for this book is available from the Library of Congress.

ISBN 978-1-4964-5847-6 (HC)

ISBN 978-1-4964-5848-3 (SC)

Printed in the United States of America

30	29	28	27	26	25	24
7	6	5	4	3	2	1

To all willing to know the truth
about their past, for the present.

"Fret not thyself because of evildoers . . . for they shall soon be cut down like the grass, and wither as the green herb."

PSALM 37:1-2

PROLOGUE

THE LETTER FROM HER MOTHER arrived in a bad way. It was buried in dirt, lying inside a rusted metal box, covered under tangled weeds and dust near her little Denver cabin. Annalee Spain picked it up with a raw disbelief—this thing waiting all these years for her to discover.

When she opened it, in the dark after a long night, she read the letter aloud then tore it into mean, jagged pieces.

Then in the same moment, she laid the bits on the dirt to read the message again—needing to see the penciled evidence that people are often wronged in life, and in the unfolding of it, they may do wrong themselves.

The letter was a confession, therefore, but also a request: *"Forgive me anyway."*

Annalee didn't know how to do that. Or know when she would be ready for something so incandescent as forgiveness. Especially for her mother. Thus, with a crooked shovel, she again buried the confounding letter, rendered into bits inside the rusted box, knowing she'd have to read it and accept it, maybe sooner than later. But she couldn't worry about that now.

Besides, nobody could stop her from digging up and shining light on other wrongs done—to her, but also to others.

This was her calling now. She exposed misadventures so wronged people wouldn't be simply dead and gone, and then forgotten. If such a journey brought her back to this box and the truth of her mother, she'd just have to accept that. She couldn't hide her own truth forever.

But for now, Annalee Spain waited for her next assignment. She felt certain it would arrive soon.

In fact, it did.

The very next evening, in a beautiful place, along came more trouble.

CHAPTER 1

"It may turn out to be of more interest than you think."
SHERLOCK HOLMES, "THE ADVENTURE
OF THE COPPER BEECHES"

JUNE 1924

THE YOUNG LADY WAS DEAD, so the little girl cried. But first the child danced. It was that kind of night.

A web of garden lights swung in the bold breeze in financier Cooper Coates' pristine garden. His little daughter, Melody, twirled in and out of glowing pools of light, her white crinoline fairly shining as she skipped and whirled with nine-year-old mischief across her father's inviolate Five Points lawn.

Hurrying into the fancy potting shed, the bespectacled child clicked shut the door, scheming certainly as she often did, to startle her coldhearted father. She'd spring from the shed to scream, "Surprise!" Just for the shock of it. For the power of gaining her important father's attention. She'd annoy him to extremes, especially during one of his eminent shindigs like the political benefit now under way on his showy property tonight.

3

Annalee Spain stood near a punch table and waited for the family's fireworks. Father and daughter were a notorious pair. She'd seen them go to blows—shouting like crazy in this same backyard—at a fundraiser Coates hosted a month ago for rebuilding Mount Moriah AME Church, burned to the ground last winter in an arson.

Now at this mid-June political benefit—with highbrow Negro citizens like himself, along with his smattering of upper-crust white guests—Coates wouldn't bear his precocious daughter's shenanigans, even if her mother had died in childbirth, her elderly greataunt couldn't control her, and her debonair father was preoccupied with his high-society life and his evening guests.

Annalee surveyed the grounds, the well-heeled crowd, the buzz of genteel but tense conversations. People with means always managed to sound tense, even when they laughed. Or maybe it was their fear. Annalee had felt fear herself—more times in her life than she could count. Why wouldn't rich people?

Even now, a string quartet—composed of four colored college students wearing matching black evening dresses—looked touchy as they set up under the spreading boughs of a majestic sycamore tree. Its leafy branches twinkled with tiny, white electric lights. The college girls, finally settled, looked self-conscious in such a setting—their ankles crossed too tight, their eyes blinking too fast. But in due time, they surrendered to softly playing their first classical number.

"Some fancy doings," Edna Stallworth, Annalee's friend and former landlady, whispered to her in a shadowy corner of the thickly fragrant garden. Her smile looked wry. "I'm surprised they let me in here."

"You and the other high-and-mighty." Annalee winked. "Look, there's a few seminary folks here too—well, one professor from Saxton." Annalee nodded to the nervous-looking young man. She'd seen him once visiting at Jack's church.

"Saxton? That theology place? It's fancy too."

4

"Small, exclusive, private—and rolling in dough. Like that high-stepping new president of theirs." Annalee gave her friend a look. "But look at you, wearing a high-stepping new dress yourself."

Mrs. Stallworth tilted her head, flounced her hem a bit.

Annalee flashed a grin. "You even match tonight's music. It's Bach. 'Air on the G String.'"

"Sounds like a funeral." Mrs. Stallworth sniffed.

Annalee tried to laugh. But a chill slid past her slim shoulders. She shook it off, trying to forget that same sensation from the night before. Her tiny garden couldn't compare to Cooper Coates' showstopper. But it had called her from inside her little wood cabin in Five Points, inviting her to pull stubborn weeds and move dirt. Then her fork hit something hard. Bone hard. She'd recoiled, not sure she wanted to know what hard thing lay buried there. Digging with her late father's crooked shovel, she found the rusty box—but quickly buried it again. Its contents were too hard to face. She wasn't ready.

Now with funereal music wafting across Cooper Coates' lush garden, she felt the same nagging chill but wasn't sure why.

She touched Mrs. Stallworth's arm. "Let's walk." Annalee gave her friend a subtle look, gesturing them across the clipped lawn. They were only here because of Annalee's growing notoriety as Five Points' new, young Black detective. Coates had invited her to bring a guest, so Annalee persuaded Mrs. Stallworth to accompany her—a sort of stand-in for Jack, who she let decline. As close friends, both women vowed that, at such a swanky party, they wouldn't fret over not quite belonging.

But now here, Annalee felt more discomfort than she expected. Mrs. Stallworth looked uncertain too.

"Walk? You mean explore?" She blinked. "In that dolled-up potting shed?"

"Right. Over there." Annalee excused them past a tight group of Denver Negro society women, not one bothering to grant her a whiff of attention. Annalee's cotton summer dress—her best for the season—didn't compare to their silky sleek chiffon and satin frocks.

Ignoring their arrogant coolness, Annalee sauntered with self-composure toward the shed, reaching out to grab Mrs. Stallworth's hand, displaying their homespun friendship. Both were sporting the beaded earrings Annalee purchased for them in Salida, Colorado, after ending her last case. A buck a pair, they'd cost her—and never mind tonight's glossy Negro society women. Annalee was bothered instead by something she couldn't put her finger on. At such a perfect party—in such imperfect times as these—something was bound to go wrong. Evil stayed afoot in their city. The Klan ran amok. Crime was having a heyday. Even churches in town were embroiled in scandals, some pastors forced to step down—for one regretful reason or another.

But tonight's wrong turn—if it was coming—could instead mean something silly. That Coates had overworked himself again while overlooking his wild child, Melody, but disregarded something dire. He was chatting up donors for the anti-Klan gubernatorial candidate he was promoting. So Melody's probable surprise would be the farthest thing from his political-fixing mind. But if Melody acted up, he'd erupt with fury.

Annalee didn't relish seeing a child get rebuked—or misbehave—or whatever Melody Coates was cooking up while lurking in her father's potting shed.

The little shelter up close looked, in fact, more like a child's dollhouse—a tiny replica of the Coates' sprawling larger home. A riot of flowers marked its spot. Trimmed shrubbery announced its importance. Blooming yellow roses dressed up the border of a gravel pathway leading to the shed door, their fragrant abundance released with every step or slight breeze.

Inside, however, the shed would feel dank, probably, and also dark. Under this cover, little Melody was likely rooting around for a hiding place. From her spot, she'd scope out the goings-on at the party without being seen.

Coates was none the wiser, therefore, when Melody shot from the door of the shed, her eyes wide as saucers, shouting not in joy on such an extravagant night but in sheer horror.

"Father!"

The scream ripped the air.

Party guests froze. Melody wailed.

"A lady. She's dead!"

"Melody?" Coates, busy talking nose to nose with a Denver banker, spun at the child. "Cut that racket. Stop it."

"But the lady. She's *dead*." She seized her father's hand.

"Stop being ridiculous." He shook himself free.

Annalee exchanged glances with Mrs. Stallworth, saw Coates turn from his daughter, shaking his head, giving Annalee a moment to walk herself toward Melody and speak with clear directness, her voice steady. "Where is she? The dead lady?"

"In the shed." Melody then screamed again.

"Stop it." Coates swung back to his daughter. "You're making a scene."

He turned on Annalee, an edgy smile plastered on his aristocratic face. "This, Miss Spain, is a political gathering, not one of your murder mystery puzzles."

"Sir, if you'd just let me check—"

Coates cut her off, pointed at Melody. "March yourself inside, young lady. Right now."

Annalee held her tongue. This was nothing, apparently, like the jokes Melody had played on her father in the middle of one of his high-society fetes.

Melody wouldn't retreat. "But the lady. *She's so dead.*" She fell to sobbing.

Coates squared his shoulders, leaned over his trembling daughter, turned back to excuse himself to the banker. "Just a moment, Warren."

"Everything okay, Coop?"

A crisply dressed Negro man turned from a knot of friends to check on Coates, who waved him away, looking embarrassed and annoyed.

"I'm fine, Otis. Get yourself a drink. Some hors d'oeuvres." Coates called over a waiter. His laugh sounded bitter. "Let's enjoy ourselves tonight."

But the look in Coates' eyes, aimed at Melody, seethed. His daughter went on the offense.

"It's your pretty garden. Father, you can help!"

"You shouldn't even be out here. Get upstairs."

His guests were staring now, many whispering, some scowling. One woman in particular—recognized by Annalee as Valerie Valentine, a well-positioned Negro society lady—looked down her nose at the commotion, shook her head at Melody.

Coates stepped up to apologize to her. He pointed Melody toward their large house. "To bed. This instant."

Melody pushed past the Valentine lady and her father's other guests, ignoring any attempts to calm her. Pulling away, Melody slammed into a punch table, upsetting a glittering set of cut-glass crystal punch cups—the disruption upsetting her father even more, provoking his shouts, making the child drop to the grass and start to sob harder. *"But she's dead."*

"Oh, my gracious," Valerie Valentine huffed. "Young lady, that's enough."

But the woman's upbraiding only riled Melody more, the child's sobbing growing more dramatic.

Guests whispered in tight groups now. *A dead woman?*

"I'm checking the shed." Annalee eyed Mrs. Stallworth.

"No, please, Annalee," her friend pleaded. "Not tonight."

"But somebody's likely hurt." Annalee frowned. "Or worse."

"Let the police handle it."

Annalee gave her a sober look.

Besides, another female guest was already rushing past them, shoving through the shed door. But just as quickly, she raced back outside, screaming louder than Melody, screeching, *"Call the police."*

Slamming past guests, the woman careened into a tuxedoed waiter, sending his silver serving tray—piled high with Coates' elaborate hors d'oeuvres—soaring into the summer night, a shower of meats and treats raining down on the silky party clothes of a starched, graying, tight-mouthed woman. Backing into the string quartet, the woman tripped over her feet and fell, upsetting the college girls' music stands—sending sheet music flying.

The college girls leaped up in unison, all struggling vainly to gather up their music, plus help the distraught woman to her feet—looking at each other, their eyes asking if they should sit instead and keep playing.

"My Bombay silks." The woman glared at the young musicians. "Ruined. Every pleat." One of the college girls grabbed a hand-kerchief from her stand and started dabbing at the woman's dress.

"Leave it. You're making it worse."

"We're so sorry."

Coates threw up his arms. "Everybody!" He waved for calm.

It was an empty gesture, not calming a soul.

"A dead woman, Coates?"

"Well, I never."

"C'mon. Let's look."

Coates tried vainly to quiet his appalled but excited guests, but several had broken off to peer inside the shed, only to exit wide-eyed and stunned.

Coates, finally taking a long look himself, slumped out looking sick and dismayed.

"I'm so sorry—" He struggled for words. "Call the police," he ordered a waiter.

Little Melody ran back across the yard, pleading with her father. "See, Father? I told you."

Coates refused to answer. "Please go inside, Melody."

"Are you going to jail?"

"Stop talking nonsense." Coates pushed her away, shook his head, confronted people still gawking inside the shed, begged them to please back away.

One man emerged appalled but excited. "Mercy, she *is* dead. Some poor colored gal." He called to his frowning wife. "C'mon, we better leave."

Coates looked heartsick. "Everyone! The police are coming. You'll have to stay for questions."

But people were gathering themselves, many taking their leave. A dead person amongst the likes of them? Denver's social finest? Guests looked horrified. This wasn't a pretty sight.

A dead body, in fact, as Annalee knew, wasn't prepared to be viewed—not as in a mortuary. Or at a wake. Stepping into the shed, Annalee was appalled, indeed, to see such an unlikely victim.

First, the dead woman looked so terribly young. Nineteen or twenty at most. She'd been dumped in a sad huddle in a corner of the shed—all the potential of her life drained away.

Her pretty face was already losing its deep glow. Her dark curls bore splotches of dirt from the potting shed floor, her pressed hair looking grimy and dusty. Her eyes, still open, were jewel-like and dark. Her lashes long. Her slim body wore a sleeveless cotton shift, revealing lovely arms and dainty hands—poised and delicate-looking, as if they didn't deserve hard work.

Now, however, her slight, cooling hand held a crumpled, unopened rose—as if to protect the bud. Or to send a signal? The rosebud's color was, in fact, remarkable. A shy red with daring streaks of fuchsia, it was nothing quite like any rose Annalee had ever seen. Simply, it was stunning. Annalee grabbed for a stray petal, inhaled its heady scent, felt its silky touch, stepped away from the young woman's still body.

Annalee searched Mrs. Stallworth's eyes. *Do you know her?*

"Poor little thing." Mrs. Stallworth shook her head. "I've never seen her."

"So, how'd she end up here?" Was she recently off a train? A long-haul bus? Mercy, a farm? If not, how'd she end up in a fancy potting shed—with slight bruising around her neck? Annalee shuddered. As if she'd been strangled.

Annalee dropped the rose petal in her small secondhand pocketbook, noticed another matter.

The young woman's dainty feet bore black patent pumps with a sweet tiny heel, a subtle gold swirl design on each toe. A charming style. Decent quality, too. But the shoes were scuffed, marred by ragged holes in each sole—as if the young woman had walked for miles in her pretty party heels.

"She's had a bad end." Annalee stiffened, her stomach tight. She knew what was coming next.

Little Melody Coates announced it to her. The child was waiting just outside the shed.

"Father says you're a detective. But you don't look like one to me. Father will probably get blamed."

Annalee took in Melody's countenance—the angry face of a distraught, uncertain, motherless child, standing before her with defiance, the girl's little lip poked out with despair, anger, confusion, maybe a dare.

Annalee bent to her level. "He won't get blamed—not if I can help it." She tilted her head, making assurances she couldn't back up yet. Maybe Coates had killed the girl.

"So, you can find out what happened?" young Melody demanded. "Working for me?"

Annalee held the child's hands. She couldn't lie to her. Or take up a case that looked like a straight-up murder while pretending her client was this little girl. It was a whimsical idea. But murder is serious business. Solving it a dangerous grind. Annalee needed her wits about her.

"I'm going to figure out what happened. Even if I don't look like a detective." Annalee released Melody's hands. "But if I work for anybody, it'll be for the pretty lady in the shed."

"But she's dead. How can she even pay you? Or speak to you?"

Annalee squeezed Melody's shoulders, but spoke to herself. "With her best truth."

Annalee stood then, looked out on the glittering rich people on Melody's father's lawn, so full of themselves, so randomly blessed, most of them, in the material circumstances of life—making Annalee unsure why she couldn't stop thinking one nagging, awful thing. That somebody here already knew what had happened to the young woman, who she was, who had killed her and why, and what the young woman's death would reveal.

Annalee held a breath.

And that somebody would kill to keep it all a secret.

CHAPTER 2

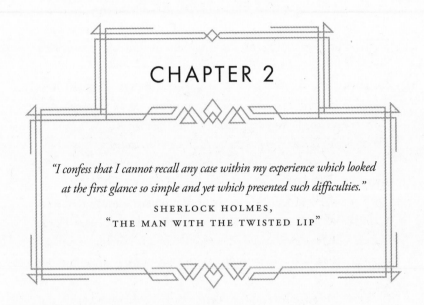

"I confess that I cannot recall any case within my experience which looked at the first glance so simple and yet which presented such difficulties."

SHERLOCK HOLMES,
"THE MAN WITH THE TWISTED LIP"

"CAN WE GO?" Mrs. Stallworth gave Annalee a look. "Enough of this garden party."

"Not quite." Annalee took a breath. "If there's been a crime here—and it certainly looks like it—we'll have to be questioned. All the guests will."

"I'm not talking to police." Mrs. Stallworth aired defiance. "They won't care about that dead girl."

But the law had arrived.

"Back off, people!" Two grim-looking white officers stomped in heavy boots across Coates' pristine yard, pushing back a crowd of guests. Not everybody had fled.

"Out of my way," one cop snapped.

"Officers, please—"

"This your place?" The older cop gave Coates a once-over.

"It is—and your chief knows me." Coates squared his shoulders.

The cop shrugged, unimpressed. He gestured to his partner, started questioning Coates, ordering him to show them the body.

Annalee turned away, despairing to see Coates diminished before his guests. His nerves looked frayed. His white society guests were probably judging him. His fancy Negro guests, too. Or that's how things looked to Annalee. How would he handle the scrutiny? Especially if, in fact, he was guilty of stone-cold murder?

The college girls plucked at their stringed instruments again, struggling to find a tune.

But Coates shushed them. "That's enough for tonight, please, young ladies." He reached inside his tuxedo jacket for an envelope. "Something for your wonderful service tonight. Divide it equally among yourselves." With shy faces, the girls looked uncertain but grateful.

Coates headed toward the potting shed, then turned back suddenly to the college girls, his eyes pained. "Keep working hard, young ladies." He wiped a sheen of sweat off his forehead with a spotless monogrammed handkerchief. "And please stay safe. Watch out for each other."

The girls mumbled thank you, stood to pack up their instruments and music.

"Nobody leaves," a cop barked.

The girls dropped back into their folding chairs, each gripping her instrument, seeming desperate to leave—let alone to not get questioned by the full force of the law not known to protect the likes of them.

At the shed, the officers glared at the death scene, spent a brief and indifferent minute looking around. They ordered Coates to stand off to the side, told everybody else to wait "while we investigate."

Annalee gave Mrs. Stallworth an ironic look. Mrs. Stallworth pursed her lips. Annalee pursed hers. But her attention wasn't on Mrs. Stallworth or even on the cops.

Instead, she let her eyes search the crowd. Who here, among the living, would know most about the young woman who lay in the dirt dead?

She felt that inquiry in her bones.

Who here is guilty?

But no. Wrong question, detective. She knew the better one.

Who has the most to lose?

She'd learned that in her first two cases. People kill people—or kill other people's dreams, hopes, and spirits, even kill their accomplishments—for fear of losing something themselves. But what was it here? Annalee sighed. Sherlock cautioned against theorizing before having all the facts. Still, she knew one thing people feared: losing another's love. She knew that firsthand. Maybe worse, they despaired at the thought of losing money. Greed was a killer, for certain. Thus, they feared losing status. The higher on the rung especially. Annalee blinked. Was that why a poor-looking young colored woman ended up paying the ultimate price? Because somebody cared more for herself—or himself—instead of for her?

"I know exactly what you're thinking," Edna Stallworth whispered to her. "Stop looking like Sherlock."

"But he'd be fascinated by this case. Especially by this crowd," Annalee whispered back.

Already Coates' guests were turning their well-heeled thoughts to other concerns. Chattering about upcoming society happenings crowding their curated calendars. Gushing over upcoming travels to all the right places. The women comparing their fancy dresses, shoes, handbags, handkerchiefs. Laughing about one insignificant-sounding thing or the other.

One man had people holding their stomachs over his barely whispered gags.

"I came to see a colored man's garden. Instead, I see a colored gal in a shed. Dead."

"Thaddeus!" The woman at his side—his wife, apparently—grabbed his arm and shook it. "Hush!"

Annalee turned her gaze on the man.

But an interruption broke into her thoughts.

"You're amused?" The sleek-looking Valerie Valentine stepped toward the man called Thaddeus.

He didn't answer.

"You didn't hear me? I said—" The woman stepped closer to him.

"I heard you." Thaddeus turned, spoke to his wife. "We're leaving anyway," he announced in loud words.

"You can't leave," Valerie Valentine declared. "Those two officers told everybody to stay—"

The man shrugged, turned his wife toward a lilac arbor across the lawn. "This way, Evelyn."

Coates rushed over. "Thank you for coming, Thaddeus. Can we talk another time?"

"About the election?"

"Well, yes. Let's talk with Malcolm, too. Is he here tonight?"

"Let me think about it. We're leaving now. And, no, Malcolm couldn't make it. He's a no-show. Good night."

Coates nodded, saving any kind of speech about not leaving before the cops said it was okay. He turned to Valerie Valentine. "The police should be finished soon."

She nodded, set her jaw, turned back to her group of associates.

"The coroner is here." Coates spoke aloud, but not to anyone in particular. "He's almost done."

Many people seemed to hear that but didn't show concern or enough worry to wait. The two cops were leaving now, too, pushing through Coates' lilac arbor, but not bothering to see if the whole contraption might fall.

Annalee approached Coates. "Did you get a time of death?"

Coates glared. "That sounds like a detective's question."

"It's important—"

"Around six this evening," he snapped. "If you must know."

"So, before your event started? Or any guests arrived?"

"I wasn't even here myself. I'd gone for a walk to relax—as I said, if you must know." He brushed invisible lint off his impeccable white tuxedo sleeve. "I didn't arrive back here until right before seven. Barely time to get a shower and dress before my gathering started at eight." Then he laughed. Or tried to laugh. "Some party."

"Did you know the young woman?" Annalee swallowed. "In the shed?"

Coates searched her eyes. "You're actually questioning me, Miss Spain. Even more than the cops."

"They didn't ask you?"

"Frankly, I don't think they cared."

"She's just a dead—"

"Colored gal. That's what they called her." He pursed his mouth. "Or maybe they called her worse."

Coates pointed toward his pretty shed. "Why here? And why her? Whoever she is." He sighed. "What a hideous ending, and on my property."

The coroner's man was backing out of the shed with a long stretcher, an assistant holding its other end. On it was the lifeless woman, her face and body covered with a faded, wrinkled, graying sheet—one black patent leather party shoe peeking out of one end.

Without ceremony, the men hauled away the body, not having to ask people to stand back. The remaining crowd parted automatically.

One of the demure college girls started to weep. A silent sob. Another tried to comfort her.

"Could I stop by tomorrow?" Annalee asked Coates. "I'll have some more questions, but tonight's not the best time."

Coates frowned at her. "Are you the investigator now?"

"Nothing official." Annalee didn't need to lie. "But that could change."

"Then I'm through with giving answers." He moved toward the college girls. "You're free to leave now, young ladies—"

"If you need me—" Annalee interrupted, then lowered her voice—"would you call me, Mr. Coates?" She searched his eyes. "Or call Reverend Blake? He could come by."

Coates stepped back. "Jack Blake? To talk to me? I don't need a confessor." He shook his head. "You'd better leave. It's getting late." He gave her a curt nod and gestured to his gorgeous lilac arbor. "This way out. Good night, Miss Spain."

With that, he turned to other guests, apologizing for the night's disturbance, thanking them for coming, seeming to ignore their questioning looks, telling them farewell, offering to walk them to the flowering bower.

Mrs. Stallworth touched Annalee's elbow. "Have we overstayed our welcome?"

"If we ever were welcome." She checked the crowd. "Have you seen little Melody?"

"Someone took her inside."

"Then you're right. Time to leave."

Mrs. Stallworth huffed. "Why'd we even come?"

Annalee grabbed her friend's hand, headed them toward the garden's flowery exit. "Because somebody important needed us." She blinked. "And the poor girl was killed before she knew it."

A half-shrouded moon shone its shadowy light on Five Points as they walked down silent streets to Annalee's cabin. The clock on a neighborhood bank showed ten, so the sidewalks had mostly emptied. A hard-eyed man stepped out of an alley, lit a cigarette, and followed them with a glare, frowning as if he owned this portion of the block. But after a moment, he swung back into the alley, melting into the dark.

"I'm staying at your place tonight." Mrs. Stallworth tightened her hand in Annalee's.

"No need. I'll be okay." Annalee pressed closer to her friend.

"Not for you. For me." Mrs. Stallworth tried to laugh. "Being alone tonight—well, by myself—not quite my choice. Even at the rooming house with other people in their rooms."

"With a killer on the loose?"

"Stop saying that." Mrs. Stallworth grabbed Annalee's arm.

"I'm just thinking what we're up against." Annalee returned Mrs. Stallworth's tight grip.

"We? Nope to that, Miss Sherlock. Isn't that what Pastor Jack calls you?"

Annalee smiled to herself. "Sometimes."

"Well, if you take this case—and I hope you don't—you're on your own. There's no 'we' in this summertime murder—especially if you're including me."

"Then you can't stay at my cabin," Annalee teased her friend, stepping off the main street onto the road leading to her rustic, one-room cottage.

"Doesn't matter." Mrs. Stallworth gave Annalee a look. "We're here. But why's it dark inside? Is your electricity working?"

"Works swell, but why leave lights burning? Besides, the moon is trying its best to shine bright."

"Unless it rains."

This was some light banter, as Annalee knew, to keep them from stewing, or admitting to stewing, over Coates' garden party and the murk they'd witnessed there—especially the still body of a young colored slip of a murder victim.

Annalee was sure that's what had happened. Murder. And the thought made her heartsick but also jittery.

She'd known murder, sadly, in just the past few months—

including the loss two winters ago of her beloved but confounding father, Joe Spain, who she'd learned a year later wasn't really her father at all. Then her second big case had dropped her knee-deep into the sad killing of another young Denver troublemaker, a barnstorming stunt pilot—a white man not much older than herself.

But tonight's killing of someone so curiously like her—young, colored, female, probably poor, so not among the higher echelons—felt personal.

Annalee wouldn't walk away from this one. Never mind that nobody had hired her to investigate. Or likely would hire her. She didn't even care about that. This was one murder she felt determined to solve because the killer—quite possibly somebody high on the social ladder—would otherwise get away with it.

Annalee clicked on the small lamp next to her tiny bed. Her one-room cabin came into focus, giving off a feeling of humble but cozy warmth, making both women sigh a bit. Annalee set the dead bolt. What a contrast to Cooper Coates' fancy digs and heady flowered gardens. But Annalee felt glad to be back in her own little place. No better spot to rest. And her best haven for asking the hard question.

"Who do you think did it?" She sat down at her little table, allowed herself to say this before she convinced herself to keep quiet. After all, it was time for sleep.

"I knew you were going to ask that." Mrs. Stallworth stepped over to Annalee's narrow bed, pulled back the summer quilt lying there, gave it a pat. "You'll think better after a night's sleep. Why not call it a night?"

"Because my mind's still churning. Besides, you observe things, Mrs. Stallworth. You were at that party. What did you see?"

"Rich people."

"And a poor-looking dead girl in Cooper Coates' shed. How in the world did she get there?" Annalee studied her room. "Do you think Coates killed her?"

"Right before hosting his fancy party? I'm no Sherlock,

Annalee, but I can't see a reason for that. It's more like somebody put her there to make him look guilty."

"That's what little Melody suggested." Annalee pointed to her bed. "Clean sheets. I put them on this morning."

"Good. You'll sleep like a baby." Mrs. Stallworth arranged the quilt. "All ready for you."

"No bossing." Annalee wagged a finger, pulled two chairs together, seat to seat. "Besides, I want to think a little before I turn out the light. Now, take off your shoes and climb into bed."

"But—"

"No arguing either."

Mrs. Stallworth nodded with her soft laugh, turned into Annalee's tiny bathroom to freshen up, took off her beaded earrings, then climbed into Annalee's bed and, with a sigh, closed her eyes.

Sleep well, my friend.

Annalee prepared for bed too—taking off her earrings, washing up in her little bathroom. She slipped on her nightclothes, made up a pallet of light blankets on the two facing chairs. But then she clicked open her pocketbook and slipped out the rose petal, admiring the stunning color, breathing in its fragrant perfume. Sighing, she placed the petal on her shelf, letting it kindly rest there as she pondered the girl's apparent sad end.

Even as she clicked off her small lamp, then snuggled into her makeshift two-chair bed, trying to quiet any pesky thoughts, she still pondered.

She was waiting, in fact, for Mrs. Stallworth to drift off and start her light snore—then Annalee could mull longer on all they'd seen that evening. But Mrs. Stallworth's loud silence spoke volumes. Her friend was still awake.

"Annalee?"

"Your mind's working too?"

"A little. Those were fancy people we saw tonight," Mrs. Stallworth said finally. "Did you see some of those dresses?"

Annalee pulled up her light blanket. "I was too busy admiring yours. Lacy white eyelet? A purple sash? You looked like a queen."

Mrs. Stallworth huffed in the dark. "A rummage sale dress. I stumbled on it at my Hearts and Hands sale last week."

"Hearts and Hands?"

"At Jack's church. You know—my women's civic group."

"Fancy you," Annalee teased.

"Nothing like that. They're good, hardworking women. Mrs. Cunningham kept pestering me to join."

"Good thing you did. You found your pretty dress."

"It looked kind of brand-new." Mrs. Stallworth sounded thoughtful. "Probably a cast-off. Maybe from one of those rich women at Coates' hoedown tonight. Imagine throwing out a nice dress like that, then seeing somebody walking around wearing it at tonight's party."

Annalee considered. "Do they sell shoes, too? The Hearts and Hands? At their rummage sale? You know—hand-me-down shoes? Like high heels?"

"Sure. You need a pair?"

Annalee gazed at the fading moonlight drifting past her cabin's little window. "Me? In fact, I might. You never know."

"Well, if you do, make our next sale." Mrs. Stallworth rustled the quilt on Annalee's little bed, settling herself. "Good night, sweetheart. Thanks for inviting me to the party."

"Good night, Mrs. Stallworth. Thanks for going with me. I'm real sorry things turned sour."

"Especially since I know what that means—that you're 'taking the case.' That's how you say it, right? You're already working on it probably—just firing up your busy brain to figure out who killed that poor girl."

"Not just who. But how."

"And also why?"

"Now you're talking, Sherlock."

Mrs. Stallworth laughed, but turned serious. "I wish I could talk you out of it. But I understand—because who is that poor girl? And where are her people?"

"Right, so many curious, unanswered questions." Annalee studied the dark. "Somebody killed that young woman. Took her life. I'm praying to find out the whole story. But for now, thanks for keeping me company. You were the best party date ever."

"You too." Mrs. Stallworth turned in the bed, but just as fast turned back again. "Did you like them, Annalee? Those rich society women?"

"Who's to say? I don't really know them, even if I've seen them around town—especially the Five Points crowd."

"Maybe you'll get to talk to some of them one of these days."

"Like I said. You never know."

But Annalee did know this: to solve the girl's murder, she'd talk to whoever it took—club woman or pauper, policeman or professor, high society or not. When? She'd start first thing tomorrow. Why in heaven wait?

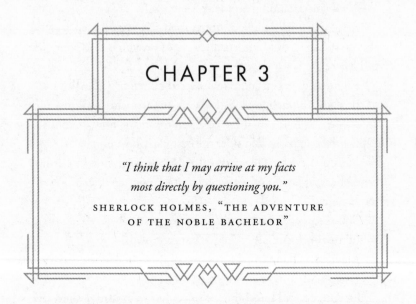

CHAPTER 3

"I think that I may arrive at my facts
most directly by questioning you."
SHERLOCK HOLMES, "THE ADVENTURE
OF THE NOBLE BACHELOR"

AN OVERNIGHT RAIN lulled Annalee into a sound, deep sleep—so deep she felt mortified the next morning to awaken way past nine and squint at sunshine pouring into her little window with Mrs. Stallworth already up, bustling about, and finishing up with breakfast. A meal for a visitor.

"Professor, you're awake. Time for biscuits."

"Eddie?"

Her young, orphaned friend, Eddie Brown Jr.—the scrappy white boy who'd been her partner during her first crime-fighting adventure—knelt down by her makeshift bed and grinned, his nose almost touching hers.

"Biscuits, Professor. With butter and jam. Wake up. Hot coffee, too. It was great."

"You're too young for coffee." Annalee threw off her blankets.

"And what are you doing here after nine—" she looked at the clock on her wooden shelf—"on a Monday morning."

"School's out. Summer vacation. I'm free." He threw wide his skinny arms.

She grinned.

"Don't encourage him." Mrs. Stallworth gave Eddie a plate. "Take this and finish up. I fried you an egg, too."

Eddie reached for the plate, sniffed the aromas in the air, sat down at Annalee's little eating table, said thank you—"You're the best, Mrs. Stallworth"—then pointed to the small clock.

"Time to get moving. We've got work to do."

"Nope, young Sherlock." Annalee shook her head. "Not we."

"But I heard about a murder last night—at that fancy garden party. What a shindig. And you were there."

"Heard what?" Annalee frowned. "Heard from who?"

"A cook at the boys' home. She's a Negro lady. She heard it from a waiter she knows. He was working the party and—"

"What cook?"

"Her name's Alice. She's real nice. She gives me extra helpings sometimes, says I'm skinny and need the extras. Anyway, she said, 'Your friend's solving a crime. There was a murder—a colored girl—and your friend's investigating.' That's what she said." Eddie blinked his gray eyes. "So that means we got another case. Right, Professor?"

"Finish your breakfast." She spoke softly to Eddie. He wasn't her actual sidekick. The pastor Jack Blake was moving into that role. But Eddie had flat-out saved her life during her ruthless first case. Now, when he showed up from the Denver boys' home— where he lived—she paid attention. Or tried to.

Watching him, she shook out her blankets and folded them, laid them at the foot of her little bed, found a fresh dress and underclothes, and stepped into her tiny bathroom to freshen up, change clothes, and fluff out her curls.

Closing her eyes a quick moment, she placed her hands on her chest and breathed deep.

I'm trembling, she realized, surprised. Looking into the small mirror over her sink, she searched her face, looking at her youth, and reflected on what Eddie just told her.

There was, indeed, a murder discovered last night at a fancy party, and the dead person was "a colored girl"—who, in fact, nobody seemed to know. But investigating—if that's what she was pondering—didn't make it an escapade. Eddie sounded downright giddy, as if solving a murder offered them a summertime lark filled with thrills and chills.

How could she explain the other side to him? A stranger was dead. Murdered. So that stranger deserved justice. *That's what I'm going after, right?* She nodded to herself. *So I need help? Explaining it that way to Eddie?*

Or did Eddie already understand?

He was tapping on the bathroom door.

"Professor? Are you okay?"

Annalee took a moment to squeak open the door.

Eddie looked sheepish. "Did I say something wrong?"

She stepped from her little bathroom but stayed silent.

"Wrong," he said, "because somebody was killed?" He glanced down a moment. "I made it sound like fun."

"Well, it can be exciting tracking down a murderer." She pursed her lips. "But *murder* means somebody died. We can't ever forget that."

"I won't."

"Then you can help me."

Eddie gave her a crooked grin. "Finally."

"Well, when I start, you can help. I don't even know who the victim is. She's young—like me, Eddie. But where on earth did she come from? She didn't just drop out of the sky."

Eddie cocked his head.

"What now?" Annalee studied his eyes.

"Just the carnival."

Mrs. Stallworth smirked. "He's trying to talk you to the carnival." She wagged a finger at Eddie. "You're a sneaky little somebody, young man."

"No, listen, Professor."

"What carnival?" Annalee pulled a chair up to her table, pointed Eddie to a facing chair.

"The Sonny Dawkins carnival." Eddie's eyes brightened. "They came last week. The colored carnival."

"Here in Denver? Who's Sonny Dawkins?"

"The carnival master. Like at the Sells-Floto Circus—you know, the big one—but all the acts with Mr. Dawkins are colored people. Clowns and trapeze artists and wire walkers and stuff. Like the Sawyer Sisters. They're young. They have a high-wire act."

Mrs. Stallworth sat down at the table, crossed her arms. "How do you know so much? Oh, I know. You sneaked away from the boys' home to check it out. Tell the truth."

"Not this time. I swear—"

"Don't you dare." Mrs. Stallworth hiked a brow.

"Are there more biscuits?"

"Don't change the subject."

"Stop arguing, you two." Annalee pulled on the boy's chair. "What are you saying, Eddie?"

"Okay, I'm saying that maybe the dead colored girl is a stranger because she just arrived in town. You know, with the carnival. Think about it, Professor."

"So you've been to that carnival? Is that what this is about? You want me to take you again? Don't kid me, Eddie."

Eddie twisted in his chair. "Well, to tell the truth, I'm chomping to go. Some boys at the home sneaked over there one night. That's how I found out about it—and to be actually honest, Professor, as I said, I'm raring to go. I want to see all the acts and rides and games. But then I heard about the dead young lady—who nobody seems to know—and for some reason, I thought about the carnival."

"Your logic is stretching me." Annalee narrowed her eyes.

"It's like you said, everybody in Five Points seems to know each other. Even if you don't know everybody, you've seen them around."

"So the dead girl is a newcomer."

"Exactly. And what's new in town except the carnival?" Eddie grinned. "Right?"

"You could be a lawyer when you grow up." She shook her head.

"But I want to be a preacher." He looked sly. "Like Reverend Blake."

"Oh, you're a shrewd one." She grinned.

"Gotcha. I'll be a preaching lawyer."

Annalee laughed and gave him a look.

"That boy has you wrapped around his little finger." Mrs. Stallworth offered Annalee the last biscuit slathered in butter.

Annalee poured herself a mug of steaming coffee, stirred in cream, and munched on the biscuit. Even cold it tasted tender and delicious.

"Thank you, Lord, for our breakfast—and Edna Stallworth for cooking it." Annalee finished and stood.

"So, we're going now? To the carnival?" Eddie looked hopeful.

"In the light of day?" Mrs. Stallworth frowned.

"For detectives like Sherlock here, and for me, it's the best time to go." Annalee grabbed her pocketbook, straightened her summer dress, and slipped on her only pair of T-strap vamps — praying that the left shoe, with its frayed strap, wouldn't finally break today. She wiggled her toes. She'd get the strap repaired soon.

"Ready, Mr. Sleuth?"

"A hunting we will go."

"Mind your manners, young man." Mrs. Stallworth wiped his mouth with a dish towel.

"With our eyes wide open." Eddie opened the door to Annalee's cabin. "Right, Professor?"

"If there's something to see, we will." She winked. "Let's go find out."

Annalee and Eddie rode the Welton Street trolley downtown, gazing from their streetcar windows at the awakening day and the morning's passersby. The city's clear air was summer fresh, the sun's rich rays warming a sparkling expanse of cloudless blue sky. At their stop, Eddie gave Annalee a grin.

"Hurry." He clung to Annalee's arm, prompting looks and frowns from some white streetcar riders.

"Calm yourself," Annalee whispered at him, loosening her arm.

Thanking the driver for their ride, she followed Eddie off the trolley in front of Denver Union Station. Then walking south, they swung westward onto the Fourteenth Street viaduct, crossed over the railyards below—while Eddie threw a pebble or two in to the gurgling Cherry Creek running alongside—and headed toward the grounds of the carnival, if one could call it that.

Gaping across the bridge, they could barely make out two sagging tents.

"Lousy." Eddie grumbled. "A two-bit outfit?"

Annalee wasn't sure. Sonny Dawkins' carnival would be modest—nothing like the swanky Sells-Floto Circus that thrilled Denver when it landed every summer. Big top and sideshows, dancing elephants and acrobats, midway games and Ferris wheels, Sells-Floto was high stepping.

But Dawkins' outfit? From a distance, anyway, not one thing impressed.

"We're not here for entertainment." Annalee squinted across

the bridge, feeling Eddie's disappointment. Scoping out a carnival had sounded exciting, but their work today was sobering.

"We're looking for a dead girl—well, somebody who knows her. Let's get moving." She gave Eddie a look. "And don't hang all over me when we get there. You never know who's watching. If cops are about, I'd rather not explain why we're together."

Eddie twisted his mouth but agreed.

As they approached, however, they saw not a soul moving at the Sonny Dawkins carnival this early Monday morning.

A sad-looking, hand-painted sign hung over an entrance gate. *Sonny Dawkins Extravaganza.*

Annalee studied the sign. Maybe this wasn't such a good idea after all. The place had a worn, neglected look.

Sawdust covered the carnival grounds in patches. A faint animal smell wafted through the air, along with a scent of stale popcorn. Three down-in-the-mouth kiddie rides—all needing several fresh coats of paint at the least—sat forlorn in the bright sun.

One called Timmy's Kiddie Whip looked downright danger-ous, especially for small children. Its metal cars leaned on warped wooden wheels barely lying flat on a metal track.

"Look. A Ferris wheel." Eddie ran at another ride, then slumped. "Nah, it's broken."

Annalee squinted at the miserable contraption. A child-size version of a giant Ferris wheel, this one offered five two-person cars attached to its center wheel, which stood near a hand-painted sign. *5 Cents a Turn.*

"Wanna ride?"

A bowlegged slip of a man sporting silky purple pants, black boots, and a man's red blouse appeared out of nowhere, sauntered over, pointed to the Ferris wheel. "It's early, but I'll get her going. It'll work."

"Mr. Dawkins?" Annalee extended her hand, but the man threw back his head and laughed.

"Me? You got the wrong cat. I'm Zimba."

"Nice to meet you. I'm Annalee."

He gave her a quick wink. "Pretty name for a pretty girl."

Annalee tilted her head, gave him a cautionary look. But he seemed regular enough. All show and bluster, but probably not much trouble.

"Thank you, sir. So, is Mr. Dawkins around?"

"Mornings? It depends on what you want."

Annalee pursed her lips. What exactly did she want? Or intend to ask? *"Is one of your circus girls missing? Maybe one of the Sawyer Sisters? Or, do you know the pretty stranger who, sadly, was found murdered last night?"*

She gestured to Eddie, meantime, taking a risk, daring to show they'd arrived together. "I'm just showing my young friend a carnival. He's been begging to visit."

Zimba glanced at Eddie, back at Annalee, then back at Eddie, but he didn't seem bothered to see a white boy visiting the carny with a colored woman. He'd probably seen far more curious social situations.

He grabbed a toothpick from his shirt pocket and chewed on it. "You should come back at night. That's when a carny comes to life."

Annalee considered that. "So everybody's resting now? They're all okay?"

Zimba crossed his arms, peered at Annalee, and finally smiled. "I don't know what you're after, pretty lady. But, yes, everybody here's just fine." He scrunched up his face. "Are you with animal control? They bother us sometimes."

"Animals?" Eddie stepped over to Zimba. "You got tigers and lions and stuff?"

Zimba laughed. "Nope, but you know something, kid? That's my secret dream. To own a fancy act with trained tigers. Ferocious ones." He raised his arms, mimicked a pouncing tiger, and made a growling sound.

"Wow." Eddie sounded impressed.

"Can't you just see me, boy? I already got the outfit. The name. The right look." He winked at Annalee. "Instead, at this here carny, all we got is him." He pointed Eddie toward a large, rusted, truck-sized metal cage sitting across from the kiddie rides.

As Eddie rushed toward the cage, Annalee squinted in that direction—her eyes taking their sweet, good time adjusting in the sunshine to see what the cage held.

A hulking shadow. Moving.

"Eddie!"

"Look, Professor. It's—"

A *bear*.

"Watch it, boy." Zimba ran toward him.

Eddie had wrapped his twelve-year-old little fingers around two bars of the bear's cage, pressed his face forward, and poked his nose through the bars to get a better look.

Annalee raced past Zimba and yanked Eddie back.

The black bear reacted in a flash, bounding from side to side, shaking the cage, his cavernous mouth letting loose a fierce roar.

Annalee jerked back, inches from the raging bear. Suddenly she felt silly for coming to this ridiculous, two-bit carnival—as Eddie had called it—and terrified also of the hulking animal huffing angry breaths at them, until she saw the bear's problem. It was chained by the neck with a metal restraint allowing it to move about only the dank back half of the cage—which was a mucky mess.

"Is it sick?" Eddie asked, trembling.

"Maybe hungry." Annalee backed away. "What do bears eat?"

The animal roared again, shaking the cage harder, making Eddie stumble toward Annalee, gripping her tight around the waist.

"It's okay," she started to say.

"Zimba?" An intently dressed Negro man burst from a small

tent, a frown creasing his sober-looking young face. Sonny Dawkins?

Zimba pushed Annalee and Eddie farther back from the bear cage, making Annalee stumble, causing the weak strap on her left shoe to snap and break. She stifled a groan and tried to pull off her shoe.

"Oh, I'm sorry, Miss Annalee." Zimba struggled to help her with her T-strap, holding on to her bare ankle.

The other man hiked a brow. "Have you lost your mind?"

"It's okay. Mr. Dawkins?" Annalee apologized. "We're just—"

"We? Who is *we* exactly? And, yes, I'm Sonny Dawkins." He glared at her in the bright morning sun. Looking at Eddie, he frowned, adding, "We?"

Annalee squared her back, settled into herself. "We're patrons, sir."

She calmed her voice, refused to feel ludicrous or in the wrong despite standing there holding a broken shoe in one hand, her toes sinking into sawdust while she kept one eye still on the huffing, restless bear.

"My name is Professor Spain—Annalee Spain—and his name is Eddie. He's an orphan, and the boy wanted to see the Sawyer Sisters—to catch their act—and I had some time this morning—" She babbled on, forcing herself to sound reasonable and feel calm while she tried to get a read on Dawkins. Friend or foe? He'd tried to dress sharp as a circus master, far sharper than his run-down carny. But his too-bright suit was mended in places, clean but not elegant. So what was he trying to say to the world? That he was still up and coming? A hardworking business owner, despite his run-down-looking operation?

"You're here to see the Sawyers?" Dawkins glared. "You and the whole world. Come back tonight for the show." He reached in a vest pocket. "Here's a pass—one for the boy and a friend. You can buy a real ticket. That's the only way you'll see them—"

"Not if you don't set up our high wire."

Dawkins jerked around.

"We need to practice, Sonny."

Two look-alike young ladies sashayed out of a main tent, looking smart, young, flush with confidence. The Sawyer Sisters, in the flesh. Not dead.

They were dressed to match, head to toe, in sleek daytime getups—tight sleeveless sweaters, mint-colored women's slacks, summer straw berets, and expensive-looking shoes all sporting the same color. No worn-out clothes for them.

They both struck a pose, as if used to having their photos taken, and flashed smiles—their white teeth gleaming, showing off pretty, perfectly made-up faces, both looking every inch of who they were. Performers. Too bad their only audience was whoever showed up for Dawkins' nightly carny.

Still, Eddie gaped. "You look just like your photos. In the papers."

"Thank you." One of the girls made a little curtsey. "I'm Maggie Sawyer, wire dancer. Middle sister."

"And Minnie here." A matching curtsey. "Elder, but wiser."

"Nice to meet you. I'm Eddie." He extended his hand, but then frowned. "Except where's your other sister? There's three of you, right? Plus other ladies in the carnival? How do you stay safe and not fall off?" He sounded confused. "And stay safe from all your fans and admirers?"

Annalee watched this. *Look at him,* she thought. *Eddie's milking these young women for the exact information we need.*

Watching the exchange, Dawkins stepped between Eddie and the Sawyers. "That's enough. Come back tonight—or another day. That pass will get you in all week." He glanced at Annalee. "Time for you two to scram. You've upset Big Bruno."

"That's the bear's name?" Eddie pointed toward the hulking animal.

Annalee stifled a smile. Eddie was working every angle. She'd better weigh in.

"C'mon, Eddie. Don't bother such a remarkable animal. It's time for us to leave. But, Mr. Dawkins, regarding my shoe?" She held up her broken T-strap. "I hate to ask this, but—"

"You want shoes?" Dawkins scowled. "From the carnival?"

"What size you wear, honey?" Minnie Sawyer glanced at Annalee's bare foot. "Come with me. I'll find you something."

Dawkins blocked her. "No patrons in the private areas."

"No worry," Minnie insisted. "This won't take a second."

Annalee whispered a silent, grateful prayer. How did Sherlock Holmes put it? Don't start by fussing over moral and mental aspects of a matter. Instead, at first, master elementary problems. Basic stuff. Her basic problem was obvious. She needed shoes.

Solving a mystery could start with the strangest thing. She grinned to herself. But look, girl, she indeed was starting.

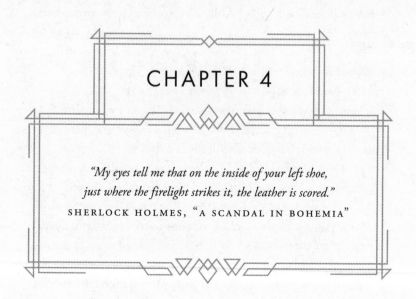

CHAPTER 4

*"My eyes tell me that on the inside of your left shoe,
just where the firelight strikes it, the leather is scored."*
SHERLOCK HOLMES, "A SCANDAL IN BOHEMIA"

A SHOE? MINNIE, IN FACT, had a trunkful. Annalee had never in life seen so many in one woman's possession—and it didn't make sense. Dawkins and his carnival looked barely on their feet. But here, in a run-down little trailer behind Dawkins' tent, Minnie Sawyer was swimming in beautiful shoes amid piles of other gorgeous things—dresses, wraps, coats, even a fur, plus hangers of sparkly circus costumes.

Annalee eyed the haul, her eyes wide.

Minnie looked sheepish. "It looks like a lot. But I didn't actually buy most of these high-rent things." She laughed. "Or steal them."

"So, somebody gave them to you? You and your sisters?"

"More or less." Minnie shrugged. "What can I say? It's complicated."

Annalee squinted. "By what?"

Minnie was handing Annalee random pairs of shoes, pointing her to a chair to try on this style or that. Annalee sat instead on a small, unmade bed because the chair was piled high with clothes, and slipped her feet into a steady onslaught of shoe options—her eyes looking around at the same time for a pair of shoes similar to the pair the dead young woman had worn.

Instead, here came oxfords, spectators, ballet flats, summer T-straps, high-heeled pumps, evening slippers with sparkly, pointy toes. The tiny trailer looked like a quickly cobbled together women's boutique. It bore the scent of one too. A summery hint of a rose-smelling cologne wafted in the air.

"We grew up poor." Minnie sat down cross-legged on the rug-covered floor and leaned against a wall of the trailer. She sighed. "In Alabama. You ever been there?"

"Just once." On a school trip when Annalee was at college in Chicago—but she hadn't planned to discuss her college life today. Not now. "I just remember cotton. Mile after mile. Field after field. I've never seen so much cotton in my life."

"Don't remind me. If I never see a boll of cotton again it won't be too soon."

"So, you ran away to the circus?"

Minnie laughed, but grew dead sober. "I ran away after a lynching."

Annalee slipped off the bed to the floor, feeling her chest tighten. She faced Minnie. They hadn't even introduced themselves, but Minnie had moved from broken shoes to murder. Annalee swallowed.

"Somebody you knew?"

"An old friend from school. Our little one-room school. We all lived within hollering distance, walked together to nursery school, first grade, up and on. So we all knew him—me and my sisters, my mama, our family, and Sonny, our first cousin. You like this shoe?"

Minnie handed Annalee a gold-colored ballet flat. Annalee

took it but didn't answer, numbed by Minnie's casual mention of a friend getting lynched. Minnie chatted on.

"Sonny and Lil' Baby—that was his name—joined the war together, trying to be men. After the war, they came home—twenty-four years old and grown, both of them, chomping to leave Alabama, fed up with all the infernal rules. Don't walk on a sidewalk with white people. Don't look white people in the eye. Don't try on clothes or shoes or even a hat in a white general store. And if you're a man, don't even think of talking to a white woman."

Annalee listened. "It's like that here, too, in some places."

"But Sonny fought in a world war—in France—with a whole country full of white women. White men, too. He couldn't care less about those stupid rules. He kept pushing at every line—he and our school buddy, Lil' Baby Mack. That's what everybody always called him, even when we all got half grown."

Minnie handed Annalee another pair of shoes. Annalee set her face. She blinked. The shoes were an exact match to the pair the dead young woman had worn. Black patent pump, sweet little heel, pretty gold swirl on each toe. But now wasn't the time to react to that happenstance. Annalee placed the shoes on her lap, gave them a gentle pat. *Mercy, what in the world is this murder leading me into?*

"What happened to him? To Lil' Baby Mack?" Annalee asked that instead.

"A white gal in town got pregnant and blamed him. Said Lil' Baby violently raped her."

"Oh, my gracious," Annalee whispered.

"The county sheriff arrested him the same day, but a mob dragged Lil' Baby out of jail, beat the living daylights out of him, hung him by the wrists in the courthouse square from a big ol' loblolly tree. Just let his body dangle. He was wearing his Army uniform. He liked to wear it around, but that didn't matter—"

Minnie froze. "Mercy, how'd I start talking about poor Lil'

Baby? Bless his poor soul." She pointed to more shoes. "Find anything that'll fit?"

Annalee wasn't sure how to react. A lynching. The crime was horrific, still happening all over the South, but up North, too. But now Minnie was running on about shoes. Annalee sucked in a breath, tried on the pumps—which didn't fit. Too wide. But Annalee refused to mention that. Instead, she held tight to the pair, picked up another.

"These are nice too," Minnie said.

Annalee slipped on the pair of mesh flats—quite pretty. But totally irrelevant compared to what had befallen Minnie's old school friend.

Minnie sighed. "They finally burned him alive."

Annalee flinched. She scrambled to her feet, holding the two irrelevant pairs of shoes. She didn't want to hear another word about the lynching of Lil' Baby Mack. But why shouldn't she hear such a thing? Lynching was a sick ritual that wouldn't seem to stop, with hundreds of people showing up and cheering, even bringing little children to watch.

"If that's why you left Alabama," she said, "not a soul in heaven or earth can blame you."

"Being on the road takes us away." Minnie gave a wan smile. "'Cause you know the worst thing? Lil' Baby didn't even know that white gal. He'd never breathed one word to her."

But who did? Minnie didn't say.

Instead, Minnie grabbed an empty shopping bag and started stuffing in other pairs of shoes. She handed the bag to Annalee, grabbed some dresses, too, adding them to the bag, dropped in a fake pearl necklace.

Annalee needed to stop her, but Minnie wasn't actually watching what she was doing. Her mind was a thousand miles away, back in Alabama. She added a pink sweater to the bag. Then a yellow one.

"We'd all be dead if it wasn't for Sonny's boss. A farmer. A white man. He helped him get away. So we left with him. Me and my sisters. Driving across the county line in the man's big ol' smoking farm truck. He gave Sonny fourteen bucks and told us to catch the first train heading north." She shook her head. "Because they would've lynched Sonny, too. Guilt by association. So we headed north with him and landed in St. Louis—no piece of cake either when it comes to doing right by colored folks. But Sonny, right off, found a colored carnival for sale for almost nothing, if we worked there for the next year for practically free. Me and my sisters learned the high-wire act. Sonny learned to run everything. Then four years ago, we started out on our own, traveling from pillar to post—with a 'dancing bear,' too—and here we are this summer in Denver, the Mile High City. It's our third trip here."

Minnie opened the door to the trailer. "Think those shoes and things will cover you?"

Annalee studied Minnie's face. She searched for relevant words. Nothing came out. "These are awfully nice, Minnie," she finally said.

"It's nothing." Minnie shrugged. "Nothing at all."

Annalee let out a quiet sigh. "Are they from a sweetheart?" A nosy question.

Minnie shook her head. "Not really."

"Then where'd they come from?"

"Fell off a truck. Santa Claus left 'em. Birthday presents. Whatever. That's another story—for another day."

Annalee didn't understand or argue. She felt sure the items weren't acquired honestly—well, not totally honestly. But Minnie had just shared the details of perhaps the worst moment of her entire life. Annalee wasn't going to debate her about a shopping bag of shoes and clothes, no matter where they came from. Instead, she'd give the clothes and extra shoes to Mrs. Stallworth's Hearts and Hands ladies. For their next rummage sale. Still, Annalee had one more snooping question:

"Won't your sisters wonder what happened? Do you three share your clothes? Like these shoes?"

"They're Milly's, but they fit me better." Minnie patted her hairdo.

"Where is she? Milly?"

"She's still in Sonny's tent. I did our hair this morning and she's probably gazing at herself in a mirror. Mercy, that child is vain. Her real name is Millicent. She's the youngest in our act. Maggie's in the middle. Then me. I'm eldest, but not by much."

"A lovely family."

"There's more back home. Five younger sisters and brothers still live with our mama. All back in Alabama."

"You three here ever been to Five Points?"

"Not this trip. We may go there today for lunch. Good folks over there. Better than those Saxton people Milly wastes her time with."

"Saxton? The seminary? Milly spends time there?"

"Whenever we're in Denver." Minnie patted her hair again. "She knows some of the hot shots there. Or, rather, they know her." She rolled her eyes.

"How'd they meet her?"

"Through this ol' carnival. You know how it works."

"I'm not sure I know anything." Annalee searched Minnie's eyes. "Any other young ladies work in your carnival? Is anybody, well, missing?"

Minnie gave her a look. "You're one curious little thing. Running around with some skinny white child, asking crazy questions, wearing broken T-straps. But I don't mind you getting new shoes. My sisters and me are the only females here, but nobody should go barefoot. I did that growing up and I never will again, as God is my helper, thank you, Jesus. Here's a nice pair of slip-on summer flats, good leather with the heel out. Paris style. They're darn cute. A nice light beige for the season. My gift to you. You can wear them home."

Outside Sonny's tent, the third sister had appeared. The missing Milly Sawyer. The youngest. She was pretty and pouty and vain looking, just as her sister described her. Still, Annalee was glad Milly was alive and apparently doing fine—despite wasting her time at Saxton seminary, of all places. But since all the Sawyers were okay, and no other women worked here, that meant Annalee wasn't any closer to figuring out a name or identity of the dead young woman in Cooper Coates' potting shed.

But now she had another question.

Why was Jack Blake here, standing inches from pretty Milly? Mercy, she could bat those lashes.

"Annalee!" Jack rushed toward her.

"Well, if it isn't the Reverend J. R. Blake." She gave him a wry wink.

Jack grinned, leaned down to push a curl off her forehead. He held her gaze. He was dressed in his weekday clothes—khaki pants and a white shirt, sleeves rolled up to his forearms. He looked relaxed. Or was that a frown behind his eyes?

"I just got here." He pointed to his car, parked amid the weeds outside the carnival gate. "Did you meet Sonny? We go way back. Served in France. I heard his carnival was in town, so I came over to say welcome."

"You know this young lady?" Sonny gestured to Annalee.

"I do—and if she lets me, I'm giving her a ride home right now. This young boy, too." Jack nodded to Eddie. "Have these two been giving you trouble?"

"Nothing I can't handle." Sonny pointed to the shopping bag, looked at Annalee. "Got yourself some shoes, I see."

"A few. Thanks to Minnie." Annalee turned and gave the eldest Sawyer sister a quick handshake. "Thank you for everything, Minnie. My name is Annalee."

"Nice to officially meet you, Annalee. Enjoy the shoes and things."

I will, Annalee thought. *When I find out where they came from.* And when she learned how a pair of shoes like Minnie Sawyer's swirly-toed pumps came to rest on a dead young woman's feet. She squinted. And maybe how Sonny Dawkins' friend Lil' Baby Mack couldn't escape a lynching from a loblolly tree in Alabama. Did that matter to her case? Possibly not. But getting answers would help her enjoy these shoes and other things far better. But first she had some serious work to do.

CHAPTER 5

*"We heard the hound on the moor,
so I can swear that it is not all empty superstition."*
SHERLOCK HOLMES, *THE HOUND
OF THE BASKERVILLES*

ANNALEE SLIPPED ONTO THE CAR SEAT next to Jack, made room for Eddie to crawl in next to her. Scooting over closer to Jack, she hooked her young arm in his, breathing the light scent of his morning aftershave or bath soap, whatever it was—but mostly leaning into the warmth of his living, war-surviving, all-in-one-piece, confident soul.

She searched his eyes, smiling, as he reached across her—pressing a bit too close—opened his glove box, and took out a small bag of caramel sweets, offering it to Eddie. "Like some candies, son?"

"Wow. Thanks, Reverend Blake."

Starting his car, Jack turned back to Annalee. "Nice to see you this morning," he whispered in her ear. "It's been a while."

"You mean since yesterday morning? At our church?"

He grinned. She did too. He was teasing her. But her smile soon fell away.

"Hey, what's up?" He frowned.

"Nothing to worry. You've got your church work—"

He tilted his head. "You mean those good folks who run me ragged, but I'm determined to love every last one of them?"

"Right. That church work."

"It never stops. But what about you? What's on your mind today?"

Jack steered the car onto the viaduct bridge to head them back downtown. Glancing at Annalee, he waited for her next thought. "I'm listening."

"It's nothing."

"Right. But let me decide."

"Well, are you safe in Denver, Jack?" She thought of Minnie Sawyer's awful tale of a lynching. "I mean, are any of us safe? Which probably sounds like a crazy question, especially coming from me—running myself ragged, too, but trying to be a detective."

He loosened his arm, reaching down to hold her hand a moment as he drove. "I know what this is about. The dead girl. The one at Coop Coates' shindig. I heard about the whole tragic mess, turning the party upside down—Coop trying to save face after a girl's murder in his own backyard."

"She looked barely my age." Annalee scooted closer. "Hardly started with her life."

Jack made a turn on Champa Street to head north. He checked his rearview mirror, turned again to cut three blocks to Welton. "I didn't expect to see you this morning. I was checking on Sonny. It's been more than a year, and he's rarely answered any phone calls or letters, but something's bothering him. Still, about the dead woman, since you're sitting right here in my car, I'm going to ask—what you planning on doing about her?" He glanced at her. "Or have you already started?"

Annalee took a moment to answer. "Here's what I'm thinking—" she began. But Jack broke in.

"Annalee?"

"What's wrong?"

"We're being followed."

She jerked to look, then stopped herself, took in an alert breath. "Followed? Are you sure?"

"Were you in the papers today?"

"She probably was," Eddie broke in. "In the midnight editions. They cover shindigs, like that garden party."

Annalee stiffened. She'd barely begun investigating. But already she was being followed?

"Let me try something," Jack spoke low. At the corner, he signaled to turn, watching his mirror. From behind them, a slim black sedan pulled alongside Jack's car. Inside was a lone driver, a man. Middle-aged, white, stern-looking. He gave them one hard glance but kept going.

"False alarm." Annalee sounded hopeful, but she wasn't.

Jack gave her a look. "You're working on something. You and Eddie. I know it."

Eddie popped another caramel in his mouth, chewed it like crazy, but stayed quiet. Annalee stayed silent too.

Jack stopped the car near East Thirty-Second Avenue—a busy intersection—and at a curb, let the car idle. "Are you two going to tell me?"

"I will if you'll help us." Annalee swallowed. "Well, help me."

"Soon as I get Eddie on the next streetcar—"

"But I'm helping with the case, Reverend Blake."

"You're a regular Sherlock. I know. But first you need to get back to the boys' home—"

"It's summer vacation."

"So they'll be looking for you—and if the head man and his people can't find you, they'll come looking for Annalee."

"Or for you, Jack." She turned to Eddie. "I'll keep you up to date. You did some great sleuthing this morning—"

"Did you see me?"

"Sherlock all the way. I'll tell Reverend Blake all about it. But for now, get back to the boys' place." She wagged a finger. "And don't start pouting."

Eddie slouched out of the car, turned back to accept streetcar change from Jack.

As he boarded the No. 64, he glanced back, looking sorrowful, but he waved.

Waving back, Jack looked at Annalee. "A young colored woman got murdered. Eddie's too young for this one."

"What have you heard?" Annalee searched his eyes.

"That's the problem. I haven't heard a peep. Not one word. Nobody's talking—not even the church gossips. For a preacher, that means something."

"Then I've got a little idea." Annalee let Jack help her out of the car a few blocks from her place.

"Right, let's walk," he said. "Hand me that shopping bag. We'll clear our heads."

"It's a muddle, yes. Let's walk and think." She even let him hold her hand a moment in public. "But maybe I've got an even better way to start."

Her plan wasn't elaborate or fancy. Just something that came to her mind after Cooper Coates' swanky party, which she now described to Jack.

"What'd you wear?"

"Don't change the subject."

"I'm not totally. But mooning about you looking beautiful means I can put off thinking about that dead girl—whoever she is."

"That's the thing. She's not from Denver. At least nobody seems to know her—or even seen her."

Explaining Eddie's theory about the carnival bringing in new people, she told Jack about visiting Sonny Dawkins' carny that morning—to ask about any missing young women who'd traveled to town with Dawkins, but they didn't find that at all.

"Dead end."

"Right. But it made me think of another way: what if the dead girl left a clue in Coates' fancy potting shed?"

"On purpose?" Jack looked skeptical. "She suspected she was going to be killed?"

Annalee stepped on a crack in the sidewalk, defying it. "No clue. But there's one curious thing. In her hand, the poor girl was still holding a red rose. Almost as if to send a message. One budded red rose."

"Not surprising. Coop's backyard is loaded with flowers of every kind."

"But not every kind." Annalee looked up at Jack. "I've been studying on plants, working on my little garden—"

"I know." Jack grinned. "I drove by your cabin a couple of days ago. You weren't home, but I saw you'd been scratching in the dirt on the west side."

"Not scratching. I'm planting, thank you very much." She paused. "Well, sowing." She swallowed. "Let's call it that."

"Sounds good. I saw a few rows."

"Right, beans and peas. Lettuce and carrots. One little tomato plant. Just to see what I can grow—if anything. I planted some marigold flowers, too, because I think they're pretty." She took a breath. "But you never know what you'll dig up."

"You never cease to amaze me, Watson." He grabbed her hand again, squeezing it.

"Gardening helps people see the world better." She squeezed back. "Well, maybe. I don't half know what I'm doing. Oh, Jack—"

"What's wrong?"

She couldn't answer. She wasn't sure how to tell him about the letter found in the dirt in a rusty box. She'd let it stay buried. For now.

"It's nothing. Growing things is a mystery. So, I'm reading about the famous flower expert George Washington Carver."

"The peanut man?"

"There's far more to him. He talks to plants." She squinted at the sky. "He talks to God first, that is. Then he talks to plants—and they tell him things. Well, God talks to him—through the plants."

Jack gave her a look. "What's this got to do with the dead girl, Annalee?" He tightened his hand, led her down rocky gravel to her cabin, took the two steps to her front porch.

"What do you want me to do?" He sat down on her top step, stretched out his legs, pulled her down next to him.

"Go back with me to Cooper Coates' backyard. To his potting shed. Tonight. After everybody's asleep."

"In the dead of night? But why?"

"To see what other clues she might've left."

Jack rubbed his chin. "Why not just call Coates? We could walk over there right now and check around with him—if he hasn't already."

"Well . . ."

Jack gave her a look. "Oh, I see—because you don't trust Coates, one of my best church members. Pays his tithes every Sunday, donates thousands to the building fund, serves on half a dozen committees, visits the sick."

Annalee scoffed. "Cooper Coates doesn't visit the sick."

"Well, he pays his tithes."

"But a dead woman was found in his backyard. If he's not a prime suspect, who is? Even if he claims he has an alibi and is innocent."

"So, we'll break in and enter? At night? On private property. After everybody's asleep?"

"Well, it's outdoors. So, when you think about it, Reverend Blake, that's not actually breaking and entering."

"Okay, Eddie." He laughed a moment, scooted closer. Then he sighed, pushed a curl off her forehead, and searched her eyes. "What time do you want me to pick you up?"

"Two a.m."

"Good gravy." Jack gave her a grin. "Only criminals and half-steppers are out that time of night."

"How do you know who's out then?"

"Guess we'll find out."

Jack stretched and stood, unlocked her door with an extra key she'd given him. He stepped inside to set the shopping bag down, then came back out and pulled her to her feet. He grabbed her by the hands and drew her close, circled her with his arms. He leaned to her ear. "What dress did you wear to that garden party?"

She looked up at him. "Just a little summer number."

"Would you wear it tonight?"

"While we're at Coates'?"

"Right, breaking and entering."

"We'll be in the dark—in the moonlight. So I'll wear something dark. With quiet shoes." She winked at him. "You'll do the same, handsome sir."

He grinned a moment. Then still looking at her, eyes wide open, he stopped to kiss her, and she didn't pull away. He was alive and she was glad to feel the urgent breathing of him, making her feel desired but also safe, and not terrified of anything—even things buried—just for now.

Because their case would start tonight, and it would be danger-ous, putting them both in harm's way. So she'd dress for danger. But would that be enough to stay alive?

———◇———

Jack swung his car down her road right on time. Two on the dot. She heard the car idling, turned the key in her dead bolt, and crawled onto his front seat—smiling at his sleuthing outfit: black sport shoes, black khakis, and a black preacher shirt, but no preacher collar.

"Hey there, Sherlock," she whispered.

He winked. "Hey there, yourself—wearing blue jeans?" His voice sounded loud to her. "You're ready to wrangle, Miss Cute."

She put a finger to his mouth. "Keep your voice low."

He grabbed her hand, kissed a fingertip.

"Stop that," she whispered lower.

"Why? Not a soul around. We're nowhere near Coates' place. He's several blocks over."

"But it's two a.m. Somebody might see us. How would you explain to your church people why you're driving around Five Points at half past middle of the night with 'that young gal professor'?"

"My gossips would have a field day."

"So, Reverend Blake, keep your voice low." She squared her shoulders, trying to look proper and purposeful—telling him, in a soft voice, how she'd started writing another article—hoping to sell it soon. "It's on the Gospel of John, chapter fifteen. God is the Gardener." She prattled on about her premise, her voice dropping, not half listening even to herself. The talking would settle her nerves, which were firing. Jack looked jittery too.

He parked his car a block from Coates' house, stopping at the curb outside a colored dentist's office. Annalee was scurrying with him in the dark, headed toward Coates' yard, when they saw a car approaching with its lights out.

"What now?" Jack whispered. Annalee slipped behind a towering, flowering lilac bush. Jack followed next to her. Moving some leaves, they peered through as the car turned into Coates' portico drive. The driver's door opened and the person sliding out turned out to be Coates himself.

Annalee gave Jack a look. The city's 2 a.m. half-steppers apparently included his tithe-paying church member—driving home in the dark without his lights on. Annalee peered harder, watched Coates step softly from the car and head for his front porch.

Then Coates stopped.

Jack gripped Annalee's hand. Saying be still? She held her breath. Coates jerked his head toward the side of the house, looking straight at the big bush where they hid—as if discerning somebody there.

But just as quickly, he stepped onto his wide porch, unlocked the impressive front door, entered his house, and shut the door. They heard the dead bolt click. Then the front porch light snapped off.

"Second thoughts," Annalee whispered. "Let's leave. I thought he'd be fast asleep, but your fancy church member's just getting home."

"He'll be in bed soon likely, snoring," Jack whispered back. "C'mon, we're here now. Let's do the deed." He searched her eyes. "For the dead girl."

Annalee nodded. "For the dead girl. But let's make it quick." She tiptoed around the bush, moved the few steps toward Coates' huge lilac arbor, put one hand on the gate, and pushed it open, keeping one ear tuned to hear Coates, praying he wouldn't return.

As she stepped through the gate, eyeing Jack to follow her, she froze. At what? A snarling growl? Deep. Angry. Chilling. Arising from inches away, somewhere in the dark garden, just as its source—a massive dog—leaped at her, barking and snapping.

Annalee jerked back.

"Jack!" Her whisper was half cry.

"Watch it." Jack steadied her. "German shepherd," he whispered.

She nodded, trembling, expecting Jack to back them away, grab her by the arm, and pull her to a run, fleeing the creature. But Jack dropped to his knees in front of the angry dog—ignoring its pacing, growling, menacing, fuming at them—desperate to keep the dog quiet so it wouldn't alert Coates, even if it simply was protecting his property. Annalee hadn't seen one hint of a dog at Coates' party. Mercy, she'd had her share of angry animals today—and she didn't enjoy the experience one bit.

Jack had turned sideways on his knees, not facing the dog straight on or looking it in the eye—maybe something he'd learned about German shepherds in the war. Annalee sure hoped so. Jack pulled on Annalee's sleeve, gestured her to kneel and do the same.

Both knelt now under the lilacs, Annalee desperate for Coates not to hear his dog snapping and carrying on.

"It's okay . . . Bullet," Jack whispered, repeating the name inscribed on the tag hanging from the dog's thick collar. He whispered the name again. "Bullet."

"*That's* the dog's name?" Annalee's whole body was shaking as she cowered before a hundred-pound canine growling from deep in its throat, its teeth showing, whose name was Bullet.

"I'm leaving," she whispered to Jack. But she knew they had to keep the dog quiet whatever it took. Jack, still kneeling, reached out his right hand, palm down, talking calmly to Bullet, calling him a good dog, telling him everything was okay.

"Reach out your hand," he whispered to Annalee. "Let him sniff."

Jack was letting the dog snuffle at his hand, forearm, elbow, shoulder, then both shoulders as the dog paced, growled, and circled him. Finally, the dog sniffed at Jack's face, which Jack allowed, still keeping his eyes down, not showing any challenge to the fearsome animal.

"Your hand, too," Jack whispered to Annalee.

Shaking worse now, Annalee extended a trembling hand, let

the dog sniff it—feeling his hot breath and wet nose, reminding her how she'd wanted a dog as a child, but her father said no. "I can barely bring home enough food to feed you." She'd thought a dog would be a sweet little fluffy pet, something she'd love so it would love her back. Now a dog named Bullet seemed half ready to eat her alive.

As Jack let the dog see he wasn't a threat, urging Annalee to do the same, the dog stopped growling, pacing around them half a dozen times. Then finally Bullet sat on his haunches, no longer on high alert, even letting Jack rub under his chin. Jack told Annalee to do the same. Still trembling, she gave the dog a little scratch, which he seemed to like.

"We're going to the shed," Jack whispered to the dog, as if he understood. "To the shed, Bullet."

"To the shed," Annalee whispered, forcing herself to sound calm. "Even though I wish I were at home, safe under my own bed." She smiled. "Bullet."

The dog cocked his head at her but didn't growl or bark. When Jack slowly stood, petting him as he walked, Bullet allowed this—even turning back to look at Annalee, as if to ask if she were coming too.

Tiptoeing slowly behind Jack and Bullet, Annalee finally reached the shed, let Jack open the door—which didn't dare squeak because every inch of Cooper Coates' property was stringently well maintained. So the door was well-oiled, quiet, and pulled open now as Jack, Annalee, and Bullet entered the shed—Bullet leading them—with Annalee knowing she'd somehow crossed a line in a murder case, and in her own life, that wouldn't let her turn back.

In the shed, they rooted around in the dirt where the young woman's body had lain and found nothing for a long time—both stopping from moment to moment to make sure Coates hadn't heard their snooping, Jack still assuring Bullet he was "such a good dog."

Believing that apparently, the dog lay down just inside the door, looking smart and well-groomed, calmly watching but still alert.

So they searched with dispatch here, there, and everywhere, not finding anything suspicious. Coates' shed was pristine. Every single thing in place. What would they even find here?

"A murder weapon." Annalee moved a neat stack of garden magazines. "Is that what we're looking for?" She was still whispering.

"Something sharp? Or extra heavy?" Jack whispered as he looked top to bottom at orderly shelving, then checked every corner of the shed. A collection of garden tools, hanging on nails in order of size, occupied one wall, but none were heavy or even that sharply pointed. Besides, what murderer rehangs a weapon in its precise place after bludgeoning somebody? None showed bloodstains, in fact. But the young woman hadn't appeared beaten or stabbed, just dead. With a slightly bruised neck. Bless her soul.

"Nothing here," Annalee agreed.

"You ready to scram?" Jack finally whispered. He'd left the shed door open, letting the faint moonlight help them to see inside. Now he grabbed the door to pull it wide so they could leave.

Jack looked up. He froze.

Annalee froze.

Above the door on a narrow shelf sat two green glass bottles, each bearing garden poison—labeled cyanide and arsenic. A few other bottles and jars also sat on the shelf, all displayed in order of size. The two green bottles sat on the end, labels facing forward, almost begging to be noticed.

"Wow, Sherlock," Jack whispered.

"So, was she poisoned?" Annalee hated the question. It sounded like some clichéd detective story plot. Except hovering above her were those two toxic bottles—both looking already opened and used. Recently? She had no way of telling.

"Something's not adding up." Jack looked at his pocket watch. "We need to move it."

"Not adding up? How?"

"A cop friend—one of the colored guys on street patrol—told me the young woman's death will be wrapped up fast. No big investigation."

"Case closed?"

"Looks like it. No suspects. She's just a dead colored girl—"

"And that's the end of it."

"She'll be tossed in a pauper's grave before the week's out."

Annalee looked down at Bullet, who was now rooting around with his front paws in the dirt.

"Let's get out of here." Jack headed out the door, but Annalee didn't move.

"Wait. Why is Bullet digging?"

Kneeling to the ground, Annalee could see in the moonlight, just under the top layer of the shed's dirt floor, the gleam of thin, gold-toned metal. She tilted her head. It was a necklace. More detective story nonsense? Yet here sat this: a shiny necklace, its tiny clasp rudely broken. It even held a locket. The annoyed policemen hadn't found it because they hadn't bothered to look that hard. Same with the coroner's people.

Annalee picked it up.

"Good boy, Bullet." She scratched the dog under his chin a moment, opened the locket, tried to make sense of the faded photograph inside.

"Is that Coates' child?" Jack knelt too, to look. "Or her late mother?"

"I'm saying no. Recognize the photo?"

Jack squinted in the half-dark. "Well there, what d'ya know? It's Valerie Valentine. My fancy church member."

"But younger?"

Bullet started to whimper then. Suddenly, without a warning— or even a fare thee well—the dog shot from the shed, headed across the yard.

"Bullet!" Coates sounded sleep weary. "Where are you, boy?"

"Gracious." Annalee slipped behind the door, jammed the necklace in the back pocket of her blue jeans, huddled next to Jack.

Jack nodded at her, put his ear to the door, probably praying that his church member Coates wouldn't find him secreted in his fancy garden shed in the middle of the night.

Coates messed about with the dog for a few minutes, letting Bullet chase around on the other side of the big yard, but didn't bring him near the shed.

Then, to Annalee's relief, she could hear Coates call and praise the dog one last time, then finally walk with Bullet into the house and shut the door behind them. A small, polite light by a back door went dark. Coates and Bullet seemed to be in for the night.

Annalee exhaled a silent breath and waited in the dark a moment with Jack. Then, as they eased open the shed door, they gestured each other across the yard—half running in the dark along a perimeter fence. At the lilac arbor, they slipped through the gate. Annalee latched it, breathed in the lilacs' delicate, powdery scent.

"All clear," Jack whispered, winking at her, reaching for her hand. She wanted to run quick as a flash. He probably did too. But he held her steady—so both of them were walking fast enough, but not fleeing like bandits. Still, Annalee couldn't wait to climb into Jack's car and speed into the night.

But as they approached the Buick, they both stifled groans at seeing a man crouching by the car, peering in the windows.

"It's Doc Hayes." Jack whispered the name.

"Hayes—the dentist?" Annalee looked down at the sidewalk, avoided Hayes' eyes, wished she could melt clean through the pavement. "What's he doing out? At two something in the morning?"

"He's probably wondering that about us." Jack straightened his back, walked Annalee to his car, not holding her hand now.

"Hey there, Doctor Hayes." Jack smiled at his church member. "Everything okay?"

The doctor half glanced away.

"I'm just—" the doctor stammered. Because he was guilty of something too? "I couldn't sleep. So, I'm just taking a walk—by myself." He wrung his hands. "Just checking on my office."

"Well, don't stay out too late. Be careful."

"Thank you, pastor. I'd better go. Good night."

The doctor touched his hat to Annalee, hurried away.

"What was that about?" Annalee whispered as Jack opened his driver's side car door.

"No clue." Jack looked in his rearview mirror at Doc Hayes scurrying fast down the block. "But I have a feeling I'll find out sooner than later." Jack shook his head. "Oh, I love my church members."

Annalee nodded at him, scrambled in, and watched Jack fire the engine, punch the fuel, and race off, heading away from Coates' place—and also away from Doc Hayes at now almost three. A couple of blocks down, he jerked the car around in a quick turn, swung back into Five Points, aiming toward Annalee's place.

Parked outside her cabin, he let out a long breath, grinning as he exhaled.

"That was crazy. And fun? And stupid and—"

"Dangerous and—"

"Eye-opening. Who knew, at all hours, my church members were coming and going across Five Points from one direction to the other."

"If we'd stayed out longer, who knows who we would've run into." Annalee pursed her lips. "I just hope Doc Hayes doesn't tattle on us. Out together past midnight. Holding hands. But we found a clue."

Annalee pulled out the necklace, clicked open the hinged locket. They both leaned to look. Annalee read aloud an inscription opposite the faded photograph: "'From Aunt Volly to my special niece, Prissy Mack. Love you always.'"

Annalee's brow wrinkled. "Mack." She whispered the name. "Prissy Mack?" The young dead woman shared a last name with Lil' Baby Mack? Minnie Sawyer's mob-lynched friend? She searched Jack's eyes. "It's like you said. Something doesn't add up."

"Especially if 'Aunt Volly' is Valerie Valentine—Miss High-Class Society Woman of Colored Denver." He pursed his lips. "And may God bless her going out and coming in." He pushed a curl behind Annalee's ear. "And may he help you crack your case."

Annalee whispered to herself amen and finally let herself yawn. "Let's sleep on it."

Jack moved aside another curl and watched her yawn again. "In our two lonely beds."

Annalee gave him a gentle laugh, scooted out of the car, and wagged a finger at Jack. "Good night, my handsome sir."

He grinned and blew her a kiss.

"Caught it." Then she let herself in, locked her door, crawled into her little bed—still holding the necklace—and before she knew it herself, she fell fast asleep.

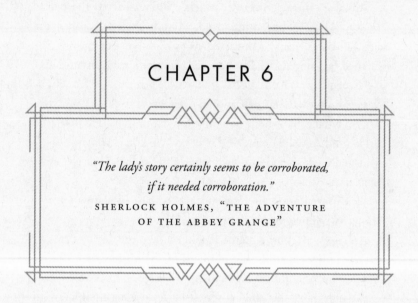

CHAPTER 6

"The lady's story certainly seems to be corroborated,
if it needed corroboration."

SHERLOCK HOLMES, "THE ADVENTURE
OF THE ABBEY GRANGE"

THE NEXT MORNING, Annalee awoke with a start and a fresh plan. It was just before ten—another late sleep for her—but no shame, she told herself, because she'd had a successful night of sleuthing with Jack and she now knew for certain her next step.

First she retrieved the necklace from inside her coverlet, brought down her first-aid kit from her shelf, and dropped the necklace inside under a stack of clean cotton bandages, away from prying eyes.

This afternoon, she'd go visit Valerie Valentine, Miss High-Class Society Woman of Colored Denver. May God bless her going out and coming in, indeed. But not before Valerie came clean about that necklace.

Annalee didn't formally know Valerie Valentine, but she knew the house where the society woman lived and had seen her often, prancing around Five Points—including almost every Sunday at Jack's church. So she felt sure that the photo in the locket, of a sweet-looking "Aunt Volly," was Valerie in the flesh, just much younger. But would the woman acknowledge that? And if she did, and the dead woman was Prissy Mack, how did Valerie Valentine connect to poor Lil' Baby Mack, lynched in Alabama? Or did she?

Mercy.

Annalee straightened up her cabin, stepped outside, and stood in her half-sown garden for a minute, telling herself not to worry about her unresponsive seedlings or anything else buried in her yard. Not yet. Thus, she came back in to work awhile on her Gospel of John paper, letting the focus of it get her ready to confront the society woman. She twisted her mouth. Maybe God would even give her a nice little detective tactic. But she shook her head. A half-baked idea.

Instead, she took a bracing bath, pouring in a drop of her only bath scent—a kind gift from Jack's landlady, Mrs. Cunningham—and changed into a summer dress, telling herself to nail down her questions for interrogating Valerie, because Prissy Mack deserved the best answers and justice. By the time Annalee walked the few blocks to the Valentine woman's house, she felt ready to take on an "aunt" who might lie—to cover secrets, not to mention the truth about a murder.

Annalee tilted her head. Valerie, for example, hadn't looked inside the shed to view the dead lady at the garden party. Because she already knew the victim?

Approaching Valerie's house, however, Annalee was distracted by three things: First, a sleek, bloodred sedan parked on the curb—the color a curious repeat of the dozen or so deep-ruby rosebushes surrounding the Valentine home in full bloom. Second, Valerie's arbors, vines, and rosebushes almost rivaled Cooper Coates' lush bounty. The house was less than half the size, but the growing things were spectacular—even though her roses didn't rival the beauty of Prissy's rose. Then third, Valerie herself was already on her porch, dressed in pale blue silks and pearls, saying goodbye to an impressive-looking white society woman who Annalee remembered seeing at Coates' party.

The woman, dressed in her own luscious silks—a blend of ivory and beige—and matching strands of pearls was thanking Valerie for a perfect lunch.

"You know every etiquette rule and follow it. I approve of your plans and will expect to talk more. I hate to leave so soon. But here's my son, Nathan—waiting for me in his fancy car." She laughed demurely, as if fancy cars were an embarrassing bother.

Noticing Annalee, the woman looked her over. "Do I know you? I am Charlotte Furness." She intoned her name, perhaps expecting that Annalee would know who she was—but not waiting for Annalee to share her name in return. She didn't extend her hand.

"Good day." Annalee gave her a nod.

"Come anytime." Valerie was gushing her airy goodbyes, not bothering to greet Annalee. "Watch your step, Charlotte."

"It's your gorgeous flowers. They take my breath away." She nodded to a bouquet of yellow roses she was carrying. "And these friendship roses from your patio garden. Spectacular. But I'd better watch where I walk and stop admiring them so much." The woman laughed. "Until next time."

On the curb, a youngish-looking man with a shock of barbered blond hair exited the sleek sedan to help the woman into the vehicle.

Noticing Annalee, he glanced at her briefly but didn't speak.

Annalee took this all in but couldn't take a measure of it. She didn't have a clue what being in society circles entailed, or whether such status was good, bad, or otherwise. All the airish talk seemed pointless. Or maybe that was too harsh. But that wasn't her worry today.

She was working on solving a young woman's murder—her questions at the ready. But Valerie Valentine cut her off.

"Well, don't just stand there. If you're here to see me, come inside the house."

Valerie turned on her heel and pushed open her scrolled screen door, letting it ease shut behind her. Following her, Annalee opened the door and stepped into the house—a well-appointed home, she had to admit, with a small but beautiful parlor. Fresh flowers in vases covered almost every surface. Prissy's rose? Annalee didn't see it here. But she could admire the gleaming room—freshly dusted, mirrors sparkling and spotless. Stacks of campaign signs lined one wall. *Vote Valerie!*

Valerie didn't offer Annalee a seat.

"What a busy morning. But my best days are. Of course, you wouldn't know about that—" And this and that.

Annalee listened to the prattle. Nervous talk. Valerie hadn't even asked her name. No courtesies, just blather. When she'd heard enough, Annalee had ditched her questions. Instead, while Valerie prattled on about the pressures of running a business, serving as acting president of the esteemed Colored Women's Civic Society, and campaigning to be voted their president, all while maintaining her gorgeous garden, Annalee interrupted.

"I'm here about Prissy."

Valerie blinked. A hard blink. No other reaction. Well, she took in a silent breath. Annalee could see that happening, watching the society woman closely.

If she were guilty of something, especially the murder of Prissy Mack—if that's who, in fact, the young woman was—this would be the moment for the color to drain from the woman's overly powdered, painfully groomed face. Or for her to act conflicted or nervous or look unsettled. Instead, Valerie picked a fallen rose petal—the ruby red—off a mirrored console table. Her nails were manicured almost a matching shade. She moved aside an embossed envelope with her name written in large calligraphy letters on the front. The return address was from the Saxton Theological Institute. The prestigious Denver seminary.

Annalee peered at it.

Valerie Valentine watched her looking at it, squared her shoulders. "And you are? That little detective?"

"Professor Spain. That is me." Annalee was determined to intone like the best of them.

"And this, who, Prissy? Is that the name you mentioned? What about her? Who is she?"

"Your niece apparently." Annalee squared her own shoulders.

Valerie glared. Annalee went on. "She's the young woman found dead in Cooper Coates' garden shed. But you already know who she is."

Valerie's mouth went tight. "I should call the police. Because you're questioning me, as if I'm a suspect, but you don't have the right, nor do you work for them. I doubt they'd have you. Yet here you are, bothering me about this unseemly problem." She waved a hand. "Look around you, Miss Spain. Do I appear as if I'd know, in any possible way, some poor girl found murdered in a potting shed? If even she was murdered." She shivered. "In fact, you need to turn yourself around and take your leave, standing there in that homemade dress—"

Annalee stepped back. *How dare she?* Then, in clear defiance, she sat herself down. *Right, Mrs. Stallworth?*

Plopping onto one of Valerie Valentine's prim parlor chairs, she settled her secondhand pocketbook onto her lap, squared her back, and pushed back a curl—which made her think of Jack, bringing to her face a self-satisfied smile. She was wearing her pretty yellow summer number, a sheath—a style she'd seen in the fancy display window at the Daniels & Fisher department store in downtown Denver. Since colored women never were sure if salesclerks would allow them to try on a garment—or show them common courtesy—Annalee had asked her friend Mrs. Cunningham to look at the dress in the window and find a pattern—maybe a Butterick or McCall's—and sew up the dress.

It fit like a glove. Jack adored it. *"Hey there, sunshine."* That was his teasing. But she'd enjoyed it—then paid Mrs. Cunningham to sew up the same pattern in pink.

Annalee, this morning, had also slipped on Minnie Sawyer's Paris-style, beige leather flats. So she felt nicely dressed, even if Valerie Valentine didn't appear to think so. The woman was telling her as much.

"As an educated woman, you should do a better job of presenting yourself—"

"I'm here about Prissy," Annalee interrupted. "Aren't you worried that a young colored woman who looked as if she'd barely started her life has been killed? On our side of town? A mere few blocks from this, your lovely home?" Annalee waved a hand too. "While she was wearing a necklace and locket with your photo in it?"

Valerie sputtered, "I don't know what you're suggesting—"

"That you have a niece, and she was murdered, Miss Valentine. But you're more worried about my 'homemade' dress?"

"I'm worried that you're a woman with potential. You also need better associates, better friends—the younger set. College graduates like yourself, not those old church women."

"Those church women? Each one is like a mother to me."

"A mother? Then they'd tell you to buy some decent dresses and stop wasting your intelligence doing 'detective work'—whatever in the world that's supposed to mean."

Annalee shoved back the chair, stood tall. "What it means is there's a dead young colored woman in the city morgue who nobody seems to care a bean about. Not even her own Aunt Volly."

"You're wasting my time." Valerie pointed to her ornate foyer. "Close my front door on your way out."

"At least go to the coroner's and look at her for yourself—"

"The coroner's. You can't be serious." Valerie stepped back. "The young woman deserves justice—whoever she is—but to think I'm related to someone like her is preposterous."

Valerie Valentine turned on her heel to leave her front room. Then she swung back. "When I saw you at Cooper Coates' event, I'd planned to inform you of our Women's Civic Society meeting this Friday afternoon. One o'clock sharp in the remodeled Phillis Wheatley Y building. I would urge you to come, start affiliating with the right people, meet some respectable young ladies. We invited a guest—an expert on gardening and plants. She's speaking on flower arranging." She sniffed. "I hear you're scratching around in the dirt at your father's old place, trying to act like a gardener, but you haven't a clue—"

"You're right." Annalee set her jaw. Valerie Valentine had cut her in a place so deep Annalee could barely see straight to retort. "So I'm a novice nobody, in the world by myself—with no connections, not even my own mother, let alone a blasted decent dress—but scratching and plowing in dirt is teaching me things." Things Valerie Valentine couldn't imagine.

"Well, keep scratching," Valerie snapped. "But you won't dig up any answers about a dead girl from me."

Such a grand speech. But when it came to digging and scratching, Valerie Valentine was working overtime pretending not to see the most important, blooming thing. Annalee Spain wasn't quitting this case. Not on her own life. If anything, after Valerie's put-downs, she'd chase this case to its murderous end.

Marching back home to her cabin, Annalee swung by the Cunninghams'. She craved breathing kind air. To hear assuring voices. She wouldn't tell Mrs. Cunningham about the necklace and locket. Nor reveal it yet to Mrs. Stallworth—who was shucking corn in Mrs. Cunningham's sun-blessed kitchen. Annalee's former landlord cooked for the Cunninghams' rooming house. She also stayed in a comfortable-looking room there. Yep, these two "old church women" weren't society ladies—but they'd proven to be true friends and they meant the world to Annalee.

So Annalee couldn't hide her anger. Valerie Valentine had grieved her last nerve. Annalee sat down at Mrs. Cunningham's kitchen table, accepted a cup of black coffee and a sweet roll, and let herself describe how Valerie Valentine had acted, sparing no details.

Mrs. Stallworth, listening, yanked at a corn husk. "I cannot abide the woman."

"You know her?" Annalee bit at her roll.

"I know how she treats people."

"I hear you, Edna." Mrs. Cunningham sniffed. "Sitting on her high horse. Acting better than everybody else."

"You're gossiping?" Annalee hadn't heard such talk from Mrs. Cunningham.

"But it's true. She has looked down her nose since the day she first got here. A Sunday at church. Overdressed like Miss Somebody Hollywood."

"So, that's her problem? We don't like what she wears?"

"It's her attitude," Mrs. Cunningham went on. "Ever since she showed up—"

"From where? When was that?"

"About five years ago."

Annalee frowned. "She came from Alabama?"

"Oh, mercy, no." Mrs. Cunningham pursed her lips. "Valerie Valentine is from Chicago. An 'important' town."

Annalee scoffed. "I mean originally. Where'd she start out? You sure it's not Alabama?" *As in Lil' Baby Mack's Alabama?* Annalee wondered.

"Who knows for sure? All she talks about is Chicago."

Annalee laughed. "But I lived in Chicago during my college years." She looked at Mrs. Stallworth. "You lived there too. For decades. Did you know her there?"

"Never laid eyes on her until I came here—and since then, all I hear is Miss Valentine this, that, and the other." Mrs. Stallworth yanked at more corn. "But will she stoop low enough to join Hearts and Hands? Never. She's too high society for us."

"And we invited her twice." Mrs. Cunningham counted off two on her fingers. "And we're a solid group of church ladies. All of us." She sighed. "Well, she invited Hearts and Hands to her civic society meeting—not to join, but for their special guest this Friday."

"Oh, that." Mrs. Stallworth scoffed. "She just wants a full house. Her speaker is some woman from 'back East.'"

"Hoity-toity." Mrs. Cunningham rolled her eyes. "But I'm going. What about you?" She turned to Annalee. "We actually learn great tips at those meetings. How to vote. Where to shop. Modern recipes—not that down-on-the-farm stuff. All the rich colored ladies attend. They even have a dress code. No home-spun. They're trying to build up people, Annalee. You might learn something."

Annalee narrowed her eyes. No homespun? She set down her cup. "I hadn't planned to attend, but now that you mention it . . ."

"So, you'll go?" Mrs. Cunningham looked hopeful.

Annalee smiled, curious about people she might find there. A young woman's killer? "In fact, I believe I will."

CHAPTER 7

"We must have something definite."

SHERLOCK HOLMES, "THE ADVENTURE
OF THE SECOND STAIN"

THAT AFTERNOON? For Annalee, it was for thinking. For working her little brain long enough to understand what she knew about the murder of Prissy Mack. *So what do I know?*

Hardly anything.

Annalee despaired of that.

But nobody had hired her to take the case. Not fancy Cooper Coates. Not Valerie Valentine's just-as-fancy civic club. Not Robert Ames, the federal agent who'd hired her in March to solve a curious case that had gotten ignored by police.

Not even Jack. Nor his church—which was up to its eyeballs with rebuilding their burned-out sanctuary, plus the parsonage where Jack had lived. Giving their church time, or even money, to help solve the murder of a young woman not known by a soul in the congregation wouldn't be unusual for Jack's generous flock. But now?

That's what she asked him when Jack stopped to hear about her visit to Valerie's.

She met him with a frown.

"Hard morning." He searched her eyes. "I see it."

"A test." She described Valerie's rudeness, her denials about knowing poor Prissy.

"Could she be telling the truth?"

"She's lying." Annalee set her jaw. "But one other thing: any idea why she'd get invited to Saxton Theological Institute for some fancy hoedown?"

"That envy I hear?"

"It might be. But either way, do you know anything about the seminary that might shed light on the young woman's murder? Saxton folks were at the garden party. Then Minnie Sawyer said her sister had connections there."

"Saxton? Seems a solid place. Strong students. Some visit Mount Moriah, ask me about my sermons. Still, I hear gossip sometimes. Rumors and whispers about the new president. Never met him, but . . ." Jack shook his head.

"But what?"

"Let's take a break first."

Annalee breathed deep. "Is that what I need?"

To answer, Jack helped her drag two chairs from her cabin out to her yard, setting them under her maple tree in the shade. She'd already changed into her jeans and a simple white blouse. Her yellow "summer number," the sheath, hung inside on a hanger—recovering from Valerie Valentine's put-downs.

Now, sitting with Jack in the shade near her cabin, sipping fresh lemonade made by Mrs. Stallworth, she wondered aloud if anybody on earth cared about the death of poor Prissy Mack.

"What about your church?"

"Mount Moriah is your church too."

"I guess that's why I'm asking. What if the church took a

stand for Prissy? The whole congregation calling for a thorough investigation—not just sweeping her killing under a rug and tossing her in a pauper's grave."

"You really want to solve this. I see it in your eyes."

"It's like you said—something about it doesn't add up. But who cares about her? Anybody?"

"The person who killed her cares. But, Annalee, here's a hard question—"

"I'm afraid to hear it."

"But I have to ask it."

Annalee sighed. "I know. What if Prissy was the one doing wrong?" She blinked. "It's a fair question. Still, my gut says no."

"Mine does too."

"But for me," Annalee said, "that doesn't matter. Nobody deserves to be murdered. Sure, the girl's a stranger to all of us, and maybe she was doing some kind of wrong, but shouldn't that make her matter more? I mean, after all, God knows her, loves her, wants her in the fold." Annalee set her jaw. "That's enough to keep asking who did it—and why—and look to others to stand up for her."

"Others at the church, you mean."

"If they're willing."

"Well." Jack tightened his mouth. "We're rebuilding now. We're making progress, finally. Foundation's in. Scaffolding's up. But our question is what are we building? And why? A monument to ourselves? Or to help folks who need us?"

"So, you'll think about it?" Annalee searched his eyes.

"It's not me. That young woman named Prissy mattered to Almighty God himself. End of sermon." Jack squinted. "But what would we have to pay you? To take the case for us—the members of Mount Moriah AME Church?"

"It's not money. Even if I need it." Annalee grinned a little. "That payment from my March case won't last forever. But most

I need allies—folks standing with me on behalf of Prissy. People who see a young dead woman as one of them, somebody who deserves a reckoning and God's good justice."

"Great sermon for real. Sisters and brothers, our preacher this morning is—"

She smiled a moment but grew sober. "It's such a challenge, Jack—this detective game."

"But you're not calling it quits." He reached for her hand. "You just need people who believe in what you're doing."

She smiled. "You understand."

"I'll talk to the trustees. Steward board, too."

"Some won't like it."

"Naysayers? I've never known a church that didn't have any."

"They'll say I lured you into it. Your 'lady friend.'"

"Some will—because that's who you are. My 'lady friend.'" He gave her a sly wink. "But I'm not worrying about gossips. That's why I'm taking you on a date tonight."

She grinned. "What date?"

"To the carnival."

"With Bruno the bear?"

"Yep, Big Bruno. But also Sonny Dawkins. He gave me a call. Something's weighing on him. He begged me for a talk. Is nine o'clock too late?"

"After our two a.m. escapade? Nine sounds great." She glanced away. "But I wish I could bring Eddie. He wants so bad to help, but I haven't heard a peep out of him since yesterday."

"We'll catch up with that boy. I have a feeling he'll be coming around soon." Jack stood. "Let's get these chairs in—in case you want to do a little gardening."

"Don't tease," she scolded, meaning it.

"Never." He picked up a chair, then searched her eyes. "You're not telling me something—about your garden. What is it?"

"Will you kiss me instead?"

Jack set down the chair. "Anytime. But what are you hiding? Tell me?"

Annalee studied a cloud overhead. "Not yet. When I'm ready?"

"I can wait," Jack said. He sat in the chair. "I'm not going anywhere."

She smiled at him. "I'm not either."

Still, looking later at her frightening garden, Annalee let herself admit she'd failed. Why couldn't she nurture a single thing in her pathetic little yard? Or the real question: why did it matter so much to her now—when trying to solve a young woman's murder but not unburying the truth of her past?

She kicked a stone, done with her fretting. Then after Jack took his leave, she walked herself around Five Points to enjoy the afternoon sunshine, say hello to kind people, maybe rest her mind. A colored patrolman gave her a wave. She waved back, trying to look at ease. Still, at the hardware store, she let herself step inside— followed her nose straight to the garden tools and paraphernalia.

At a table of Burpee catalogs, she was grateful to see Five Points' stationer, Raynard Robinson. He was loaded down with yard gear—a lawn hose, two rakes, half a dozen packets of flower seeds.

"Growing something pretty, Mr. Robinson?"

"Not as pretty as all the Five Points ladies. But I'm trying." She laughed. She'd known Mr. Robinson most of her life and enjoyed his banter. A kind white man who loved all his neighbors—colored people, too. He seemed rare, but maybe he wasn't. She hoped not.

"At least you know what to grow." She gestured to his haul. "New seeds?"

"Ready to sprout. What about you? How's your garden?"

"A total failure—as everybody in Five Points seems to know." She sighed. "I can't figure my mistake."

"Maybe you're growing the wrong thing."

"Peas, mustards, lettuce? What's wrong with that?"

"But what do you love? What makes your heart sing?"

Annalee sighed. "Lilacs." She smiled. "Bouncing in the wind. Dancing in the breeze. I adore their pretty fragrance."

"Anything else?"

She searched his eyes. He actually was listening to her. She loved that about Mr. Robinson. When you talked to him, he took time to hear.

"Well, climbing vines—like clematis. The purple ones." She reached for his lawn hose to help him carry it. "Do you remember Sister Nelson? Our neighbor from years back? She used to grow clematis. I have a soft spot for them."

"They're easy to grow, too," Mr. Robinson assured. "Why struggle to grow peas and mustards?"

"I have to eat."

"The soul does, too. Feed it. Look at me—buying all these trappings and whatnot." He stepped toward the register to pay. "So, grow something pretty—like your bouncing lilacs."

"I wouldn't know where to start."

"Just find a sunny spot, dig a hole, and drop them in the ground. I'm busy at my store, but I'll come by one slow day—early fall, the best time to plant them—and I'll help you. Now off I go."

She thanked him, watched him head home, studied him. She wondered what he'd say about her mother's unearthed letter. She wouldn't know how to ask. So she walked the long way to her cabin, stopped at the corner grocery store on Welton for a few items, and headed home.

A Sherlock afternoon? It didn't feel like it. But things change fast.

CHAPTER 8

"Do you know him?"

SHERLOCK HOLMES, "THE ADVENTURE
OF THE BERYL CORONET"

JACK PICKED HER UP A LITTLE BEFORE NINE, looking Tuesday-night casual—except for a worry simmering behind dark, brooding eyes.

"You talked to your church people." Annalee scooted across his car seat.

"All but a few. Most are on board." He winked at her. "Pretty dress, Professor."

She gave him a scolding look. "Flattery will get you—"

He laughed. "I'm serious."

She beamed, moved aside her pocketbook—a larger one she didn't usually carry. She'd tied a pink ribbon on one strap for whimsy. She was glad Jack liked her dress—also pink—but she had a deeper question. "Now it's you frowning. About . . . ?"

"Sonny. He called me three times today. Something's up—he's worried sick."

"Some bit about the war?"

"Well, it's complicated."

"Oh, mercy. A secret?" She glanced at Jack.

"It's not secret to everybody. The war's over—or supposed to be. But let's get to the carnival first. Let me talk to Sonny."

At nine on a Tuesday night, the little carny was hopping with action—the weedy parking lot filled with cars and farm trucks and Denver taxis, the grounds bustling with smiling, joyful people.

Walking under Sonny's big sign, Annalee found herself smiling joyfully too. A nighttime crescent moon, plus countless strings of glowing lights, transformed the carnival's faded daytime murk into a magical, even romantic-looking wonderland.

Couples walked the grounds holding hands. Jack reached for Annalee's too, weaving his fingers through hers. The warmth of his strong hand, and his gesture, steadied her. She studied the modest promenade.

"Everything looks so different here at night." She glanced at Jack. "Unless I'm missing something."

"You're not. It's the deception—which works like that. Things can look different than they are."

"That sounds awfully cryptic, Reverend."

"Just saying—"

"Oh, look." Annalee pointed up ahead.

Little children aboard the Kiddie Whip squealed and laughed on each jagged turn—one tiny blonde girl screaming her little head off, then crying like crazy, calling for her mommy, then squealing and laughing again as the crazy-car ride whipped her and the other little passengers around.

"In the daylight, that ride looks like a death trap. But tonight . . ."

"Sonny's doing a bang-up business," Jack noted. "So, why's he worried?"

Jack then told Annalee to watch her step. She'd almost collided with another couple. "I wasn't expecting this crowd," he said.

"It's Zimba." Annalee pointed to Dawkins' carny man. Dressed in a velvety red getup, his head wrapped in a silky towering turban, he sprayed fire from his mouth—like a true fire-eater—as he strolled the grounds, drawing his own big squeals. Swirling a concoction in his mouth, he spit it out in a spray, lighting the effluence with a blazing wand—the flames rising a foot or more high.

"Well done." Annalee gave Zimba a thumbs-up.

Rushing over, Zimba waved his hand in a flourish, bowing deeply. "Miss Annalee!"

She curtsied back.

Zimba laughed, then unhooked a small megaphone from his belt and shouted an announcement. "Ladies and gentleman! Cast your eyes up! To the sky!"

"Gracious," Annalee whispered. She grabbed Jack's arm. "It's the Sawyers."

The three Alabama sisters—Minnie, Maggie, and pouty, pretty Milly—were toeing their leather-stockinged feet along a cable, one sister behind the other, as they cavorted on the impossibly thin wire stretched between two wooden platforms erected at least three stories high.

Each held a long pole, for balance apparently. But they didn't seem to need it. Instead, they looked to be taking a stroll in the park, except they each wore a skimpy, glittery, body-skimming suit—in white, silver, and bronze—showing off remarkably fit bodies and trim, gorgeous legs as they slid along the wire. Their hairdos looked perfect. Makeup dramatic. They were ready for the limelight—the piercing spotlight pointed at them by Zimba.

Annalee had heard of high-wire acts, but she'd never seen one performed. She gripped Jack's hand. "Please don't fall," she whispered at the sisters.

But she was mesmerized by the act—gaping at Minnie lying flat on the wire while her sisters hopped over her, none of them losing their cool or balance. Each trick was more daring, it seemed, and Annalee couldn't take her eyes off their show.

I wish I'd brought Eddie, she kept thinking, *so he could see this,* especially when Milly took to Maggie's shoulders, riding piggyback while Maggie traversed the thin wire, making the crowd utter a collective, stunned *"Oooooh!"*

"Can you believe—" she started to whisper to Jack.

Except, as she noticed, Jack wasn't looking at the Sawyers or the high wire. Instead, his eyes were scanning the crowd—watching the people watching the Sawyers. Or looking perhaps for Sonny?

So Annalee now did the same, looking over the crowd—seeing not just young couples, holding hands as they gazed skyward at the daring wire walkers.

Instead, her focus shifted in a curious direction.

"Who are all these white men?" she whispered to Jack.

"That's what I'm wondering."

Their question wasn't nasty or judgmental—just stating the obvious fact. Sonny Dawkins' carny was a Negro man's business. Almost all his customers were colored people too. A few white families had brought their children, drawn probably by the carnival lights shining from across the bridge to downtown.

But also in the crowd were half a dozen serious-looking white men—not the type to be attracted by cheap, twinkly lights. Some even wore business suits, looking out of place on a summer night. They also weren't standing together.

Hovering to one side was the young man who Valerie Valentine's society friend, the haughty Charlotte Furness, had said was her son. What was his name? Oh right, Nathan.

Jack squinted.

"A seminary fella?" He shook his head. "Well, I see a couple I know about."

"Saxton seminary?" Annalee looked at the men's faces. "Why in the world would they be here?" She couldn't guess their motives, but she'd make it her business to find out. Because also among them was the one mottle-faced man she'd seen—and heard—at Cooper Coates' garden party. He was, what, Thaddeus? She could still hear his voice, complaining.

"I came to see a colored man's garden. Instead, I'm seeing a colored gal in a shed. Dead."

Such a strange thing to say. But why?

Like the other men, this Thaddeus was standing alone. Huddled near the back of the crowd, munching on some probably stale popcorn, he gazed at the Sawyers' acrobatics.

But not with glee.

As with the other gentlemen, he looked not joyful watching the Sawyers end their act and take dramatic bows.

Unlike the other men, however, the man named Thaddeus looked afraid. But more than that, he looked angry as sin.

"Let's find Sonny." Annalee moved with Jack against the crowd, heading toward Dawkins' tent at the back of the carny grounds. On the way, Annalee was shocked to confront another frightened face, but much younger.

It was Eddie Brown Jr.

"Step right up. Win big." He sounded tentative, his voice jittery. Then he froze.

Seeing Annalee, Eddie jerked a hand over his face and ducked down, trying vainly to hide. But she'd already spotted him standing front and center behind a game of milk-bottle toss. Eddie was running the game, offering customers small orange-colored balls, a nickel a throw. Worse, he had help—from nine-year-old Melody Coates, who was collecting money from their customers.

"Son?" Jack frowned.

"Melody." Annalee stiffened. "What in the world are you two doing?"

"Professor. I'm working." Eddie swallowed. "Earning my keep. School's out for the summer—"

"Same here. I'm helping." Melody fidgeted. She sounded brash but looked nervous.

"Not any longer—you're not helping." Annalee pointed them both toward the promenade. "Come out from behind that counter. Both of you." She frowned at Melody. "Where are your eyeglasses?"

"They sorta fell off." Melody looked sheepish. "When I was on the Kiddie Whip."

"Young lady . . ." Annalee sighed. "Does your father know you're here?"

"He doesn't care what I do."

"Don't you believe it." She gave Melody a reproving look. Gave the same to Eddie. "Who 'hired' you two anyway?"

"Zimba." Eddie and Melody both spoke the name as if employment by Zimba made everything they were doing okay.

"This place isn't safe. Not for kids." Jack grabbed each by a shoulder. "It's after ten. You should be home. Asleep in your beds."

"You still need to find Sonny?" Annalee asked Jack.

"Wait for me here—" Jack tried to finish, but out of nowhere, Minnie Sawyer—still wearing her high-wire costume—almost knocked them all over.

She grabbed for Annalee. "Help us!"

"What's wrong?" Jack glared.

A tear slid down Minnie's face.

"What's happened now?" Annalee tried to sound calm, but Minnie's eyes showed a sober terror.

"It's Sonny." Minnie gulped a sob. "He's dead."

———————◇———————

Jack flinched. Annalee gripped his arm. "Have mercy." This life of hers—solving curious murders—meant she encountered death at horrible times in the worst ways. This was one of them. As twinkling lights glowed and Zimba ate fire, strolling the dusty midway accepting tips, Annalee reached for Minnie.

"Take us to him."

"I can't." Minnie was sobbing full out now. "I don't want to see him like that."

"Where?" Jack sounded heartsick.

"In the cage. With Bruno."

Annalee stiffened, turned to Eddie and Melody, pointed to a nearby wooden bench. "Sit there, both of you, and don't move—"

"But I can help you, Professor." Eddie protested. "I've been feeding Bruno. He knows me now."

"I helped feed him too," Melody piped up. "He likes us."

Annalee shot a glance to heaven. *Oh, these children.* "How does Bruno know you two?"

Eddie cut in. "I'm sorry, Professor. I sneaked back to the carnival yesterday—truly I'm sorry. Zimba taught me to feed him. Then Melody and I spent the whole day with Zimba, today. Getting ready for tonight. So, Bruno knows us. We're practically experts, right Melody?"

Annalee gave him a look. She couldn't begin to guess what shape Sonny was in. Torn to shreds? Mauled to the bone? Yet Eddie and Melody had befriended Big Bruno?

"We'd better find Sonny," she said to Jack. She helped Minnie sit on the wooden bench. "Wait here. We'll be back."

Grabbing each child by the hand, Annalee followed Jack along the promenade, avoiding unaware patrons. Then they took a corner to the big bear's cage. Sure enough, there lay Sonny—face up on the cage floor, eyes staring at nothing, his body stone still. No breathing. No sign of life. And watched over by Bruno.

The bear hadn't mauled him, by all appearances. Not a scratch, scrape, or claw mark was evident on Sonny, still wearing his too-fancy but worn-looking circus master's suit, and still not looking comfortable in it. Not even in death.

"Who did this?" Jack hissed through pain.

Annalee felt his sorrow. "I'm so sorry, Jack."

"He served in a war—and he dies like this? In a carny bear's cage?"

"Bruno." Eddie called out to the bear.

"We're here, Bruno," Melody chimed in, too loudly for Annalee's comfort.

"Don't rile him." Annalee gripped Eddie's hand tighter. Melody's too. Both children felt warm and sticky.

"Cotton candy?" Both Eddie and Melody squirmed. Bruno, meantime, had hulked to his corner.

"Who can get Sonny out of there?" Annalee asked the children.

"Here comes Zimba." Eddie pulled Annalee toward the carny man. "Help us."

Zimba's big circus smile greeted them but vanished when he saw Sonny in the cage.

"Mr. Dawkins? Sir?" Zimba turned to Annalee. "What happened? I'll call a doctor—"

"Show me to a phone." Jack sounded angry. "Any stores nearby? I'll call the police."

"Cops are already here." Zimba pointed to the crowd. "Some colored patrolmen. Sonny hired them. They're in uniform. While you find them, I'll pull Mr. Dawkins from the cage—"

"Sonny." Maggie Sawyer rushed over, wearing a short robe tied at the waist. Her fancy costume peeked out from the top. "What happened? Help him, Zimba. Open the cage."

"Watch the bear." Annalee still gripped the children's hands.

"Bruno's not dangerous," Eddie said, but he didn't look totally certain. "Right, Mr. Zimba?"

"Get back, everybody." Zimba tossed down his fire-eating paraphernalia and waved back a growing, curious crowd. Grabbing a set of keys from a pocket in his outfit, Zimba approached the cage door—talking low to Bruno, assuring him. But Zimba's hands were shaking with fear.

Bruno stood and huffed in his corner. His eyes roamed the crowd, then zeroed in on Zimba.

Annalee turned to Eddie. "What do bears eat? Did you find out?"

"They eat berries, Professor. Isn't that strange? A big bear like Bruno eating little berries?"

Annalee released the children's hands.

"Actually, that's not strange at all." Annalee opened her pocketbook, reached inside for the item she'd purchased earlier at the corner grocery store in Five Points.

"Berries?" Eddie grinned when he saw what she'd brought.

"A half gallon of them. Blueberries. I called the Denver Zoo." She eyed Bruno. "Where shall we put them? So Zimba can get inside the cage?"

"Here, toward the back," Melody chimed in again. "I can do it."

"No, we'll feed him together." Annalee gestured the children toward the cage, praying with all her might their approach didn't alarm Bruno. "Walk naturally, slowly."

Both children nodded, joining her in a casual approach.

"Talk to him, Eddie," Annalee said. "Quietly."

"Nice boy, Bruno. Look, berries."

Annalee smiled at the bear but felt completely ridiculous. Did bears even understand a human smile? With one swipe, he could take out the jittery three of them.

Instead, Bruno seemed to tilt his head as Annalee and the

children—all holding the stash of berries with trembling hands—pushed the package slightly inside the cage.

Melody let go first, jerking back her hands. Annalee and Eddie did too, meaning the berries ended up not on the edge of the cage in one neat pile but rolling out of the container like a tiny rivulet of fruit, all of it twirling one by one toward Bruno.

The big bear sniffed then started picking up the berries with his big paws, jamming the purple fruit in his huge mouth.

Seeing the distraction, Zimba opened the cage door, slid to the floor, eased like a silent snake toward Sonny Dawkins' still body, and pulled out his dead boss—a hand under each shoulder. Zimba laid Sonny down in the sawdust, ripped off his turban and placed the fabric over Sonny's face after closing his eyes for dignity. Then, in a flash, he closed the cage door and, with trembling hands, locked it.

"Oh, poor Sonny." Maggie Sawyer knelt by her cousin's body, rocking herself, moaning over him.

"I'll get Minnie," Zimba said.

But Minnie had pushed her way through the crowd. Seeing her still cousin on the ground, she fell over his body, sobbing. "I'm so sorry."

Annalee watched all of this, not sure why she felt confused by it, but trying to keep herself and the children from adding to the distress. Still, she had a question.

"Is Milly around? Shouldn't you tell her?" she asked Zimba.

Minnie jerked up. "Milly's gone! She left right after our show—with Malcolm Kane. That man from that seminary—"

"The Reverend Kane?" Annalee asked again. "The seminary president?" What was going on over there? At the so-called Saxton Theological Institute of Denver?

Annalee looked around for Jack. Breathing relief, she saw him hurrying back with two police officers, both young colored patrolmen.

"Get a tarp," one told Zimba. "Got a stretcher?"

"Yeah, we do." Zimba headed toward a back tent. "It's in case a girl falls off the high wire."

In the same moment, Annalee heard an ambulance siren. The drivers turned out to be young Negro men too, both dressed in their ambulance whites. She looked up proudly at them. She couldn't imagine how they got their jobs. But she felt grateful for their employment.

Then in a rush, the body of Sonny Dawkins was ferried away—leaving Minnie and Maggie Sawyer clinging to each other, sobbing, looking stunned and broken.

"Not poor Sonny," Minnie moaned.

"But what about us?" Maggie gripped her sister's hands. "What'll we do? We've got a couple more weeks in this sorry town."

"That's long enough," Annalee whispered to herself. But for what?

To figure out why newcoming strangers to Denver are dying? Long enough for her to stop the killings? She blinked. She had to stop it. Dead cold.

CHAPTER 9

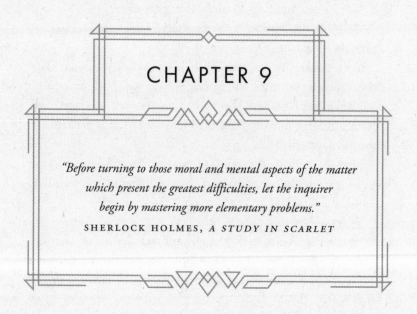

"Before turning to those moral and mental aspects of the matter which present the greatest difficulties, let the inquirer begin by mastering more elementary problems."

SHERLOCK HOLMES, *A STUDY IN SCARLET*

In Jack's car, Annalee and Jack drove Eddie and Melody away from the carnival, away from the night's odd incident. On the way, Annalee thanked them both for helping her distract Bruno the bear with the blueberries.

"I couldn't have done it without you, and I want to thank you."

"Thanks for letting us help—" Eddie started to say.

"But—" she turned herself to the back seat to give Eddie and Melody a full-on look—"am I pleased about you 'working' at the carnival?"

The two sat silent.

"Why'd you do it?" Annalee asked. "What were you thinking?"

"Actually, Professor—" Eddie started in.

Annalee shot up a brow. "No funny business, Eddie."

"Well, we thought it would be exciting," Melody piped up. "And fun—"

Jack interrupted. "How'd you two meet each other anyway?"

To explain, Eddie unfurled a convoluted story about wanting to see the fancy backyard of Cooper Coates after reading about it in the papers. So he took himself there, saw Melody out front playing hopscotch and—after she showed him her father's garden and the shed "where the dead lady was found"—he invited her to go to the carnival with him.

"Without asking her father?" Annalee could hear the fury and disappointment in her own voice.

"Well, he's hardly ever home," Melody tried to explain. "He doesn't care where I go."

"Not another word on that," Jack chimed in. "I'll talk to Brother Coates."

"I will too." Annalee swung to face forward. Then she turned back to Eddie. "So, was it fun? Working at the carnival?" She gave them a look. "I assume Zimba 'hired' you to work those games."

Eddie sighed. "His part-time worker didn't show up, so he asked us to help. I thought it would be exciting."

"I thought so too." Melody nodded at Eddie.

"But a lot of it isn't exciting at all, right, Melody?" Eddie sounded conflicted. "Not fun either."

"Meaning what?" Annalee searched his eyes.

"Well, the games, Professor. They're crooked. Those milk bottles? They got weights inside, so they won't all fall during the toss game. Then the ball hoop—it's not round, and it's kind of smaller than the ball—"

"So you can't really score a basket," Melody said.

"And the balloon game—that's crooked too. The balloons are underinflated—"

"And the darts are real dull," Melody added.

"They weigh less than normal darts," Eddie added. "So, getting a balloon to burst is pretty much impossible."

"But not impossible to steal from people? Because that's what you were doing, right?" Annalee didn't wait for an answer. "It's 'Step right up! And let me take your money.' Is that what you were doing?"

"I know, Professor." Eddie didn't argue. "That was wrong."

Melody sat silent.

"I'm glad you both understand," Annalee finally said. "Thank you, Eddie—for telling the truth about the carny scams. Both you and Melody. Did you have even a moment of simple guilt about it?"

"Actually it felt horrible." Eddie half laughed. "It's cheating people. I don't know how Zimba does that every night."

"Well, let's not repeat it. Right?" Annalee ended that discussion. "Here's your house, Melody. Let's get you inside."

Cooper Coates was already on the porch, pacing with Bullet. When Coates saw Melody climb out of Jack's car with Annalee, he looked relieved but furious. Annalee stepped to the porch with the child.

"Inside now." Coates hissed at Melody. "Where are your spectacles?"

"I lost them. I'm sorry, Father. I'll get them back."

"I doubt that—"

"It wasn't her fault." Annalee tried to explain.

"You've been driving around late at night with my daughter? I'm calling the authorities."

Melody jumped in to protest. "Miss Annalee didn't do anything wrong."

"Upstairs. Now."

Annalee pushed Melody toward the front door, watched her slink inside, stood there while Coates fumed. Bullet watched this, then moved closer to Annalee. With a contented sigh, the dog lay down at her feet.

Coates reached to jerk the dog's collar. "I'm calling child welfare—"

"Actually, Mr. Coates," Annalee finally said, "I was downtown with Pastor Blake at the carnival when we saw Melody there—essentially by herself. We could've called the authorities ourselves on you. Instead, we're delivering Melody home, safe and sound—believing you'd be glad to see her."

Coates bristled. "What exactly are you implying?"

Jack had exited the car. He stepped to the porch. "It's late, sir. We didn't think Melody should be at the carnival alone late at night, so we brought her home. It was an upsetting evening. The carnival master was found dead—"

"Killed?" Coates looked alarmed. "Somebody else, Blake?"

"Melody will probably tell you about it," Jack said, "if you're not too hard on her. That's all we're saying." He gestured to Annalee. "We'll leave you now."

"Yes, good night." Annalee nodded to Coates, patted Bullet's head, stepped off the porch, and walked with Jack to his car. Neither turned to look back. Instead, Jack opened his driver's door and let Annalee scoot inside in a flash.

Still she heard Coates yell, "How do you know my dog?"

But Jack had fired the engine, hit the fuel lever, pressed the accelerator pedal, and taken off. On the dark street in front of Coates' beautiful home, they left Cooper Coates behind—a man, it seemed, with a confused heart and more than a few unspoken answers.

"Can I stay at your place tonight, Professor?" Eddie sat crouched in the car's back seat. "Or with you, Reverend Blake?"

Jack had taken a right turn onto the wide street leading to Eddie's boys' home. "The child authorities wouldn't approve, son."

Eddie stayed silent.

"We're trying to keep you safe and stay out of trouble ourselves." Annalee looked back at Eddie. "It's frustrating, I know. But as we've told you many times—" she started to say, but she held her tongue. That's because, to her surprise, Eddie had begun to cry.

He rarely did that. At twelve, he'd seemed to have outgrown a younger child's emotional makeup.

Except right now, sitting alone on the back seat of Jack's big car, Eddie had run low, apparently, on his twelve-year-old bravado. Tears spilled and were running unabated down his face.

Annalee glanced at Jack, blinked hard. Finally, after a while, she reached in her purse for her pretty handkerchief. She turned to give it to Eddie. He took it and wiped at his face.

"I'm so sorry," Annalee finally said.

"It's not fair," Eddie answered in a whisper. "After everything's over, everybody's got a home where they can go—except me."

Annalee listened. Nothing made her feel more miserable or helpless than Eddie's despair about not having his birth family—and now being denied the family he'd come to want.

With both of his young parents dead—his mother from illness, his pastor father from Klan mischief—Eddie had bonded like printer's glue with Annalee, developed a loving respect for Jack. He'd turned their romance into a dream that would end in their marriage, with him as the child they'd joyfully adopt and take in.

In his mind, in fact, Annalee and Jack already were his family. He'd told her as much. But as she'd explained to him countless times, no Negro couple—even legally married—could adopt a white child. The laws absolutely refused it.

Annalee and Jack were breaking the law even conducting a relationship with Eddie, made worse by Eddie breaking rules so often at the boys' home they all could face heat. Sneaking out.

Staying away late. Talking up his crime-fighting escapades with Annalee.

White couples probably came to the home often, looking for a child to adopt. But Eddie hadn't made the cut, even if he'd wanted a home with a family of folks he didn't know.

He sighed, threw Annalee's handkerchief onto the car seat. "Grown-ups make their own rules all the time, even if they're bad rules—or bad people." Eddie kicked the back of the car seat. Annalee felt the kick but didn't fuss.

"Don't think about that tonight," she finally said. She asked Eddie to hand back her handkerchief and told him thank you.

"Here's your place, son. Next block," Jack said. He pulled to the curb, cut the lights on his car. "Need help out?"

Eddie shook his head. He clicked the car handle but didn't move to depart.

Annalee reached back, touched Eddie's cheek, let her hand rest there a moment. "You look exhausted. What's on the books tomorrow at the boys' home?"

Eddie shrugged. "A fishing trip. Some church club is taking everybody to Sloane's Lake."

"I like the sound of that," Jack reached back and gave Eddie's door a push. "You'd better go on in, son. Get to sleep—before they find out you came back late."

"Yes, sir." Eddie slumped away, then rushed back to Annalee's open car window. He searched her eyes, as if he wanted to tell her something.

She smiled at him, reached for his hand again, waiting—but he stayed silent.

"Have fun tomorrow." She tapped his nose. "Show those fish who's boss."

He nodded, wiped away the last of his tears, gave her a little wave. She waved back. Too soon, she thought, he was in for the night.

———————◇———————

At Annalee's wood cabin, she and Jack sat outside on her two front steps and watched the stars. A blaze of meteorites flashed neon green, every now and then, through the black sky, doing their best to please them. It was almost midnight.

"Look. Another one." Annalee pointed up.

Jack pointed too, then gently grabbed her hand and held it in his lap.

She didn't pull away but let him thread his fingers in hers, leaned closer to him, felt him brush a curl off her forehead, and breathed in his strong presence and maybe whatever he was going to say.

"I should've headed to the carnival sooner—to talk to Sonny. Now he's gone. I could kick myself—"

"You feel guilty? Well, you and the kids. They feel guilty too."

Jack gave her a look.

"You're good with kids, detective."

"Mercy, I'm trying." She glanced at him. "With Melody and Eddie, I mean. I know how they feel, I guess—to not be wanted as a child, especially if you don't understand why. Like with Melody. Why is Mr. Coates so harsh with her? So unloving?"

Jack sighed. "As his pastor, I know why. He and I have talked. It's nothing illegal, just something complicated."

"Life and its troubles." She studied the dark sky.

"Right—but he's working on it."

"Kids are work for sure. But for most—"

"Would you like your own?" Jack interrupted.

"My own what?"

"Your own kids."

Annalee opened her mouth but couldn't produce an answer. She blinked once, letting his words take their purchase.

"Our kids, Annalee. Would you like to have kids? With me?" He searched her eyes. "Have my babies? Well, our babies."

He squeezed her hand. She let him hold it, feeling warmth rising between them.

"If I say yes, is that what you want to hear?"

He held both her hands now. "If you say yes, is that what you mean to say?"

His questions were agonizing. She felt so unsure. Her own mother's letter lay buried nearby in the ground, and she didn't know how to tell Jack all that it meant she might not be. Because of what her mother wasn't. But Jack was asking about her—and for now. But why? Because his friend Sonny had died? Because life, indeed, can be so short?

Finally she simply whispered in the dark, "All we can be together, and all we can have together, I want that."

He gave her a look, pulled her close, pointed skyward. "Another shooting star."

The flare seemed beyond beautiful.

"Maybe it's a sign," she said.

"Or just a bright light," Jack told her. "We'll need that."

Annalee tilted her head. "Especially if we name a kid Sherlock." She bit her lip, trying not to laugh.

"Right." Jack held his laugh too. "And if our next one we name Watson."

Then they both grinned and collapsed into each other's arms, allowing the laughs they needed.

"Oh, God, help us," Annalee whispered in his ear.

Jack held her close. "I have a feeling he will."

Before Jack left, he and Annalee reflected on Sonny Dawkins. Also on Prissy. She thought he'd say more than a few idle words. Sonny, after all, was a war buddy. Without explanation, Sonny was now dead. So she invited Jack to tell her how he was feeling. He just said he wasn't sure. She understood. Didn't press him.

Instead they agreed to let the police handle the case—not certain that Denver cops would give a Negro man's death much attention, but she and Jack agreed that she should focus now, first, on the killing of Prissy Mack.

"It could be related—to Sonny's death?" she asked. "Don't you think? One right after the other?"

"I'm not sure what I think yet." Jack stood in the dark, walked over to his car, leaned on the passenger door. "Let's start with Prissy."

"Right. Tomorrow, I've got a visit to make." Annalee narrowed her eyes.

"Where?"

"Out to Saxton."

"Ah, the seminary." Jack tilted his head. "Something's cooking at that 'theological' place?"

"And to think I used to dream with all I could muster of getting a position there—which never would've happened anyway. Now I just want to know why at least two of their people ended up at a colored carnival tonight—one who was at Cooper Coates' garden party." She pondered. "And why young Milly Sawyer, the high-wire acrobat, goes to visit their president." She squinted. "And what these things might have to do with Prissy."

"Let me go with you?" Jack asked. "I could break away late in the day tomorrow."

"Nope, I'll head over there first thing in the morning."

"Watch your every step."

"I have a nice pair of new shoes." Annalee wiggled her toes and stood. "I'm praying to step just fine."

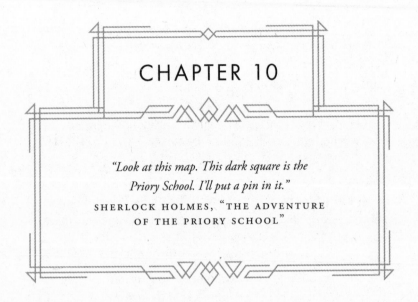

CHAPTER 10

"Look at this map. This dark square is the
Priory School. I'll put a pin in it."
SHERLOCK HOLMES, "THE ADVENTURE
OF THE PRIORY SCHOOL"

AT SAXTON THEOLOGICAL INSTITUTE, HOWEVER, Annalee could barely get in the door. She'd stepped off the streetcar near the seminary's private front gate on its property just inside Lakewood, southwest of Denver. Awed by the seminary's manicured green lawn, leafy and carefully placed trees, well-tended flower displays, and understated complex of academic buildings, she'd taken the front steps to a brick, three-story administration building, passed under arched pillars on a long stone porch, and pulled open the heavy front door.

"Wrong entrance!" A steely-eyed, high-chested receptionist barked rejection—despite a large *WELCOME DESK* sign hanging above her bright-blonde head.

And here we go, Annalee thought. *Please, God. Not today.*

"Pardon me?" Annalee kept walking toward the desk.

"Deliveries in the rear."

It was such a common insult in a colored person's life that Annalee almost spoke the words *"Deliveries in the rear"* herself for the aggrieved receptionist. Instead she took a deep breath to simply explain, "I'm not delivering."

She stood inches now from the welcome desk.

"For whatever reason you're here, you're at the wrong location." The receptionist swiveled in her desk chair, turning her back on Annalee, then glared over her shoulder. "You can turn right around and leave."

But Annalee wouldn't retreat. She'd ridden a long hour on a slow streetcar. She set down her pocketbook—the big one that had held the blueberries for Bruno the bear—on the seminary's welcome desk.

The receptionist's neck stiffened. With a huff, the woman swung around on her chair and pointed to the front door. "That way. Out—"

"I'm here to speak to Reverend Doctor Kane."

"I beg your pardon."

"I am Professor Annalee Spain, and I'm here to see the president, Doctor Kane."

The receptionist sniffed, reared back, reached across her counter, slapped open an appointment book, ran her finger down a page—then down a second page, a third page, and, for good measure, a fourth page. She looked up with a satisfied smile. "No one by that name is on his schedule."

"He's not expecting me, but I'm here to talk to him—about a murder."

The receptionist looked apoplectic. Pressing her mouth, she slammed shut the appointment book, swung around, stood with disdain, and marched toward a suite of offices at the rear of the reception area. The woman's high-heeled pumps clicked with defiance against a black-and-white marble floor.

As she disappeared behind a large office door, Annalee gave herself permission to do two things. First she turned around the appointment book to see who Dr. Kane was so busy seeing now. Among three names, she only recognized one—Thaddeus Hammer. The man from the garden party? He'd had a 9 to 10 a.m. appointment, which would be over now. Annalee would give her eye teeth to know what they were talking about.

Setting right the appointment book, she allowed herself the second thing—the right to explore the impressive reception space. Big, airy place. Handsome polished woodwork. Stately lighting and furnishings. Those marble floors. She felt drawn, in fact, to a long corridor holding framed portraits of seminary board members.

Annalee stepped closer. *I know some of these faces.* She'd seen their photos in the papers. A cattle rancher, a horse farm owner, a dozen or more "high-and-mighty," as Mrs. Stallworth would say. They included some of Denver's most known movers and shakers, politicos, business owners, and rainmakers—a top automobile dealer, a mortician, a high-flying hotel executive, three accountants, one senator, two city council members, one big restaurateur, a department store proprietor, four or five pastors of "important" churches, and three lawyers, one who appeared to be the youngest trustee of all.

Annalee squinted.

She'd seen that young lawyer, and she knew exactly where. He was the carefully barbered blond son of Charlotte Furness—Valerie Valentine's fancy society friend. Annalee recalled the young man's quick glance at her and, just as quick, his look away. He'd done the same thing at Sonny Dawkins' carnival the night before—given her a quick glance, then turned away as if not wanting to be seen noticing her.

Studying the name label next to his portrait, Annalee confirmed that the young man's name was Nathan Furness. More than a young lawyer, he was a partner with a large, well-known law firm in downtown Denver.

The only other trustee Annalee had personally encountered was the man Thaddeus. Last name indeed Hammer, according to his name label. He'd joked his way at Cooper Coates' party and also was in the crowd the night before at Sonny Dawkins' carnival.

Thaddeus Hammer turned out to be *Executive Director of the Western States Agricultural Association*—whatever in the world that was. Annalee hadn't heard of the outfit, but she'd make it her business to learn more about it.

Stepping back from the wall of framed portraits, she considered all of the men—who, altogether, appeared to be a well-heeled collection of esteemed Colorado leaders. Yet more than a few would be Klan members, since so many in Colorado were dues-paying followers of the "civic" hate group, including the governor, Denver's mayor, county sheriffs, jury commissioners, and many well-regarded churchmen and their parishioners.

Only one person didn't smile down from a portrait with eminence—the Rev. Dr. Malcolm Kane, the seminary's venerated president. A label was affixed to the wall, but his portrait was missing. Curious.

He consorted with Milly Sawyer but would refuse to see her now.

His receptionist had returned, found Annalee in the corridor examining the trustee portraits, and rushed over to marshal her away, ordering her to leave the premises immediately.

"President Kane will not be seeing you today—or any day—for any reason. If you don't leave now, our security officer will be called to escort you off the grounds."

The woman pointed to the front door again.

Still standing there, Annalee studied her. "You're quite good at your job."

The woman crossed her arms. "Indeed, I am. Thus, I insist. The door—"

"Although," Annalee interrupted, "it must be annoying protecting Doctor Kane from all the people pressing to see him."

"You're out of order here—"

"Men, of course, and many women, I'm sure. Maybe more women than men." Annalee let that sink in for good measure.

"That's it. Security! The woman half called down the hallway, pointed again to the door, but not so forceful now.

"I'm taking my humble leave, yes." Annalee stepped forward then. She clicked open her pocketbook and pulled out her business card. "But if you ever need to talk to a detective about anything, here's my card. I can be reached at that telephone number. It's in Denver."

Annalee placed the card in the woman's already outstretched hand with a gentle but firm touch.

As the woman glanced at it, Annalee stepped toward the front door, not bothering to look back, not waiting to hear if the receptionist's heels were clicking with defiance on the black-and-white marble floor because the woman had followed her, making sure Annalee was leaving.

But Annalee heard nothing.

The woman hadn't seemed to move.

As Annalee knew, the woman probably was thinking. Thinking hard. About a lot.

Out on the sidewalk, Annalee stood in dappled sunshine for a moment, thinking. Such a beautiful place. The seminary campus was quiet—since, after all, this was a late morning during the summer session. Not many classes, if any, would be under way. Few people moved about, letting Annalee give herself permission to walk around the grounds and take a leisurely look at everything.

The administration building—three stories of red brick with mullioned windows and spiky turrets—occupied the centermost position.

Three squatty, smaller buildings—barely more than huts actually, likely for classrooms—were set off to one side, looking a bit like afterthoughts.

Still, elaborate flower displays adorned the entrance to each building on the grounds—including a garden shed that looked not that different from the potting shed at Cooper Coates' place.

Largest of the three long huts turned out to be Saxton Library, although it looked more like an army barracks. Still, Annalee couldn't help herself. She couldn't resist entering. *Ah, books.* She loved them. Loved libraries, too. She couldn't imagine the volumes that would be on the shelves at a place like Saxton.

Glancing around—grateful that nobody had noticed her—she pulled open the library door, peeked inside, and stepped into a narrow foyer, expecting to breathe in the lovely, well-worn scent of shelf after shelf of leather-bound books.

Instead she smelled something else. A young woman's bright perfume.

Annalee froze.

From an opened door off a hallway, she heard the tinkle of laughter. Not happy laughter. This was laughter marked with a tinge of discomfort or uncertainty in it. A young woman's laughter. Annalee recognized it because she'd laughed that way herself at times in her past. Trying to sound knowing and confident—but, in the laughter, revealing herself to be immature and uncertain.

"Maybe we shouldn't—"

The man's voice, coming from the same door, sounded older, coaxing, persuasive, impatient, angry, then demanding.

"But we will."

Annalee figured what she was hearing—in this place filled with shelf after shelf of important books that not one soul, on this summer morning, seemed to be reading.

She was hearing a forced seduction, and on the grounds of a prestigious Christian seminary, she especially loathed the sound of it.

That meant she faced a choice. She could slip away, her presence never known. Or, as the young woman's voice grew more frightened and alarmed, Annalee could interrupt whatever was going on and give the woman an opportunity to break away and flee.

The young woman cried out.

Annalee did the same.

"Are you okay?" Annalee rushed to the open doorway, looked in, and sighed with disappointment at what she'd encountered.

The woman was colored, pretty, young—barely twenty at the most, similar in age to the timid college girls in the string quartet at Cooper Coates' garden party. This girl's eyes, however, looked not shy and nervous but horrified. Her blouse was opened, and when she saw Annalee, the young woman grasped her clothes together, grabbed her small handbag, and rushed across the room and through the door—looking embarrassed but grateful beyond words for this chance to escape.

Annalee had never seen her before.

And the man?

He'd looked so proper and respectable in his photo displayed on the trustee gallery of the seminary's main administrative building, not to mention appearing so high-society important in Cooper Coates' flowery garden.

Now Thaddeus Hammer looked heated, disheveled, and angry. Angry enough to kill.

Annalee decided not to hang around to find out if he would.

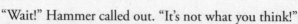

"Wait!" Hammer called out. "It's not what you think!"

Annalee didn't wait. She swung around and ran after the girl. Whatever she'd interrupted, she was 100 percent certain it was more wrong than she wanted to hear about or imagine.

Across the grass, she saw the young woman racing from the seminary complex. Stumbling at one point—apparently while trying to fix her clothes—the young woman still never stopped. She'd been given a merciful way to break free of Thaddeus Hammer and she wasn't stopping even a second, it seemed, to delay her getaway. But at the front gate, the young lady appeared confused about which direction to go.

"Are you okay?" Annalee cried out again, trying to make her voice loud, not sure the young woman could hear her, but hoping she would stop so Annalee could find out who she was and how in the world she'd ended up at the seminary.

But just then, a streetcar pulled to the stop near the seminary's front entrance. The young woman bounded up the steps, and the streetcar pulled away.

Annalee looked back, expecting to see Thaddeus Hammer chasing behind to run her down, demanding she stay quiet about what she'd seen—or offering some cobbled-together excuse.

But she saw no one. The seminary sat quiet in the afternoon's still air. A few songbirds had the audacious, hopeful nerve to chirp from trees. A few bees buzzed. Traffic on the main road by the gate seemed miles away, drivers unconcerned about whatever might be unfolding on the stately-looking theological grounds.

This seminary—rippling with lush, outdoor floral displays, a parade of mature trees, and green and weed-free lawns—seemed a picture of what such a place should be, a home where ideas were seeded and planted, where moral philosophies were sown and nurtured. So beauty was appreciated here. God's lovely nature. But what else was growing here?

Annalee didn't know. But one day soon, she told herself, she would find out. Then another thought came to mind:

Prissy Mack, if she could, might be first to thank her.

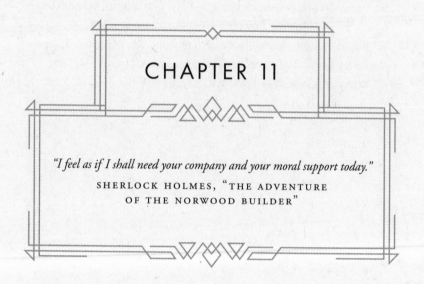

CHAPTER 11

"I feel as if I shall need your company and your moral support today."
SHERLOCK HOLMES, "THE ADVENTURE
OF THE NORWOOD BUILDER"

RIDING THE STREETCAR BACK TO FIVE POINTS, Annalee pondered the morning's disturbing, disappointing, but somehow not surprising events. For all the hubbub and dissatisfying trouble, she still hadn't spoken to the highbrow President Kane, or even seen him—but his presence as top dog of the seminary seemed to hover over every inch of the Saxton campus. As the chief actor at the private institution, Kane had managed in a short tenure to amass, or keep, an impressive collection of prominent Colorado men as his board of trustees. But Thaddeus Hammer, for one, had shown himself morally hollow. Were other trustees as lax? Not to mention Kane, too?

Why, indeed, were young colored women involved? And could any of this connect to Prissy Mack?

Annalee had a curious guess who could provide an answer. The young trustee Nathan Furness.

He'd only glanced at her when she first encountered him at Valerie Valentine's place. Volumes were spoken in his quick glance, but she couldn't read them.

She saw the same look in his eyes when she'd noticed him at the carnival the night before. His eyes following her, then quickly looking away.

What was he trying to say? To her in particular? She hadn't a guess. Nor did she have a clue how to talk herself into his fancy law office to question him.

On such a balmy summer afternoon—and after the sad shock of Thaddeus Hammer's sexually suggestive wrestling match with the young colored woman in the Saxton library—her mind needed a break from fretting over things that might explain how Prissy Mack was found dead on Sunday night.

Back at her cabin, she decided to give her questions a rest while she changed clothes, pulled on her late daddy's work gloves, and meddled around in her little yard—raking up dead leaves and brambles on the east side of her humble place, not bothering herself with the failed rows of vegetables and things on the west side.

The spot holding her mother's box didn't get even a glance. Likewise, she let Nathan Furness fade from her mind. Prissy Mack, too. Malcolm Kane, Thaddeus Hammer, the fleeing young woman, the wall of trustee photos at Saxton seminary. As Jack had told her—and Sherlock Holmes stories, too—sometimes the best way to unlock a puzzle is to stop stewing over it. Let the answers find their way to you.

Besides, she was appreciating the look of her leaf cleanup. Stepping back to admire her humble work, she'd even started to hum a melody—something the choir sang on Sunday. "Savior, Like a Shepherd Lead Us."

Thus, as she knelt over a big pile of leaves, pushing them onto a tarp to move to the riverbank and burn, she almost didn't notice when a shadow fell over her.

The shadow didn't move.

She froze. Still kneeling, she let herself take a deep, silent breath.

A danger? If so, Lord, I'd appreciate your protection—especially from Thaddeus Hammer? Was the shadow his? If anybody had a reason to stand looming over her now, it was him.

Or maybe Malcolm Kane? His starchy receptionist? Valerie Valentine? One of the Sawyers?

As she turned to look up, she saw instead the one person she'd wanted most to talk with and question—but thought would be hardest to find.

It was Nathan Furness.

"Good afternoon." He stepped back, giving her room to stand. "I'm sorry to interrupt, Miss Spain. Do you have a minute?"

She stepped back too, giving him a quick once-over glance. Head to toe, he looked impeccable—his summer seersucker suit spotless and neatly pressed, his tan-colored tie perfectly matching and knotted. A little dust from her yard lay on the toes of his brown-and-white spectator shoes.

But he looked born to dress well, and on this summer afternoon, he was doing exactly that.

"My name is—"

"Nathan Furness," Annalee answered for him.

He gave her a nod. "Of course. You already know. That's exactly why I wanted to find you and talk to you."

"About the seminary?"

He twisted his hands. "Is there somewhere we can talk?"

Annalee wasn't comfortable inviting him inside her little cabin—for both of their sakes. Neither would feel at ease, especially if someone discovered him inside with her.

"I'll bring out some chairs—if you don't mind sitting in the yard."

He agreed, offering to help with the chairs. They weren't fancy—her simple wooden chairs. But Jack had repaired every loose bit and botch on each one, so the chairs sat steady and sturdy. A wave of gratitude for what Jack had done washed over Annalee as she watched aristocratic-looking Nathan Furness sit in one of the plain chairs to face her under the small maple tree near her cabin. Her father had planted the tree, and she loved everything about it, especially its dappled summer shade.

"Take your time." She looked at Nathan evenly. "I'm not in a hurry."

"Do you have a certain fee? For your services?" Nathan blinked. "As a detective?"

"You want to hire me." Annalee couldn't hide her surprise.

"There's nothing I want more. To help save our seminary. But also my family—my wife. My mother, too, especially." He frowned. "But I know I'm not making any sense." He tried to laugh. "And I'm a lawyer."

"Our lives get complicated. Believe me, I understand." Annalee gave him a neat-enough smile. She'd have to coax him to say more. "Can you tell me your biggest concern? Why would you need a detective?"

Nathan swallowed. "Can I ask you a theology question first?"

Annalee searched his eyes. *What now?* Still, she nodded.

"Well," Nathan began, "we're not supposed to judge others, as you know."

She stayed silent.

"But I'm aware of a situation. Let's call it that, and—"

"You don't want to make a judgment about it?" Annalee gave him a sober look. "Is that your concern?"

"That's it exactly. Won't God judge me?"

"I can't answer for God." Annalee took a breath. "But this

'situation'—is it wrong? From all that you understand about right and wrong?"

"Wrong doesn't begin to describe it. I have no question it's wrong. Yet I'm stuck. Do I speak up? Because my actions and my motivation to speak might be questionable too?"

Annalee sat straight in her chair. "This is confidential—our talk. So I'd like you to feel free to tell me—"

"It's Malcolm."

"President Kane? At the seminary?"

"He has this scheme—with a lot of young women."

Annalee listened. She felt wary but was willing to hear. "What's going on? What exactly is the scheme?"

"Have you heard of our Welcome Ambassadors?"

Annalee shook her head. "Ambassadors?"

"They're all young women." He looked sheepish. "Attractive young women. Every one of them."

"How many?"

"About thirty or so."

"My, that's a lot. Who do they welcome?"

"New trustees and top donors. Malcolm recruits talented young ladies to serve as Welcome Ambassadors for the seminary— to welcome Saxton's supporters with deep pockets—"

"Who are all men."

Nathan nodded, blinked hard. "But with the young ladies, Malcolm makes it feel competitive, exclusive, prestigious to be selected to be a Saxton ambassador. The girls are all coeds from colleges around town, hardly more than eighteen years old, most of them. But all are poor. Always poor."

"So, they're paid?"

"Not exactly. They're promised scholarship money if they complete the program, plus the prestige of calling themselves Saxton Ambassadors, with special events, a clothing budget, fundraising trips out of town. They're each assigned to one prominent male, whether he's married or not. She meets him first on campus, gives him a tour, stays on call for him, starts running his errands, finds out what he likes to eat, wear, places to visit to relax, hosts him at special campus events and programs. He, in turn, is her 'mentor.'"

"Sounds like a lot of time together." She left it at that.

"Unsupervised time. Then the inevitable happens—well, with a few of the men."

Annalee folded her hands, studied Nathan Furness. Never in life had she entertained a more unlikely guest—this young man offering her curious dirt on a seminary, of all places. What was his game?

Nathan shifted in his chair. "From the outside looking in, one would think President Kane would see the problem with these 'arrangements'—that they encourage both parties to cross a dangerous line." He looked pained. "I know—because that's what happened to me." He twisted in his chair. "I'm married, and—I'll just be honest, Miss Spain—I went too far with my welcome girl." He looked away. "Her name is Stella."

Annalee listened, just as a question came to mind. "Nathan, is this about blackmail?"

He gave her a hard look, nodded. "That's why I wanted to talk to you, yes."

Annalee pursed her lips. What was young Furness asking?

"So—" she tried to explain it out loud—"President Kane sets up each prominent man with a welcome girl. Then, if the relationship turns tawdry, which one or two do, he . . . ?"

"Calls you in for a private meeting. Acts disappointed beyond words. Mercy, that man must've acted on vaudeville in his not-so-recent past. You should hear him. 'My dear Nathan, I'm sorry to tell you this, but it's come to my sad attention that you and your Welcome Ambassador have crossed a regrettable line.' Then he twists the knife—saying he's sure I'd flat-out die if my dear wife Edith learned of my 'assignations' with Stella, not to mention if the partners in my law firm caught even a whiff of such scandal."

Annalee crossed her arms. "How much? What did you have to pay him?"

"First a 'small' donation to make the whole thing go away. For me, twenty-five thousand dollars."

"Not so small, Mr. Furness."

"He's come back twice for different amounts—ten thousand, twelve thousand. The money goes to the Saxton Foundation that Malcolm started and operates, supposedly for seminary support." He scoffed. "But for him, it's more like an open checkbook. He pays himself for 'expenses.'"

Annalee shook her head. "His fancy trustee board lets that pass?"

"We do if he's got enough of us under his thumb." He winced.

"Curious," Annalee said. "The trustee wall in the admin building looks so esteemed."

"But not everybody on that wall is still on the board. Some have left." Nathan stood. "I've said enough. I came to ask if you'd figure a way to expose Malcolm's scheme—acting privately for me. I'd pay you a fee—"

"Please sit down a moment. You mentioned your motivations. Is something else bothering you?"

Nathan sank in the chair again. "My mother, Charlotte Furness. I believe you met her briefly at the home of her Negro friend, Valerie Valentine."

"Is Malcolm blackmailing your mother, too?"

Nathan laughed a bitter laugh. "Worse. He's asked her to marry him—and even worse, she's said yes."

"You didn't warn her about him?"

"I'd have to explain to her what I'd done, and Mother's disappointment is more than I could bear." He winced. "There's been other talk about me—that I'm a gambler, with debts. Breaks Mother's heart."

"Is it true?"

"Me, a gambler? Of course not." He set his shoulders. "But compared to Malcolm, I look like a worry. She thinks Malcolm Kane walks on water. He's only been at the seminary for three years, but he's quickly 'turning it around.' Winning fellowships. Luring top faculty. Malcolm has a flair about him. Tall, strapping, handsome guy like that. All that silver hair. Smooth Southern drawl. But you've met him—"

"Actually, no. I've never seen him." Annalee blinked. "Not even in the papers. I just hear about him all the time, see articles about him reviving the seminary. Where is he from? How can I learn more about him?"

"His background statement is printed on seminary fundraising material. I'll send something to you. But his photo isn't on that either." He shrugged. "He seems to hate getting his picture taken. He plays the modest leader." He sighed. "Mother's fallen under his spell."

"She's a widow, then?"

"And worth an obscene pile of money. Father's people sold munitions during the War between the States—"

"Oh my." Annalee exhaled her whisper.

"Made a fortune during a horrible war. Father himself traded in steel. Made another fortune. I'm an only child and I inherited much of it. But Mother's still sitting on a pile of it, which Malcolm gets his oily hands on the second Mother says, 'I do.'"

Annalee stood. "I can't take your job, Mr. Furness. I wouldn't be the right person." She gripped her chair. "Anyway, a church in Five Points may be helping me investigate something else—"

"The colored girl? The one found dead?" Nathan stood.

Annalee felt a chill. Why was he asking about Prissy? "Did you know her?" she asked. "Her name was Prissy Mack. At least, I'm pretty sure that was her name."

Nathan looked confused. "I'm certain I wouldn't know her. Although I heard that Malcolm had secured some young Negro ladies as behind-the-scenes ambassadors—not acknowledged in public but granted similar benefits—as recommended by Valerie Valentine. She's catering Mother's wedding—if it ever happens."

"Valerie sent young girls to Kane?"

"She's like my mother. Malcolm has charmed her, and she's fallen for the prestige factor, like so many others. She's big on self-improvement for the colored race. I'm sure you've heard of that. She probably promised the young ladies greater status by associating with Kane and his people—giving them a way up in life. She'd believe something like that."

Annalee searched Nathan's eyes. This entire story raised her hackles.

"What about Thaddeus Hammer? What's his role at the seminary?"

Nathan looked grieved. Or confused? "Long-standing trustee. An agriculture man—well, he advocates for them, farmers out West. That sounds good. But I wouldn't trust him as far as I could throw him. He acts like a friend to colored people in town—says he despises the Klan. Then behind closed doors, he's the one telling race jokes."

"And people laugh?" Annalee studied him. "People at the seminary laugh?"

Nathan nodded. "Actually, some do."

His answer made Annalee ask one more question.

"So if you hire a detective, what will you ask that person to do?"

"To expose the dirt that President Kane is building a legacy on at Saxton. It's reprehensible. True, I was involved in the worst of it, let myself fall off a moral wagon. As for my ambassador, Stella, I've apologized to her more ways than I know how. I promised to pay the remainder of her college tuition, books, fees, and expenses—but she turned me down." He shook his head. "I even promised to confess to my wife, Edith—but Stella begged me not to do that. She left the program to start over fresh, even returned the clothes to me, transferred to a different college somewhere on the coast—in California, I believe. So, good for her."

"That is good." Annalee hiked a brow. "And you?"

Nathan sighed. "I'm still a trustee. I want to keep an eye on things out there, especially with Kane poisoning the atmosphere. May he never get a chance to marry into my family. I'd be devastated." He squared his shoulders. "But in the meantime, I'm working hard as I can to rebuild a better life with Edith. To be the husband she deserves." He smiled at Annalee. "Also, I've rediscovered a far better pastime. I'd always dabbled in painting. Portraits. I also paint nice, pretty flowers. In watercolors and oils."

"I like the sound of that." Annalee searched his eyes. "I'd love to see your work."

Nathan reached in his suit jacket, pulled out a business card, handed it to her.

Annalee glanced at the printing.

Nathan Furness, Attorney at Law & Partner
Willis, Jones, Gracey, Smith, and Furness
900 Seventeenth Street
Main 2222

A prime exchange, Annalee thought, wondering how the law firm managed to acquire it.

"Painting—the artistry of it—lifts my soul," Furness was saying. "It's wholesome, so it relaxes me. Some say I'm getting pretty good at it. They bring me bouquets to paint. A couple of my floral paintings are hanging in my law office—in the foyer. Every time I walk in the door and look at one, I thank the good Lord for getting me back on track."

She gave him a look. What a curious young man. His words sounded heartfelt, his story intriguing. But had he told her the whole truth? And if not, why? She pointed him toward her gravel sidewalk.

He nodded. "Time for me to go."

"Thanks for trusting me with this information."

"I believed you'd keep my confidence—from what I've read about you in the papers." He stepped back. "It also helps to get things off my chest."

"You've given me much food for thought."

The remainder of the evening, in fact, she let her mind weigh all that Nathan Furness had told her. The Rev. Dr. Malcolm Kane was running a scheme, exploiting young women, tempting prominent men, and blackmailing their guilty souls. All in the name of God. She pursed her lips. If this was true about Kane, he was a menace. But she didn't feel sure.

Either way, what about Prissy Mack? Had she known Kane— as a Welcome Ambassador? Sent by Valerie Valentine? Then, for some awful reason, did he kill Prissy?

Troubling questions. But Annalee kept returning to the worst one: on top of everything else, *why wouldn't a peril like Kane kill me too?*

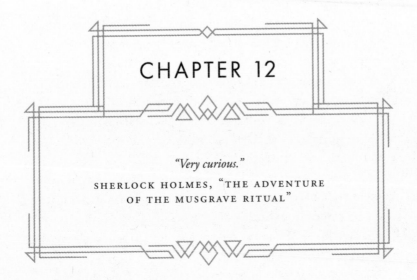

CHAPTER 12

"Very curious."

SHERLOCK HOLMES, "THE ADVENTURE
OF THE MUSGRAVE RITUAL"

WITH THAT NASTY QUESTION, Annalee set her sights on heading back to the seminary the next day—a summer-hot Thursday. That business about Malcolm Kane, and what she'd observed of Thaddeus Hammer, nagged at her like a sore thumb.

That's how she explained it on Thursday morning to Mrs. Stallworth. She hadn't talked to Jack because he'd be busy helping the Sawyers handle details of Sonny's death. Instead, she stood in Mrs. Cunningham's kitchen, talking to her friend.

"Will you ride with me? To the seminary?" Annalee asked. "We can take the streetcar."

Mrs. Stallworth set down a massive platter she was washing. An apron was tied over her dark cotton dress. She'd been cooking— her regular job here in Mrs. Cunningham's rooming house, where eight hungry, paying tenants kept the kitchen hopping. She'd just put a roast in the oven to slow cook for that evening's dinner. The potatoes were peeled, sitting in the icebox in cold water. She'd made a dressing for the salad. Three apple pies were cooling in the pie safe.

The pleasing scents of homemade cooking wafted through the kitchen, but Mrs. Stallworth looked aggravated.

"What about my corn bread?" She put her hands on her hips. "I can't go gallivanting with you all over town. You have no idea how much work it takes—"

Mrs. Stallworth picked up the platter again, put a hand to her forehead, blinked hard with annoyance, gasped as the wet platter almost slipped from her hands.

"Watch it." Annalee rushed across the kitchen, catching the platter just before it fell and shattered.

Mrs. Stallworth let out a bewildered groan. "Oh, Annalee . . ."

"Let me do these dishes. Dry your hands and sit down a minute."

Annalee helped settle Mrs. Stallworth at the kitchen table. Something was grating at her. That was evident. But first Annalee wanted her friend to sit herself down and take a good, long, deep breath. If she didn't calm herself, she'd drop a dish, maybe slip on the wet wooden floor and fall, injuring herself.

Mrs. Stallworth protested. "That's my job. What would Mrs. Cunningham say if she finds me sitting around while you do the wash up?"

Mrs. Cunningham took on the question the second she heard it.

"What would I say?" She stepped through her kitchen door.

Annalee had moved to the sink, plunged her hands in soapy water to tackle a dish pile.

"There's the question," she said. "Mrs. Cunningham?"

"I'd say there must be a good reason, Edna, for you 'sitting around'—if that's what you call it—and I want to hear it." Mrs.

Cunningham plopped down to face Mrs. Stallworth. She reached for her nearest hand. "If you're not feeling well, tell me."

"Tell me, too." Annalee glanced over her shoulder.

Mrs. Stallworth glanced away. "It's that dead girl . . ."

Annalee set down the plate. "The dead girl?" She frowned. "Prissy Mack?"

"Is that the poor child's name?" Mrs. Cunningham scowled. "I don't know a soul by that name."

Annalee grabbed a chair. "What about the dead girl?" She sat down across from the two women. "Do you know something? Did somebody talk to you?"

Mrs. Stallworth sighed. "Sister Barnes. She runs a rooming house."

"Sister Louise Barnes?" Mrs. Cunningham eyed her. "Sister Louise Barnes in our club?"

"Who lives in the yellow house? That Sister Louise Barnes?" Annalee looked at the two women. "What'd she say?"

"She's in Hearts and Hands—our women's club," Mrs. Stallworth said, almost in a whisper.

"I've known her for years," Mrs. Cunningham agreed, nodding. "She adores Hearts and Hands. One of our best people."

"That's nice." Annalee felt her impatience. She tried to sound calm. *What was this all about?* "Can you tell me what she said to you?"

"Well—" Mrs. Stallworth looked up—"I saw her at the grocer's yesterday—"

"The one on Downing Street?" Mrs. Cunningham interrupted.

Annalee watched the two women. They were talking like the good friends they had become. So they were not hurrying, which was making Annalee frustrated as all get-out. What did Sister Louise Barnes say? But Annalee took a silent breath. This might take a while. She sat straight in her chair, gave Mrs. Stallworth and Mrs. Cunningham their time and due. *Just listen.*

"I was picking through the string beans."

"For tonight's dinner?" Mrs. Cunningham asked.

Annalee stayed silent.

"They have such nice produce at that grocer—"

"Truly, they do. Young Jacob Hill took over from his father when the old man died and everybody worried the grocer's would go down in quality—do you know what I mean, Annalee?"

Annalee nodded. *Oh, I know.*

"So, Louise Barnes was there?" Mrs. Cunningham picked up the conversation, turned it back to Mrs. Stallworth.

"In the produce, yes. That's where we ran into each other. So, we started talking about Hearts and Hands—"

"Mercy, she loves that club. You'd think she'd started it herself. But I admire her devotion." Mrs. Cunningham pursed her lips.

"That's what she and I were talking about," Mrs. Stallworth said, "just how much she loves Hearts and Hands, and how she'd simply die if she was kicked out and lost her membership."

"Who would dare?" Mrs. Cunningham looked aghast.

Annalee chimed in, curious. "Right, who would dare kick your Louise Barnes out of her own club?"

"Valerie Valentine." Mrs. Stallworth spit out the name. "She lives down the block from Louise—on the other end. The fancy end."

"She's not even in Hearts and Hands." Mrs. Cunningham bristled. "Don't make me have to call that woman—involving herself in our club business. Why's Louise Barnes worried about her anyway?"

"Because of the dead girl." Mrs. Stallworth's voice dropped.

Annalee's breath caught. What was Mrs. Stallworth saying? *Lord, please.*

"What about her?" Mrs. Cunningham looked confused.

"She was living at Louise Barnes' rooming house."

Annalee pulled her chair close. "The yellow house?"

"Right, the narrow corner house over on Emerson Street. The yellow one." Mrs. Cunningham's voice softened too. "So, she was right in our neighborhood? How'd Louise know she was the dead girl?"

"Because," Mrs. Stallworth finally started explaining, "the young woman showed up out of the blue a few weeks ago. Said she'd come up from Alabama and was looking for a place to stay. Louise likes references. This young woman didn't have any, of course—although she thought her aunt, her daddy's sister, might have moved here—"

"Did Louise Barnes know the aunt's name?" Annalee hated interrupting, but she was desperate for a solid detail.

Mrs. Stallworth turned from Mrs. Cunningham to consider Annalee. "I'm trying to tell you what I know."

"I understand, and I'm grateful." Annalee slipped that in.

"Thank you." Mrs. Stallworth shook her head. "Anyway, she'd just arrived in Denver, didn't know a soul—except maybe that aunt. But she'd heard Colorado was better for colored people. So, she got on a train and brought herself here, where Louise rented her a room, took her in."

"Then what happened?" Annalee and Mrs. Cunningham asked the question at the same time.

"I'm trying to tell you." Mrs. Stallworth wrung her hands. "The young lady started looking for a job, couldn't find anything. But something strange happened, Louise said."

Annalee waited, mouth pressed tight.

"The young woman suddenly had suitors."

"Suitors? A white man?" Annalee couldn't help herself. She had to ask.

"Don't be ridiculous." Mrs. Stallworth rolled her eyes. "Of course he wasn't a white man—although, now that you mention it, Louise didn't say either way. She never actually saw who it was. But somebody started sending beautiful flowers to the young woman, if you can believe that—beautiful flower arrangements in glass vases, to a young woman who just barely got into town. Sometimes more than once a day."

"Gracious." Mrs. Cunningham was listening intently. "I never heard of such."

"But that's not all." Mrs. Stallworth looked confounded. "The young woman stopped looking for a job."

Annalee nodded. "But she always had money."

"Enough to pay her rent at Louise's place, but she wasn't working anywhere—and Louise didn't like the look of that."

"Well, I can understand that." Mrs. Cunningham set her jaw. "Did she tell her to leave?"

"Louise gave her notice, told her to find another place to stay. That was last Saturday." Mrs. Stallworth frowned. "Then, on Sunday night, the young woman didn't come home—and she hasn't been back to Louise's place. When Louise heard a young colored stranger—a young woman—had been killed, she had a gut feeling. You know how that can happen—"

"Oh, I know." Mrs. Cunningham straightened her shoulders, looking certain about gut feelings. "Sometimes you just know."

Annalee stood. "Has she cleaned out the young lady's room?" She prayed right then that Louise Barnes hadn't touched the room.

"She's afraid to bother it. She also won't contact the police. She doesn't want her name in the papers regarding a dead girl. 'Folks would shun me,' she said. Her rooming house would lose business."

"She's right," Mrs. Cunningham said. "Who'd want to room where a dead woman lived?"

Mrs. Stallworth sighed. "And now that she's told me about it, I guess I'm involved too—which, as you know, Annalee, is the last thing I wanted because I don't want anything to do with the police." She blinked. "Or hardly with a murder. I'm washing my hands."

Annalee pursed her lips, gave both women a firm nod. They sat silent, looked at her, waiting—it seemed—for her to chime in, so Annalee did.

"But what if the dead girl was your daughter?"

Mrs. Stallworth looked pained. "What in the world are you saying, Annalee?"

"Oh, mercy." Mrs. Cunningham looked despairing. "What are you trying to say?"

Annalee searched their eyes. "I'm saying the young lady has no one fighting for her."

"That's not true, Annalee!" Mrs. Stallworth protested. "The good Lord fights our battles."

Annalee sighed. She refused to get into a complex theological argument today with Edna Stallworth.

"True," she simply said, "but he uses his servants' help." She crossed her arms. "If we stop making excuses and give him a hand."

That hit home. She could see it in their faces.

"You want us to do something?" Mrs. Cunningham sounded worried but willing.

"I need you to march over to Louise Barnes' rooming house with me—right now—and tell her we need to see Prissy Mack's room. There's evidence there—I can feel it in my bones—and getting to it before somebody hauls it away will help solve that girl's murder."

"But what about Louise's reputation?" Mrs. Cunningham still sounded worried.

"She'll be a hero if she helps us crack this case. Besides, the girl wasn't killed in her room or anywhere in Mrs. Barnes' rooming house. I feel sure of that. Evidence will help confirm your friend's innocence."

Annalee stood. "Any more questions?"

Mrs. Stallworth stood too. "What about Valerie Valentine?"

Annalee scoffed. "Valerie Valentine doesn't run the church clubs and auxiliaries and women's boards and choir guilds of Mount

Moriah AME Church. Even if she tries, Pastor Jack Robert Blake will put a stop to that right quick. I'll see to that personally." She set her shoulders. "Now, are we ready?"

"My roast is in the oven." Mrs. Stallworth glanced at the kitchen's big stove.

"I'll leave a note for Mr. Cunningham. He'll check it."

"What does he know about cooking a roast?" Mrs. Stallworth pulled off her apron.

"He'll figure it out—if he wants to eat supper tonight." Mrs. Cunningham grabbed her pocketbook. "Besides, we won't be long, right, Annalee?"

"Not if we can help it." *Please, don't let us be long.* It was a prayer they'd need more than they knew.

CHAPTER 13

"Obviously the business was a bad one."

SHERLOCK HOLMES, "THE ADVENTURE
OF THE REIGATE SQUIRE"

LOUISE BARNES OPENED THE FRONT DOOR to her rooming house looking hard-pressed and fearful. A worried frown creased her finely powdered face. She straightened her spotless white summer housedress and stepped back in her doorway, looking as if she wanted to hide from whatever was knocking inconveniently on her door. She was a neat woman, head to toe—hair recently washed and pressed, her brogue shoes perfectly laced and polished. Her yellow house was neat as a pin too. The siding was recently painted. The house looked happy enough. Yet she looked unable or unwilling to bear a frightening disturbance, especially one involving a murder.

She shook her head at the three women standing on her spotless front porch.

"Irene?" She frowned at Mrs. Cunningham, then at Mrs. Stallworth. "Edna?" She blinked with fear at Annalee, turned back to Mrs. Cunningham. "You brought the pastor's friend? The little detective?"

"We can't stay long," Mrs. Stallworth said.

"Edna's got a roast in the oven." Mrs. Cunningham's voice sounded casual, as if they'd been out on a stroll and were making a friendly house visit.

"But what do you want?" Mrs. Barnes' voice betrayed her duress. So did her surroundings. Her rooming house looked painfully well kept. Porch swept. Flower boxes bursting with blossoms. A porch swing bearing two fluffed blue-and-white cushions hung from the porch rafters, ready for her lodgers. Annalee could imagine Mrs. Barnes easing her nagging worries by throwing herself full bore into her house management duties.

Not a speck of dust could probably be found in the entire three-story property. Well, except for the dead girl's room. Well, hopefully. Dust would say the room hadn't been touched.

"I'm awfully busy," Mrs. Barnes added. "Just finishing up my cleaning, Irene. This isn't a good time. . . ." She glanced at Annalee.

Annalee gave her a nod. But she'd tell it to her straight.

"We need your help, Mrs. Barnes."

Louise Barnes shrank back in her doorway. "I can't help you. I don't want any trouble." She whispered at Mrs. Stallworth, "What'd you tell them?"

"I'm sorry, Louise. But we need to see the girl's room."

"I haven't been in there myself—"

"And it might be worrying you like crazy," Annalee said, her voice low. "But there's evidence in there, and if we find it, we could help solve the girl's murder."

Mrs. Barnes stiffened. "But what will people say?" She still whispered. "That dead girl was living right under my roof—no, right under my nose." She tightened her jaw. "My name will be in the papers. My tenants will all leave, and I'll never get another paying lodger—after working so hard to keep up this place after my husband died. God bless his hardworking soul." She took in a deep breath. "*Oh, Lord Jesus.* I don't know what to do."

"Your name won't be in the papers." Annalee couldn't promise that, but she felt determined. "None of us will mention one word about you."

"Well, one of you already has." She turned on Mrs. Stallworth. "Edna, why'd you take what I'd spoken confidentially to you and tell everybody—"

"Because murder is bad business." Mrs. Stallworth made her pitch—*sounding like me,* Annalee thought. Mrs. Stallworth kept at it. "That poor girl came all the way up here from Alabama, probably traveling by herself. Then in a matter of weeks, she's dead."

"So we have to help her, Louise," Mrs. Cunningham chimed in. "If there's evidence in her room, Annalee can use it to crack the case."

Mrs. Barnes pressed her mouth. She looked as if she'd rather be doing anything else in the whole wide world than letting two fellow club members and her pastor's girlfriend-turned-detective snoop around her house. But she stepped back and pushed back her freshly painted front door.

"Will it take long?" She still whispered.

"We'll watch the clock," Annalee said, knowing she didn't even own a watch. She stepped inside before Mrs. Barnes could change her mind.

"Edna's got a roast in the oven," Mrs. Cunningham said again. "We can't stay all day."

"Wipe your feet." Mrs. Barnes pointed to a recently fluffed rag rug.

Stepping inside, Annalee wiped her shoes on the nice rug and gestured to Mrs. Stallworth and Mrs. Cunningham to join her in following Mrs. Barnes to a wide staircase just off the foyer.

"Please stay quiet," Mrs. Barnes glanced over her shoulders as they took to the stairs. "Some of my lodgers are still in their rooms."

At the landing, a door to the right opened and a middle-aged colored man wearing overalls stepped out.

"Morning, Mr. Riley." Mrs. Barnes nodded at the man. Her voice sounded nervous.

"Morning, Mrs. Barnes." The man gave her a quick look, wondering perhaps what was bothering her, or if her three female visitors were part of the problem.

"Morning, sir." Annalee spoke softly, gave the man a nod. She hadn't seen him at Mount Moriah, so maybe his membership was at a different church.

Mrs. Cunningham and Mrs. Stallworth gave him a brief hello too. He touched his hat but didn't disclose inappropriate interest at the three women trooping up the stairs behind Mrs. Barnes—so Annalee kept following her, trying to look as if whatever they were up to was right and proper.

Suddenly, however, Mrs. Barnes glanced back.

"Oh, Mr. Riley," she called out.

"Ma'am?" The man looked back up the stairs.

"Will you be back for supper?"

"Not tonight, ma'am. I got me a temporary job. Won't be back 'til maybe midnight. Is that too late?"

"I'll ask Mr. Montgomery to sit up and let you in. He helps me when somebody's late." Mrs. Barnes looked oddly curious. "What kind of job?"

"Sorry for the trouble. It's downtown by the river, and the streetcars don't run much after ten."

"I understand. What's the job—if you don't mind me asking?"

"Janitorial, ma'am," the man said. "At that carnival."

Annalee blinked but didn't flinch, studied Mrs. Barnes' face.

"The carnival? Oh, I heard about that." Mrs. Barnes said. She still sounded distracted. "Well, have a good evening."

Mr. Riley nodded, glanced at the women one last time, and disappeared down the stairs.

Annalee watched him leave, wished like crazy she could talk to him, ask what and who he'd seen there. But Mrs. Barnes took them to the third-floor landing—Annalee and the two women following.

Annalee was burning to ask Mrs. Barnes if Mr. Riley had any dealings with Prissy Mack while she lived here. But one thing at a time. Where in the world was Prissy's room? At the top of the world?

"Are we almost there?" Mrs. Stallworth called out in a half whisper. She was bringing up the end of the line, her breathing heavy.

"It's on the fourth floor," Mrs. Barnes answered, her voice low.

"Fourth?" Mrs. Cunningham sounded surprised.

"Well, it's the attic."

"Gracious." Mrs. Stallworth didn't hide her surprise.

Mrs. Barnes didn't respond. She was unlocking a small door at the end of the third-floor hallway. Then up a half flight of narrow stairs, she brought them to a tiny, unpainted, rough-looking space under the eaves. As they crowded behind her, she explained, "This was the only space I had left when the young lady came for lodging. I tried to talk her out of it since it's not actually a proper room—just a lean-to closet with a rickety spare bed and a rack for a dress or two." She wrung her hands. "I brought up a washbasin. I only charged her half price."

"Well, she had a window." Mrs. Cunningham walked to the small opening, looked out. "You can see clear across town from up here."

"And treetops." Mrs. Stallworth looked out the small window too. "It's a pretty view actually."

"Will you be quiet up here?" Mrs. Barnes sounded nervous. "And not take too long? As you can see, I haven't touched a thing. I brought up my brooms and rags to clean." She pointed to some cleaning things. "But to tell you the truth, I hated being up here in this room by myself." She shrugged. "Dust is already settling in. I wasn't sure what to do."

"We're not either." Annalee tried to sound assuring, despite her countless questions for Mrs. Barnes. "So we'll just look around. It shouldn't take long."

"Don't worry, Louise." Mrs. Cunningham also offered assurance. She walked over to a small, unmade bed. "We won't speak to a soul about this."

"We'll just look around." Mrs. Stallworth gave Mrs. Barnes a quick hug. "Everything will be fine."

"I'll be in the dining room—setting up for dinner—if you need anything."

With that, Mrs. Barnes turned and walked back down the stairs, closing the door behind her. Her muffled footsteps faded as she descended. They now were alone.

Annalee looked at her friends and they returned the glance. *What are we doing?* their eyes questioned her. *And what do we do now?*

Annalee had never actually examined a deceased person's surroundings in this way, but she noticed something right away.

"I thought it would feel sad in here." Mrs. Stallworth said it best, and Annalee agreed. "Instead, it feels like . . ."

"A whisper." Annalee said. *Why is that?*

"Too many secrets." Mrs. Cunningham eyed the bed.

Annalee then scanned the tiny space, noticing what they all couldn't help but see.

Those flowers.

Flowers sat on almost every surface. In glass vases. In half a dozen teacups. Hanging in bunches from the rafters. On the dusty windowsill. Wrapped in gift paper and lying on the bed.

"From an admirer?" Mrs. Cunningham asked.

"That's a lot of admiring." Mrs. Stallworth sniffed.

"With cards attached. Signed by somebody, I hope." Annalee picked up a vase. Its flowers, like the others in the tiny room, were wilting and dried or simply gone dead. Water in the vase—and most of the others—had evaporated to a few muddy brown inches.

The card—from High Plains Floral, a place downtown—offered a handwritten message: *To my pretty Prissy.* No signature.

"Declaring love, without your name?" Mrs. Cunningham scoffed. "Like I said—secrets on top of secrets."

That set Annalee to collecting other cards lying next to vases, teacups, and other vessels. All were from High Plains Floral, according to a scrawled business name on each note. Annalee didn't trust that removing piles of evidence from the room would be a smart thing. So as much as she longed to drop, clandestinely, at least one card into her purse for her own investigating, she resisted the urge. She'd stop by High Plains Floral later with a question or two, try to finagle from somebody working there who had ordered all these flowers for a Five Points delivery.

The arrangements were beautiful, even in their dried-out state.

"White hollyhocks, yellow roses, and pale pink carnations." Mrs. Stallworth put a finger on her chin, perusing a vase. "Now, that is beautiful."

"And rich." Mrs. Cunningham picked up a different vase. Cut crystal. "Whoever sent these flowers has money to burn."

Annalee thought of Malcolm Kane. Was he the admirer? If so, how'd he meet Prissy? Or was it Thaddeus Hammer? But that left the same question. How in the world would Hammer meet her? As his secret Welcome Ambassador? Or through Valerie Valentine, like perhaps the young woman he was assaulting in the seminary library? But according to Mrs. Barnes, Prissy had only arrived in town a few weeks ago.

Annalee shook her head. None of this made sense. She was grateful to have her two friends' help—even if Valerie Valentine scoffed at them for being "old church women."

Mrs. Stallworth had moved to the washbasin, looking it over. It sat on a small, rough-looking cabinet with two warped drawers. Mrs. Stallworth finally wrestled open the top drawer but shrugged at not finding much. "Some clean underclothes. One pair."

The second drawer held a pilled white sweater, also clean—and something odd. A man's black leather belt, the gold-plated buckle a fancy design. Accepting it from Mrs. Stallworth, Annalee let a thought push from somewhere deep in her mind to her lips. "Look at that fancy buckle. Who would wear a belt like this?"

Mrs. Cunningham made an offer. "I could ask my husband. As a cabbie, he sees all manner of men—young, old."

"Or middle aged," Annalee said aloud, and her words brought to mind someone they all knew: Cooper Coates.

"Have you ever used garden poison?" she asked.

"Never," Mrs. Stallworth was quick to answer.

"I have a couple of bottles," Mrs. Cunningham moved a vase. "I should dump them. Those liquids are dangerous, and I don't use them that much."

"They don't work?"

"Oh, they work alright." Mrs. Cunningham hiked a brow. "Got a stubborn weed and drip a couple drops of arsenic on it, that weed is gone before you can turn around good."

Annalee listened. "What happens if someone got dosed with one of those poisons? I've never researched it." She also hated the question—and the idea of poor Prissy getting poisoned that way. *Mercy.*

"Horrible things, so I hear." Mrs. Cunningham scrunched up her nose. "Depending on the poison, someone could suddenly stop breathing. Their throat would close up. Heart stop beating. Makes me sick to my stomach to think about it."

Annalee cocked her head and suddenly blurted out, "Everybody. Stop."

"What?" Mrs. Stallworth set down a vase, watched Annalee rush over to Mrs. Barnes' stack of cleaning things, search through them, yank out a couple pairs of gloves.

"Put these on." She handed a pair of gloves to each of the women.

"You think there's poison sprinkled around in here?" Mrs. Stallworth jerked back her hands.

"Probably not, but put on those gloves anyway."

"But look here—" Mrs. Cunningham clicked open her pocket-book. "I have a pair of white cotton church gloves from Sunday." She pulled them on, handed back the other pair to Annalee. "Here. You can wear Louise's work gloves." Then she frowned at Annalee. "Are we almost finished in here?"

"That's my question too." Mrs. Stallworth pulled on the gloves. "I need to check on my roast." She let her eyes search the room. "I'll be glad when we get out of here. What are we looking for anyway?"

"If we knew, we'd go straight for it." Annalee grabbed a broom, handed over some rags to the two women. "Instead, we have to hope and pray some hidden, perfect clue falls, miraculously, from one of these cobwebs." She pushed back a curl. "Let's make one more pass through everything. Maybe something will show up."

At that, she bent down, pushed the broom across the wooden floor, then under the bed, pulling out clumps of dust, a pencil stub, flower petals, and—*look at this, detective*—a small, dust-covered white envelope.

"She received mail?" Mrs. Stallworth asked.

"There's no stamp on it." Annalee stood. She checked the envelope. Empty. The penciled handwriting on the front was smudged.

"Was she writing to somebody?" Mrs. Cunningham stepped over to look.

"Curious," Annalee whispered, looking at the name on the front. "It's to Malcolm Kane Senior."

"Who's he?" Mrs. Stallworth asked. "What's the address?"

"Must be a relative of the seminary president? His father?"

"Well, that is curious." Mrs. Stallworth sounded suddenly like a detective herself, Annalee thought.

"The address is 220 North Circle Road." Annalee stared at the envelope. "But I don't know that location."

"That's not a Denver address." Mrs. Cunningham looked closer.

"This says Mississippi." Annalee read through the smudged name. "Some town called Bramble Creek—wherever in the world that is."

"Never heard of it, but it sounds like a clue to me, right, Annalee?" Mrs. Stallworth grabbed for a second broom and pushed back the bed. "Maybe something else is under there."

"Maybe . . ." Annalee knelt down again to look but stood when she heard knocking. She pushed the envelope inside the bodice of the summer shift she was wearing. Somebody was at the little attic door.

"Why is Louise knocking in her own house?" Mrs. Cunningham moved to the steps, started down toward the door.

"Wait," Annalee whispered.

Mrs. Cunningham stepped back up. "What's wrong?"

Annalee put a finger to her mouth. In a flash, she grabbed a kerchief hanging on a nail, wrapped it around her mouth and nose, tying it tight behind her head. Watching her, Mrs. Cunningham grabbed a handkerchief from her purse, made a quick triangle and did the same. Mrs. Stallworth followed suit with a handkerchief from her purse. The three would look like cleaning ladies—or a trio of bandits—and Annalee prayed to God himself right then that it wasn't the latter.

Annalee started down the steps and reached for the door, but Louise Barnes had already opened it. Louise's eyes glared big as saucers, her body rigid with a fear that Annalee hated seeing—because behind Mrs. Barnes stood three angry-looking white men in uniform. Cops.

Annalee's mouth went dry. She kept sweeping, but she actually was praying again under that kerchief, her mouth not moving, because three scowling cops were staring her dead with cold menace. What, then, does one pray while that is happening? *God, in your mercy* . . . Annalee's mind went blank. She swallowed. *We need your protection and divine help—or whatever else we need in this instance—and we need it right now.* She blinked. *In Jesus' name, amen. Please!*

She blinked again. But was God listening?

Lord of heaven's armies, she prayed so.

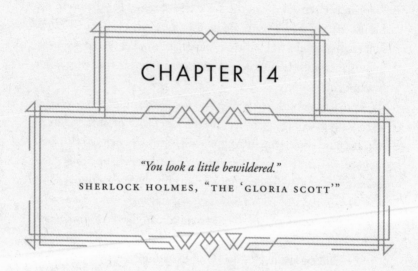

CHAPTER 14

"You look a little bewildered."
SHERLOCK HOLMES, "THE 'GLORIA SCOTT'"

"Is this what you wanted to see, officers?" Louise Barnes' voice sounded like her throat was trapped in a vise. Strained, terrified, threatened. But she kept talking, eyes blinking fast as if sending her friends a secret, coded message. She blabbered along. "I've got some nice church ladies cleaning for me." She pointed at Annalee, Mrs. Stallworth, and Mrs. Cunningham. "You're still cleaning up here, ladies? Not finished yet?"

Mrs. Stallworth and Mrs. Cunningham stood stiff as stones, not uttering a peep.

Annalee nodded to Louise Barnes, but could feel the white envelope inside her bodice scratching her skin. *Don't dare peek out, little envelope.*

"We're making progress, Miz Barnes—"

"Not anymore." A cop pushed past Louise—almost knocking

her over—took the steps, and hunched up to the attic. He was bony looking and tall—too lofty to stand to full height in the cramped space.

"Drop that broom. You're coming with me." He hovered over Annalee. "All of you."

Jerking around, the cop pointed to Annalee and her friends—then back at Louise. "You too." Her face lost all color. If misery had a look, Louise was wearing it.

"She has lodgers, sir," Annalee broke in, talking under the kerchief, trying to give Mrs. Barnes an out. "This is her rooming house—and her husband died. She runs it by herself. She's fixing supper. That's why we came to help clean. We brought our gloves and—"

The cop looked livid. "Drop that broom!"

"Sir, we just cleaning ladies—" Mrs. Cunningham had found her voice.

Mrs. Stallworth stepped forward, pulled down her kerchief, pulled off her gloves. "And I got a roast in the oven—"

"Handcuffs." The cop gestured to his men. "All of them."

Mrs. Barnes sank to her knees. "Oh, Lord, no. Oh, Lord Jesus. Help me, Jesus."

They were going to jail.

Annalee let that sink in. She shut her eyes tight a moment, made herself think harder than she'd ever thought about anything in recent memory about what was happening—and most important, why. But she already knew why.

Somebody with an inkling of Prissy Mack's lodging location had alerted the Klan-run cops—probably the police chief himself—warning him that evidence in Prissy's room could point to an upstanding white man. So send some cops over there now. Clear out the place.

The lead cop turned on Annalee. "Open your hands. Take off those gloves! What'd you steal?"

"From here?" She pulled off the gloves, crossed her arms. "Dust?"

"Cobwebs?" Mrs. Cunningham yanked off her gloves, pulled down her kerchief. She wiped her forehead with it.

"And these—" Mrs. Stallworth picked up a dirty vase. "Bunch of dead flowers."

Her friends were giving the cop their best what-for. It was now her turn again.

"Look around yourself." Annalee nodded to the washbasin, the bed. "Plow through the drawers, search under the bed, look under every flower vase—"

"Enough," the cop snarled. His two partners pushed into the room, both carrying handcuffs, all of them—suspects, cops, and Louise Barnes—now jammed together in Prissy's tiny sleeping space.

The atmosphere on a June afternoon was stifling, and the cops—in their heavy uniforms, their angry handcuffs clanging— were sweating. Louise Barnes, still huddled on the floor, leaning against the wall, turned from it all, still moaning, "Jesus, mercy. Help me, Lord."

"Hands behind your backs." The lead cop issued orders, turning from woman to woman.

The other cops mimicked him. "Hands behind your backs. Cross 'em!"

"I certainly will not." Mrs. Stallworth pulled to her full height. "I have a roast in the oven. Besides, I refuse to let my dear friend Louise Barnes get taken downtown to a jail, not to mention let a kitchen burn down."

"Handcuffed for what?" Mrs. Cunningham did her bit now. "On what grounds? If you arrest me, I'll have our pastor contact the NAACP—Denver chapter!"

"Of all the—" The cop reached for Mrs. Cunningham, who promptly swung back around, screeching, "No" at the man.

Annalee knew what they were doing—giving her a chance to rid herself of that envelope scratching like crazy against her skin.

While her friends ranted, she yanked off her kerchief and threw herself into a fit of sneezing, pressing the kerchief against her face, then her chest.

"All this dust." Mrs. Stallworth grabbed her pocketbook, pulled out another handkerchief, pushed it at Annalee. "Here, use this."

"Enough!" The policeman grabbed for the kerchief.

But Annalee had yanked it from Mrs. Stallworth's hand, wiping at her own forehead and face with it—still sneezing and coughing. "These dead flowers." With a moan, she turned dramatically, bending from her waist to genuinely sneeze, held both kerchiefs to her chest, and let the envelope slip from her bodice into one of them.

She let it all fall, moving her foot to push the envelope back under the bed, using the back of her hand to wipe sweat from her forehead, because she actually was sweating for real now.

"Resisting arrest." The policeman glared. "That goes for all of you." He pointed to Louise. "Her too."

Mrs. Barnes, still moaning, covered her face with her hands.

Annalee turned on her heels, held her hands behind her back. She'd heard enough.

"Well, if we're getting handcuffed, get on with it."

Mrs. Stallworth and Mrs. Cunningham both took the same stance. Hands behind their backs, wrists crossed.

"That's right." Mrs. Cunningham spat out her words. "Get on with it."

"But if my roast burns . . ." Mrs. Stallworth glared at the policeman.

"Wrists tight." The cuffs locked. Cold steel. Heavier than Annalee expected. She sucked in a breath.

The cop swung around, huffed at Mrs. Barnes. "Stand yourself up, sister."

Mrs. Barnes shook her head, protesting. "I'm sorry, but I'm feeling sick." She tried to stand but sank down again. "My legs won't hold me."

The cop cursed. "Carry her down," he snarled at the other cops. "Get moving."

Annalee held a scowl. This had become one of those problems that simply couldn't have a good ending. If neighbors saw Louise Barnes carried like a sack of spuds out of her hard-earned house by cops—hands behind her back in handcuffs—she'd never recover, even if her reputation didn't completely unravel.

Annalee hated the prospect of going to jail. But she would survive whatever amount of time she'd be kept there. Same for Mrs. Stallworth and Mrs. Cunningham.

But Louise Barnes wouldn't last one day, if even one hour. Annalee felt sure of it. The experience would kill off the sensitive, hardworking Louise—mind, body, and spirit—before the sun went down.

She needs help.

Her prayer sounded impotent to Annalee's ears, so it probably sounded that way also to God. But she couldn't ponder that now. Not at a moment like this. Instead she just wanted God to help. *Good grief, Jesus. Please.*

Walking down Mrs. Barnes' stairs, from attic to foyer—with hard-faced cops following their every nervous step, and two of the cops lugging Louise Barnes down without a shred of concern for her dignity—Annalee kept repeating whispered pleas until it became a question. *Please?*

Perhaps that's why at the bottom of the stairs stood her answer.

Nope, not Jack Blake.

Not Eddie Brown Jr.

Not Mr. Cunningham wearing his sharp-looking cabbie cap.

Nor was it a half dozen other folks who could've come to the rescue—including the entire membership of the Hearts and Hands Women's Civic Club of Mount Moriah AME Church.

Instead it was the same curious man who'd sought out Annalee the afternoon before. He was standing astride the rag rug in Louise Barnes' carefully dusted, mopped, and swept foyer.

And he was a lawyer—Nathan Furness.

Annalee blinked. Nathan Furness looked professional and sounded furious.

"What's going on here?" he snapped at the police officers.

"Get out of my way," the top cop snapped back.

"I will not. These are my clients."

"Attorney Furness?" Annalee gave him a grateful, confused, hopeful look.

Nathan nodded at Annalee. "I dropped off my mother, Mrs. Charlotte Furness, at Miss Valerie Valentine's home—at the end of this block—but all I could see were your police cars parked all over the lawns in such a nice neighborhood."

Nathan saluted Mrs. Stallworth and Mrs. Cunningham, freed a sobbing Mrs. Barnes from the two cops, and helped her sit down on a parlor chair in her foyer, even though her wrists were still shackled.

Mrs. Stallworth and Mrs. Cunningham nodded at him, spoke their clear thank-yous—as if they'd been acquaintances for years with Nathan Furness, who happened to turn up just when they needed him.

He turned now on the cops. "Uncuff these ladies." He glared at the lead cop. "Right now."

"I've got orders to bring them all in."

"You have no such orders," Nathan scoffed. "On what grounds?"

"This is a murder investigation."

"You can investigate until the cows come home, but you have no right to take these ladies to jail for no good reason—especially for a murder investigation. These women haven't murdered anybody."

"How do you know—?"

"I know wrong when I see it. More wrong than you could know. But these ladies haven't killed anybody or hidden a murderer or committed any other horrible crime. Now, uncuff them."

"But the chief—"

"I'll call the chief myself. Where's the telephone?"

"On the table?" Louise Barnes' soft voice sounded unsure, as if she shouldn't reveal where her lodgers' telephone rested. "At the end of the hall?"

"Never mind." The lead cop cursed again. "Unlock those cuffs. Men, we're leaving."

"But the chief—" a second cop cut in.

"It's over," the top cop grumbled. "Let's go."

Annalee didn't look that cop in the eye for fear of gloating. Instead, she turned, squaring her back to let her cuffs get removed—which didn't happen gently. The other women did the same. Louise Barnes did too—turning in her prim parlor chair.

Clanging away with their handcuffs and sweaty breathing, the cops stomped out of the house. One kicked Louise Barnes' rag rug to the side, a final insult. But never mind, they were gone.

Annalee let out a long breath. She heard the other ladies breathe deep too. They all rushed to Louise Barnes, embracing her, asking if she was alright.

"I think so," Louise whispered, but suddenly she commenced to weep while telling God, "Thank you, thank you, thank you."

Annalee turned to Nathan Furness. "I don't understand how you ended up here just when we needed you, but we're indebted to you."

"You were right on time." Mrs. Stallworth reached to shake Nathan's hand. "You're a lifesaver—and a lawyer?"

He shook her hand. "Nathan Furness, ma'am. Attorney at law."

He shook the others' hands too—including Annalee's. He nodded to all three. "And like I told Miss Spain yesterday—"

"You talked to him yesterday?" Mrs. Cunningham broke in, looking surprised.

"He's working on the same case." Annalee decided to put it that way.

"And working on myself too." He shrugged. "When I saw all those police cars—one of them parked on the lawn, doors wide open as if some crazy villain was on the loose—something didn't look right. Not with so many truly bad things going on in town these days."

"Can I show you something?" Annalee pointed up the stairs. "In the attic?"

He agreed. So she took Nathan Furness to the dusty fourth floor, showed him the humble room that Prissy Mack had rented—with all the dried-up flowers, unsigned cards, and under the bed, the envelope addressed to Malcolm Kane Sr.

Nathan took in the space, staying silent. Then his focus shifted in a flash to the man's leather belt.

"What's that doing here?" His eyes showed alarm.

"You recognize it?"

"It's mine."

Annalee frowned. "I don't understand."

"I don't either, but this is my belt." He picked it up. "See the design on the buckle? That's our family crest. My father sketched it on a paper napkin when he started his first company. His neckties bore the design. Then a few years ago, my tailor suggested I order some buckles for my coats and belts." He pointed to the belt he was wearing. "See? Same insignia."

Annalee listened and watched. Was Nathan telling the truth?

"But how did it end up here?" She frowned. "Unless somebody was scheming to frame you."

"But who—?"

Annalee put a finger to her mouth, grabbed a couple High Plains Floral cards, dropped them in her purse. She recovered the white envelope from under the bed and dropped it in as well. If she was going to steal evidence, she might as well make the most of it. "Let's get out of here."

"What's wrong?" Nathan looked panicked. He gripped the black belt.

"I don't know." Something felt wrong but she couldn't explain it. Nathan searched her eyes. "What are you thinking, Miss Spain?"

"I'm not—thinking. Not clearly. But when that changes, if I need to talk to you, you'll know."

After Nathan Furness left, Annalee and the women helped Louise Barnes take to her bed, offering their help. "I'll finish preparing dinner for your lodgers," Mrs. Stallworth assured her. "Give yourself a break this evening."

"Thank you, Edna," Louise whispered. She still looked wan and weary from the day's ordeal. Mrs. Stallworth brought her a cup of hot sweetened tea with lemon and, after sipping it with trembling hands, Mrs. Barnes nudged herself under her bedcovers and fell into a sound sleep.

"She probably hasn't slept well since her husband died," Mrs. Cunningham said. "After today, she deserves a good, calm rest. Sleep well, my friend." She patted her hand.

As Mrs. Stallworth headed to the kitchen to start dinner for her friend's lodgers, Annalee asked Mrs. Cunningham to help her finish cleaning up the attic.

"Isn't it evidence?"

"Those cops didn't care about evidence—not to help Prissy. I'm worried about Louise Barnes now. If we clean everything, she won't have to worry herself with it."

Mrs. Cunningham agreed.

So back went kerchiefs over their faces—and gloves on their hands—as the two swept, dusted, washed, and aired out the attic room, clearing it of dead flowers, dirty vases to wash, and bedsheets, plus Prissy Mack's few clothes to launder.

By dinnertime, Mrs. Barnes was awake and back on her feet, wearing a fresh dress and a smile of relief on her face as she welcomed her lodgers home for their meal.

"Corn bread smells right good," said one elderly man, and other lodgers agreed. Louise Barnes looked grateful.

"Let's go home to our burned roast," Mrs. Stallworth said to Annalee and Mrs. Cunningham.

But when they arrived and opened Mrs. Cunningham's front door, the best-smelling roast that Annalee could recall awaited them—with Mr. Cunningham, wearing one of his wife's aprons over his cabbie clothes, carving the meat, mashing summer potatoes, buttering green beans, and stirring brown gravy.

"You made gravy?" Mrs. Cunningham grabbed a spoon to taste and nodded approval, amazed. "When in the world did you learn that?"

"At my mother's knee." Mr. Cunningham, a round-faced man with a twinkle in his eye, gave his wife a wink.

"But you never made it for me."

"You never asked."

Annalee laughed then—the first light moment she'd had all day—and the others laughed too.

"Sit down, everyone," she said. "I'll set the table and serve."

Annalee also said grace.

It was heartfelt but short. After their close call with going to jail, she felt grateful but wouldn't nag God's ear with some dramatic, long prayer. *Thank you, Father* said it all—especially when her work to find a murderer was hardly over.

She winced. Not by a long shot.

CHAPTER 15

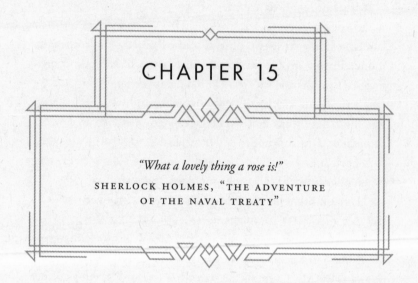

"What a lovely thing a rose is!"
SHERLOCK HOLMES, "THE ADVENTURE
OF THE NAVAL TREATY"

BACK AT HER CABIN, Annalee huddled alone in the dark at her little table and tried to make sense of the day—and where things stood. First, and most important, she hadn't gone to jail. *I'm forever grateful, heavenly Father, in Jesus' name. Amen.* For all her bravado—and her confidence she could survive prison—she knew for sure that jail was the one place she never wanted to find herself. Not ever, thank you very much. End of discussion.

More than all, after today, she wanted to find out who'd courted Prissy Mack by swamping her with boatloads of gorgeous fresh flowers—so that this flower-giver could then maneuver a way to kill her?

What kind of monster would do that?

Tough question, but she already knew the answer. The monster was somebody with something monstrous to hide. She swallowed. Or an evil lust to monstrously fill.

Shuddering at the thought, Annalee clicked on her small lamp to take the gloom off her room. Back at the table, she snapped open her pocketbook to plow through its contents and clean it out. This seemed to be her ritual with every case. Now here she was again, dumping out her purse on her little table, picking through all the detritus of the investigation that she'd collected so far.

Those cards from High Plains Floral caught her eye first. The endearments would have turned the head of all but the most level-headed young woman.

You take my breath away, Prissy.

Thank you, sweet Prissy, for a scrumptious afternoon.

You're the answer, lovely Prissy, to my prayers and dreams.

Heady words. Not even Jack Blake himself had written such love notes to Annalee. So were they a young man's words? Or the carefully crafted seduction of an older, experienced lothario? She thought of Thaddeus Hammer. Or the evasive Malcolm Kane. She tilted her head. Or was the note writer just a cunning killer, no matter his age?

She'd sniff around at High Plains Floral tomorrow and see what came forth. But something else. She'd also ask Jack to write a love note to her one of these days—a counterpoint to the harsh words she often heard from the world, but also a contrast to the letter still waiting in the rusty box she'd buried in her yard.

She let herself sigh.

More digging was needed, meantime, to figure out why Prissy was writing to a Malcolm Kane Sr. in Bramble Creek, Mississippi. That person surely would be the father of Malcolm Kane Jr., the elusive or cryptic president of Saxton seminary. She set the envelope aside.

Then those flowers in Prissy's rented room nagged at her too.

For all the piles of petals and multiple vases of blooms, not a single one matched the distinctive color of the budded rose that Prissy had held in her cooling dead hand. That rose was a stunning red streaked with fuchsia, one of the prettiest roses Annalee had ever seen.

Glancing at her small shelf, Annalee let her eyes take in the single rose petal. Drying naturally, it still retained most of its gorgeous color.

But where in the world had it come from? Somebody at High Plains Floral might know that too.

For now Annalee brushed debris off her little table, set her kettle on for tea—it was too late for coffee, as much as she'd love a steaming hot cup—and sat down with nice, random reading matter. So she finished a Sherlock story she'd started a week ago, enjoying the blithe detective's discernments. Pondering God and his goodness, thus, Holmes had pointed to flowers.

"What a lovely thing a rose is!" he remarked in the story, holding in his hand "the dainty blend of crimson and green," a drooping stalk of a moss rose.

All other things, Holmes then observed—food, powers, desires—are needed for our existence. "But this rose is an extra. Its smell and its colour are an embellishment of life, not a condition of it. It is only goodness which gives extras, and so I say again that we have much to hope from the flowers." ·

Thinking on his words, she opened up a gardening article by George Washington Carver. What might the famous "peanut man" teach her on this summer night?

He was a simple man, said one writer, who "found God in the hills and fields." If a problem stumped him, he didn't fret. Instead, the next day he'd arise at four o'clock—his daily practice—then go into the woods and talk with God.

"I never grope for methods," he said. "The method is revealed the moment I am inspired to create something new. I live in the woods. I gather specimens and listen to what God has to say to me. After my morning's talk with God, I go into my laboratory and begin to carry out His wishes for the day."

What intriguing men, these two, Annalee thought—Holmes and Carver—both in their own way searching for God's mysteries in his creation. "Not we little men that do the work," Carver wrote, "but our blessed Creator working through us."

Annalee set down the article on her shelf, pondering its various wisdom, but especially the faith that Carver expressed in an always-working, all-knowing, and ever-present God.

She thought of her little garden and her vain and empty efforts to get anything to grow there—notwithstanding the actual letter she'd discovered from her missing mother. She still didn't know how to talk to anyone about it, including Jack—not because he wouldn't understand, but because she herself didn't quite know how to say what it meant. *Life for us can be the same way,* Annalee thought, *with our vain, empty efforts to make things happen with our sometimes confounding families.* But also with her work—her struggles to solve another crime.

This thought then whispered to her.

God knows who killed Prissy Mack.

God also knew *why* Prissy Mack was killed.

This God of mysteries also would share these secrets—as the humble George Washington Carver insisted—if she asked for answers.

Annalee, huddled at her table, pondered the matter. She finished her tea, freshened up in her tiny bathroom, changed into her nightclothes, and clicked off the lamp on her shelf.

In her small cabin, lit now only by the faint moonglow passing through her one tiny window, she knelt by her bed. The words of a plea took a while to find their way to her lips. But finally, after reflecting on her day—and all that she and her friends had seen and experienced—she let her thoughts form.

"You care about Prissy Mack, Lord." Her voice was a whisper. "She was your child—just as we all are, including even me. Somebody lured her, and used her, and stole her life, and tried to pretty it up with a covering of flowers."

Annalee shook her head.

"But you already know all this, heavenly Father—just as you know who did this awful thing to pretty Prissy in her swirly-toed shoes. So help me to hear what you know. Speak to my heart, O Lord. If it's my call to find and reveal the truth of this killing, would you show me a sign? A little, bitty nudge, Lord. Am I on the right track?"

Annalee lay across her small bed.

"We almost went to jail—and that can't happen again. So would you keep us safe—my friends and me? Especially Louise Barnes, bless her precious soul. But all of us."

She ticked off her friends' names on her fingers, speaking them aloud. "And Eddie Brown, too, Lord. And little Melody Coates." She twisted her mouth. "And all the people at that Dawkins carnival. Whatever in the world they're doing here and however they're involved—if they are—in Prissy Mack's demise, please can you show me? So I can solve this thing? If it's your will."

She curled under her covers.

"And Jack, O Lord." She whispered the young pastor's name with a sigh. "I am in love with this man." She hugged her blanket. "So will you keep him safe? Safe from awful things and bad people?"

She closed her eyes.

"And me, too, Jesus." She yawned. "Guide my feet."

She wiggled her toes.

"And thank you for my new summer shoes. They're really pretty.

"In Jesus' name," Annalee added, "amen."

———◇———

Early the next morning, Annalee dressed in her jeans, a simple shirt, and oxfords. Then after eating toast and jam with coffee, she pulled on her late daddy's work gloves and stepped outside.

The morning was glorious. The sky pink, its wispy clouds fading into dawn, the air warming itself in the early sun as chickadees and robins and finches flitted from tree to bush to tree.

"Good morning, kind birdies." She gave the birds a little salute, grateful for their cheerful, busy singing, their humble digging at the dirt, their tiny joy—making the day look and sound as if it could turn out to be delightful.

Walking around her cabin, she was caught by surprise at the sight of a growing plant. Well, it wasn't something she'd planted. But it seemed awfully sweet—a white-petaled flowering plant that could've been a weed. Or was it a flower?

She picked one of its stalks and laid it on the top step to her door. Maybe the speaker at today's Colored Women's Civic Society meeting could identify it for her. Thinking about that event, she pulled a couple of other plants. Flower or weed? She wasn't sure, so she laid them all on her top step. She'd wrap each in a hanky or wax paper and take them to the afternoon meeting.

In fact, she'd wear her pretty pink sheath and little white church gloves, act her society best while meeting Valerie Valentine's fancy friends—seeing if any had met a young woman named Prissy Mack, plus getting the chance to see her beloved pals. Both Mrs. Stallworth and Mrs. Cunningham, and maybe even Louise Barnes, would attend the gathering—so much better than huddling in a jail cell.

I'll be grateful to see them today.

A happy yellow flinch flitted by her with a song.

This day was looking bright, indeed.

So Annalee had a song on her lips as she rode the streetcar to

High Plains Floral. Just east of downtown, it occupied a full city block and now, in mid-June, was in full glory. In aisle after aisle, every possible variety of blooming plant, flower, bush, or tree likely to thrive in Colorado's high, dry summer sunshine was on display and offered for sale.

A busy army of salespeople—each wearing High Plains Floral canvas aprons tied at their waists—bustled about. None offered to help Annalee, which she expected. So she roamed the aisles—lost in her own thoughts as she strolled through the bountiful displays, many flowers and plants giving off glorious aromas.

A lemon balm display on a long wooden table smelled so heavenly that Annalee picked up a pot and lifted it to her nose, breathing in the lovely citrusy scent.

"Are you buying that?" A salesman stopped. No smile. His balding head had been pomaded and combed within an inch of its life, his dark bushy eyebrows hairier than the hair on his head.

Annalee searched his eyes, saw the sad hate that so many seemed to carry these days. She set down the plant and made a decision.

"Actually, no. I'm looking for my friend. He works here. A colored man."

"Colored?" He scowled. "You mean Leroy?" The salesman gestured over his shoulder. "He's out back. But he's busy. Don't dare bother him."

The man straightened the lemon balm pot that Annalee had set down and marched away.

Annalee watched him go, lifted the pot one more time, breathed in the heavenly scent again, replaced the pot, and turned toward the back. She'd made a calculated guess. An enterprise this big would have at least one colored worker—toiling, yes, out back.

Walking by rows of plant displays, she finally passed a stack of rakes and shiny metal watering cans, stepped into a darkened storage area, and saw a graying colored man pushing a pallet of large, heavy-looking flowerpots.

He looked up, saw her, and touched his hat. The brim was soiled. A weathered straw. His apron from High Plains Floral looked even more weathered. How long had he worked here? Decades, it seemed.

"Help you, miss?" His voice sounded weary. He spoke low. He pointed to a gate behind him. "Looking for the way out?"

"Mr. Leroy?" She took a step toward him, offered her earnest smile.

He looked confused. "You looking for me?"

"You're Mr. Leroy? Yes, I was told you worked here?" Annalee smiled again.

He nodded. "Did you need something? I'm kind of busy." He pushed the pallet along. "Watch your feet."

She stepped back. He wasn't unkind or rude, but he was, in fact, working. It wasn't her intent to interrupt him or, worse, get him in trouble at his longtime job.

"Just a quick question. Is this from your company here?"

She clicked open her pocketbook and brought forth a card written to Prissy. She'd chosen one with fairly tame wording.

Enjoy the bouquet, dear one. Scrawled at the top was the name High Plains Floral.

Mr. Leroy frowned. "Ain't one of ours—that card."

Curious. "It says High Plains Floral."

"Our cards is printed. Paper's nicer too." Mr. Leroy frowned again. "Why you asking?" He stepped back. "I'm busy anyway. You better leave, young lady. There's the gate."

"I'm leaving now, sir, thank you." She looked quickly in her purse again. "Just one more thing. Is this one of your roses?" From her purse, Annalee lifted Prissy's rose petal, wrapped in her pretty lace hanky.

His eyes went wide. "Mercy, where'd you find that?" He looked closer. "What a beauty. Look at that color—"

"Leroy!"

Annalee froze. Leroy flinched.

It was the salesman, glaring at both of them.

"Those pots, Leroy!" The man pointed to the cash registers. "Up front! Today, if you don't mind."

"Coming, sir. But look at this here petal. This color—"

The salesman's eyes widened, then narrowed. He glared at Annalee. "What do you want?"

"A friend received this from an admirer, and—"

"What admirer?" The man furrowed his bushy eyebrows. He reached for the petal, but Annalee pulled it back just as fast.

"I don't recall his name. But the color was so unusual, I thought someone at High Plains Floral could tell me the name of the rose. And if you deliver it. Do you sell this variety here?"

The man didn't answer, swung instead back to Leroy, his voice harsh. "Can you not hear? Take those pots up front now."

Leroy blinked hard, grabbed each side of the pallet with a gloved hand and pushed the pile of pots out of the storage area, saying nothing more to the salesman, but touching his hat as he passed Annalee.

"Thank you," she whispered. Folding her hanky over the rose petal, she dropped it into her pocketbook, clicked it shut, turned to follow Leroy through the big store and out the front doors.

"Just one minute." The salesman barked the order.

"I'm done here." Annalee glanced back at him.

"Actually, you're not done. Stealing a rare cultivar is a serious infraction in the floral industry—"

Annalee swung around on her heel. "I'm not a thief. If I were stealing this here—" she shook her head at him—"*cultivar,* I surely wouldn't come into this gardening store with a sample of it and ask about it. Now if you'll excuse me."

She turned her back to leave.

"Stop right now!" the salesman called out.

But Annalee kept walking. She'd had enough this week of

being suspected of doing wrong. So why the slight smile on her face as she walked away?

She'd learned something vital at High Plains Floral.

Prissy's red rose wasn't some garden-variety flower by any stretch of the imagination. It was apparently the creation of a floral expert, and if well received "in the floral industry," it was probably worth a tidy sum.

So who in Colorado bred rare roses? That was her next question to tackle, but she had a good guess who could help her answer it.

Leroy, the High Plains Floral worker, was pushing his pallet into position near the row of cash registers at the front of the gardening store.

Annalee opened her purse, took out a calling card, dropped it on Mr. Leroy's pallet—without skipping a step—and breezed through the garden center's open front doors, but not before hearing him whisper, "I might can help you." She nodded once, just barely.

Outside the sun was still shining.

So Annalee was smiling to herself as she headed back downtown to catch the Welton Street trolley to Five Points. But a church bell sounded. It was 12:45. She'd have to scramble to make it to the Phillis Wheatley YWCA on time for Valerie Valentine's 1 p.m. civic club meeting.

Where was that streetcar? Looking down Welton, Annalee saw no car in sight.

She'd just have to walk fast and hope the doors weren't locked to latecomers—if locking doors once a meeting started was something Valerie Valentine mandated, which it probably was. Annalee rolled her eyes. *Oh, that woman.* So she picked up her pace, hurrying now down Welton in her summer pink sheath.

"Hey, Miss Spain." A couple of children were playing hopscotch. "Will you play with us?"

"I'm late for a meeting," she told them, but she hopped from square to square on their chalk-drawn game—stirring up their laughter—before rushing down their block.

"You touched the line!" one of the girls called out.

"I know. But I'm late!"

The girls giggled.

Four more blocks to go—and more playing children to rush past, not to mention women sweeping sidewalks, schoolboys mowing lawns with mowers going *clickety-clack*, *clickety-clack*, plus two young men in a car whistling at her. She shook her head.

At the Y's redbrick building, she ran up the concrete front steps, wiped perspiration from her face with the backs of her hands, straightened her dress while watching the door slowly closing as she reached forever and a day for the handle.

She put her foot in the door.

"Sorry. You're late." It was a Valerie Valentine acolyte—a younger version of the society woman decked out in white summer silk and perfect strands of pearls adorning her bodice. "The meeting is starting." The young woman set her mouth.

Annalee grabbed the doorframe and stepped inside.

"Gosh, you look so pretty," Annalee told her, gave her a smile, and ignored the young lady's rejection. "Look, there's still one minute to go."

"Well, I . . . thank you . . ." Not expecting the compliment, apparently, the young woman stepped back, which allowed Annalee to push past her and ease inside the door to glance over the crowded room—every seat taken, it seemed—as Valerie Valentine stepped smartly to the podium to start the meeting.

"On special occasions like these, dear ladies—" Valerie intoned her most high-society voice. She was dressed to the nines, head to toe in pale peach silk. She cleared her throat to start again. "As I said, on special occasions like these—"

"Excuse me." Annalee whispered her way down a row of seated women. Mrs. Stallworth was waving to her from the opposite end of the room, pointing to the saved seat between hers and Mrs. Cunningham's wooden folding chairs. This was in one of the back rows. The front rows seemed to be occupied by fancier women— probably associates of Valerie Valentine. Their chairs were nicer. Upholstered and plush.

"Excuse me." Annalee kept pushing herself down one of those fancy rows, apologizing to the seated women—some cutting their eyes at her, which Annalee ignored.

I shouldn't be late anywhere, she admitted to herself. But she couldn't change that now. *Just let me get to my seat.* "Excuse me, please." She kept her whisper low.

"Ladies!" Valerie Valentine, reacting to the commotion, looked up to give Annalee an icy glare.

Annalee held up her index finger, as older ladies at church did when they arrived late—an old-fashioned gesture that made Valerie press her mouth into a thin line of pure ire.

"On occasions like these—" Valerie started again.

"No matter, my lady."

Valerie swung around. She put up a hand as a humble-looking little colored man in a painfully worn-looking suit stepped forward.

"Excuse me! Oh, sir! Let me introduce you properly—as our special guest."

"Allow me, first, to say a humble hello." The man stepped to the podium.

Annalee slipped to the back of the room, settled between Mrs. Stallworth and Mrs. Cunningham, and looked up, her eyes finally taking in the stage. She stifled a gasp, not believing who she was seeing. She gripped Mrs. Stallworth's hand.

"What?" Mrs. Stallworth whispered. "You okay?"

Annalee held her other hand to her chest. "I'm not sure."

The little man was speaking, a smile gracing his glowing face.

"I was in town, dear ladies," he was saying in the most curious high-pitched voice, "so I volunteered to serve you when your planned speaker had to cancel." His voice truly was high in tone, but it wasn't unpleasant. He laughed at himself.

"I wish I had a radio voice."

Some women in the audience huffed at that. Others looked unsure who was speaking to them.

The little man went on. "But, mercy me—I'm getting ahead of myself. The good Lord stopped me in your beautiful city of Denver just when I was needed here. So I'll say a few words to you about flowers." He smiled. "And maybe a few words about peanuts."

"Peanuts?" A woman in the front row gasped.

At that, the air seemed to leave the room as the women seemed to suddenly understand who was addressing them. A buzz of whispers erupted as the women stood as one to gasp, fan their faces, and applaud. Annalee leaped to her feet too and put her hands to her face, realizing then that a tear was running down her cheek— even before the small man shared his name. *I am crying, yes,* she told herself. But why? *I'm crying for myself. Crying, yes, for Prissy.* Crying for any little girl who found herself in the world without someone to tell her she was beloved and good and deserving of a flower—or a mother. Such a child would never have been given a beautiful rose because she was deserving of it simply because of who she is—a daughter of God himself.

"That is right," the famed man was saying. He nodded to Valerie Valentine, to the young lady still keeping watch at the door, to the audience of surprised women—to whom he then offered a gallant bow from the waist. Finally, with a twinkle, he let his bright eyes scan the room as he confirmed his identity.

"My name, dear ones, is George Washington Carver."

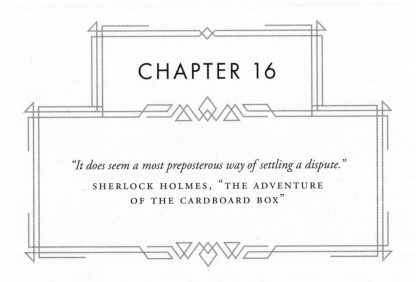

CHAPTER 16

"It does seem a most preposterous way of settling a dispute."
SHERLOCK HOLMES, "THE ADVENTURE
OF THE CARDBOARD BOX"

ANNALEE STIFLED A CRY. *George Washington Carver,* in Denver? Standing in this room right before her eyes? She couldn't decide how to respond, and that rattled her. She wasn't one to gush over famous people. She'd seen plenty of the "high-and-mighty" at Mount Moriah AME Church—renowned national speakers, singers, politicians, preachers. The gamut. All seemed to love to strut their stuff across a grand stage at an "important" church.

Jack let them come, not endorsing any of them but opening his pulpit to famed people because his parishioners, in out-of-the-way Colorado, seemed eager to meet such celebrated people.

But Carver seemed different. She would hang on his every word, she told herself, precisely because he didn't seem important. He sounded and looked like a humble nobody. His threadbare woolen suit had been brushed within an inch of its fraying life, offering only one bright note—one tiny pink posey in his worn buttonhole.

He was reflecting now, in fact, on the simple glory of such a posey, and how he so dearly prized them.

"Is there anything lovelier, dear ladies, than a precious flower—awakening at dawn while lifting its pretty face to the sun?"

The audience of women beamed, all of them still standing, gaping simply at the sight of their guest. As Negro women, they'd likely heard as much about Mr. Carver as about any other renowned person of their shared, beleaguered race. Surely knowing that, Mr. Carver invited them to "please take your seats, dear ladies. I'd like you to stay awhile." All sat down but one. Thus, he turned to Valerie, the only one still on her feet, retaining her "I'm in charge" command position.

He smiled kindly at her. "You, too, Miss Club President."

Valerie nodded proudly at that acknowledgment, even though she still was vice president of the civic club—and hadn't been elected yet to the top spot. Mr. Carver seemed to be saying such titles didn't matter that much.

"Sit, please," he said to her again. "Any chair will do—that little wooden one by the window." So finally, Valerie stopped fussing with her pearls, her hair, the oversize diamond ring on her finger, and reached with resignation for the plain wooden chair and sat down.

Mr. Carver closed his eyes a moment, testing the atmosphere apparently. Then, looking over the audience again, he spoke.

"We've come a long way, haven't we, ladies?"

Most were nodding, understanding exactly what he meant, after the brutal sorrow of slavery, the terrors of the Ku Klux Klan, the flight from places down South where many thought nothing of snuffing the life out of any random colored person for not "staying in their place." Then even up North, one faced countless daily insults. Getting looked down on by most in their nation—"from the White House to the outhouse," as some of their preachers often said—those in this room had arrived in a place like Denver to find themselves at odds, too often, with even each other.

"Have you formed different social and civic clubs?" Carver asked. "So you see your club as better than somebody else's?"

Annalee nodded with understanding and let out a long sigh. She hadn't a clue what Carver was going to talk about, but he went straight to the heart of so much that challenged her world—and maybe to the heart of her current case, and so to the heart of why poor Prissy Mack didn't survive her escape from down South and now, like many, somehow was dead.

"Teach us, Professor," Annalee whispered.

Mrs. Stallworth squeezed Annalee's hand, gave her friend Mrs. Cunningham a meaningful look, turned in her seat to glance at various Hearts and Hands friends sitting in nearby wooden chairs—all of them crowded into the back of the Phillis Wheatley Y meeting room because they weren't the "right" people, not "good enough" to sit up front. Especially not with fancy colored people.

Like Annalee and Mrs. Cunningham, Mrs. Stallworth moved to the edge of her chair, as if ready to leap from her seat to show thanks for Carver's fearless words.

He went on. "Some of you have arrived sooner than others. So you have more. You've accomplished greater. You dress better—"

"Mercy, Jesus."

One of the Hearts and Hands members stood to her feet, fanned at her face. Her humble, homespun dress was clean, but it marked her as a "lesser" person than the Valerie Valentine crowd. The woman lifted her hands, as if she were in a church service—grateful to hear rightly divided truth. Around her, other Hearts and Hands members stood too.

In solidarity, Mrs. Stallworth and Mrs. Cunningham stood as well. Annalee arose to stand kindly beside them. If the good Lord sent Carver here to speak some truth, she'd do her best to show she affirmed it.

Valerie Valentine, meantime, scowled, Annalee noticed, toward the back of the room—her face a grimace.

But all eyes were probably on Carter.

"I understand," he was saying, "the hunger to be found 'good enough.' Or acceptable enough to others—if not to oneself. I've traveled that road myself."

Many in the room were nodding, including women up front. The young woman seated by the door moved to the edge of her seat to nod agreement too.

"But hear me now." Carver stepped forward. "It is not the style of clothes one wears, neither the kind of automobile one drives, nor the amount of money one has in the bank that counts. These mean nothing." He smiled. "Does anyone here agree?"

But he didn't have to ask. As he spoke, Annalee watched Mrs. Stallworth, Mrs. Cunningham, and what appeared to be the entire Hearts and Hands contingent applaud warmly, wildly, wonderfully. True, they were guests here. They'd come to hear about flowers—a few words, yes, about how to create from almost nothing a beautiful floral arrangement.

But Carver had discerned a problem in the room, and he'd spoken directly into it. They couldn't thank him enough—even if Valerie Valentine looked fit to be tied. Her mouth was a wrathful, thin line. Why was she bound so tight? Determined to be queen bee, lording over everybody else?

Carver didn't seem worried about her. Instead, he acknowledged the applause he was getting. Stretching out his hands, he gestured everyone to sit back down—which they finally did.

"I'm here," Carver said, "to give service. Simple service. That's what matters most. And, as God knows, for that I am grateful." He chuckled. "So now, let's talk about flowers. What questions do you have?"

Hands flew up. Carver spent an hour or more answering a stream of often shy questions. He was Negro royalty, even if he didn't look like it, so the club women spoke with deferential respect. Working from a small table on the raised podium, he demonstrated how to arrange flowers in a simple milk bottle to show them to best effect.

Annalee was riveted.

In Prissy's room, the vases of blooms had seemed gracious and beautiful—with their tall, showy flowers in the center, filler flowers around the middle, and spiller flowers at the edges. So what was missing in the vases that Prissy received?

"Love."

Carver said the word with reverence, mentioning what he called the main ingredient in a beautiful floral arrangement. "Love for the person receiving them. Love for God, who created them. But also love for yourself, as a child of God.

"So start with the vessel that will display your flowers. No, not the vase," Carver said. "Start with yourself. Start your day with prayer. Clean your heart of envy. Love your neighbor. Then select a simple, lovely container for display of your pretty blooms." He smiled. "Like this."

He picked up a tin water pitcher. Set it aside. No cut crystal, apparently, for him.

"Then organize your blooms by color," he added. "They will please the eye." He laid a selection of roses in varying pinks in small piles on his table.

"But first, lay a bed of greenery into your vessel—cutting its stems at an angle so each can sip the warm, fresh, clean water awaiting it."

His movements were gentle as he built up his floral display, "using what was growing around your Y building here—plus these precious flowers, each one a gift from one or two of the ladies in our meeting today. And how much did I spend? Nothing really. Just the small effort to show up. But look how lovely."

He held up his arrangement. In his hands, the tin water pitcher had become a marvel almost impossible to stop admiring. He managed the same with the milk bottle, using it to display greenery from lilac bushes—probably from the row of lilacs growing behind their Phillis Wheatley Y building. An assortment of other purple blooms all faced left, their attention on a single white rose placed amid them.

"If nobody else sees this but me, it gives me more joy than I can measure."

He let his eyes roam the audience, a deep look of regard on his face.

"You each deserve that. In fact, I'll tell you a secret. Day after day, I spend time in the woods alone in order to collect my floral beauties and put them in my little garden that I have hidden in the brush not far from the house. That's because it was considered foolishness in the neighborhood to waste time on flowers."

He laughed.

"Can you imagine? Foolishness?" He scoffed. "Even if your garden is secret, water it and let it grow."

Annalee thought of her dirt yard and what she'd reburied there, but blinked hard, kept watching Professor Carver—grateful for him.

He moved the milk bottle and tin pitcher aside. "Now come shake my hand before it's time I take my leave."

A rush of women moved toward the podium. Carver stepped down and began greeting admirers—each woman looking as if the famed botanist only had eyes for her.

"No pushing!" Valerie Valentine shoved past women to the front of the line. "Give Professor Carver room."

"I'm fine, Miss Club President," Carver said. "Besides, one last lady has arrived." He was gesturing now at the door, which had just been pushed open.

Annalee smiled. *Lord, thank you.*

"It's Louise!" Mrs. Stallworth gave a little clap.

"Our Hearts and Hands member!" Mrs. Cunningham proudly announced to anyone within hearing distance that Louise Barnes, of her beloved civic club, had arrived.

"Hearts and Hands!" Another member of their club shouted out, gesturing to Louise. "We're back here!"

"I'm sorry I'm late." Louise Barnes seemed to be apologizing to everyone, especially to the young woman who still guarded the door as if manning exits and entrances was her one purpose in life.

Valerie Valentine set her mouth, looking peeved.

But Louise didn't seem to notice or seem worried to be wearing a clean but plain cotton dress. Her hair was neatly curled and she clung tightly to her pocketbook as she made her way to the back of the room to join her beloved Hearts and Hands friends.

"Are you okay?" she whispered to Annalee, Mrs. Stallworth, and Mrs. Cunningham—who each assured her they were fine. "Is it okay that I came?"

"Did those officers return to your rooming house?" Annalee spoke low.

"None of them. Are we in the clear?"

"I'm sure we are." Annalee gave her an assuring nod, even though she wasn't sure one bit. In some ways, danger seemed closer than ever regarding the Prissy Mack affair. That's why she'd attended Valerie's fancy meeting—to get a break from the pressure but also to perhaps learn something new from the society women who shared Valerie's inner circle. The surprise gift was Professor Carver and his calming presence and remarks.

She'd needed his peaceful assurances about flowers and making things beautiful, but also his wisdom.

She got in the line to shake his hand.

The line wound around the room and seemed to take forever and a day to come to the end, with Annalee dead last in the queue. Approaching the table where Carver was offering his goodbyes to the woman preceding her, Annalee reached out her hand to him.

"The line is closed." Valerie Valentine stepped between Annalee and Carver, cut her eyes at Annalee, swung around, and grabbed Professor Carver by the elbow. "You'll miss your train."

Carver stepped back, releasing his elbow. He searched Valerie's stern face. A frown had deepened over her eyes.

"What is the matter, Miss Club President?"

"I don't want you to miss your train."

"Actually," Carver spoke softly, "something else is bothering you. I could feel it the moment I stepped into your meeting room, see it in your face, hear it in your voice, see it in the way you're doing everything in your power to stop me from speaking to this lovely young lady."

He gestured to Annalee, reached out, and softly grabbed her gloved hand. She didn't pull away. She also didn't want to argue with Valerie, especially not in front of the esteemed professor.

"May I speak with you now?" Annalee asked him instead.

Valerie bristled. "Sir, you'll miss your train—"

"Another train will come along. They always do. That's the nature of transportation, dear lady. If you'll wait for me outside, you and I can talk on the way to the station. I won't be long." Carver pointed Valerie to the door, ignoring her stiff departure.

He turned to Annalee. "Now, who are you, young lady? And why were you crying when I was introduced?"

She swallowed. "You noticed me? In the back of the room?"

"When we watch the world well," Carver said, cocking his head, "we see what needs to be seen."

Annalee could understand that. Her own watching could use refining. "Thank you for your time," she told him. She felt both nervous and humbled. He was showing her such kind interest. "I'm not sure where to start—"

"Start at the beginning." Carver gestured them to two chairs—the simple, plain ones. They sat facing each other. Carver seemed to Annalee deeply interested in what she had to tell him, even if she couldn't understand why. *So, I'll just be honest.*

"There's been a murder."

Carver winced, but nodded. "In your beautiful city. Someone you know?"

She told him about Prissy Mack. "At least, I feel sure that's her name. No one seems to know her, but it appears she came to Denver from the South. Maybe from Alabama."

"Alabama? That's where I teach—at the Tuskegee Institute, but you already know that." He shook his head. "A beautiful place, Alabama, but, Lord, so much is dirt poor. Entire counties are practically starving. Families, too. Then the lynching and carrying on. Colored folks are leaving in droves. Like your Prissy." He studied her eyes. "But how are you involved with her killing?"

Annalee blinked. "I'm a detective."

Carver blinked too. "A detective who cries?"

"I'm at a loss." She told him about her garden—a dusty failure. Her struggles at being a detective—in a world that turned its back on her, ridiculed her, where she didn't seem to count. *Well, except with Jack.* But she decided not to mention him. "So I cry, I suppose, for myself. But I also cry for Prissy. What a sorrow to be alone in the world, without a single soul saying they know who you are."

Carver searched Annalee's eyes. "Is that your story too? You're alone in the world?"

Annalee swallowed. "But you are too. I know about your mother." He hadn't seen the woman, according to the news and biographies about him, since he was a mere infant.

He sat still as a stone.

"I grew up without a mother too." Annalee went on. "No need to tell you the story. But for her and for me, I suppose I cry." She shook her head. "A mother would tell me how to grow green beans." She half laughed. "All I'm growing is dirt."

"Well, I can help with that." Carver gave her a smile. "How old are your seed packets? No, I'll tell you myself. You found them in a box that's decades old."

"They were my late father's." Annalee kept it at that. "So I decided to plant the seeds—in honor of him."

"But they're not growing, dear lady, are they? Not a one. So tomorrow you'll go to the hardware store and buy fresh seeds." He tilted his head. "We harvest what we sow." He patted her hand. "Now what else?"

"Weeds. They're everywhere."

Annalee opened her purse, took out a folded piece of newspaper, unfolded it to show Carver a weed from her garden.

"Purslane," Carver said, "and it's edible. The flavor is lovely. Prepare it like spinach, cooked with other greens. Or it's equally acceptable as a raw salad."

"Raw?" Annalee knew she sounded doubtful.

"Just don't confuse it with common spurge. The two plants look alike. But with spurge, the sap oozes white. That's your warning not to eat it. Or any plant with white sap. Stay away."

Annalee tilted her head. "So spurge is poison?"

"Well, it'll turn your stomach inside out. But it can be fatal too." Carver pressed his mouth. "I hope I'm not frightening you."

"You're helping me. Maybe regarding Prissy."

"Lord, you think the poor girl was poisoned?" He shook his head. "My soul reels at such evil. Plants with poison are simply protecting themselves. They're not meant to harm. If you learn their signs, the flowers will tell. *Don't touch me. Don't eat me.* So what else did you bring me?"

Annalee showed him another weed. "Can I eat this?"

"It's wild asparagus. Also edible." He smiled. "You have a good eye, Miss Detective."

"I'm trying to learn—just as you said. But you must catch your train."

"I'd like to, but you're still frowning. How else can I help you?"

"With this." Annalee opened up a corner of a plain cotton handkerchief to show him the pretty white flowering plant she'd found in her yard. "Wild onion?"

Carver leaped from his chair.

"What's wrong?" Annalee saw his panic.

Carver had grabbed the handkerchief, twisted it in a ball, looked for a place to toss it away. "Is a garbage can outside, miss?"

Annalee led him out a back door, into the bright Denver summer sunlight, to an alley and a row of rubbish bins.

With one deft toss, Carver dispatched the flowering plant along with Annalee's humble handkerchief. "Where'd you find this plant?"

"A few blocks from here—behind my wood cabin. A little patch of it is growing in the sunshine. It caught my eye because I hadn't seen it before, and the little flowers—running up and down the stem—are so pretty."

"Then you need to know about that 'pretty' plant. It's not wild onion, although it looks like onion. It's called death camas—and it will kill you." He pointed to her hands. "It's a good thing you're wearing your church gloves. Peel them off and drop them in the bin. Same with your pocketbook. Anything of value in there?"

"Just this." Annalee reached in her purse and brought out the rose petal. She told him about finding its bud in Prissy's hand.

"Every flower tells," Carver whispered.

"But what does that mean?" Annalee sounded desperate.

"Find the person who provided her this hybrid—as it appears to be—and thanks to this flower petal, you'll find your killer." He sounded certain.

"Can I write you if I have questions while I investigate?"

Carver nodded soberly. "Send your letter to Tuskegee. Address it to me. But one more thing."

"What is that, Professor?" Annalee asked.

"Mark it urgent."

CHAPTER 17

"Really, Watson, you excel yourself."
SHERLOCK HOLMES, *THE HOUND OF THE BASKERVILLES*

SOMEBODY TRIED TO KILL ME. That was Annalee's awful dilemma. Jack needed to know. She wanted to talk about it. But Jack was busy with church work, rebuilding Mount Moriah, dealing with a dead friend, and certainly more troubles, Annalee thought, than she could imagine or probably realize. So for the rest of this Friday and much of Saturday, she focused on ridding her yard by herself of the nasty death camas.

Following a booklet on toxic weeds she'd found at the Five Points hardware store, she dug up each plant—bulb, stalk, little flower, and leaf—all while wearing protective clothing, gloves from the store, and even a face mask fashioned from one of her plain cotton handkerchiefs. Then she tossed the whole shebang in a double burlap sack, jammed the protective clothing in another burlap sack. She wrote *Danger: Poison!* in big letters on the outside of both.

Then Mr. Cunningham put the sacks in the trunk of his cab—laying them on newspapers spread out underneath—and drove the entire haul with her out to the city dump. And good riddance. Annalee hoped never to lay eyes on anything like death camas again.

Still, she had that bigger problem.

Somebody tried to kill me. Right?

"It's a fair question," Annalee told Mr. Cunningham. "But how and when?"

"During the dead of night, I guess." He squinted. "You must be a sound sleeper."

"Makes me embarrassed."

"Why?" He'd turned his cab around, heading them back to Five Points.

"Because it was a simple ploy. Whoever planted the weeds figured I'd notice them, which I did. But they guessed I'd also touch them, then eat them—mistake them for wild onion or something like that—which, thankfully, I didn't."

"God's keeping watch, little lady." He straightened his cap.

"I'll never have enough thanks." Annalee nodded. "I've been threatened before while 'detecting' a case. But planting a poison plant where I'd find it? That's attempted murder." She pursed her lips. "Professor Carver, before he left, told me the plant usually grows wild in meadows and prairies. Ranchers have to monitor their pastures for that plant. Entire herds can die—"

Annalee froze.

"What's wrong?" Mr. Cunningham frowned.

"A rancher? Two or three ranchers sit on the board at a seminary where I've been snooping around." She squinted, trying to remember the portraits on the Saxton gallery wall.

"You think one of them came all the way to town just to plant that nasty weed? In your yard?"

It was a ludicrous idea, she could admit. Some rancher—hearing about her visit to Saxton—driving long miles into town in the dead of night and planting a deathly dangerous plant in the dirt outside her window.

"Or—" she sat up in the taxi—"they hired somebody to do their dirty work. So you know what's next for me."

"Find out who did it."

Annalee squared her back. "What's the time? The streetcars are still running, right?"

"You bet. They run 'til midnight. But it's Saturday. Almost five. You're not going out to that seminary this afternoon, are you?"

"Closer to home, in fact. I'm going downtown to the carnival."

"Now? Why?"

"There's a curious lady there I need to talk to. She knows things. Knows people too."

"Well hold your horses. I'll give you a ride." Annalee checked her reflection in Mr. Cunningham's passenger window, moved a wayward curl off her face, smoothed her plain white blouse, and brushed off her blue jeans. She didn't look professional, but she looked serious. Why? She was.

At the carnival, however, the crowd looked upbeat and light-hearted. Not a serious-looking face in the Saturday crush of folks. Not one soul showed concern for a young woman killed barely one week before or, if they'd known, a stitch of concern for the attempt to plant poison in Annalee's sorry-looking garden.

Annalee kept her eyes down, feeling self-conscious walking alone on the dusty promenade. But she wasn't the only one with nerves. Passing the milk-bottle game, she saw the worried-looking man running it—Mr. Riley, the lodger she'd seen earlier this week at Louise Barnes' rooming house.

He was sweating. Annalee figured she knew why. The summer evening was warm, especially for Colorado. But Mr. Riley would've been coached to cheat—meaning every interaction with carnival customers probably vexed his soul.

He was wiping his brow repeatedly, his voice cracking. "Step right up! Win your sweetheart this . . . Kewpie doll."

Poor man. Annalee could relate. But she felt uncertain.

Nathan Furness had told her of the Welcome Ambassadors scheme involving seminary men. It sounded preposterous. Despite Nathan's kindness, she couldn't quite get a fix on him. Was he the seminary man trying to get her off his trail? A trail intersecting the carnival? She kept walking. The whole thing was still a conundrum. But who could help her unravel it?

"Miss Annalee!"

Annalee heard her name and turned. "Zimba?"

"You're okay?"

Annalee took the measure of the fire-eater, surprised that she felt genuinely grateful to see him. "Shouldn't I be?" She meant that. What on earth did Zimba know?

"Well, a cop was here—asking for you."

"What cop?" Annalee shook her head. "When?"

"Night before last. Tall, angry-looking guy." Zimba shrugged. "He seemed so put out over you, really angry about something, that I felt worried for you."

"What'd you tell him?"

"Nothing. We're from out of town. What would anybody here know about you? Like that you're a detective. The cop told me that much." He gave her a look. "Is that right, Miss Annalee? You're a detective?"

"Well . . ." Annalee hesitated. "Sometimes I am. But this policeman—did he talk to anybody else here? Your booth workers?" She pointed at the milk-bottle man. "Or janitorial folks?"

"Not sure about that. But he probably talked to the Sawyer

sisters. Everybody does. Minnie's in her trailer. You can ask her. Do you remember which one?"

Annalee thanked him, pushed past the crowd to the relative quiet of the personal staff area.

"Minnie?" Annalee stood at the trailer door. She tap-tapped. Nobody responded.

"It's Annalee." She tapped again. "Do you have a minute? I just have a question—"

"It's you?" Minnie opened the door to peek, almost as if she feared Annalee would visit. She gave Annalee a half smile. "You'd better come in."

Annalee stepped inside. Minnie's trailer looked the same. A riot of fancy clothes. A trunk filled with shoes. Scarves, beads, and baubles flung in every corner. Seeing Minnie in all the chaos, Annalee did something that surprised even herself. She reached out and gave Minnie a hug.

Minnie received it, hugged her back. They were two young colored women living in a complicated, inhospitable world. Neither needed to explain a need for comfort. Minnie's cousin Sonny was dead with no explanation. Annalee, among other things, was being hunted by a cop.

Annalee cut to the chase. "Somebody tried to kill me, Minnie."

Minnie nodded as if she wasn't in the least shocked. "I didn't know you were a detective. That's probably why."

"Well, that's part of it." Annalee pushed aside a pile of dresses on a fussy boudoir chair. She sat down, not bothering to ask permission.

Minnie sat opposite, facing her, on a narrow bed. "What are you investigating, Annalee? Sonny's death?"

"Actually, no. But it is a killing." She told her, finally, about Prissy Mack.

"Mack? That's her last name?" Minnie looked pained. "Like Lil' Baby Mack, our lynched friend?" She sighed deeply, hugged herself, searched Annalee's eyes. "So, a coincidence?"

"Hardly." Annalee scoffed. "I wouldn't trust coincidence as far as I could throw it. So no, it's not coincidence. But what is it? How are Prissy and Lil' Baby Mack connected? Or even Prissy and Sonny?" She wrinkled a brow. "Is there a way for you to find out? To maybe write to somebody in your hometown and ask?"

Minnie sat silent for a long time. "Digging up the past won't change a single thing. That's what my mama would say. I can hear her now. Leave it be." She pursed her lips.

Annalee nodded. "Some things should stay buried." She frowned hard. "But I'm solving a murder."

"Is that what you're doing? Is that why somebody tried to kill you?" Minnie shuddered. "Mercy, am I supposed to help you?"

"I'd say the one you're supposed to help first is yourself."

Minnie swallowed. "I don't know where to start." She whispered the words.

"You do know where a lot of bodies are buried. I'll put it like that." Annalee hiked a brow. "Well, not bodies per se. But secrets. You know a lot of them about a lot of people, right, Minnie?"

Minnie nodded slowly. "I keep them for Lil' Baby. Use 'em when I can."

Annalee gave her a look. "You're blackmailing people?"

"Getting even. That's what I call it. These rich guys come sniffing around the carnival, looking for 'clean colored girls.' So sure, I go out with them. My sisters too. Then when we've got enough dirt to hold over them, I let 'em have it. Pay up. For our silence." Minnie twisted her mouth. "And the clothes, shoes, watches, jewelry? What I can sell, I send the money to Lil' Baby Mack's mama and daddy. I send money to my mama, too." She grimaced. "Yesterday, I sent money to Sonny's mama. One of these men owns a fancy department store. I've got more clothes, dresses, furs, shoes than I'll ever use. He'd give me all his inventory to keep me from blabbing to his wife."

Minnie sounded defiant, but a note of defeat had crept into her voice.

"What would it take for you to leave this path?" Annalee wanted Minnie to reconsider. She was letting herself get used. Why on earth would she walk such a road?

"Leave this?" Minnie sneered. "Now that I know about Prissy Mack too? It would take the guilty person getting justice, which I may never see—not in my lifetime anyway."

"Even if 'vengeance is mine—'"

"'Saith the Lord'?" Minnie rolled her eyes. "You expect me to accept that after so many good colored folks—men, women, boys, girls—have been lynched despite being innocent, but just Black. Like Lil' Baby. Why would I believe a God who allows that? Then he says vengeance is his? Not mine too?"

Annalee listened. "You're not really asking me, so I'm not going to lecture one word about trusting God—"

"Don't you dare preach the Book of Job at me." Minnie glared. "You smart people think folks like me don't know these things. How many colored preachers have I heard spouting those words? 'Though he slay me, yet will I trust in him.'"

"And maybe preached at the hardest times." Annalee would ask Jack to explain that. Did hurting folks want to hear Job preached while they're suffering? It may be the proper thing to do, but would Joseph's story be better—from the pit to the palace? But Annalee had a deeper, far more urgent concern.

"You're in danger, Minnie—just like me. You realize that, don't you? If you keep on with your 'paybacks'?"

"Of course I'm in danger." Minnie set her jaw. "But maybe I don't care about that anymore. And don't give me some fancy lecture for saying that too." She studied Annalee. "But with you? Somebody wants you out of the picture—as in dead and gone. Do you know why, Detective Annalee?"

Annalee searched Minnie's eyes. "I've gotten too close to something." She squinted. "You probably have too, even if you don't know what that something is. But it's like you said, Minnie: it's no coincidence that Prissy's last name is Mack—like your school friend. She was from Alabama, it seems, like you and your sisters, and Sonny, and Lil' Baby, too. Alabama people—"

Annalee moved suddenly to the edge of her chair. She let out a long breath. "What else is in Alabama?"

Minnie laughed. "Cotton."

Annalee nodded. "I understand. But what else are people in Alabama doing?"

"Doing? They grow cotton. Or they grow something else. Corn. Hay. Oranges. That's what people do."

Annalee wrinkled her nose. "Have you ever heard of death camas?"

"Sure. A weed. But it's bad." Minnie shrugged, made it sound as if the weed was something any person would know about. "Have you ever seen it?"

Annalee didn't answer.

"It's a pretty little plant. Dainty flowers up and down. The stalk looks like wild onion. But any part will kill you. We always stayed away from it. My mama taught us that. It's not like common camas. You can eat that—but Mama didn't want to make a mistake between the plants, so we just left it alone. Daddy always dug it up if it came up in the fields."

Minnie gave Annalee a look. "Why you want to know? About death camas?"

"What kind of person would know about it? Anybody at the seminary? Any of those men on the board? You've met some of them?"

"A few. Ranchers. Farmers. A banker—"

"And Malcolm Kane? The president?"

"Nope. Milly just mentions him a lot."

Minnie leaned over to a dresser, opened a drawer, and pulled out a thick brochure. The name *Saxton Theological Institute* was printed on the front—over a color photo of the leafy Saxton campus. Minnie opened it to the center pages, a double-spread with a gallery of photos.

"My sister waltzed home one night with this. Here's the board. The lot of them." She squinted at the page. "Who would know about death camas?" She counted off the best candidates—a total of nine of the twenty or so on the page.

Annalee sighed. "Mercy, that's a lot of people. How would I narrow down that list?"

"Oh, that's easy actually." Minnie handed the brochure to Annalee, pointed to different photos. "These four have resigned the board in the past year or so, or so says Milly. Their term was up. This one moved to Europe two years ago, or so I heard. I never met the man. This one's on a round-the-world trip with his wife. So he's out of the country."

"That's six." Annalee looked over the portraits. "What about the other three? Any chance one might've been introduced to Prissy Mack?"

A crazy question? But she asked because seminary people were at the garden party and were involved with the Welcome Ambassadors. Then she'd overheard Hammer seducing the young colored woman.

Minnie studied the photos. "Introduced to Prissy Mack? Probably none of them. Not this rancher, that rancher, or this farmer. From what I know, they're all on the up-and-up. Or trying to be."

"But what about him? Thaddeus Hammer."

Minnie pursed her lips. "Curious guy, Hammer."

"What makes you say that?"

"He's hard to nail down. I've seen him around. He's top dog at some agricultural outfit. But he's not a farmer."

"A rancher?"

"Nope. Probably doesn't own a single cow. Besides, he lives in the city. Comes from city folk, I hear. He lives in a fancy city house—"

"So he wouldn't know about death camas?"

"It's hard to say. He runs that agricultural group. How he got picked for that I don't know—a city man who knows nothing about farming? You could go see him and just ask." Minnie hiked a brow. "My sister Milly knows where he lives." She sighed. "C'mon. Let's go find her."

Minnie stood, but Annalee reached for her arm.

"Not Milly. I'd rather not bring her into this. But does she have an address book? Do you?"

"Now that you mention it." Minnie swung from the bed and stepped to the chest of drawers. Going drawer to drawer, digging through a stash of silky underthings in each one, she finally pulled out a purse-size black notebook. It was alphabetized. Minnie went straight to S.

"Saxton. Thaddeus Hammer. He resides on Clarkson Street." She made that sound fancy. She repeated the house number. "Want me to go with you?"

"Not for this." Annalee stood to leave. "But a prayer would help."

"They do. Even when I'm frustrated." Minnie sighed. "So go with God."

"I'm trying." Annalee banged open the door to Minnie's trailer. "Trying more than you know."

CHAPTER 18

"Knowing what I know, I have sent for you and not for the police."
SHERLOCK HOLMES, "THE ADVENTURE
OF THE DEVIL'S FOOT"

EDDIE BROWN JR. WAS WAITING FOR ANNALEE on her tiny porch when she got home. He sprang from her wooden steps, hugged her quick and tight. She returned the embrace. He seemed grateful to see her, but he looked preoccupied. Such a grown-up-looking face on such a young boy. She kept her mood lighthearted.

"How was the fishing?" She stepped back to look him over.

"Not bad. I caught two catfish."

"Outstanding."

"Plus a trout. Miss Alice, the cook, fried up the haul. I caught a lot of weeds too. But it was fun."

"So what's the secret? To landing your catch?"

"A light touch, I guess. Don't go slapping around, making a lot of noise, scaring the fish."

"I'll have to remember that tonight."

"You're going fishing? Tonight?" Eddie studied her face. "Oh, for your case?"

"I shouldn't have mentioned it." Annalee stepped back.

"Please let me go."

"Absolutely not."

Eddie's shoulders dropped.

"Too dangerous. This fish is ruthless. Sly and cunning."

"You're going to meet him? It's a man?"

"Just look at his house. After it's dark."

"Breaking in there?" Eddie looked alarmed but excited.

"Nothing like that." Annalee quickly glanced at her dirt garden, but just as quickly, she turned away and stepped off her porch. "I'll just walk around his block—for starters. It may be a complete waste of time. Not sure what I'll find. But I won't know if I don't go."

"You have his actual address?"

"It's on Clarkson Street. The swank part of town." Annalee mentioned the block number.

"Man, that's a fancy neighborhood. Not far from Sidney Castle's place." Eddie looked hopeful. "I could meet you there. They're having some boring speaker at the boys' home tonight. I could duck out."

Annalee gave him a half laugh. It would be irresponsible for her to bring Eddie along to case Thaddeus Hammer's private home. She didn't have a plan. She just wanted to see the place, get more of a measure of the man—then hop on a streetcar and head back to her side of town, clean as a whistle.

"Well, I hate to say it, but you're already dressed for a little nighttime adventure." Annalee pointed to his dark pants and a black T-shirt. "Does that explain your clothes? You were hoping for some detecting tonight?"

"That garden-party murder isn't solved, right? I haven't seen anything in the papers. You always say it's best to solve a case sooner than later. So, going into week two, I figured you and Pastor Blake might have something cooking tonight—and you'd let me ride along." Eddie blinked; then he got serious. "Please, Professor? With you and Pastor Blake? I won't ask anything about you two getting married."

Annalee shook her head and laughed. "Pastor Blake isn't coming along tonight."

"How come?"

"He's busy with other things." Annalee unlocked the door to her cabin, gestured Eddie inside. "Let's get something to eat. Then off you go—back to the boys' home."

"No thanks. I'll leave now." Eddie slumped.

"Let me cook you something." Annalee opened her little icebox and removed two eggs to fry up with a potato.

"Naw, no thanks." Eddie still stood in her doorway. "Alice the cook is making us a surprise dinner—and rumor says it's steak. A thick one for each boy. A rancher near town donates beef once in a while and—"

"A rancher?" Annalee tried to sound casual. "Do you know his name?"

"Benson, I think."

Annalee tilted her head. Was Benson a rancher on Saxton's board? She didn't recall seeing his name.

"When his truck comes to the boys' home," Eddie went on, "it says Benson's Beef." Eddie backed out of the doorway, still looking disappointed. "Well, so long."

"Don't leave pouting."

"I'm not, Professor. But Pastor Blake's not going with you tonight. What if you get in a jam?"

"What jam?"

"I don't know. But somebody killed that young colored lady." Eddie searched her eyes. He looked vexed. "That's what I'm angry about. Somebody's out there killing people. Even little kids. Lynching them and all. I saw it in the papers. We have to stop them."

But what exactly was her plan? What had she done to help God clean up the world's dirt so more people could find him—not to mention find each other?

"You're the best helper a detective could have. If there's steak tonight at the boys' home, make sure Alice gives you the thickest, tastiest, best cut of the batch. Hot mashed potatoes, too."

"Then I'll jump on the streetcar and meet you at Clarkson Street." Eddie set his back.

"Too dangerous."

"Did that stop us before? From letting me help you? Did it, Professor?" His persistence rattled her. He usually backed down when she said no, even if he felt miffed. She tried a different tack.

"Scoping out Hammer's place isn't just dangerous for you—"

"That's his name? Hammer?"

"Forget I said it." Annalee shook her head. "On second thought, I've changed my mind. I'm not going to Hammer's tonight."

"I don't believe you, Professor!" Eddie grabbed the door handle. "But it doesn't matter. I'm going to that Hammer man's house tonight whether you go or not."

"Wait." Annalee ran to the door. "If you get caught—" But Eddie had already swung to her porch, jumped the two steps in front of her cabin, and run down the road heading back to the Five Points streetcar.

She didn't call after him. She knew why.

She was going to Hammer's tonight herself. And if Eddie was there?

The two of them would just have to sleuth together.

The streetcar she rode stopped three blocks west of Clarkson. It was after ten, but on a Saturday night, the trolley was still running and packed. The sidewalks too. Annalee whispered prayerful thanks. With so many people out and about, she'd blend in as best she could. Well, as the only colored woman on the trolley.

She sat on a back row. Quiet as a mouse. Dressed all in black now in an ordinary skirt and cotton blouse, she turned toward the window, watching the nighttime street life with seeming indifference. But her senses and nerves were firing. What would she see? Or find, or hear, or learn? She didn't have a clue what to expect around Hammer's place—or even if she'd run smack into Thaddeus himself. She just hoped to gain some sense of him, and whether he grew flowers. Or killer weeds.

At her trolley stop, she stepped off with other riders, all taking off in varying directions—some to taverns and restaurants on the main drag called Broadway, others toward townhomes and apartment buildings lining the bustling street.

Annalee kept walking south, finally turning east on a tree-lined avenue. Right away, the hubbub of Broadway fell away as she walked deeper into the uptown, leafy neighborhood.

Nearer to Clarkson, a stately quiet hovered over the gracious blocks. A long row of grand homes—each set back from the street on a sweeping lawn—conveyed the wealth and prestige of those who owned them. Glancing at the street address of the home closest to the corner, Annalee figured the Thaddeus Hammer residence would be three properties to her left.

Sure enough, at the place she expected, she passed a three-story, Georgian-style, white brick home marked by two granite pillars framing a large, double-sided, wrought-iron gate—each side joined together to form an oversize scroll-letter *H*.

"Welcome," Annalee whispered to herself, "to the city estate of Master T. Hammer."

She kept walking, ignoring the occasional barking of a large-sounding guard dog.

Just what I don't need. A Clarkson Street version of Bullet.

Walking along the block, Annalee saw a heavy curtain move. So she picked up her pace, walking with purpose, then headed a few blocks east before circling back to Thaddeus Hammer's block one more time. Passing by the alley running behind the homes on Hammer's side, she took a deep breath and ducked into the alleyway.

Standing behind a garage, she let her eyes adjust to the lack of lights, then crept along the fence behind that first property. No dog. Nobody milling about in the backyard. Annalee let out a breath and scurried behind a fence bordering the second yard, which—*oh my goodness*—wasn't quiet.

A swimming pool took up half the yard, and on this warm summer night, a raucous pool party seemed to be underway—with splashing, laughing, drinking, dancing. Annalee had never in life seen such a gathering. A swimming pool at a private house?

And in the pool?

"Thaddeus!"

Annalee froze.

This wasn't the home of Thaddeus Hammer. What was he doing there? His estate would be the next property. But his neighbors, apparently, were hosting Hammer and a crowd of Saturday night partygoers at their highbrow digs. Annalee refused to gawk through a slat in the ten-foot fence. She hadn't been to a highbrow splash party before, but she felt certain how the people would look—women sporting their modern swimming costumes and even wearing their diamonds, men showing off, leaping off the diving board, going on about their latest business deals and entrepreneurial triumphs, laughing at each other's risqué jokes and mimicry of colored people and the poor.

"Thaddeus! Stop that!"

"But the night is young!"

"It's just ten o'clock. He's just getting warmed up!"

More unruly laughter.

Annalee stood behind the oversize garage, still as a stone, and listened.

To the merriment. To the joke-telling. To the casual disregard for "lesser" people by folks who had amassed far more than any of them needed.

She turned in the dark, moving herself toward Hammer's property. But a whisper jolted her.

"You shouldn't be here."

Annalee jumped.

It was Jack Blake.

"What in the—?" she whispered.

He put a finger to her lips. "I came to get you."

She grabbed his hand. "How'd you know?"

"Eddie. He found me at People's Church. He wanted me to come with him, but I sent him home."

"Thank goodness."

"So, I'm here for you." Jack's dark eyes shone in the moonlight. "C'mon. Let's get out of here." He grabbed her hand, pulled her away from the garage, away from the swimming pool shenanigans, and started walking toward the other end of the long alley.

"Wait." Annalee stopped short. "There's a big guard dog down that way—"

"I know." He looked wry.

"Besides, I need to check the next property."

"Why?" He glanced at Hammer's place. "It's just a big, oversize house. Windows all dark." He was still whispering.

"Not the house," Annalee whispered back. "I want to look around the yard."

"Inside the fence? It's got a conservatory on it."

She cocked her head. "A glass conservatory? Like a greenhouse?"

"I think that's what it's called."

Annalee felt excitement. "Jack, I have to get in there—to look around. I'm sorry I don't have time to explain, but I've got to look." She pushed past him. "The owner's next door at that swimming party. Now's my chance."

Jack looked wary, but followed her, both stepping with stealth on gravel underfoot. Alongside the Hammers' large brick garage, Annalee lifted the latch on a metal gate—surprised and grateful it wasn't locked—and entered the property. Jack followed, halted, then turned back to close and latch the gate.

In the dark, wearing his black Sunday pants and a dark T-shirt, he looked strongly handsome as usual, but if anybody had asked, he also looked up to no good. They both did. Annalee pushed back a curl and started to smile at him, to ramp up her courage, but as she cleared the garage, her jaw dropped.

A stunning conservatory sat front and center in the Hammers' rear yard. Two stories high, covered in a metal framework with glass panes, it was a dazzling private showpiece of garden architecture.

"Mercy," Jack whispered.

"That's some greenhouse." Annalee set her jaw. "Help me." She pulled a pair of white church gloves from a pocket in her dark skirt, along with a second pair she'd brought for Eddie—assuming he would disobey her and show up. She offered the gloves to Jack, but she could see they were too small for him. Annalee stuffed the extra pair back in her pocket.

Jack finally grinned. "Don't break anything."

"Lord forbid."

Annalee turned the handle on the greenhouse door with a gloved hand and stepped inside. Jack followed, closing the door behind them with his elbow.

The air inside was fragrant and humid, heavy with moisture. Annalee thought of one word: *tropical*. Leafy things grew from floor to ceiling, blocking any light from a pale sliver of moon above the conservatory's glass ceiling—or even light from the glittering swimming party next door. From behind the ten-foot fence separating the properties, the pool fete was muffled and distant, which to Annalee felt perfect. *Time to get to work.*

She squinted in the dark, walking between row after row of wooden tables bearing potted plants, flowers, fruit-bearing trees, and vines.

Every specimen was labeled with its generic and Latin names, making the greenhouse look scientific—as if maintained by a renowned and serious horticulturalist. Like Thaddeus Hammer?

He seemed too frivolous.

Yet here stood Annalee on Hammer's property inside a stunning conservatory featuring flora of countless types, sizes, colors, and categories.

"What are you looking for?" Jack whispered from a few tables over.

"Something pretty—and something poison." She was looking for Prissy's rose—well, the one that dead Prissy had held in her poor hand. As for poison, Annalee had on her hunting cap for that deadly weed, death camas.

"Poison?" Jack looked confused. "What's the story?"

"It's a weed. Green stalk with little lacy flowers. If you find it, don't touch it."

"I'm glad you told me because here it is."

"Death camas?"

"That's what the label says." Jack pointed to a table of death camas, chained off and set up in a corner. A sign hanging over the pots and a half dozen other plants—also chained off—said COLORADO POISONOUS PLANTS. WARNING! DO NOT TOUCH!

Annalee scooted two tables over to the display, shaking her head.

"That's it, yes." She'd hoped to never see that weed again. Now here was death camas growing nice as you please—protected as if it were precious and valuable—in Thaddeus Hammer's fancy conservatory.

"You going to tell me what this is about?" Jack pulled her back. "As soon as I get us out of here?" He reached in his pocket for his chain watch. "Now?"

"Let me find just one more thing."

Jack shook his head. "Oh, right—something pretty." He tried to smile, but his face showed his nerves. She could tell he was ready to get moving.

"It's a rose, Jack. Like the rose that Prissy Mack—"

She froze. Jack did too.

A flashlight was shining in Hammer's yard.

Annalee stifled a groan. Jack gestured to a nearby wall of shelving piled high with empty pots, garden tools, bags of soil and fertilizer, and a huge bucket holding rakes, hoes, shovels, and whatnot. A corner to hide?

Annalee glanced at the pile, doubting it was a good hiding place, but the crazy light in the yard was bouncing around.

Was it Hammer?

Unlikely. The swim party was at a high pitch. Annalee could hear not muffled sounds now but high laughter, joking, loud music blasting on a radio. Partygoers were singing along to a popular song, "Hinky Dinky Parlay Voo?"—known for its silly spelling—and Hammer's voice seemed to be loudest, his wife playacting annoyance.

"Stop that silliness, Thaddeus," she yelled above the commotion. "If you don't stop, I'm taking you home."

"You'll have a fight on your hands." Another woman offered that point and everybody laughed.

Meantime, the flashlight pointed toward the conservatory door as the handle turned.

"Stand over here," Jack whispered to Annalee. But she shook her head.

"We're fine." Annalee stepped fast toward the greenhouse door.

"Wait," Jack whispered.

But she'd already swung wide the door, staring into the beam of the flashlight.

"Turn off that light."

She heard a click. Then she saw a worried face. Of course it was Eddie.

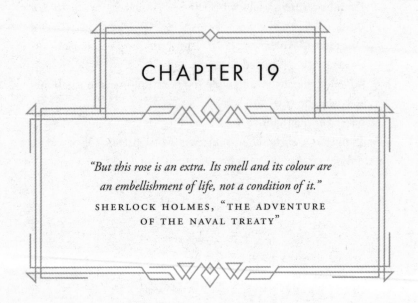

CHAPTER 19

*"But this rose is an extra. Its smell and its colour are
an embellishment of life, not a condition of it."*
SHERLOCK HOLMES, "THE ADVENTURE
OF THE NAVAL TREATY"

ANNALEE REACHED FOR THE BOY. "A flashlight? Whose is it?" She
grabbed the small light, shoved it in her purse.

"The janitor's." Eddie's whisper sounded frightened and small.
"At the boys' home."

"You borrowed it, son?" Jack slipped over to the door. "Never
mind." He turned to Annalee. "Time to go. We're pushing it here."

Annalee nodded. Jack was right. Eddie was here because she
hadn't insisted he stay away. Not really. Besides, she hadn't found
Prissy's rose—but Hammer sure had a boatload of others. If she
made just one more walk around, she could find the hybrid she
felt certain was growing here.

Jack searched her face, looked as if he understood what she
wanted, but he held open the door. "Now," he whispered.

She knew he was right. Her little escapade to Hammer's place could go wrong in a second and in a thousand ways. Found on Hammer's property—especially with an underage white child—she nor Jack would have a single good excuse to explain themselves.

She gave the conservatory one last glance, slunk behind Jack through the door—pulling Eddie along by the hand as she closed the door behind them—and then scooted behind Jack along Hammer's garage. Jack lifted the latch on the back gate into the alley, and Annalee hurried Eddie along so they could follow him.

"Nobody speak." Jack pointed them toward the far end of the alley.

"Guard dogs," Annalee whispered.

"There's just one," Eddie whispered back. "He's not that big."

Annalee started to scoff but froze.

An overwhelming floral scent wafted at her from the opposite side of the garage.

Jack turned. "Your rose."

Annalee dropped Eddie's hand, scurried to the opposite corner of the garage. She swallowed. There it was. Prissy's rose. Not some fancy hybrid carefully cultivated behind a chain in Hammer's greenhouse, this rose made that huffy guy at High Plains Floral dead wrong. Prissy's rose was a wild vine—audacious and a glory, and alive and free.

"Mercy, it's beautiful." Jack stood behind Annalee, his hands on her shoulders.

"Oh, Jack." Her whisper caught. She could've stood under this vine all night, admiring it, fingering the silky petals, breathing in its rich, heady, audacious scent. She plucked off the largest bud she could find and held it to her face. Her eyes tingled.

"Is that the dead lady's flower?" Eddie grabbed Annalee's hand.

She nodded. "This is it—growing right here in front of God and country behind a silly garage." She wiped away a tear. "In an alley—"

"Hey!"

Annalee jerked, felt Jack start running. She shoved the rosebud into the bodice of her blouse and dragged Eddie from the yelling, prompting him to a run too. Annalee glanced back, daring a quick look.

Some teenager in swim clothes and beach shoes, a towel around his neck, called after them.

"Hey! Wanna swim?" The boy laughed. He was holding a teen girl's hand, his other hand gripping her waist.

"Trouble." Jack picked up his pace.

"Hurry, Eddie." Annalee gripped Eddie's hand tighter, felt him move faster.

Good thing, because the next voice Annalee heard was unmistakable. It was Hammer.

"Stop! Thief! Police!" Waving his arms, throwing down a towel, and looking awkward in too-tight swim clothes, his feet bare, he tried to take off after them but stumbled. He grabbed his foot.

The guard dog pounced onto a gate, barking like crazy.

They were steps from the alley's end. Across a wide street was the south end of a park.

"Stop! Thief!" Hammer screamed now, sounding boozy.

The guard dog snapped, snarling and growling.

"This way." Annalee pointed Eddie toward downtown, looked at Jack for a sign she was heading them the right way—back to the main drag. Streetcars would still be running. If they could make it to Broadway, they could jump on one before getting stopped.

Jack grabbed Annalee's hand and reached to catch Eddie's hand on his other side—and they all three turned on the gas.

Hammer was still yelling, but they'd soon put distance between him and his drunken threats. Still the three kept moving. If Hammer called the police, they'd be toast.

"Eddie," Jack called to him. "Run ahead and catch a streetcar to Five Points. Got any change?" Jack pulled two nickels from his pants pocket. "Get off by Mason's rooming house. My car's parked outside. It's not locked. Climb in the back, huddle down, and wait for me. I'll drive you home when I get there."

"And don't make a show on the streetcar," Annalee told Eddie. "Just sit and ride. Don't talk to anybody and don't look back."

"I won't, Professor." Eddie pocketed the nickels. "Thanks, Reverend Blake—"

"Here's the janitor's flashlight too. Make sure he gets it." Annalee gave Eddie a look.

"I will, Professor."

"Hurry, son." Jack pointed Eddie toward Broadway. Annalee gave him a quick hug and Eddie took off.

Jack and Annalee then cut over a few blocks, headed west on a darkened side street and walked fast toward Broadway too. A police siren screamed into the night. In the shadows, under a massive weeping willow tree, Jack stopped them, pulled Annalee under its leafy canopy, then held her close, waited for the siren wail to fade. He searched her eyes, his emotions on high. Moaning, he sighed and kissed her, his longing plain.

"You make me crazy with these escapades."

"I'm sorry," she whispered. "I cut it too close. Bad trouble."

"This isn't trouble. Not yet." He pulled her tighter a moment, kissed her again, defying the night's dangers. "Let's get moving. We'll catch two different streetcars on Broadway."

"And I'll stay at the Cunninghams' tonight," she told him. "I'm sure that'll be okay with them."

"Right. Then I'll see you in the morning." He hiked a brow. "At church. I have to preach."

"On what?"

"'Fret not thyself because of—'"

"'Evildoers.'" She blinked. "Psalm Thirty-seven."

He hugged her quick again and glanced at his pocket watch. "Let's get moving."

At almost eleven o'clock, the side streets weren't as crowded, but the main drag—Broadway—was still bustling. Annalee gave Jack a quick look, moved away, and stepped onto the next trolley to Five Points.

She didn't look back but adored the feeling that he was watching her pull safely away in the streetcar, leaving behind any infernal trouble. After a few stops, she'd be away from downtown—far from Thaddeus Hammer's neighborhood and his boozy yelling at them to stop.

Annalee let out a breath, held on to a smile. She closed her eyes. *I found Prissy's rose.*

She held her hand to her bodice, felt the rosebud lying against the rise of her breasts. Warmth from her body released the bloom's outrageously heady scent. The aroma was intoxicating.

Opening her eyes, she saw a young man in stained overalls sitting across from her—looking weary as he rode home after a long day of work. He gave her a shy, grateful smile. She blinked and responded with a kind look. She wasn't flirting. Far from it. But the scent of the rose seemed to ignite the attention of people seated near her.

"Is that your perfume?" A man yanked off the golf cap he was wearing and scooted closer to his wife—a petite, smiling, curly-haired woman in a red summer dress. "You smell delicious."

The woman laughed. "Hold on to your hat, mister. We've already got five kids at home."

"One more won't hurt." He laughed. Other people near them laughed too.

The woman giggled and elbowed her husband. They looked happy together, riding home perhaps from a rare Saturday night out on the town. The woman snuggled closer to her husband. He put his arm around her shoulder, kissed her ear.

Annalee smiled, watching the couple. But breathing deep, she didn't know whether to laugh or cry. Poor Prissy. She had discovered the gorgeous scent of the wild rose too. Maybe she'd secreted herself to Hammer's house, eager to ask him something about it—whatever that something was—but look at what Prissy got from her confrontation.

She was dead.

Annalee hugged herself. She was grateful to see complete strangers appreciating the lovely scent of the rose that Prissy had held as her last act on earth. But she was past ready now to get to her stop and deboard this streetcar. How many more stops?

She glanced out the window as the trolley turned onto Welton. Almost there.

But her heart thumped. *Mercy, Lord. Not this.* She swallowed. *Please not this.*

Three cops were standing on the trolley tracks, two cop cars and a paddy wagon parked on the tracks behind them.

Their red police lights glared, lit up the inside of the streetcar. The driver—a middle-aged white man—groaned. "What now?" He brought his trolley to a stop, opened the front door. "Help you, officer?"

Three cops stomped aboard and pushed past him, ignoring him. "Stay in your seat," a cop snapped at the driver.

An ugly tension consumed the trolley.

The young man in overalls slumped on his bench, jerked toward the window. He'd maybe had dealings with cops before, so he showed no interest in a run-in tonight. Same with the man with the golf cap. He slapped on his cap, pulled it down over his eyes.

Most of the folks now on the streetcar—almost all colored people—surely just wanted to be left alone. To get home to their families, lives, hopes, dreams, not to mention home to their beds—to their cold-water rentals or shotgun houses or wherever they were fighting to live, and not have to answer a string of indicting questions from Denver's Klan-ruled cops.

The officers carried batons. Their nightsticks. The big ones.

The youngest-looking cop was one of the three who'd shown

up at Louise Barnes' house. He swung his nightstick, making sure to look menacing, eyeing the streetcar riders, swaggering. Annalee didn't shirk or look away. She had nothing to hide—well, except trespassing on Hammer's property. Still, the young cop didn't seem to even recognize her as the woman he'd almost arrested two short days ago.

An older cop had taken charge anyway. The third cop stayed silent.

"Okay, gals." The older officer glared at the women on the trolley. "Open your pocketbooks."

A chorus of female groans erupted.

"Shut your racket! Open those purses."

Annalee pressed her mouth into a tight line. She was carrying her small, secondhand purse—with not much in it, thankfully. A plain handkerchief, three nickels. No lipstick. None of her calling cards sat crunched down inside. Nor even her almost-new driver's license, which would also reveal her name. She'd left it at home.

She clicked open her purse, set it on her lap, waiting for the older cop to rumble through the women's purses, making his rounds, getting ever closer to her bench. This was an illegal search. No doubt about it. But who on the trolley would dare protest?

Stopping at her row, the cop gave her a once-over—which she ignored.

"Open it," he growled. "Wide."

She held up her purse. The cop grabbed it, turned up his nose at her measly contents—which clearly weren't worth his time. With a snarl, he threw the purse back down on her lap. A nickel rolled out, fell onto the floor, but the cop didn't pick it up.

Stomping past Annalee, the cop jerked to the woman sitting with her husband. The wife was shaking like a leaf.

"Your purse!" the cop barked.

"She didn't bring it." The husband spoke up.

"Shut up! Your purse!" the cop snarled back at the woman.

"I don't have it—not with me, sir." The woman's voice trembled. She held out her empty hands. The cop slapped both her hands down.

Her husband flinched.

"Where is it?" The cop was standing over the woman, legs spread wide. He hovered too close. The woman's husband shifted in his seat. This cop had touched his wife. The man looked furious and pulled off his golf cap, twisting it in his hands, surely knowing he couldn't intervene.

"Why not?" The cop was still dogging the woman. "Where is it?"

"My husband carries our money. I didn't need no purse—"

"You're lying." The cop turned to the younger officer. "Take her in."

"No!" the woman screeched.

Her husband leaped to his feet. "That's my wife. Leave her be." He grabbed for her, pulling her from the cop.

The cop jerked them apart. "I'll take you both in."

"For what? We ain't done nothing—"

The younger cop swung his nightstick at the husband, missed the man's head, landed the baton on a windowpane—which instantly shattered.

"Hey!" the streetcar driver yelled from the front of the trolley, leaping up to stop the trouble, but the third cop grabbed him around the neck.

"Officers, please." A distinguished-looking colored man in a seersucker suit jumped from his seat on the front row. The third cop pushed him back down.

"Bring the woman!" the top cop ordered. "Her man too."

"But our kids!" the wife screamed, pleading. "We got kids at home—"

She reached for her husband's arms, but the younger cop reared back, gritted his teeth, and swung his stick—cracking it hard on her hands. Bones split, fractured. The sound was unmistakable, sickening.

Annalee jumped in horror. *God, no.* Others did too. Everybody pleading, begging the cops to stop.

The woman's face had gone blank. Her arms hung limp. Both her hands swelling and turning blue. The woman dropped to her knees.

The husband hollered. Two men leaped over to hold him back.

"Move!" the top cop yelled at the woman, but she seemed frozen to the spot. So the cop yanked at one of her hands. Her wail was a horror of unmitigated pain. But the cop ignored that, pulled on her other hand too, dragged her along the floor of the trolley. Her dress had hitched up around her underpants and her husband was screaming like a madman.

Others were screaming too. *"Stop!"*

Annalee could hear herself screaming along with them. Her heart pounding, her eyes wet with rage and disbelief.

She couldn't bear what she was seeing, hearing, witnessing. So when the cop dragged the woman down the trolley steps by the feet now, letting the woman's head slam, again and again, against the metal risers, Annalee refused to grasp in that moment what she was watching. A woman was being killed.

The woman had left her purse at home—and God alone knew why that simple infraction had indicted her on this particular night—but she was being killed for it. She was already dead now, in fact. Annalee was sure of it.

Like the other streetcar riders, Annalee had rushed to the windows to see what was happening.

The woman lay prone across the trolley tracks, not moving. Her red summer dress was bunched and twisted above her thighs, her pretty legs exposed, one shoe off.

"Resisting arrest!" the top cop yelled into the night.

The woman's husband ripped himself from the streetcar riders holding him, fell down the trolley stairs, and lay across his wife's lifeless body, his wails splitting the air.

"Downtown! Take him!" The two other cops grabbed the husband away from his dead wife, handcuffed him, threw him in the back seat of a cop car, and locked the door. The car shrieked off.

The pure meanness of this set the trolley abuzz. Men cursing. Women crying.

"Let me out." A man in the back pushed his way to the front, jumped off the trolley, and headed down Welton Street. Other riders followed.

The cops yelled at people to stop, but they'd spent their rage on the dead woman and her husband and nobody seemed to pay them any attention now. What were they going to do? Arrest and kill everybody?

Annalee was one of the last to exit the trolley—along with the older man in the seersucker suit. They both stood by the woman's body, but the cops ordered them away.

"Move it!"

"But you killed her." Annalee looked the cop dead on, eye to eye. He didn't reply.

"What about their kids?" Annalee dared whisper a question that needed an answer too. But the cop was throwing open the doors of the paddy wagon. They were going to throw the body inside, dump the woman at the morgue, and drive home to their families.

Annalee knelt on the tracks by the woman, touched her pretty cheek, her hair, her shoulders, tugged her dress down to give the woman her modesty.

The cop glared. "I said get moving!"

Annalee stood to leave, but before she did, she pulled open her bodice—not caring what the cop or anybody else was thinking—and pulled out Prissy's trembling rosebud.

She wanted to cry now more than anything. But she couldn't spend energy on crying as if she couldn't do more.

Instead she bent to thread the rose in the woman's lovely curly hair. The flower looked so beautiful that Annalee could barely stand to look on the horror that its petals adorned. Pushing back her own curls from her face, she let the man in the seersucker suit help her move off the tracks.

"You need help getting home, miss?" the man asked.

She thanked him but told him no. "I'm almost there." She turned onto the dark street.

But she knew that wasn't true. In this town, to get to truth— not to mention to justice—she still had a horrifying long way to go.

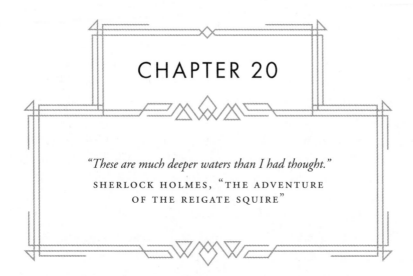

CHAPTER 20

"These are much deeper waters than I had thought."

SHERLOCK HOLMES, "THE ADVENTURE
OF THE REIGATE SQUIRE"

AT MRS. CUNNINGHAM'S HOUSE—one block from the streetcar stop on Welton—a small but welcoming light flickered on the front porch. Annalee tapped on the screen door.

Mrs. Cunningham answered right away. She was waiting up for her husband, wearing a simple nightdress under a cotton house-coat. On Saturday nights, his cab business kept him out late. It was good money, she'd admitted, but she couldn't rest until he was safely home.

Seeing Annalee, Mrs. Cunningham pushed open the door and let her inside. "You alright, honey?"

"I need a place to sleep."

"Come in, baby." She gave Annalee a warm hug, stepped back, moved a curl off Annalee's face. "Are you hurt?"

Annalee blinked. "Can I explain in the morning?"

"Don't worry about it, sweetheart. I'll get you some blankets."

Annalee followed Mrs. Cunningham to the back of the house, where Mrs. Stallworth was already in her darkened room, asleep for the night. Her former landlady snored lightly on her bed. Annalee curled up on a small sofa under a window and told Mrs. Cunningham good night. Pale moonlight slipped through the blinds.

Annalee pulled a clean, light blanket up to her chin—thankful for Mrs. Cunningham's stellar hospitality—and fought to calm her thoughts. Her heart pounded still, her mind struggling to assess all she'd seen, done, and experienced in the matter of a few hours on this night.

Well, it actually was early morning—about 1 a.m.—but her eyes still glared wide open. She'd seen a woman die right before her eyes, and she could identify the killer. Everybody on the streetcar could. But who would they tell? Would she? Nothing would come of it anyway.

Resisting arrest—that would be the cop's own verdict. It wouldn't be overturned. *That's just how things are,* Annalee said to herself. But something else about the evening felt horribly wrong.

I don't even know her name.

For all that had transpired—from Annalee trying to uncover some clue about Thaddeus Hammer to stumbling upon Prissy Mack's rosebud to encountering people on a city streetcar who'd been captivated by the scent of the mysterious rose—Annalee had watched helpless as a second colored woman in a week had come to an awful end right in her town.

And I don't even know her name.

Annalee felt her anger burn, even at herself. She'd failed that woman on the trolley. What if the cops were hunting for her? But she stopped herself. She hadn't done one wrong thing. No felony, anyway. If anything, she'd given the woman and her husband a gift, letting the scent of a rose waft around the streetcar, granting to those breathing it in a certain joy, before all hell—because that's precisely what it was—broke loose.

Lord, what a horror.

She felt desperate for Jack to know what had happened. He'd be asleep now, she was sure, and a call to his rooming house so late at night would be out of line. Tomorrow, in the morning, he'd be caught up with his church service.

Annalee turned on the little sofa, trying to find a comfy position—not to mention some peace. She could hear Mrs. Stallworth snoring away nicely. The Cunninghams' house felt and sounded quiet too—all Mrs. Cunningham's lodgers probably in for the night, along with Mr. Cunningham.

So now what, Lord?

That wasn't even remotely a prayer.

But that's all I got. Now what?

As if in answer, a cloud drifted over the moon, and through the blinds, the orb's pale light dimmed to an empty black.

Oh, swell, Annalee thought. *Even God is turning out the lights.* She lay in the dark, knowing good and well that's not what happened. But that's how she felt. So she let her theologian's mind cast about for a psalmist's plea or a disciple's prayer—something to stir in her belly a shred of peace.

Or she could go to the reliable. The Twenty-third Psalm. She pursed her lips. From a Bible she knew almost from front to back, that's the best she could come up with? It would feel rote and unimaginative to repeat such familiar words. Besides, she didn't feel them. Not tonight.

But that's all I got.

"'The Lord is my shepherd.'" Her voice was a whisper.

She sighed.

Blah-blah-blah. She sighed again.

On through the psalm she repeated the memorable words, arriving soon at that time-honored line:

"'Yea, though I walk through the valley of the shadow of death . . .'"

Her voice caught. *How dare I pray those words tonight?* But she went on:

"'I will fear no evil: for thou art with me.'"

She stopped. More iconic words were in the psalm. Comforting and timeless words. But she'd found the place to stop.

"For thou art with me."

You could've been with that woman, Lord, on the trolley. She needed you—more than I do curled up on a silly sofa in Mrs. Cunningham's nice, safe house. She blinked. *Yes, I'm fussing. Because I'm so angry at what happened. And there's not a thing I can do about it—that's how it feels, anyway.* She twisted in the blanket. *Jack doesn't even know about it—if he even got home safely himself. But "thou art with me"?* She swallowed. *But thou art with us?*

She'd gone deep now in her prayer—to a place she didn't usually go. Her anger at being a target in a world that, by law, said she didn't matter. She ranted along. *But "thou art with me"?* Not even noticing the cloud had passed over the pale moon and its soft light was, once again, working its way through Mrs. Cunningham's venetian blinds.

That would be a good thing, sure, when she finally noticed it. But more than all, she wanted the young woman on the streetcar to still be alive, not to be lying cold in the back of a stupid paddy wagon. Her little children never to have her with them again. Her husband furious and frustrated that there was nothing he could do to stop the awful thing that, in a flash, had simply happened.

But thou art with us.

Annalee didn't know how to even start believing that again. Not tonight. But she needed to go to sleep. She also needed to say thank you. *Because I'm still here.*

That wasn't the luck of the draw or by some crazy chance. She was here because God intended her to be here and keep working, doing her little part, however much it added up to.

She closed her eyes. She breathed in the faint remaining scent of Prissy Mack's crushed red rose, no longer inside her blouse. Then by God's strange grace, she did what the psalm invited her to do. By God, indeed, she went to sleep.

When Annalee awoke, she looked at the clock on Mrs. Stallworth's small chest of drawers and moaned. The time was 9:35. Jack's church service started at 10.

She threw back her covers, rushed into the kitchen—where Mrs. Stallworth was cleaning breakfast dishes—and begged her to wait for her.

"You were sleeping so hard, I hated to wake you." Mrs. Stallworth poured Annalee a cup of coffee. "Get dressed. I found a clean change of clothes. They're yours. You left them here some other time for some reason."

Annalee grabbed the clothes—a plaid summer dress with a silly bow at the neck and clean underclothes, all freshly ironed. "You spoil me. Thank you."

"You can wear that to church this morning. Drink your coffee and let's go."

"I'm already moving." Annalee gulped the coffee. In a flash, she was dressed.

They were half running, in fact, trying to get to People's Church—the temporary home of Mount Moriah during its rebuilding—in time for the doxology. On the way, Annalee decided to tell Mrs. Stallworth about the woman on the streetcar, but Mrs. Stallworth already knew.

"Mr. Cunningham heard about it last night while he was out driving his cab. He told us this morning. Some people mentioned you were on the trolley too." Mrs. Stallworth shook her head. "Oh, Annalee. Things are getting too dangerous. I hope the cops don't come back looking for you."

"Don't worry. I almost wish they would. I've got a thing or two I could say to them."

"Well, for now, let's get to church. We'll be late."

"I'm hurrying."

But when they rushed up the steps and into the secondary, smaller sanctuary at the church, they saw right away that neither Jack nor the choir had formed a procession to start the service. Instead, around the congregation, the strain of tense voices cut the heavy summer air. Nearly every seat was taken.

"What a crowd." Mrs. Stallworth grabbed Annalee's hand. Annalee accepted two hymnals from an usher.

"Let's sit here." Annalee pointed her to an already jammed pew, left side, halfway toward the front. A dozen Hearts and Hands members, including Mrs. Cunningham, had claimed seats there, and as Annalee and Mrs. Stallworth worked their way down the row, the women grabbed for their hands, saying hello—showing their common fellowship while squeezing closer to make room.

For a mid-June Colorado morning, the weather was sultry. A sea of church fans were beating the air. Overhead, ceiling fans whirred. One of the Hearts and Hands ladies had a small stack of fans in her lap and passed one each to Annalee and Mrs. Stallworth as they passed by her.

"You're going to need this," the woman announced. Annalee didn't argue, taking the fan, putting it to use right away. Moving along the pew, Annalee noticed Louise Barnes seated near the end between two friends. Seeing Annalee, Louise gave her a grateful wave and a smile.

Up front, a large, gold-toned metal cross sat on a makeshift altar table covered in washed white linen. Vases of yellow and white roses sat on each side of the cross. In the heavily fanned air, a petal fell, and Annalee noticed Valerie Valentine almost jump up from a front-row seat to remove it. The roses were from one of her home gardens, Annalee figured, so Valerie would monitor their use and appearance throughout the entire service.

"Yep, God's people. But I love them," Jack always said. Annalee wanted to smile to herself, hoping one day she could learn to love all folks without judgment as well. But on this day, to be honest, she didn't feel it. Besides, Valerie looked on the flowers with a half-hearted glance. Perhaps last night's trouble had shaken the starch right out of her. If so, Annalee could understand.

Finally she and Mrs. Stallworth were seated—Annalee making sure not to crane her neck to watch Jack process down the aisle in his preaching robe, behind the choir. As he passed her row, however, she noticed an alarming look on his face. It was horror. Or defiance. Or maybe determination. Whatever it was, she was sure it would help explain why he was starting service a good fifteen minutes late—something she'd never known him to do.

Looking out over the congregation, he invited all to stand, spoke the call to worship, led them in the doxology—"Praise God from whom all blessings flow; praise him, all creatures here below . . ."

He led the opening hymn, citing a page number in the hymnal, leading all in the room into "A Mighty Fortress Is Our God."

A bulwark never failing.

As the first verse ended, Jack leaned his body into its words:

For still our ancient foe doth seek to work us woe;
His craft and pow'r are great, and armed with cruel hate,
On earth is not his equal.

Annalee hugged her hymnal, preparing to sit after the first verse. But Jack kept singing, giving the pianist a gesture to keep playing and the choir and people to keep singing, and so she opened to the page and sang out through the second verse.

And the third verse.

And the fourth verse.

Then for good measure, the fourth verse again.

Then finally, the hymn's closing words were sung with a fervor that seized Annalee's soul, the singing rolling from the rafters as all voices in the sanctuary, with Jack leading, seemed to be fairly screaming them:

The body they may kill: God's truth abideth still.

Then, together, they sang the closing line:

His kingdom is forever!

Jack looked across the congregation. He knew that they knew—that he knew—what had happened in Five Points on the streetcar the night before. Someone must've come to his rooming house to tell him—probably one of his trustees, or maybe his chief steward. Annalee was grateful that he knew. His congregation needed to hear his thoughts, wisdom, prayers—something that would console them.

Annalee searched Jack's eyes, waiting and listening for what he would say. Finally he spoke:

"His kingdom is forever. Do you know, God's people, what *forever* means?" Jack's voice was a whisper. But heads nodded.

"Then let us pray."

Annalee watched heads bow as Jack led the congregation in the prayer that they didn't know they needed. It started not with woes or worry. Instead Jack began by thanking God—"for who you are, Lord."

He said that three more times. "For who you are—yes, Lord."

A sort of hushed surrender began to wash over the congregation. For anyone who'd come into the sanctuary with angry questions—which was probably most of them—Jack was inviting folks to turn that anger over to God, "for who you are, Lord."

"I know that's hard to think about this morning. Two terrible things have happened in our neighborhood of Five Points in just one week—one of them last night."

A murmur rumbled through the room. These people knew about the streetcar killing. Word spread fast. But Jack still described, in his prayer, what happened for the few who didn't know. Or perhaps, Annalee thought, Jack needed to say it out loud to remind even himself of the awful outcome on the trolley.

"The family's name is Burch. Sammy and Nellie Mae Burch. They've got five children at home—the youngest a baby, the oldest fourteen. And, no, they aren't members of our congregation—if you're worried about that. But they're members of God's world and our community, and Mr. Burch will need a lot of help to keep his family together. Hearts and Hands will organize meals and a help calendar, right, Mrs. Cunningham?"

"That's right, pastor."

Still, Jack was praying.

"But you'll walk with us every step, blessed Lord, as you always have."

"Oh, yes; please, Jesus." Several people in the sanctuary moaned aloud their hope.

Then Jack petitioned the people's God to "calm our hearts, ease our hurts, heal our pain. Wrap your arms of love and assurance around the Burch family."

Jack prayed for wisdom and resources to help Mr. Burch and his children find peace and forgiveness so they could heal. He asked God to bless the memory of Nellie Mae Burch, "a very sweet woman by all accounts." He then thanked God "in advance for all you are going to do for this family—and in our neighborhood—and in our world. And also in us."

After he said amen, he took a seat on the podium, letting the choir sing the morning's second hymn, "How Firm a Foundation." All five verses.

Opening her hymnbook again, Annalee sang along with the choir—her polite alto voice finding strength. Almost all in the congregation sang too. She sat quietly afterward, as Jack led the responsive reading, using a portion of Psalm 37—the part he'd told her last night he would preach. "Fret not thyself because of evildoers, neither be thou envious against the workers of iniquity. For they shall soon be cut down like the grass, and wither as the green herb. . . ."

Annalee listened to all of it, her hands crossed with purpose on her lap, her church fan quiet.

She knew Jack would now preach sustenance and hope in a time of despair and hurt. She believed him, in fact, that God doesn't manufacture the evil that some men and women do. God, instead, is your hope, Jack preached.

"So, 'why art thou cast down,'" Jack intoned, "'O my soul?'" His eyes flashed. "'And why art thou disquieted within me?'" He leaned over the pulpit. "'Hope thou in God.' Isn't that right, God's people? For yet we shall praise him!"

A sigh of moans and amens—a combination of hurt and hope—formed a reply across the sanctuary.

Annalee let her eyes roam the room. Jack was preaching the kind of sermon that brought broken colored people to churches in droves every Sunday. Hope in God, he thundered. Trouble comes. But hope anyway.

"Amen." Annalee declared that now. All around her, others shouted out too.

"Down and out?" Jack asked the crowd. "Then hope!"

"Hope!" the congregation responded.

"Can't find your way?" Jack shook his head. "Then hope!"

"Hope!" People jumped to their feet.

"Hit a brick wall?" Jack pumped his arms. "Then hope!"

"Hope!" Folks were applauding, shouting, crying. "Preach, pastor!"

"Get knocked down?" Jack pounded the pulpit. "Then hope!" He wiped his own wet eyes. "Hope in the one who is hope."

Amens rocked the sanctuary. Annalee nodded at him, not worried that he wasn't looking at her. He was trying to reach every single person in the room. Annalee nodded again. "Preach, sir!"

Jack picked up a clean white handkerchief from off the pulpit and wiped his face. All over the sanctuary, people were still on their feet—still saying amen and crying, still shouting out the preacher's audacious marching order: hope.

"Hope!" Mrs. Stallworth joined the shouting.

"Hope!" her Hearts and Hands friends were calling out too.

But Jack didn't look put off. He had the people's attention. His own, too, in fact. His next words were simple and honest.

"I know it's hard." He wiped his face again. "In this life, we've been asked to do things—and put up with things—that no child of God should have to endure."

Heads nodded.

"Downtown at the coroner's office, in the basement—"

"Have mercy!" a woman moaned.

"In the basement," Jack repeated, "a young colored woman, probably no older than nineteen or twenty years old, is laid out on a slab with a tag on her toe: *deceased unknown*."

Many in the crowd moaned.

"But that label is wrong. God knows who she is."

"Yes, he does!" many shouted.

"But that's not all. Somebody in this room may know who she is." A silence met that remark. Jack cast his eyes across the congregation. "Several of you may know the young woman. I'm not sure. But here's another question: do you know who you are? Because if you do, you won't stand for that young woman— another dead woman—to get tossed in a pauper's grave tomorrow at one o'clock p.m. without coming forward and telling what you know."

The gauntlet. Jack had thrown it down. Annalee sat stiffly, listening.

"One o'clock." Jack repeated the time. So he knew, Annalee realized, the coroner's plan for disposing of an "unknown" young woman—actually Prissy Mack—unless somebody stepped forward. "Will you let that happen?" He gripped the pulpit.

"These 'stand up' things in life," Jack went on, "are about hope. Like prayer, we hope with our boots on. And that's all I'm going to say about it." He set down his handkerchief. "But you know where to find me if you have information. No judgment. Just come. Tell me and talk."

Jack looked over the congregation. "One of our members is working on the case. She's a detective."

The congregation shifted in their seats. Annalee felt every eye had turned to look at her. She let out a long, silent breath. A single bead of sweat traced down her back. She didn't blink.

"If you have a solid tip," Jack was saying, "let her know." He cocked his head. "Boots on."

Jack suddenly smiled big. "But for now, does any soul in here want to join the church?"

At that, a man and his family came down the aisle. Jack looked pleased for them, shaking the hands of all the family members—even the youngest child, a tiny girl probably no more than two.

Jack picked the child up and lifted her before the congregation. "Our newest family member." Applause rang out. "Let us hope great things for her life."

"Boots on, pastor!" an elderly trustee shouted from the front row.

"Help us, Lord," Jack said. Then soon, following the offering and Jack's benediction, the service was over. As Jack processed out of the sanctuary, Annalee saw him look down her row. He nodded once. She did the same. She knew what that meant.

He had called up his church to join her fight for Prissy Mack. With their boots on. His already were.

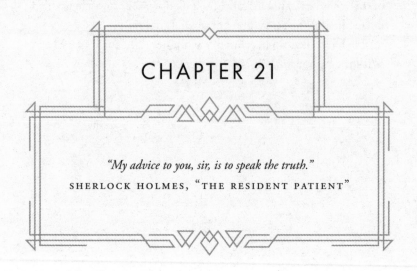

CHAPTER 21

"My advice to you, sir, is to speak the truth."
SHERLOCK HOLMES, "THE RESIDENT PATIENT"

A RUSH OF PEOPLE PRESSED TOWARD THE EXIT DOORS of People's Church. The crowd noise was electric. Happy faces had replaced sorrowful. Hurt had given over to hope. People's Church was their temporary home. But Jack's sermon had stirred among them fresh identity and purpose.

"What a service!" Mrs. Stallworth squeezed Annalee's hand. "Pastor even mentioned you." She winked. "I pray you get some solid tips. With everybody's help, you're going to solve this thing." Her friend then scurried off, eager apparently to meet Mrs. Cunningham and her other Hearts and Hands ladies to plan how to help the Burch family.

Jack stood on the top step outside of the church, in the doorway, to shake hands with parishioners as people departed. Annalee could see him greeting and talking. She headed in the opposite direction, aiming for a side exit. She would see Jack later, their frequent Sunday arrangement. They didn't like to socialize openly right after the service.

So, moving through the departing crowd, she enjoyed hugs or a warm hello from this person or that. Many were church members she'd known since her childhood. "Nice to see you, Sister Morton." "Have a blessed week, Miss Kinsey." She chatted with a couple of choir members she'd known in her grade school days and stopped to admire a little girl's truly beautiful white dress—then grinned to discover the little girl was Melody Coates.

"You look charming, Miss Melody."

"Thank you, Miss Spain." The girl beamed, pushed a new-looking pair of spectacles higher on her nose. "I got this dress for obeying Papa better."

"I'm glad to hear it. Where is your dad?" Annalee looked around the crowd. "I see him." Her eyes locked with his.

Cooper Coates approached, extended his hand, surprising Annalee. She returned the courtesy, giving him a nod. He was dressed to the nines too, in crisp summer whites.

"I hear your daughter is obeying better these days."

"Maybe we both are. I'm finding more ways for us to spend positive time together."

"He didn't feel like church today." Melody fluffed her dress. "But when I wanted to come, he got dressed up nice and came with me—right, Papa?" Melody leaned closer to Annalee. "You know how you just feel like going to church some days?"

Annalee nodded, smiling. "I know exactly what you mean." They chatted a minute more, then told each other goodbye—Annalee reminding Melody to stay on the straight and narrow. Melody said she would.

Coates turned back to Annalee. "It sounds like you're working to solve that situation in my garden."

"I'm trying. But I need a breakthrough."

"Maybe we can talk sometime soon."

"You have information?"

"You could call it that." Coates glanced down.

"May I come by to see you this week?"

They agreed on the next day—Monday—in the late afternoon. Annalee watched him leave, eager to hear what Coates might tell her. She then listened and chatted with a woman who'd been crying—her eyes still teary as she asked Annalee what it takes to be a detective.

"Being stubborn," Annalee finally said. She could've said more, but just then a church usher touched her shoulder.

"Pastor Blake would like to see you. He's in his office."

Right now? That surprised Annalee. Tongues would wag.

But the usher insisted. "Follow me, please."

Annalee said goodbye to the woman, followed the usher. She kept her head down, trying to keep a low profile. Church folks didn't miss a beat. A church was like a small village. Annalee tried to act casual and look informal in her plaid, not fancy, summer dress—on her way to the pastor's office. But the usher was parting the waters, pushing lingering people aside, acting as if he were leading her on the most critical of missions—that is, straight to the office of Pastor Jack Robert Blake.

What in the world did Jack want that couldn't wait?

She saw right away as the usher turned into a hallway and tapped on a closed office door.

Jack opened it. He'd removed his pastoral robe, but he still wore his collar with his long-sleeved white shirt and dark pants. He didn't actually smile, but his dark eyes were gleaming—his demeanor still bright after preaching on hope. Maybe still trying to feel hope himself. He invited her in, told the usher thank you.

"Good day, Pastor Blake." Annalee spoke softly, not wanting to act familiar. That was a good thing because Jack was pointing to another person in the room.

"You two know each other, I believe?"

Sitting behind the office door in a stiff wooden chair was someone Annalee should've predicted would be there.

Valerie Valentine was crying. Her face was wet.

Annalee pursed her lips. Every meeting she'd had with the woman had been ugly, with Valerie saying the most insulting things possible to Annalee. Her clothes were handmade. Her friends were uncultured and old. Her vocation—detective work—was a waste of her time.

But now Valerie sat on the wooden chair, weeping. She held out her hand to Annalee.

Annalee took it. *Mercy. What a life.* From highs to lows. From a heart-stirring Sunday service sitting on a pew with loving friends to holding the hand of the meanest woman in the neighborhood. But God says love. So Annalee didn't release her hand.

"I know her," Valerie was whispering. Her voice broke. "I know Prissy Mack."

"Yes, ma'am." Annalee knelt next to Valerie's chair. "You're her auntie. Aunt Volly."

Valerie wiped her eyes and nodded. "I lied."

"It can happen." Annalee touched Valerie's shoulder. Jack moved over another chair, helped Annalee sit beside Valerie.

"We've all lied at some point." Jack stood by the desk. "Most of us more than once."

"I said I didn't know her." Valerie wiped at her face again, turned to Annalee. "But she's family. My niece."

"A brother's child?" Jack asked.

"Or a sister's?" Annalee added. "Is she from Alabama? That's your home?"

"She's from Mississippi—well, originally." Valerie blinked. "Like me. I say I'm from Chicago—and I did live there for a short minute. But I'm from Mississippi. Born and bred. Reared in the woods deep in the country—near the Tennessee border." She winced. "I've never told anyone this. I guess I try to be more than my beginnings."

"We all probably do." Annalee gave her a look.

"Prissy's my half brother's child. A sweet girl, not like her hot-headed daddy. I haven't spoken to him in years. He and I have the same mother. But Amos—that's his name, Amos Mack—and I never saw eye to eye. After Mama passed, he and I came to blows after he accused my dad of stealing his inheritance—which, believe me, wasn't that much—and selling it to a white man trying to build a lumberyard."

Annalee listened. She still didn't know what this had to do with Prissy. *But just be quiet.*

Valerie then dropped her bomb. "The white lumber man is a Kane—"

"Kane?" Jack asked.

Annalee stiffened. "Like Malcolm Kane, the seminary president?"

"Same family." Valerie laughed a bitter laugh. "Like the saying goes, it's a small world."

"Too small," Jack said.

Annalee agreed. "So, did you know a Kane was in Denver when you moved here?"

Valerie bit her lip hard. She sat silent for several moments. "If I tell you, Annalee—and tell Pastor Blake—do I have to tell anybody else?" Her eyes searched both their faces. "Because it's confidential."

"We're just trying to help Prissy," Annalee said. "Please say what happened. It probably can stay between us."

Valerie shook her head. "Like I said, I came from nothing. Mama had taught herself to cook for private homes. I'd go with her to serve, taught myself to cater big dinners and act 'society.' But Amos hated me 'sitting on a high horse,' acting 'prissy.'" Valerie smiled sadly. "That's how Prissy got her name. When she was born, she looked so fancy and dainty. I gave her that nickname. I called her Prissy right off, and everybody else did too. She'd follow me around. Trying to act 'like Aunt Volly'—like 'a lady.'" Valerie looked pained.

"What went wrong?" Annalee was trying to understand.

"Bad money." Valerie untwisted her long pearl necklace, pulled it from around her neck. "After Mama died, Daddy took Amos' little land that Mama had left him as her only son and sold it to the lumberman, Malcolm Kane Senior."

"Oh, my gracious," Annalee whispered.

"Worse, Daddy gave the money to me. 'Leave Mississippi,' he insisted. 'Nothing good here for you.' Amos had a family, but Daddy gave me the money. Said I'd do more with it. It wasn't that much, but once I had it, I caught the first train north and never looked back."

"On stolen money." Annalee just said it.

"Well, I suppose, yes."

"So, your nice home. Your lovely clothes and jewelry. Your fancy ways and society manners, all bought with seed money from your half brother's stolen legacy?"

"Well, yes."

"And Prissy?" Annalee longed for her story.

"She followed me here, still wanting to be like Aunt Volly." Valerie stiffened. "But wrong money wrecks all. In fact, I heard Ol' Man Kane bought a whole batch of land underhanded—every acre from struggling poor folks. Colored. White. He didn't care. One white man's sick wife died, and her husband sold her grown son's land—to give to his own child. Shrewd, he said. But Kane did the deal. Said he loved doing business with canny people."

"Then God fixed it," Jack said.

"As he wills." Valerie twisted her necklace.

"So, what happened?" Annalee asked.

"Kane's only son gave himself to God, became a preacher. Told his old man he was doing wrong." Valerie searched Annalee's eyes. "Truer words were never spoken. That money pestered me like a vise around my neck, even though I tried to pay it back. Amos refused to take it. Then I came to Denver and learned from the papers that Malcolm Kane's son—Malcolm Kane Junior—was appointed at the seminary. I found the campus, managed to see Malcolm, introduced myself—I'd never met him—and asked him to help me put the past behind me, redeem my stolen gain, do good in this world. Could I serve his campus, even do some catering? He said not at the moment, but if I knew any young colored girls trying to go to college, he could help them with a program—"

"Welcome Ambassadors."

"Right."

Annalee shook her head, confused. "And Prissy?" she asked again.

"She came west. She'd moved to Alabama to be with her daddy. Then she heard I was here. She tracked me down, asked for help. I sent her to Malcolm. She went once but refused to go back. Refused to see me too. Said her daddy was right—that I couldn't be trusted. But she was cozying up to one of the board members at the seminary." Valerie looked pained. "Or he was cozying up to her."

"Which one?"

"I never could find out. Just heard a rumor—from one of the girls I sent to Malcolm."

"Did that board member kill her?" Annalee asked the question.

"At the garden party? A board member? But why? I can't imagine how she ended up dead." Valerie's voice broke. "When you told me about her little locket, my heart sank. I held Prissy in my arms on the day she was born, had the locket made when she was just a girl. Then I panicked. Prissy dead? I acted as if I didn't know her, trying to make the murder go away. But all I was thinking was how

220

I'd tell Amos—who already hates me—if I sent his baby girl home in a coffin. *God, in your mercy.*"

She turned to Jack. "Pastor Blake, will you tell me how to contact the coroner's office?" She gripped Annalee's hand. "Oh, God, what a nightmare."

"I'll go with you, Miss Valentine." Annalee spoke with certainty, although she'd never once stepped foot in a coroner's office. That didn't matter. Valerie had come forward, spilled her sad truth. Annalee would walk with her. "You'll have to identify the body."

"I'm not sure I can." Valerie shuddered. "Amos will have my head."

"He's still in Mississippi?" Annalee asked.

"He moved to Alabama a couple of years ago. He has cousins in that state. I'll send Prissy's body there—if that's what he wants. I'll have to make a long-distance telephone call to talk to him." She let out a long breath. "I guess this will make the papers."

"Doesn't matter about the papers," Jack assured her. "Sure, some may gossip. But most folks, here in Five Points anyway, are busy just trying to stay ahead of their own troubles—"

"Just like me." Valerie looked despairing. "I've worked myself to the bone trying to rise above my beginnings, above my family, struggling to be important and 'better.' But my past keeps dragging me down—back to everybody and everything I've tried to leave behind. So what was the point?"

"The point?" Jack smiled at her. "To God, you were always enough. We all are. The lie is that we aren't."

"I hear that, pastor. But I've stolen from family, been unkind to church people, acted uppity. Even to Miss Annalee here. I'm sorry, Miss Spain."

Annalee touched her hand, held it a moment.

"I put myself on a pedestal," Valerie went on. "Looked down at folks—even at women from Mount Moriah. Good women. Once they find out who I really am and what I've done, I doubt they'll even speak to me." She dabbed at her eyes.

"Actually, the women may surprise you," Jack told her. "Do you know why?"

Valerie shook her head.

Annalee interrupted. "Because we all have a past. We try to leave it behind, and for a while we may. But we can't outrun it. Moreover, only God can redeem it. So we might as well give it all to him."

She sounded like her teacher self when she talked like that. But Annalee knew her words were sound and held truth.

"But will God forgive me? I keep asking him." Valerie still looked despairing.

"He already has then, Miss Valentine." Jack's voice was assuring. He looked to Annalee. "Something wrong?"

"Just one thing. It's about Malcolm Kane Junior—and what he does with his Welcome Ambassadors."

"The young ladies I sent to the seminary?" Valerie looked confused.

"Did they stay with the program?"

"All but one. Why?"

"Well, I'm sorry, but I've heard the program is a scam." Annalee then explained to Valerie and Jack what she'd been told about Malcolm Kane Jr. exploiting young female ambassadors, conspiring to tempt trustees—then blackmailing them.

"Who told you that?" Valerie looked pained.

"A solid source." Annalee squinted. "At least I think he is. So would you work with me to bring Malcolm Kane Junior to heel? If he's exploiting the girls? I know who can help us. Nathan Furness—"

"Nathan? Not on your life." Valerie shook her head. "That young man unsettles me. He's a gambler. Owes money all over town."

"Just gossip, I hear," Annalee offered.

"Perhaps, but if Charlotte Furness, his mother, finds out, I'll lose my best client."

"You won't have any clients, or a life—or church friends, or your women's club connections or anything else," Annalee told her, "if Malcolm Kane isn't stopped, especially if he turns out to be a killer and you just sat on your hands."

"Nathan Furness." Valerie looked uncertain. "I wish he didn't have to be involved."

"I'll speak to him." Annalee stood. "He gave me his card."

"Let me go with you." Jack moved to the door of the office. "Taking on the leader of one of the state's prominent private seminaries won't be easy, no matter who helps you. Or both of you."

"I'll give him a call first. I can use Mrs. Cunningham's phone." Annalee grabbed her small purse. "I'll let you both know what he says—if I can reach him." She blinked. "And if he'll talk to me again."

But looking at Valerie's anguished face, she suddenly wondered if that might be the wrong worry.

CHAPTER 22

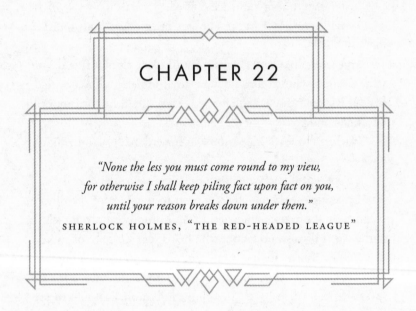

"None the less you must come round to my view,
for otherwise I shall keep piling fact upon fact on you,
until your reason breaks down under them."
SHERLOCK HOLMES, "THE RED-HEADED LEAGUE"

AFTER SPEAKING WITH A CHURCH MEMBER waiting to talk to her, Annalee returned to her little cabin, grateful to be home, but wary to find a surprise visitor.

"Good afternoon, Miss Spain."

She narrowed her eyes. She should've felt pleased and perhaps even relieved to see her guest, especially since his name had just come up in Jack's office. First, however, she felt confused. That's because her visitor was Nathan Furness.

He was standing in her side yard with a brand-new garden hoe, digging in the dirt where the death camas had been dug up.

"I brought you some lilacs."

She studied him, also noticing a feeling of sudden, unsettled panic, except she couldn't understand why. She shook it off.

"Lilacs? What a surprise."

Nothing surprised her more, however, than seeing Nathan picking around in her yard. His pressed tan slacks and matching leather sports shoes weren't gardening attire. In the afternoon June heat, his short-sleeved, white linen shirt still looked crisp. A cool customer. He'd been wearing a tan straw hat, but it sat now atop a small boulder under her leafy little maple tree. He patted his forehead with a white linen handkerchief and set it atop his hat.

"I'm sure you're wondering what I'm doing here." He dug in the dirt again.

"I'm sure you'll tell me." She looked him over. "Would you like a glass of water?"

"That would be nice."

Unlocking her cabin door, Annalee stepped inside and then did an odd thing, in her mind anyway. She locked the door behind her. *That's the kind of world we live in now,* she said to herself. *You can't give a thirsty visitor a cup of cold water without worrying that person may try to hurt or cheat you. Mercy.*

She took down two clean glasses from her little shelf, poured in cool water from her tiny icebox, unlocked the cabin door again, and stepped across her yard to hand a glass to Nathan. He emptied the glass neatly and thanked her, handing back the glass.

"I didn't expect it to be so warm this afternoon."

She searched his face, watched a single drop of sweat form above his brow. "What are you doing here, Nathan?"

She used his first name. He wasn't that much older than she. More important, she wanted to hear from his own lips why he'd come to her place, and to plant lilacs, of all things.

"I'm not sure myself why I'm here." He glanced around her yard, then searched her eyes. "But I heard talk of a colored woman dying at the hands of police last night in Five Points. One of the attorneys in our firm was at the jail when the woman's husband was brought in. The poor man was hysterical, screaming that they'd killed his wife, saying she hadn't done anything, wasn't guilty of anything and neither was he. It was quite a commotion. The man was released early this morning without charges, thankfully, but the attorney at our firm was sick about it." Nathan sighed. "Things in this town just seem to go from bad to worse."

"And the lilacs?"

"I can't explain it really. I wanted to do something for somebody in Five Points, and you're one of the few people over here I know."

"Why not help Mr. Burch? That's the man whose wife was killed—"

"I couldn't look him in the face. What happened was horrible, from the way it was described to me. The last thing he probably wants to see today is a stranger, a white man, coming to 'help.'"

"So you're helping me?"

"I noticed your yard was in bad shape. Last time I was here, I noticed. Everybody loves lilacs. Well, most people do. In the spring, they're just so pretty." Nathan shrugged. "My wife loves them, and I do, too, actually. So I picked up some seedlings and brought them over. You weren't here, so I started—"

"Please stop." Annalee had heard enough.

"What have I done?"

She bristled. "You want to help colored people in Denver? To help me? Then help run the Klan out of town. Tell the mayor to cancel his membership. Campaign against the KKK candidate for governor." She stood her ground. "Nathan, hire some colored people." She kicked at the dirt. "Sure, I love lilacs. They're gorgeous for the few weeks that they're in bloom. But these lilacs—" she gestured at the young plants he'd set down in the ground—"aren't ever going to help me or Sammy or Nellie Mae Burch or their five motherless children."

Annalee turned on her heel, headed for her cabin. She was shaking her head. She hadn't intended to unload on Nathan Furness. But the state of affairs in Denver was a broken-down mess. Lilacs weren't going to fix it. Years would pass before these plants even bloomed.

Right now, meantime, she'd promised Valerie Valentine to go with her to the coroner's to identify Prissy Mack. Nathan wouldn't even know that.

"Please, wait," Nathan was calling after her.

Annalee stopped, turned. "I've had a long week."

"Have you figured out who killed the young woman found in Cooper Coates' garden?"

She listened to the question. It was the most important thing anybody had asked her in days, because the answer was a flat-out no.

"I have some leads." She thought of Thaddeus Hammer and his wild vine of climbing roses. Or possibly Malcolm Kane? "But I haven't nailed anybody down as the killer." She frowned at him. "Unless you help me."

"What could I possibly do?" Nathan laid down his shiny new garden hoe.

"Get me into the seminary. I need to talk to Malcolm Kane."

"Kane?" Nathan scoffed. "He's a schemer, not a killer."

"That's my question. What do you think?" Annalee had walked back under the maple tree. She stood in the shade.

Nathan took a step closer. "If it's anybody at the seminary, I'd put my money on Hammer. He's a cheat and a liar. He's known to pursue colored girls. He's paid off untold amounts to Kane to keep his foibles under wraps. His moral compass is in tatters. Maybe your Prissy Mack was blackmailing him."

Annalee studied Nathan, considering his theory. Was it genuine, or was he steering her away from Kane by tarnishing the bumbling Hammer? Even accusing Prissy too? Whatever his game was, she'd play along.

"But I'd need proof on Hammer, and the closest I've come to that is a rose."

She told Nathan about the rosebud she'd found crumpled in Prissy's hand and finding its match—the rose vine growing with wild abandon on the north side of Hammer's garage.

"You've been to his house?"

He looked disapproving.

"Well . . ." Annalee pressed her mouth. *Hold your tongue, girl.* She could be saying too much. She had zero evidence she could trust Nathan Furness or anybody else at the seminary. Or anywhere else. Maybe Prissy's killer was a colored man. Maybe Cooper Coates.

"Or maybe a woman . . ."

"What are you saying?" Nathan squinted. Then he smiled. "I admire the way you think, Miss Spain. You're leaving no stone unturned."

"Nobody in the city is pursuing Prissy's death as a homicide. But if I keep at it, and get good help, I can crack this killing."

"You're determined."

"I am, but that's what detection takes. At least, that's what I've learned so far." She picked up the garden hoe and handed it to Nathan. "I appreciate your kindness of planting lilacs. Last week another plant was here and, well, let's just say that lilacs are far better. Even if it's the wrong time to plant them."

"It is?" Nathan looked surprised. "Nobody told me that at High Plains Floral."

"That's where you purchased the plants?"

Nathan stuttered. "Well . . . after church this morning, I went there after an early service. We're Episcopalian. Our service is only an hour. Afterward, I stopped at the floral center and looked around. I love painting flowers, but I don't know much about them."

"Neither do I." Annalee wrinkled her nose. "But I heard a wonderful lecture about flowers a couple of days ago, and I'm finding new ways to think about them."

"You sound like me." Nathan smiled at her. "We may have more in common than you might think."

"I'm not sure." Watching Nathan walk back to his sleek red car parked on the road by her cabin, Annalee realized she wasn't sure about most things—including Nathan Furness—especially when it came to Prissy Mack and what had happened to her.

"But I will find out," she said aloud. She poured water from her drinking glass onto the lilac plantings that Nathan had placed in her yard. Then she went inside her cabin.

Annalee then made sure to do the next best thing. She locked the door good and tight.

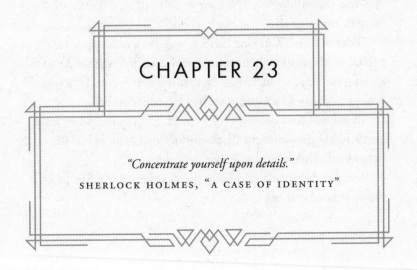

CHAPTER 23

"Concentrate yourself upon details."
SHERLOCK HOLMES, "A CASE OF IDENTITY"

LATER, ABOUT 6 P.M., Annalee joined Jack for dinner. He'd chosen a little place on Curtis Street called the New Night and Day Café. *Meals at all hours; home cooking; strictly first class; prices right.* Sunday dinners were served between 6 and 8 p.m. Private booths were a popular feature.

Annalee followed him to a booth in the back and scooted onto the blue leather bench facing him. He handed her a menu, touched her hand, then reached to hold it tight. She didn't pull away.

"Thanks for coming." He squeezed her hand.

"You preached our strength this morning, pastor, sir."

"I needed it as much as anyone." Jack hiked a brow. "Maybe more."

She waited for him to reflect deeper, revealing more, but he was quiet. Pensive. He'd just come from the Burch family's home.

Sammy Burch and the children appeared to be in shock, Jack finally said. He spoke low. Another couple was sitting in the booth behind them. Discussing church business wasn't something Jack did in public. Annalee understood. She didn't press him.

"That was kind of you—going to see them." Annalee spoke low too.

"The Burch family aren't church members anywhere, but we'll make them our members, even in name only—well, if Mr. Burch approves. The Hearts and Hands women were already at the house when I arrived. They've got meals, laundry, and cleaning lined up for weeks. Of course, that's not the primary thing the family needs. Sammy wants his wife back, and the children want their mother."

Jack's voice caught. He looked heartsick.

Annalee searched his face. For a moment, she thought he might weep. Jack was still wearing his preacher collar, but he'd left his suit jacket at his rooming house or maybe at the church office. So he looked "off hours." A few church members were dining in the café, but none stopped at their booth to ask for help or a prayer. Still, as a pastor, he looked more distraught than she'd recalled him looking even after his church was burned to the ground by arson. The Burch situation appeared to be, for Jack, just as personal. For everyone in Five Points, the killing of Mrs. Burch was perhaps personal.

A pall hung over the little café. Annalee didn't want to give in to it—even though she'd been present at the actual killing. She told Jack, in fact, more of what she'd witnessed firsthand on the streetcar last night. He looked sickened.

"Worse," Annalee said, "I don't have a clue why the cops stopped the trolley. What in the world were they looking for? At first I thought they were looking for me." She dropped her voice, whispering. "Especially after what happened in Hammer's alley. But those men on the trolley were looking for something else."

"Thieves." Jack gave her a look. "At the colored carnival."

"Last night?"

"Right before it closed, about ten. A white customer said a colored couple robbed her at gunpoint and the colored woman stuffed the money in her purse. The white woman chased them, according to the account I heard, but the pair got away, jumping on a streetcar just as it pulled off."

"Who told you all this?" Annalee was curious.

"A church trustee. He visited the carnival last night with his wife. But he didn't know if the story was true or not."

Annalee sat silent a moment.

"I hate to ask this," she said, "but do you think the colored couple, if that's what happened, was the Burches? Mrs. Burch didn't have a purse with her. That's what started the trouble with the cops."

"But the Burches weren't at the carnival." Jack sounded certain. "They were downtown at a movie show. Sammy Burch's boss gave him a pair of tickets in reward for taking on extra work and doing a great job. A couple of workers confirmed that Sammy and his wife were at the movie show the whole time. His boss said the same. He was there with his wife, sitting on the main floor in the white section, but he saw Sammy and Nellie Mae go upstairs to their seats, saw them during intermission, and saw them in the crowd when the movie ended. They even talked to each other about the picture—some war comedy."

"I wonder where Sammy works. Is he a laborer?"

"He's in janitorial. He works for a big plumbing outfit on the west side. They won't let him do plumbing because he can't get in the union. No colored men allowed. But last night, he dressed up to take his wife out on the town. She wore a dress she'd sewn herself. A red one."

Annalee nodded. She'd never forget the sight of that red dress on sweet-looking Nellie Mae Burch.

Jack went on. "So Sammy took her to a restaurant in Five

232

Points, then they rode a trolley downtown to the movies. It was the first time they'd been out like that in years, he told me." He looked pained. "As for the carnival, they never made it there on any night. Not even to take their kids. Tickets for seven would be too much."

"So they didn't steal anybody's money at the fair."

"Their alibi is solid. But that carnival . . ." Jack shook his head. "It's been a load of trouble almost since the day they pulled into town." He let out a sigh. "Poor Sonny Dawkins."

The couple in the booth behind them stood to leave. Jack looked relieved to see them depart, but the woman stopped at their booth and spoke to Annalee.

"Thanks for working on that girl's killing. It's a doggoned shame. I hope you get some tips."

"I could use them." Annalee gave the woman a smile. "If you hear anything, please let me know." She reached in her purse and handed the woman her card.

"I'll tell my friends, too." The woman turned, linked her arm with the man waiting for her, and they left.

"A lot of folks want to help 'the detective.'" Annalee watched the woman walk away. "I hope I don't let them down. They're hungry for the truth."

"Well, we think we want to know." Jack signaled a waiter. "Let's eat."

Jack said little during their meal, a simple pork chop platter. Annalee didn't press him. Something was bothering him. She could see that. *But not my place*, she told herself, *to analyze or nag*. She had enough to worry over. Instead, she let him finish his meal in peace—and herself the same. As they left the café, she let him grab her hand.

"I need to make a stop by People's Church." He threaded his fingers through hers. His grip on her hand felt comforting. "I left something in my office there. Would you go with me?"

He didn't wait for her answer. Instead Jack steered them down

Curtis Street and into Five Points. The evening sky had lost its purple, the summer stars rising to shimmer. Walking at dusk down a path of tree-lined sidewalks toward the church—the air fragrant with summer flowers—Annalee felt grateful for such a gorgeous night, for the moment of quiet and calm, for the daring hope that things in her life could always feel this good and right.

But why, she wondered, did she often worry such moments wouldn't last?

Inside the church, Jack walked them to his office, flicked on the small lamp at his desk. The chairs still sat where they'd had their meeting with Valerie Valentine. The room's air felt close. Jack straightened the chairs and opened a window. He sat then at the desk, pointed to the chair opposite, invited Annalee to sit too.

She searched Jack's face. "I'm trying to think how I'm feeling now." She perched on the chair. "I'm not sure what I expect you to say."

"I understand. It will be okay." With that, Jack opened a drawer in his desk, pulled out a stained brown envelope, and handed it to Annalee. "Open it."

She blinked.

"Please, Annalee."

She took the envelope and set it on her lap. Was it something to help her case? But the envelope looked decades old—as old as the torn-up letter buried in her yard. She swallowed, pressed back the metal closures. She could hear Jack's breathing, close and urgent. So she opened the flap and pulled out a yellowed newspaper clipping, just one paragraph. That's all it was. Torn from a paper called *The Colored American*, the clipping was dated June 22, 1901.

"That's today's date—June twenty-second."

Jack nodded.

Annalee read aloud the headline, her voice barely a whisper. "Negro 'Streetcar Woman' Dies in Prison." She swallowed again, uncertain how to keep reading, but Jack wasn't giving her a break or a choice. His eyes insisted. So, speaking aloud again, Annalee read the little article, her voice still low. Outside the open window, she heard a police siren several blocks over.

The colored woman serving a life sentence for fatally stabbing an intoxicated man—a prominent white businessman whom she accused of attacking her on a New York City streetcar on Christmas Eve in 1898— has died in prison. Naomi Day, age 19 at the time of the altercation, was found dead of unknown causes in her prison cell at Westfield State Farm, a women's prison opened early this year in Bedford, New York. She will be buried in a pauper's field on the prison grounds. She leaves behind one child, a son, now age four.

Annalee held the news clipping with trembling hands. She turned it over, looking for—what? More information? But the clipping was only a tattered sliver. On the back, a yellowed advertisement showed women's dresses. So she turned the article over again. Silently she read the news notice one more time, then looked across the desk.

"Jack?"

He sat still. Annalee placed the article back in the stained brown envelope. A frown furrowed her brow.

"Who is this woman? Naomi Day?"

"I want you to know," Jack said. "That woman was my mother."

Another siren cut the summer's night air. Annalee sat still, waiting for the infernal blare to fade. Besides, she didn't know how to react. Jack never had talked about his mother, and she'd never asked him for a single detail. They'd started their relationship in fits and starts, making mistakes—then landed on a hard discovery: she was abandoned as an infant by her mother. So the story of his beginnings got left on a shelf. Perhaps it seemed too much to take down and unravel while she tried to sort out her own life, make her way in the world, solve other people's hurts and crimes, and whatever else she had managed to handle.

She'd told herself Jack was a young war hero and a pastor and the man who made her feel loved in many complicated but amazing ways. But now she held in her hand the truth of Jack and of every last person on earth: we each have a past—with beginnings and ends, and starts and stops, and good and bad, and highs and lows. Not unlike the Burch family. Or her family. Or a million other families, no matter their race. Nothing was simple and perfect. With Jack, he'd had a mother in prison who died.

"In 1901," she finally said. "You were a little child then." She carefully set down the stained envelope. It sat on Jack's desktop between the two of them. She looked up, searched his eyes, her voice still low. "So, what happened to her? Your mother? To you? What about the Blakes? Your aunt and uncle. I thought they raised you—as family."

Jack ran a hand across his brow. They'd had a long day, but he clearly wasn't done with it yet. The Burch family's tragedy had unleashed something in him. Whatever it was, he had to tell it.

"The Blakes took in foundlings, told me to call them Aunt and Uncle, raised me and other boys—most who drifted away. But I stayed, watching over time as Reverend Blake and First Lady Blake created their carefully planned life in Negro high society in New York City with their perfect young 'nephew,' me. From my uncle, I learned to preach right. From my aunt, I learned to talk and act 'proper.' In the war, while young men and women died in the mud around me, I learned to ignore the huge hole in my heart that I'd been taught to disavow my entire life." His voice broke. "My mother was innocent and helpless and young and dared to try to protect herself from a drunk rich man groping at her on a streetcar—who wouldn't stop despite her protests. He was wrong, but she took out the sewing kit she kept in her little purse and stabbed him with her scissors, and she was found guilty. The state of New York charged her with premeditated first-degree murder and took her away—said the man approached her before and she'd armed herself with scissors, planning to attack him. So she was the one at fault. Life in prison."

He looked squarely at Annalee. "I never saw her again. The Blakes discouraged any talk of her, and over time, she was barely a name to me, not even a memory."

"Who gave you this newspaper article?"

"I found it in Aunt Jessie's things a couple of years ago when I helped her and Uncle move back to New York. It was stuck in the back of a dresser drawer. A note in my aunt's handwriting was attached with a paperclip. The note said *Jack's mother.*"

Annalee listened. Jack's mother. Questions fired in her heart and mind. She didn't know how to talk to Jack about mothers. Not his. Not her own. Not anybody else's. Nor about what he'd just told her, so she asked a question she didn't trust to be right, but she asked it anyway.

"Why are you telling me this now?" She paused and shook her head. That sounded harsh and uncaring. She started over, asking her question in a different way. "What happened is horrible. Your mother, Jack. But are you telling me now because, before, you didn't want me to know that your mother was in prison? Did you think I'd see that as a reflection on you?"

"Your heart's not like that." Jack touched the envelope for a moment. "I'm telling you now because—until the Burch woman's situation—I'd buried so deep what had happened to my mother, and therefore to me, so I wouldn't have to admit just how much I missed her, and not having her, and how much we're all up against." Jack searched her eyes. "You're working impossibly hard trying to be a detective—trying to make these wrong things right."

"I don't know any other way to work."

"But everything's stacked against you. Mercy, against us. Even if you figure out who killed Prissy, will anything come of it?"

"Do you want me to give up?" Annalee sat up in her chair.

"Never. Not unless you want to. But do you understand what you're fighting?"

"I'm working as hard as I can to understand it. With the Klan and their poison, that's clear as day what I'm fighting." She set her jaw. "Then there's that other thing we're fighting."

"Right, each other." He winced.

"Exactly. Lord, help us. Look what happened with poor Valerie Valentine. She'd been willing to let her own niece get buried in an unmarked grave for fear that claiming Prissy as family would hurt her climb upward."

Jack nodded. "I saw it in New York with my aunt and uncle. Everything they did was to break into that Negro society world. But to the rest of the world, we're still just 'colored.' To each other, some are like frogs in a kettle of boiling water—crawling over each other to make it to the top and escape what's below."

"Your mother didn't do that. She just tried to defend herself."

"With nobody to help her. I was too young. With no dad. I don't even know who he is. But I can make a difference now." Jack looked defiant. "For her, I can make a difference—"

"I'm so sorry." Annalee cut in.

"You don't have to say that."

"But I mean it. It's not on me, nor on any of us, that these horrible things have happened all these years—and still are happening. Lord Jesus, when will it all stop?" Annalee gripped Jack's desk. "But I still want you to know, from the deepest place in my heart, that I'm sorry this happened to your mother, Naomi Day, and to you, Jack, her only son. May God bless her memory. Thank you for trusting me to tell me."

"Thanks for not holding it against me that I waited." Jack stood, walked around his desk, and pulled Annalee to her feet. He searched her eyes. Then he embraced her for a wonderful long time. She felt his breath in her ear.

She snuggled closer. "The window's open and all of Five Points is watching what you're doing right now."

"Let them watch." Jack held her closer. "The Lord brought you to me, but I believe my mother would approve, open window or not. She'd be happy for me, actually for us. So folks in Five Points should be happy too."

With that, he kissed her, his breath so warm and sweet and honest she could've cried for both of them. She kissed him back. Then he turned off the lamp in the office, closed and locked the window, and walked with Annalee back to her cabin.

On the way, he told her he'd be busy the next few days.

"But find me if you need me. I'll be on the construction site all day tomorrow, but I'll be keeping close watch anyway."

"I'll look for you."

"I'll count the minutes."

She liked the sound of that. He gave her a wink, reached in his watch pocket for his car keys, and handed her his extra key, wrapping his hands around hers.

"In case you need to drive somewhere these next few days. The car's at Mason's rooming house—in the garage. Mr. Mason can unlock the door. Carry your driver's license too. Then you can drive."

"I can barely shift gears."

"You shift fine." He ran a finger down her nose, let it rest a moment on her mouth. "I don't want you or anybody else riding the streetcars right now." He gazed into her eyes. She held his gaze.

Please don't go. That's what she longed to say. Instead she just whispered an okay.

Jack left her then inside her cabin and gave her a wave from her road. She waved back. Then as she watched, he walked into a new night.

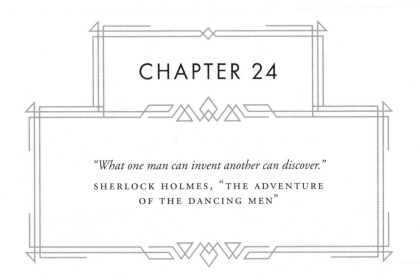

CHAPTER 24

"What one man can invent another can discover."
SHERLOCK HOLMES, "THE ADVENTURE
OF THE DANCING MEN"

THE NEXT MORNING DAWNED CLOUDY. Nasty and thundery. Annalee squinted through her little cabin window at the Colorado gloom. Denver days were rarely cloudy, especially early in the morning. But a gray overhang met her sleepy eyes, leaving a feeling of dank, impending sorrow.

Annalee turned from the window and shook off the murk. She couldn't allow gloom to drag her down. Not today. This was the morning she'd promised to go with Valerie Valentine to the coroner's office to identify Prissy. *Be alert and on the job,* she told herself. But the honest truth? *I dread going.* A coroner's office sounded like the least appealing place in the whole wide world. But as Sherlock Holmes observed in the story of his that she'd recently studied, "For strange effects and extraordinary combinations we must go to life itself, which is always far more daring than any effort of the imagination."

Annalee didn't know what she'd imagined at the coroner's office. She'd already seen poor Prissy's body, crumpled in a corner of Cooper Coates' garden shed. But now, in the clinical environment of the Denver coroner's office, she'd have to look on the sad remains again.

Mercy, I need help. But that was the wrong prayer. *Lord, help Valerie.* The poor woman must be an emotional wreck this morning. So Annalee prayed for Valerie. *Let me be the help she needs. Or if I'm not enough help, make me enough. Or send some help with hope.* She then prayed for Amos, the father of Prissy, who'd have to receive his baby girl's body when it finally made its sad way to Alabama. But at least the grave awaiting would have her name on it.

All Annalee had to do was make her way to Miss Valentine's and walk this journey with her. Jack wouldn't be with them, granting his calming pastoral presence. Annalee couldn't fill his shoes. But she'd do her best to be a peaceful help.

She climbed into a simple outfit—a white blouse and tan skirt—telling herself that Valerie would hardly be worried today about what kind of clothes Annalee was wearing. Minnie Sawyer's mesh flats would've matched. But a less daring shoe seemed more fitting. So Annalee slipped on her plain, low-heeled black pumps, grabbed her pocketbook, placed a handkerchief inside, and unlatched her door.

"Oh?"

She broke into a smile. Outside she saw help.

"Are you ready?" Mrs. Stallworth stood on Annalee's steps. Standing with her was Mrs. Cunningham. They both wore simple Sunday dresses. They also carried umbrellas.

"You can't go alone." Mrs. Cunningham looked determined.

"Bless God. I won't have to," Annalee said, feeling grateful for her two "old" friends. They'd help her on this hard day.

"Did you eat?" Mrs. Stallworth pulled an egg sandwich wrapped in wax paper from inside her purse.

"I had coffee." Annalee accepted the sandwich. "I'll eat on the way." She stopped to lock her door. "How'd you know about today—where I was going?"

"Pastor Blake told me." Mrs. Stallworth handed Annalee a paper napkin. "I saw him yesterday at the Burches'. Word travels. People saw Valerie Valentine going into his office after church service yesterday—followed a few minutes later by you. So I got pastor in a corner and flat out asked him—did Valerie come forward about Prissy? To identify her body? Her case is burdening you, I told him, and I demanded he tell me. He begged my confidence, told me you were going with Valerie this morning to the coroner's office. I decided right then that Irene Cunningham and I would go with the two of you."

"Mr. Cunningham is driving us," Mrs. Cunningham said. "In his cab."

"God bless him. I'll show him where Valerie Valentine lives."

"No need," Mrs. Cunningham said. "Everybody knows her place. The pride of the neighborhood."

Valerie hardly looked prideful, however, when Mr. Cunningham pulled his cab in front of her showy, ornate house. Valerie was locking her front door. She closed her screen door and turned, revealing a face that spoke of shame, uncertainty, and a sleepless night. She wore a clean dress, but it wasn't ironed well. Her normally well-coifed hair was pulled back in a simple bun.

Annalee stepped out of the cab, took the steps to Valerie's front porch, reached for her hand. "We've got a ride, Miss Valentine. I'm going downtown with you. A couple of Hearts and Hands ladies are going too."

"Church ladies?" Valerie searched Annalee's eyes. "I was praying to keep this quiet."

"They're here to help. It's Mrs. Cunningham and Mrs.

Stallworth—Irene and Edna—and Mr. Cunningham is driving us. He owns a cab."

"So many people . . ."

"Good people." Annalee guided Valerie to the cab and into the back seat, settling her between the other two ladies. Both greeted her kindly.

Mr. Cunningham touched his cap. "Morning, Miss Valentine."

Mrs. Cunningham placed her hand atop Valerie's and let it rest there, assuring her, letting her know she wasn't alone. They were in her corner.

"I'm sorry—" Valerie, right off the bat, tried to apologize.

Mrs. Stallworth hushed her. "Let bygones be bygone. Plus, it's a hard day. None of us want to go to a coroner's office, to tell the truth. But you're going, and we're going with you."

"I don't deserve your help," Valerie whispered.

"Nobody deserves most of the good things we get." Mrs. Cunningham glanced at her. "But the good Lord sends them anyway."

"So true, Irene." Mrs. Stallworth sounded determined and convinced.

Annalee listened to their words. They were right. Life's good, bright, and wonderful things don't belong to any of us de facto because we've done the hard work to receive them. Instead, as Mrs. Cunningham said, the good Lord is good. Even when somebody has done a horrible thing. Killing Prissy. Attacking and killing Nellie Mae Burch.

Annalee's stomach gripped at the awful horror of these incidents. To counter them, she and her friends would go now with Valerie to the Denver coroner's office so Miss Valentine wouldn't faint from the horror of it all alone. God would go too—but even more, already be there. If nothing else carried them through today, the truth of that goodness would.

Mr. Cunningham steered them safely west of downtown to the

sprawling brick complex of Denver General Hospital and Home for Nurses at Sixth and Cherokee. In the basement of one wing of the massive building, the city coroner's office did its trade. This was Mr. Cunningham's understanding, anyway.

Valerie and her contingent piled out of Mr. Cunningham's cab, opened their umbrellas. A drippy rain dribbled soggy gloom. Thunder rumbled. After a bit of debate, Annalee was appointed to walk into the building, find the coroner's wing, and explain that a family member was here to identify a young colored woman brought in eight days ago on a Sunday night.

The task, on its face, sounded simple. It wasn't. Annalee had never in life stepped one foot inside the big hospital. The facility was segregated. Negro doctors couldn't practice there. Colored people needing critical care weren't treated there except in some rare cases, but in a completely separate area—usually in the basement—and only after white patients had been treated first.

Annalee walked into the building knowing she'd face a fight. She did. At a reception desk she was ignored. Doctors, nurses, and assistants rushed by in a flurry of activity—pushing people in wheelchairs and on gurneys, none having a second of time to talk to a young colored woman trying to find the coroner.

Finally she walked to the end of a long hallway, found a staircase going down, and took the steps to the level below. Her black pumps echoed on a black-and-white linoleum floor. She passed a half dozen hospital departments, all located behind closed doors. Few people passed her in the corridor. Only one young woman, a petite blonde nurse, asked if she was lost.

"The coroner's?" Annalee asked.

"Take the hallway, next right. It's at the end."

Telling the nurse thank you, Annalee took more echoing steps and passed more closed-door departments. Finally she saw a small sign: *Medical Examiner and City Coroner's Office*.

Annalee took a deep breath, pushed open a heavy swinging

door, and almost gagged. A nauseating smell—of death, trauma, pain, the piercing formaldehyde, and sorrow—assaulted her. The only greater shock was seeing the person waiting alone on a bench at the opposite end of the big room. It was Louise Barnes. She'd gripped a handkerchief to her face.

Annalee rushed to her. "Mrs. Barnes, are you okay? What are you doing here?"

"I came to identify Prissy." Mrs. Barnes' voice trembled. She looked up at Annalee with her huge brown eyes.

Annalee reached for her and hugged her. "But you shouldn't be here. You're not family."

"Pastor said to help if we knew who she was—and she lived in my rooming house for six whole weeks." Mrs. Barnes set her jaw. "I know what she looks like. I couldn't live with myself if I didn't do my part to tell the authorities who she is, so her poor body can get back to her family—in Alabama or Mississippi, or wherever she's from." She sat taller on the bench, making her petite self look more determined.

"How'd you get here?" Annalee hugged her again.

"On the streetcar. I came early this morning."

"Has anybody here spoken to you?"

"A man in a white coat told me to wait. He said Prissy's body might already be gone for burial."

Annalee moaned silently. "I'll find out."

She marched across the big room. At a reception desk, a white-haired woman sat behind a groaning stack of manila folders, three-ring notebooks, carbon copies, and reports in metal boxes. Typing furiously on a carbon form, she finally looked up a millisecond.

"You people still here?"

Annalee ignored that. She'd already decided not to spar with anybody today.

"We're here to identify a body. A young colored woman. She

246

PATRICIA RAYBON

was brought in eight days ago—actually a Sunday night. Her aunt has been located."

The woman chomped a bite from a candy bar, looked across the room at Louise Barnes. "That her? The aunt?"

Annalee started to explain no when the swinging door opened and Mr. Cunningham led in his wife, plus Mrs. Stallworth and Valerie Valentine. All four grabbed for handkerchiefs to cover their noses and shook out their wet umbrellas.

"Louise?" Mrs. Cunningham ran to her Hearts and Hands friend.

Seeing the crowd, the wet floor, the emotion and hugging, the reception woman scowled.

"I'll be back." The woman stood. But before she could leave, a steel door behind her opened and a starched-looking man in a white coat and face mask gestured toward the group in the room.

"Come back now." He glared. "Who's next of kin?"

Annalee weighed the question. Next of kin? As in one's people? No question spoke more deeply perhaps to any conscious mortal. Annalee felt that with certainty.

"Kin? That would be me." Valerie Valentine removed her handkerchief, her voice low but pained. Walking with slow grief across the pungent-smelling room, she found whatever grit she needed to make the walk. Still, she looked soul sick.

Louise Barnes jumped suddenly from the bench, rushed to Valerie's side, and spoke up to the man. "I'm next of kin too."

Valerie turned to her, looking confused. "She was my lodger," Louise whispered. "So she was family." Louise linked her arm in Valerie's. Valerie gripped her hand.

"Okay. This way." The man swung back the steel door. Valerie's knees seemed to sink. Louise Barnes held her tightly.

"Sir." Annalee stepped forward.

"You too?" The man glared. "Make up your mind."

247

"I saw the deceased on the day she died." Annalee swallowed. "I can help."

"Well, get in here. Hurry. We're busy."

Annalee stepped toward the steel door. With Louise on one side of Valerie, Annalee took her other side and held her by the waist. Together, then, they followed the man down a narrow hallway to a tiny room with an interior window covered by a drab gray curtain on the other side.

The man left them there as he walked away to the other room and pulled back the drape. Annalee steeled herself for the appalling sight of poor Prissy's dead body. Valerie began to moan. Annalee tightened her grip around Valerie's waist, felt Louise do the same. As the curtain opened, they were confronted with the corpse.

Prissy lay on a steel table, covered to her neck in a white sheet, her eyes closed.

"Oh, Prissy!" Valerie sobbed softly.

Annalee looked briefly at the young woman's ashen face, confirming that she was the same young woman she had seen in Cooper Coates' garden shed. She nodded at the man standing behind the window. Louise Barnes did the same.

"He's waiting," Annalee whispered to Valerie.

Valerie gulped down a sob, gripped at her chest, nodded.

In a flash, the man yanked the curtain closed. Annalee and Louise Barnes gathered Valerie, got her turned around, helped her exit the horrible room, and they retraced their steps to the steel door. As they opened it, the receptionist pushed a clipboard at Annalee.

"Signatures by the X." She handed Annalee a pen. "One of you fill out Part A."

Annalee knew this process could've been kind. Even sympathetic. But for them, it wasn't. She could protest and make a show, but her concern was for Valerie Valentine and Louise Barnes. Helping them back to the bench, she gave the Cunninghams and

Mrs. Stallworth a stoic look as she showed Valerie where to fill out Prissy's name and information.

Valerie gripped the pen, spelled out with a shaky hand Prissy's legal name—Letha Lucille "Prissy" Mack—of Birmingham, Alabama. Her mother's name—Lucille Minerva Mayweather, but Valerie noted her as deceased. Prissy's father was Amos Ruford Mack. Valerie's hands trembled as she completed the rest of the form and signed it.

She'd listed a Five Points mortuary as responsible for the remains. As if on cue, a colored mortician who Annalee recognized from the neighborhood stepped in wearing a somber black suit and passed the room's swinging door with a couple of assistants, both also in their black. The death cavalry.

Poor Prissy, Annalee thought. Her escorts from the sad confines of the coroner's office were three men who'd probably never laid eyes on her. Valerie thanked them for coming. She searched in her pocketbook, pulled out a wallet, asked their fee.

"Don't worry about that now." The mortician handed Valerie his card. "We'll meet with you later today."

They walked toward the steel door—the reception lady had apparently seen the men many times before. She gestured them inside. They stepped back, however, as the man in the white coat returned, handing Valerie a small package wrapped in brown paper and twine.

"The deceased's effects. Clothing and shoes."

He asked to see the form and started writing on it.

Annalee approached him, spoke low. "Is there a cause of death?"

The man glared. "Of course." But he didn't say.

"The family is desperate to know, and I'm aware of only five ways a person can die—"

"Well, if you know so much—"

"Actually, I hardly know anything at all." She only knew those five categories for death by reading her Sherlock stories—observing that folks died by homicide, suicide, accident, natural causes, or unknown. But she'd test it. "I'd heard she was strangled—the young lady. Or poisoned?" Annalee was trawling, trying to provoke a reaction.

"Doesn't matter what you heard." The man sniffed and handed a paper to the reception lady to type. "This is official city business." He pushed past Annalee. "Next of kin get the report in due time." The man turned on Valerie Valentine. "You should leave. Take all these people with you—"

But Valerie had already headed out the swinging door, followed by Louise Barnes, the Cunninghams, and Edna Stallworth. Annalee met them in the hallway, and together, arms around each other's shoulders, they left the hospital.

Outside, the rain made one final try at ruining the day. But the morning's angry clouds were breaking up. Sun broke through. The day looked again as a Colorado day should. Annalee shoved her crumpled handkerchief in her pocketbook, took in a deep lungful of fresh air.

"If we come to my house," Mrs. Cunningham said, "I'll serve us iced tea on the back porch."

Once there, the ladies gave each other time to silently reflect on the morning, few words spoken. No need to talk over their shared pain of identifying poor Prissy. Just standing together seemed to matter far more. Valerie began, at one point, to thank everyone. But Mrs. Stallworth hushed her.

"No worry now. We help each other. Let's drink our tea."

Annalee sipped hers, glancing across the top of her glass at the other women's faces. Valerie seemed content finally to sit in a chair on a wooden back porch among Annalee's "old" church friends— those women accepting her.

Annalee took in the summer sounds of the scene. A duo of hummingbirds darted around the yard among Mrs. Cunningham's red zinnias and tall salvia. Mr. Cunningham had turned on the lawn sprinkler—since the morning's thunderstorm hadn't tarried—so a spray of water twirled in a sunny corner. Then, seeing they were settled, he'd left in his cab.

We must enjoy this moment, these hours, this sunshine, Annalee thought to herself. *Because, with murder, things get worse before they get better.* Then right away, of course, they did.

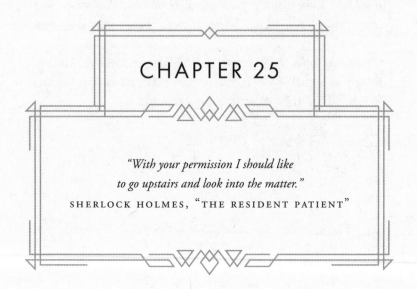

CHAPTER 25

*"With your permission I should like
to go upstairs and look into the matter."*
SHERLOCK HOLMES, "THE RESIDENT PATIENT"

THE DOORBELL AT MRS. CUNNINGHAM'S HOUSE RANG. And rang.
And rang again. Somebody was giving her bell a fit.

"Who is that?" Mrs. Cunningham excused herself from her
back porch tea to answer it. In moments, she was back for Annalee.
"The boy Eddie is here. I left him in the parlor." Mrs. Cunningham
frowned. "He's spitting mad."

Annalee rushed through to find him. Eddie leaped from a
chair and paced across a rug. He was twisting a newspaper in his
hands.

"A stupid special edition." Eddie's breath seethed. He shoved
the newspaper at Annalee.

"What's happened? How'd you know I was here?" She grabbed
the paper.

"I ran into Mr. Cunningham out by the boys' home. He was

dropping off a quick fare. When I asked where you were, he told me you were here and he'd give me a ride, then he left for another pickup."

"Did anybody see you get in his cab?" Annalee didn't want the Cunninghams or anybody else she knew to land in hot water for befriending a white child. Eddie should've known better, but she couldn't fix that now.

Eddie shook his head.

"There's something in the papers?"

She looked across the headlines. Just regular news. Wheat prices. Railroad fights. *Republicans Pick Coolidge. Democrats Debate Smith.* This thing. That thing.

"No, look inside. Page two."

A police blotter running down one column cited sad case after case of crimes and misdemeanors. Mercy, folks and their troubles. Eddie pointed to the last item. Annalee read it aloud.

"The death of a colored woman, about age twenty, whose body was held by the Denver coroner's office for the past eight days, was ruled on Monday morning a homicide. Cause of death: blunt trauma."

Annalee stiffened. Of course Prissy's death was a murder. But blunt trauma didn't kill her. Her body had looked untouched. Yet the City of Denver was making that claim. No wonder the coroner's man spurned them. He'd been forced to lie to protect the real killer. Some rich Klan man? Indeed, a seminary man? That was Annalee's best guess anyway. As Sherlock would say, the game is afoot. Annalee kept reading.

Next of kin identified the woman as Letha Lucille "Prissy" Mack of Birmingham, Alabama. Her death was reported on June 15, 1924, when her body was found in a garden shed in the Denver backyard of the colored political adviser Cooper Coates, who resides in

a Five Points manse. It's expected he'll be questioned
soon and thoroughly by Denver police and . . .

"Oh, Eddie."

"I know! Melody's dad's in hot water. Professor, you have to
help him."

"I'll grab my purse. Let's go."

Telling her friends goodbye, Annalee rushed Eddie out of the
Cunninghams' house and ran with him the five blocks over and
two blocks down to Coates' place. Well, she half ran. Her black
pumps were tall enough to make sidewalk running a chore. She
huffed. Why was she always wearing the wrong blasted shoes?

That worry faded, however, as she turned the corner for Cooper
Coates' grand house. A swarm of Denver police cars had seized his
property, vehicles parked willy-nilly—across his lawn, tires digging into Coates' manicured bluegrass, cars dripping oil on the
flagstone path under his portico. Several cops swaggered around,
glaring at the house, swinging billy clubs.

Coates stood on his front porch gripping a leash holding
back his dog, Bullet. The big German shepherd strained at the
leash, pacing around his owner, barking with furor at the commotion in the yard. Annalee saw Melody watching from behind
the home's big glass security door. She was crying. Seeing Annalee
and Eddie approach the yard, Melody pushed open the door and
called out.

"Miss Annalee! Help us!"

"Stay inside, Melody." Coates stepped to the edge of the porch.
"Who ordered this?" he yelled into the din. "Move these vehicles."

One cop approached the porch. Bullet leaped for him, almost
pulling down Coates. The dog barked with rage, bared his teeth,
growled at the cop.

The policeman jerked backward. "Stand down your animal!"
he yelled at Coates.

"What do you want?" Coates didn't move or restrain Bullet.

"Got an order to bring you in."

"For what?"

Melody yelled through the door. "Leave us alone!"

Annalee ran up on the porch. "Stay back, Melody. Your dad knows what to do." She didn't know that, but it sounded right enough.

Coates told Bullet to sit. The dog instantly obeyed, sitting on his haunches, but his bark was still fierce. Annalee spoke softly to him and scratched the dog's head. Bullet let her but still growled deep from his throat at the cop.

"We're taking you in." The cop glared at Coates and wiped sweat from his brow. "My men'll search your property too."

"They'll do no such thing." Coates looked cool and sounded like it. "I've called my lawyer. He'll be here momentarily. But even if he isn't, I'm not leaving this house, not with you. Neither me, nor my 'animal,' nor anyone else on this porch."

"Do you want me to leave?" Annalee spoke low, searching Coates' face.

"You may stay if you'd like. I'd like to talk to you later."

"Who's this?" the cop barked.

"A family friend. She's not your worry."

Melody opened the door, ran to Annalee, and wrapped her arms around Annalee's waist. The child wore another frilly dress— this one a ruffly yellow party frock. *Say what you want about the Coateses*, Annalee thought, *but they're some of the sharpest-dressed folks in town.*

"Are you okay, Melody?" Eddie called from the yard.

The cop glared at Eddie, back at Coates. "I don't know what's going on at this house, but I want answers now—"

"Sure." Coates pointed to his lilac arbor. "I've got all the answers you want. Come in my yard and look around. Again. Your superiors already checked. You think you can find something else, come right ahead. I'll be taking close mental notes of every single thing you touch."

Coates stepped off the porch with Bullet and headed to the lilac arbor, pushed open the gate, and headed with the dog toward his garden shed. Melody ran after him, followed by Annalee and Eddie.

The cop called for help. Coates jerked around. "Just you— assuming you have a search warrant."

The cop fumed, yanking a folded paper out of his pants pocket.

"I'll see that please." Coates grabbed the paper, ignoring the cop's glare. "Trumped-up nonsense." He crumpled the paper, threw it at the cop, hardly waiting to see if the policeman picked it up. Approaching his garden shed, Coates threw open the door and marched in with the dog.

"Come right in," Coates yelled at the cop. He ordered Bullet to sit and stood, arms crossed, while the cop entered the perfectly organized shed.

Annalee stood outside the door beside Melody and Eddie, but she didn't need to enter. She knew exactly what was inside that shed, including the garden tools and two bottles of poison—unless Coates had made a decision to move them. The way things were going today, she wouldn't blame him. But nothing stored in the shed on the night after Prissy was killed, Annalee felt sure, would cause blunt trauma.

The cop stepped around Bullet, giving the big dog as much room as possible. Bullet, still baring his teeth, gave the cop no margin.

Watching this, Annalee nodded to herself, impressed by Coates' bravado—perhaps because she understood it. He'd anticipated a frame. Now here it was. But he wasn't going down without a fight. Klan cops in Denver wouldn't care one fig if Coates hanged for a killing he didn't do. But Coates wasn't having it.

"Find anything?" Coates mocked the cop. He didn't wait for an answer. "Nothing here. Because nothing *is* here. Now let's check the house."

Annalee stepped back as Coates turned toward his lavish house, his dog beside him. Melody and Eddie ran after him. Using that moment, Annalee stepped in the shed after all. It looked as she recalled it. Everything in its place. Garden tools still hung by size on their nails.

Annalee took a breath. She looked up.

Coates hadn't even removed the garden poisons. He was playing hardball. No fear. *I'll have to do the same,* Annalee told herself. *Starting right now.*

Inside Coates' house, Annalee found him giving a thorough tour to the Denver cop. They'd started in the kitchen—a sprawling scullery connected to a back staircase. But the cop found nothing. Leaving there to walk room to room, Coates stopped to open every cabinet, drawer, cupboard, nook, and cranny. As with the shed, the home was immaculate, organized, not one item seeming out of place.

"Help yourself." Coates pointed the cop to a wall of shelves. "I'll wait."

The policeman continued his search, looking undone by the task.

"I'll need help," the cop mumbled his protest. "This is a big house. I'll call in my men."

"Not without supervision." Coates wouldn't budge. Bullet still stood guard.

The cop pulled a wrinkled handkerchief from a pants pocket and wiped his brow.

Annalee spoke to him. "You seem bothered, officer. And not just by the dog." She stepped closer to Bullet, scratched the dog's head, recalled the anxious, white-coated man in the coroner's office. "Who's pressuring you? And everybody connected with this case? Are you here to find something in particular?"

"Who are you again?" The cop glared, still wiping his brow, back of his neck, his hands. He shoved the handkerchief in his pocket.

"I'm a family friend—as Mr. Coates said. So I can tell you, Mr. Coates isn't a perfect person."

Coates focused on Annalee, but she went on.

"None of us is perfect. But he didn't kill that young woman found in his garden shed." Her voice sounded sure, even if she wasn't. But Coates shouldn't be railroaded.

"What do you know about it?"

"I was here the night she was found. But further, I know about your department—the Klan runs it. The chief is a member. Maybe you are too. In either case, Denver police are working overtime to pin the young colored woman's death on Mr. Coates, a Negro man. So as he says, look around. Bring in another officer. I can supervise a second officer's search. Is that okay with you, Mr. Coates?"

Coates studied her. "Perfectly fine. There's nothing here— whatever it is you're looking for. But you won't waltz around my home, ransack my belongings, and plant sinister evidence, if that's what you've been pressured to do."

The cop looked away, didn't reply.

"Well, let's go." Annalee walked toward the front of the house. "Call your man."

But to her surprise, most of the other cops had left in their cars. The officer cursed, stepped on the porch, gestured to a remaining cop, someone named Watkins, and told him to search the home's second floor "with this gal." As the first cop put it, "You know what we're looking for. I'll keep looking down here—and in the basement."

Melody and Eddie had moved to the foyer, both begging,

"Can we go with you?" Annalee agreed. She could keep an eye on them.

"Kids?" Watkins shook his head, half chuckled, headed up the steps. Annalee and the children followed him, all turning behind him into a front bedroom—a pale blue wonder, dressed with white lace but seemingly unused. A vase of fragrant lilacs and yellow roses sat on a dresser bureau. Watkins opened closets, dresser drawers, and a chifforobe and threw back the bedcovers without remaking the bed until Melody insisted he set things aright.

"This was my mother's bedroom, and Mother died when she was birthing me, so leave it just like you found it." Melody blinked. "Right, Miss Annalee?"

Annalee glanced at a framed photo on a dresser top. A demure-looking young Negro woman wearing a lace dress and holding a small bouquet of sweet william sat in a cane chair in a flower bower, looking lovely despite barely smiling.

"Your mother? She's beautiful, Melody." Annalee straightened the picture frame on the bureau. "I'll help you with the bed, Officer Watkins." Annalee grabbed one end of the bedcovers and helped the cop make the bed, something she'd never in life expected to do, but they got it done.

Watkins then looked under the bed, finding nothing, and then into a tiny, attached bathroom—also finding nothing that he thought mattered.

"Where's your bedroom, Melody?" Annalee followed Eddie and Melody into a wide, carpeted hallway.

"This next one." Melody waltzed into an oversize room filled stem to stern with dolls, toys, children's books, wooden blocks, a painting easel, a Lionel electric train set on a brass track, and all manner of playthings and children's whatnot. Eddie's eyes flashed wide. The haul looked mostly girlish, but it also invited a world of play to any imaginative boy.

"Wow." Eddie summed it up.

"You two find something to do in here. I'll be with Officer Watkins." Annalee left the children to it and followed the cop down the hallway to an even larger bedroom across the hall—surely the haven of Cooper Coates.

Walking in, Annalee shook her head. *Here I go again,* she thought—another foray through a rich person's private living quarters. Her cases seemed to always land her in these settings. This time, however, she let herself not first search but marvel.

Coates' bedroom was a handsome knockout. Mahogany, glass, gold, upholstered comforts, lush carpets. Coates had spared no expense. His life in politics—securing campaign financing, votes, endorsements, and favors for top-tier candidates, then getting compensated for his efforts—had surely paid him well.

But the upcoming election was critical. The Klan's hand-picked governor was struggling to outlast a progressive centrist eager to move the state beyond race and religious hate. The progressive was Coates' man, so the Klan's police chief had every reason to kick Coates clean out of action with a murder conviction. Politics was a nasty, murderous game, but Coates apparently didn't plan on losing or dying because of it.

His fancy bedroom said exactly that. *"Come right in and look around. But you won't find one single thing to implicate the Negro political operative who lives here."*

Officer Watkins seemed to sense that. No murder weapon would be found here not because Coates had moved or hidden it, but because Coates hadn't killed Prissy. Annalee felt sure. He had no obvious motive, Annalee thought to herself—and indeed, that was the question hanging over the entire case.

Who had reason to murder poor Prissy?

Annalee let the question follow her as she walked with Watkins around Coates' grand bedroom. The cop opened drawers and closets without disguising his frustrated interest. Everything in the room was so precisely stored that not a single thing stood out as suspicious. Same with the bathroom. Watkins seemed reluctant to even touch anything.

Opening one dresser drawer, Watkins looked at the carefully rolled men's socks—arranged by ascending color and weight—and let out a groaning sigh. He didn't even open the other drawers. Why bother? The cop did peek under the large bed and behind Coates' expensive, embroidered window drapes and made a quick survey of Coates' gleaming bathroom and a nearby hallway bathroom. But with that, Watkins looked done.

"The child's bedroom? Did you want to look there?" Annalee pointed across the hall.

"Guess I'd better."

Melody and Eddie had arranged the Lionel train set into an elaborate vignette—propped on an oversize low table at the far end of the bedroom—complete with a painted porcelain village with snow-topped mountains, tunnels, a train depot, cars, streetlights, fire station, crossing gates, clock tower, a church with steeple, tiny shops, and little people all sized to scale. Eddie pressed a switch and the train snapped to a nice clip around the track toward the village, its little headlight shining bright.

"Where's the coal car?" Watkins stepped to the train table and stood over the setup.

"One wheel is broken." Eddie picked up the car. "I couldn't fix it."

"Let me see." Watkins knelt at the table between Eddie and Melody. He pulled a Swiss Army knife from his pants pocket, extracted a little tool, and started working on the broken wheel. "My boys have a Lionel. Not this fancy. But I'm familiar with the parts and cars."

"How old are your boys?" Eddie, with his fascination for families and their children—especially families that were intact—leaned in toward the cop. Watkins answered right away and started talking about his wife and kids and the toys his three boys enjoyed.

"What about you?" Watkins asked Eddie. "You live around here?"

"Not really." Eddie glanced away. "I live at the boys' home."

Watkins took that in. "Your parents—"

"They're gone." Eddie didn't explain. "It's just me," he said to Watkins. "Melody's my friend, but she can't be my family—'cause of the rules."

Melody piped up, "I always wanted a brother, too."

"Maybe one day." Watkins spun the wheel on the little coal car. "You never know. Here, let's try it now."

As Watkins assisted the children, Annalee walked herself around Melody's elaborate bedroom. It was a perfect place to hide almost anything. Dusted, of course, the room still was an explosion of half-opened cabinets, drawers, toy chests, baskets, closets with open doors revealing a riot of Melody's fluffy, frilly dresses—enough ruffles and fluff to hide any number of weapons and murderous whatnot. Annalee didn't open any cabinets or plow through to look, however. Cooper Coates simply wouldn't hide a murder weapon in his child's bedroom, even if he had killed somebody.

Still, Annalee found the room fascinating. She knew rich people and their children owned much, but if there was any child's accoutrement that Melody didn't own, Annalee would be hard pressed to say what it was. Melody had been given essentially everything, perhaps as compensation for losing her mother—whose photo was framed in different places around the bedroom. Photos of Coates, in gleaming frames, stood center stage too.

Annalee let her eyes study the various photographs. Coates seemed to enjoy having his photo taken, not just at high-society showdowns and balls, but also in casual gatherings, at picnics and mountain cabins, at fishing parties, and in his own backyard, of course.

"How'd you learn to fix broken things?" Eddie was still questioning the cop Watkins.

"In the Army." Watkins had reattached the Lionel coal car onto the electric train, watching it properly run.

"Father was in the Army too," Melody mentioned. "See, there's his photo. It's a snapshot. I found it in a photo album. He's wearing his uniform."

Annalee smiled to herself. Melody sounded proud. Meantime, Annalee didn't know Coates had served in the Army. Jack didn't mention that, but maybe he didn't know.

"Was he a war hero—like Pastor Blake?" Eddie sounded casual too.

"Probably he was a hero, right, Miss Annalee?" Melody ran for the photo, skipped across the big bedroom, and shoved the picture in Annalee's hands.

"Well, I'm not certain." Annalee glanced down at the photo, started to return it to Melody. But she froze.

Melody didn't notice, grabbed the photo, set it on a nearby bureau, and returned to the train table to play. She, Eddie, and Watkins were setting up the village anew, debating where to position the little fire station and tiny church.

As they played, Annalee walked to an open window in the bedroom and looked out at the clearing sky for a long time. Sometimes one gets so close to a problem it's hard to see what's right in front of you. Sherlock Holmes stories had taught her that. Holmes scolded Watson for not seeing sharply in one of his very first stories, "A Scandal in Bohemia." Giving Watson a warning, Holmes told him, "You see, but you do not observe. The distinction is clear."

The same had happened to her with Cooper Coates, Annalee suddenly realized. She'd seen a lot while researching the case of Prissy Mack's death. But she hadn't observed enough of what she'd seen.

Now she stepped to the bureau and looked again at the photo of Coates. The picture was telling her a lot. But how in the world would she use it? She could barely wait to discover how.

CHAPTER 26

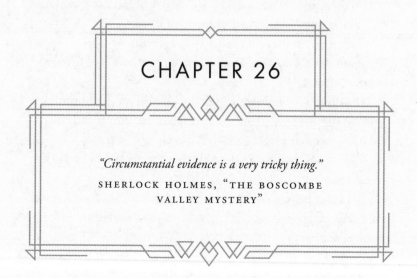

"Circumstantial evidence is a very tricky thing."
SHERLOCK HOLMES, "THE BOSCOMBE
VALLEY MYSTERY"

IN THE PHOTOGRAPH, Cooper Coates' military uniform was French, which made sense. Scores of colored Americans in the U.S. Army were conscripted by the French to help them fight the Germans, with hundreds of Negro soldiers earning the Croix de Guerre, the French war medal. Jack had earned the medal too.

But Coates' uniform wasn't what took Annalee's breath away. In the photo, Coates was standing with some of the same men Annalee had come to encounter since Prissy was killed.

There stood Coates with a narrow-eyed Sonny Dawkins, Jack's friend from the traveling carnival—but in the photo, Dawkins wore a military uniform. Then next to Dawkins stood a smug-looking Thaddeus Hammer, also wearing a military uniform—U.S. Army–issue. Next to Hammer stood a white man Annalee

264

didn't know, also in uniform. Then finally stood a slightly built young colored man, not in uniform except for his Army cap.

Annalee turned over the photo, looking for the names of the men to confirm what she was seeing. In simple handwriting, someone had written out the men's names: Cooper Coates, Sonny Dawkins, Thaddeus Hammer. Then, what a surprise—or maybe not. The fourth man—the other white man—was identified as Malcolm "Mal" Kane. As surprises go, however, the saddest and the youngest-looking was identified as Lil' Baby Mack.

Annalee gripped the photo, walked to the train table. "Melody, do you mind if I borrow this photo? I want to ask a friend if she knows one of the soldiers."

"Sure." Melody didn't look up. Annalee opened her pocketbook and dropped the photo inside. Melody was busy setting up tiny people in the train village. "Look, Eddie, here's a dog. Let's name him Bullet."

"Is he barking his head off at everybody?" Eddie laughed.

Melody and Watkins laughed too.

"Stand down your animal!" Watkins mimicked his cop supervisor.

The children laughed harder. Watkins joined in. "That policeman downstairs, Captain Goss—that's his name—he's scared of dogs. He's glad as pie Denver doesn't have a canine unit like some cities. He'd be too chicken." Watkins winked at the kids. "Don't tell him I told you."

"Stand down your animal!" Eddie followed suit, mimicking Goss too. Eddie picked up the tiny dog and started making barking sounds, growling like crazy.

"Stop it, Bullet," Melody scolded the tiny toy dog.

"You're saying it wrong." Watkins stood and put hands on his hips. "Like this—like a scared bully. 'Stop it, Bullet!'" He cracked up and the kids did too. Watkins knelt back to the train set, picked up the tiny dog.

Eddie and Melody took his place, leaped up from the table, and mimicked Watkins, hands on their hips. They laughed harder, Watkins egging them on.

"Stop it, Bullet—"

"Something funny?"

Captain Goss stood in the doorway of Melody's bedroom. He glared at Watkins. Watkins scrambled to his feet. "Sir."

"What the heck are you doing?"

"We finished our search, sir. I didn't find anything." Watkins blinked. "Me and the kids, we're just playing—"

"Playing?" Goss's disgust was front and center. "Get yourself together. We're leaving. How thorough was your search—"

Annalee broke in. "We turned over every rock."

Coates walked through the door, still holding Bullet's leash. Goss stepped back from the dog.

"You two have finished your search, I'm sure. Then downstairs." Coates pointed a finger toward the hallway. He turned and descended the stairs. Goss followed.

Annalee turned back to the children, told Eddie it was time for him to head back to the boys' home.

"I can drop you off, son." Watkins straightened a tiny streetlamp in the train village. He looked at Annalee. "You okay with that? You seem to know this boy."

Annalee gave Watkins a long, hard, take-no-prisoners look. She felt responsible for Eddie for more complicated reasons than Watkins could begin to imagine. If Watkins wasn't on the up-and-up and Eddie ended up hurt or compromised, he'd have to answer personally to her. Answer to Jack too.

"You're going straight there? To the home?" She held Watkins' gaze.

Watkins nodded, took a card from his wallet, and handed it to Annalee. "Here's how to reach me. I'll take him straight there.

And no worries, I won't grill him on his life story. Just a ride to the home. I know where it is. I don't live far from there."

"Thank you, officer."

Eddie gave Annalee a thankful hug, told Melody goodbye and thanks. Annalee thanked Melody too.

"Your bedroom is quite magical, Melody."

Melody curtsied in her fluffy yellow dress. "Glad you liked it." Annalee gave her a smile and curtsied in turn.

Her search here had given her the best lead she'd had since Prissy's killing. Now she had serious work to do, even if doing a silly curtsy was how she got started.

In Coates' second-floor hallway, Annalee checked her pocketbook. Jack's car keys were sitting in the bottom left side of her purse. Her driver's license lay there too. A good sign. She needed transportation tonight, and thank the good Lord, she could use Jack's car.

But first she needed to scurry from Coates' house. Now wasn't the time to talk to him. She wasn't sure yet what she'd say, not after seeing the photo. *So just leave,* she told herself, taking the back staircase down to the kitchen. She pushed open Coates' back screen door, hurried through his backyard, yanked open the gate under the beleaguered lilac arbor, and fast-walked from Coates' property away from his block.

The heat of the summer day hung heavy in the air. Water sprinklers made weary twirls on several of the street's small lawns. Puddles had formed along some sidewalks, forcing Annalee to jump over several, bemoaning again her choice to wear her infernal high-heeled shoes. But she couldn't tarry.

At the next corner, she made a quick turn deeper into Five Points, moving swiftly the few blocks over to the Mason Rooming

House, where Jack was a lodger. Annalee tap-tapped on the front door, grateful to see it opened by the owner, Mrs. Mildred Mason—a no-nonsense fellow church member who'd lost her only son in the war. She'd also advised Annalee over critical matters during her last case.

Mildred Mason knew things about Annalee that Annalee hadn't even told Mrs. Stallworth. So she knew Annalee had almost let another young man turn her heart from Jack. In turn, Mrs. Mason had disclosed a secret to Annalee that the young detective would take to her grave. They'd started out on a prickly basis, but Annalee's last case had changed all of that, and the trust between them was especially deep.

"Come in, honey." Mrs. Mason searched Annalee's face. "Mercy, what is it now?" She pulled a hankie from her dress pocket, wiped Annalee's brow. "You're flat out sweating. You looking for Jack?"

"Actually, his car, for now. He said I could use it."

"For your case?" Mrs. Mason pushed wide her screen door and gestured Annalee inside. Annalee gave her a grateful hug. Her little coterie of church-lady buddies had become a priceless, trusted treasury of commonsense wisdom, help, and friendship. If the best detectives had trusted sidekicks, she could claim a good half dozen, not even counting Eddie. Mildred Mason and her husband were members, for certain, of that circle.

"Want some dinner? It's after five. We haven't talked in a while." Mrs. Mason led her through a spacious, neat dining room toward her kitchen.

"Aren't your lodgers coming home from work?" Annalee followed. "They'll want a meal?"

"We eat at six. I'll make you a quick plate first. Then I'll show you where Jack parks his fancy car."

Annalee chuckled, sat down at the kitchen table. Mrs. Mason poured her a tall iced tea, then laid out her "fixins"—a plate of cold sliced ham, potato salad, carrot curls, and a small bowl of peach cobbler. Annalee said nothing for the next ten minutes, grateful to be eating. The food was a marvel.

"You're a wonder. I didn't realize I was so hungry."

"How's the case going? I heard Jack's announcement on Sunday. Had any tips?"

"Just a rather simple breakthrough today—after a hard morning."

Annalee told Mrs. Mason about going to the coroner's with Valerie Valentine, about the news clipping identifying Prissy Mack, wrongly saying she died of blunt trauma, and about watching cops search Cooper Coates' home.

"A total bust. Then out of the blue, Coates' little daughter, Melody—who's playing in her fancy bedroom with Eddie—hands me this photo."

Mrs. Mason cocked her head. "Our Eddie?"

Annalee pulled the snapshot from her pocketbook, pointing out the uncanny coincidence that almost everybody she'd encountered while researching Prissy's death had been photographed together years ago during the war.

"They all knew each other." Mrs. Mason pulled the photo closer, turned it over to read the names. "So could this mean what I think you think it means?"

"I believe it does." Annalee searched Mrs. Mason's face. "One of these men killed Prissy."

"But why?" Mrs. Mason shook her head. "Prissy would've been a child during the war. It doesn't add up."

"That's what Jack said almost from the beginning."

She told her Jack's warning to her about the case and about staying off streetcars for now. "He lent me his car keys. I didn't expect to use his car, but I need to question somebody at the carnival grounds tonight. I feel safer having my own transportation."

"I wish I could go with you." Mrs. Mason hiked a brow. "Do you want me to ask Mason? He'll go with you."

"Dinner ready?" Mr. Mason had walked into the kitchen.

"Almost. But Annalee needs a ride. Out to that Dawkins carnival. Jack won't be back 'til late."

"Hi there, Mr. Mason."

"Hey there, young lady."

"Jack said I can use his car."

"Good to see you. It's in the garage." Mr. Mason pushed open the back door. "Hand me the keys and I'll back it out for you."

Annalee was grateful for his help. She carried her dishes to the sink and washed them while watching Mr. Mason maneuver Jack's car into the alley.

"Who're you seeing at the carnival?" Mrs. Mason dried Annalee's dishes.

"Somebody who knows more than she's admitting. My gut tells me that, at least."

"Mercy, what a case."

"It's a puzzle. And it'll get solved—even if I don't see how to unravel it now. But I will."

"If you don't quit."

"That word? Not a chance."

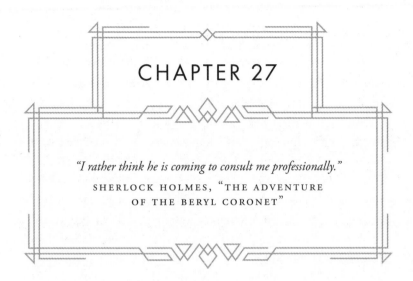

CHAPTER 27

"I rather think he is coming to consult me professionally."

SHERLOCK HOLMES, "THE ADVENTURE
OF THE BERYL CORONET"

THE DRIVE TO THE CARNIVAL gave Annalee a mile to clear her head. Driving Jack's car helped. He had an urgent meeting tonight, Mrs. Mason said. Still, Annalee could almost feel him, scooted close next to her. He'd wanted her to be safe. No riding on city streetcars. Not yet. She also felt relieved she wasn't fretting over Jack's sudden busy schedule. So Jack's absence wasn't on her worry list. Not tonight. She had other important things to hold her attention—that is, she had somebody she needed to question.

She saw that somebody as she parked Jack's car in the lot outside the carnival.

Minnie Sawyer sat perched atop the high wire, smiling down at a crowd looking up to applaud and admire her. She beamed with confidence. Or was it defiance? Sitting so high above the world and its awful troubles, Minnie seemed to dare anybody or anything to climb as high and match her moxie.

Annalee stood by Jack's car and watched her. Minnie's glittery outfit, cut too high on the thigh and too low on the bodice for actual modesty, shone in the carnival lights. Minnie flexed her arm muscles, and the crowd laughed.

Annalee twisted her mouth. She had no patience tonight for Minnie's schmoozing and drama. Once a bit intrigued with Minnie's strength and daring, Annalee now could see Minnie's game—a lot of smoke and mirrors when it suited her—when, tonight, Annalee needed real talk. Plain truth. She set her jaw, grabbed her purse, slammed the car door tight, and marched toward the carnival entrance. She barely watched as Minnie scrambled up to stand firm upon the wire, ignoring its jerky bouncing. Applause erupted. Walking without a balance bar, Minnie then slid her feet across the rope—stopping from time to time to jump up a few inches above it, daring gravity and common sense.

Then back on the bouncy cable, Minnie slid her way, inch by inch, to the opposite end and leaped with flair onto the wooden platform to more applause and cheers. Curtsying far deeper than Annalee or Melody Coates even knew possible, Minnie finally took her last bow and scrambled down a ladder, rung after rung, to solid ground.

Admirers rushed to shower praise. They begged for autographs, pressed closer to gape at the fancy getup she wore. Smiling and posing, Minnie was still chatting up her fans when Annalee walked up.

Annalee caught her eye. "We need to talk."

Minnie averted her gaze. Then she finally excused herself from her adoring fans and linked her arm in Annalee's. "Let's go to my trailer."

Annalee released herself and followed Minnie through her door and into the chaos inside.

"One more week." Minnie rolled her eyes. "Next stop: Kansas

City." She grabbed a white cotton robe from the clothes pile on the bed, pointed to a calendar pinned to a tiny corkboard, and threw the robe around her shoulders.

Annalee watched her, then spoke clearly. "I need your help. Tonight."

"Still working on your case?" Minnie pulled her robe tighter. "I've been worried about you. That death camas is no joke."

"Neither is this." Annalee pulled Melody's photograph from the bottom of her purse and handed it to Minnie.

Minnie's face went slack. "Sonny?" she half cried. "Lil' Baby, too?" She shook her head and took a soft breath. "These are Army friends? That Thaddeus Hammer? Who's the other colored man?"

"You're saying you don't know him?" Annalee felt Minnie's sorrow, but she didn't have time for games. "That's Cooper Coates. He's a high roller in Denver. A political man. His garden party eight days ago was the scene of the crime. Prissy Mack's dead body was found in his garden shed—"

"Garden? What kind of garden? What does he grow?" Minnie's interest seemed genuine.

"Grow? He grows flowers. Lilacs, daisies, pretty roses all in a row. You name it." Why was Minnie asking her this? "Does that surprise you?"

"I'm not sure." Minnie gazed at the photo another moment, handed it back to Annalee, pulled the robe from her shoulders, and tied it on. "I'm not sure what I think. Milly got flowers sometimes from admirers." She pushed a pile of clothes to the side of her narrow bed. "Don't be angry at me, Annalee. I don't know everything, even though I act like I do. I have to act strong—you know what I mean? So much bad has happened."

Annalee didn't argue. Minnie went on.

"All I know is they grow a horde of flowers out at the seminary. All over the campus. Just makes me think if your Cooper Coates has anything to do with it. You ever been out there?"

Annalee pressed her mouth. "Doesn't matter."

"Let me see that photo again." Minnie squinted at the photo. "So that's what President Malcolm Kane looks like."

"You've never met him?" Annalee doubted that.

"Actually, I haven't. I told you before—"

"Are you sure?"

"It sounds crazy, I know. Milly spends a lot of time out there. But that's between her and him, and she's—"

"Is Milly working the carnival tonight? I'll ask her to look at the photo—"

"She's not even in town. She and Maggie went home to Alabama. They got cold feet after Sonny was found dead, worried Denver wasn't a safe place. They went home to see our mama. They're catching up with us in Kansas City—or that's what they said."

Annalee rubbed her eyes. This case had so many holes, so many trails she couldn't seem to follow.

"Minnie, did Lil' Baby Mack have cousins?"

"In Alabama? Everybody's got cousins. I got more cousins than I can count. Folks I don't even know about are probably my cousins."

"What about Amos Mack? You heard of him?"

"Not sure."

Annalee shut her eyes tight, trying to think.

"Mayweather." She opened her eyes. That was Prissy's mother's maiden name—the one Valerie had written down on the coroner's paper. Annalee repeated the name. "Mayweather. Minnie, do you know—"

"Mayweather." Minnie suddenly looked alert. "Yeah, I know some Mayweathers. A big family a couple of counties over. Mama went to school with Mayweathers. One of her friends was, let's see, Lucille. I'm sure that's her name. But she got married and that's the last I heard of her."

"She did." Annalee blinked. "She got married." She took in a breath. "Minnie, can you call your mother? Does she have a telephone? It's a long-distance call. I'll pay."

"Call Mama?" Minnie looked confounded. "What do you want to ask her?"

"The simple truth." Annalee held Minnie's gaze. "What happened with Prissy? What did Prissy know? Something odd maybe. Or curious. Or out of line. I'm betting your mother knows." Annalee's eyes pleaded. "I mean, what one thing could get Prissy killed?"

"Tough questions." Minnie twisted her mouth. "But Mama won't talk to you. She doesn't believe in looking back. I'm starting to believe it's time I did the same—stop looking back. I'm ready to try that."

Annalee stepped toward the trailer door to leave. If Minnie and her mother wouldn't help nab the killer of a dead friend's daughter, based on some new life philosophy, Annalee was finished here. Still, she turned back.

"You're a beauty on the high wire, Minnie. So where do you look—when you're three stories high?"

"You mean, so I don't fall?" A look of odd amusement crossed Minnie's face.

"You don't look down? Is that the secret?"

"It's not hard, really. It's how you stand—as tall as you can. Proud. Head high. But knees bent a little." She lifted her shoulders to demonstrate. "Zimba rigs the rope tight, but with a tiny bit of give." Minnie smiled. "You can't walk this life without some give—right, Miss Detective?"

Annalee listened, intrigued despite her frustration with Minnie. But she didn't answer.

Minnie grinned but then grew sober. "I don't want to die, Annalee. Not in a stupid fall. So on the wire, I look two places— first right here." She pointed to her heart. "That helps me stand tall. I look inside. To find the confidence that's already there. Then I walk the rope to show it. At least, I pray I can."

"You pray?"

"Before I walk the cable? You better believe it."

"Then what?" Annalee seriously wanted to know.

"Then I look where I'm aiming to go—to the end of the line, to that platform on the other side. Zimba painted a small red circle dead center on the other platform. If I look right there, I end up where I look. I can't explain it. It's like I'm pulled there." She set her shoulders. "I could look down. Lots of wire walkers do. But when I walk with my pole, slide my feet toward the red circle—my eyes on the point where I'm going—I make it every time."

Minnie sat down on the side of the bed and looked up at Annalee. "Walking that rope is the only thing I've ever done in life that lifts me above the crowd. Nobody can stop me up there. No stupid rules. No bad boyfriends. No mean white people. No lynch mob. I won't do this forever, walking a tightrope. But just doing it tells me nothing can stop me. I already know what I'll do next—start my own business, something exciting." Minnie set her jaw. "I'm not above being a maid, like my mama. She raised nine hardheaded children cleaning other folks' houses. That's not what she wanted to do, but that's about the only thing folks in Alabama let her do. I want more."

Minnie turned on the bed, looked at herself in a mirror on the wall, fluffed her pressed and curled hair. "The sky is the limit. That's what the tightrope teaches me. So I can try anything. Fearless me." She pointed to Annalee. "Like you. You're a detective. That's brave. Exciting, too."

"Sometimes it is." Annalee could acknowledge that. "But that's not why I do this." She thought then of her murdered father. "I solve crimes because victims deserve it."

Minnie stood. "You're saying I'm walking away from Prissy Mack? Well, I'm not. Neither is Mama."

"Maybe not." Annalee grabbed a business card from her pocketbook. "But if you change your mind and want to help me, you know where to find me."

Annalee ran her hand through a pile of glittery, unmatched earrings scattered across a dresser top, picked one earring up, and jammed its post through her card, tacking it onto Minnie's corkboard. Then she left. The night was still early. For Prissy right now, she had vital things to do.

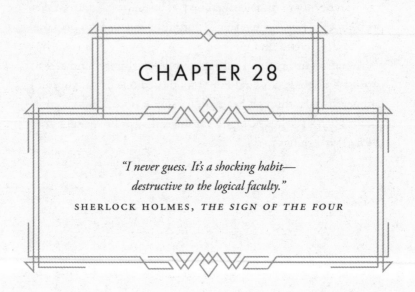

CHAPTER 28

"I never guess. It's a shocking habit—
destructive to the logical faculty."
SHERLOCK HOLMES, *THE SIGN OF THE FOUR*

THE CARNIVAL GROUNDS WERE JUMPING WITH CUSTOMERS. A full house. The late Sonny Dawkins was still pulling folks in, Annalee could see, minus poor Sonny—and never mind it was a Monday night. She pushed through the crowd, aiming for the exit. Her car—well, Jack's car—sat no longer alone in the dusty carnival parking lot.

The car was instead surrounded on all sides by other cars, parked helter-skelter. A big Caddy facing hers was pulled right up to the front grill.

Annalee grabbed open the door, realizing only then she hadn't locked it. But too late for that. She threw in her purse and climbed in, reflecting on her standoff with Minnie—a tightrope daredevil who climbed three stories high every night to conquer the cable, but somehow managed to never look down.

So what about you? Annalee frowned. *To solve Prissy's murder, look right in front of you.*

Or maybe right behind her. She heard the angry voice first.

"Where's my photo?"

Annalee flinched. Her heart thumped. Cooper Coates was sitting in the dark in the back seat of Jack's car.

"Get out of my car."

"It's not your car, but I'm hardly going to argue about that."

"What do you want?" Annalee twisted on the seat to look back at Coates. He was stationed behind her, looking dangerous and irritated. But she didn't feel fear. She'd had a grueling day, her feet hurt in her infernal high-heeled shoes, and she'd run out of patience for nonsense, including Coates' improper demands. Hiding out in Jack's car to surprise her was clearly out of bounds.

"What do you want?" she asked again.

"My photo."

"Where is Melody? Did you leave her at home again by herself?"

"If that's any business of yours—which it's not—Melody is with a college girl. But you? You had no right to talk her out of that photo—"

"Melody said the photo was hers. She let me borrow it."

"Give it back to me. Now."

"And if I don't? You're going to attack me? Hurt me? Kill me?" Annalee rolled her eyes.

"Actually, none of that." Coates' eyes glowered. "But if you keep it, I can't protect you."

"What in the world are you talking about?"

"When word gets out—and it will—that you're flashing a war photo around town and who's actually in that war photo, you're very likely to end up like Prissy Mack. Maybe you won't be dead in my garden shed, but you'll be dead just as well. Only God knows where you'll be found."

Annalee took in a deep breath, slammed open her car door, and stepped outside.

Coates did the same, slamming open his back door. They faced each other in the dark. Carnival lights sparkled in the distance beyond them. Their faces reflected the twinkly lights, but Coates' face spoke a dull, hard defiance.

Annalee searched his gaze. "Who are you protecting?" That's what she wanted to know first. "And why?"

"I can't tell you, Miss Spain. The people in that photo have shared a past—and a secret—that can only end in another murder."

"Then why'd you keep the photo?"

"I didn't know I had it. I can't even remember who took the blasted picture. Melody must've found it in a photo album—searching for more photos of her mother. She asked me one day, when I was rushing to a meeting, if she could have my war photo. She wanted to display it in her room. I thought she meant a regulation photo of me in my uniform—that she'd found one of those. I said yes without looking at it. I'd forgotten all about it. Then right after you left today, she asked me why Miss Annalee wanted a photo of me and my 'Army friends.' Right away, I recalled what photo she meant—but worse, who was in it."

"What are you saying?"

"Bad things happen in war." Coates set his mouth. "The people back home don't want to know those things. They just want to cheer their heroes, wave their flags, watch us march in parades." He squared his shoulders. "Prissy stumbled on something she shouldn't have discovered. I'm sorry from the depths of my heart that happened. It cost her life—"

"No, somebody took her life. She was murdered—probably by somebody who's in that photo." Annalee squared her shoulders too. "Was it you?"

"I've done a lot of things—like you told that cop today. I'm not perfect. But I'm not a killer. I followed you in my car from my house, saw you ended up at the Mason Rooming House. What a surprise when you drove yourself here in Pastor Blake's car. I didn't know you could drive, especially a big car like this—"

"Right." Annalee shook her head. "You have no idea what I've learned in it."

"My daughter thinks the world of you. Even if she didn't admire you, I couldn't stand by and let you get killed because of something from the past. You helped me today when the cops did their search. I appreciate that. But I want that photo. Now."

Annalee crossed her arms. "Your concern feels oddly touching. You say you're worrying about me, and I appreciate that. But either way, there's still the matter of Prissy. She was a somebody too—loved by her family, deserving of her life, which one of your Army buddies cut short because she got in the way. That's how it seems anyway. So, it goes without saying, Prissy deserves justice. Neither you nor any of your 'buddies' seems to understand that."

"You're awfully stubborn." Coates shook his head. "If only you understood."

"I understand alright." Annalee climbed back in the car, pushed the starter, retarded the spark, hit the lights, and slammed the door. "That's why you're not getting Melody's photo back. Now move your big Caddy out of my way." She gunned the engine.

Coates gave her a look. "Don't say I didn't warn you." He climbed in his Cadillac, backed it up, made a way through the chaos of parked cars, and sped away.

Annalee watched him in the Buick's rearview mirror. Then she spoke to her reflection. "I'm warned and I'm scared. But I won't turn around."

She straightened the mirror. "Besides, it's late. Time to get home and take off these ridiculous shoes."

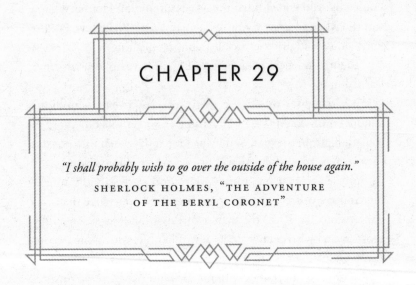

CHAPTER 29

"I shall probably wish to go over the outside of the house again."

SHERLOCK HOLMES, "THE ADVENTURE
OF THE BERYL CORONET"

MR. MASON PULLED JACK'S CAR INTO HIS GARAGE and escorted Annalee into his wife's rooming house. Mrs. Mason was dishing up cobbler in her kitchen. She looked Annalee over.

"You're safe. Thank God." Mrs. Mason pushed a chair to her kitchen table. Annalee sank in the seat and closed her eyes a grateful moment. Mrs. Mason set a bowl of cobbler at her elbow. Her lodgers would've eaten dessert earlier and retreated to their rooms—or up front to the parlor, or to the front porch swing, watching the night. The house was quiet.

"Jack's not back yet."

Annalee took a lovely bite of cobbler, wishing Mrs. Mason wasn't scowling, but she understood it.

"Folks are jittery, Annalee." Mrs. Mason shook her head. "They won't ride the streetcars, even hate walking down the street. Things feel dangerous."

"They are." Annalee studied the pie, reflected on her two face-offs tonight, first with Minnie Sawyer and then with Cooper Coates.

"Was it a trial?" Mrs. Mason asked.

"I was in a public place, so I was safe enough. Now, can I have a favor?" Annalee took another bite. Mercy, Mrs. Mason was a good cook.

"I already fixed the daybed for you, if that's what you want." Mrs. Mason pointed to a back room. "You can sleep here tonight."

Annalee wanted so bad to say yes. She'd be safe here. A good night's sleep would do her good. But she didn't want the Masons to get heat because of her case. If Cooper Coates was right, and Annalee was sure he was, a target was already on her back. Staying at the Masons' could draw these good people into her orbit.

"I don't have a change of clothes here—"

"I've got clean nightgowns. They'll be too big." Mrs. Mason laughed. "But you can take your pick."

"And a bath too?" Annalee asked quietly. "Or maybe not. Your hot water is precious."

"Not a worry. Mason's got enough hot water heaters and furnaces and contraptions downstairs in the basement to bathe the whole block."

"But how can I pay you back?" Annalee stepped to the sink to wash her dessert bowl.

"By staying safe. Like tonight. You want to sleep in the room next to Jack's? It's cozy up there."

"Absolutely not." Annalee gave her a look.

"You're right." Mrs. Mason hiked a brow. "But Jack's got you on his mind. He called here tonight—asked, if I saw you, to offer you lodging. Said he'd pay for it. Tongues will wag, but he didn't care. 'Keep her safe,' he said, adding he wants to talk to you tomorrow afternoon. He has an early meeting."

Annalee wanted to talk to him too. She had questions—especially about the war and all that had happened in France. Just for starters, did Jack know Cooper Coates over there?

She yawned. She was too exhausted to think. Besides, the steaming, soapy bath in Mrs. Mason's small first-floor bathroom was indulgent perfection, and Annalee sank in with gratitude. She soaked herself head to toe, using for a light just one worn-down candle. Then she cleaned the tub, climbed into Mrs. Mason's too-big, clean nightgown, snuggled into the daybed—two whole floors away from Jack's room—and slept like the dead. Well, the contented dead. It was sweet sleep.

Little did she know how much she would need it.

Arising before dawn the next day, Annalee got herself dressed—in a pretty summer sundress Mrs. Mason had ironed for her, left behind by a former lodger. Then Annalee fixed herself a quick breakfast, aiming to leave before the Masons' lodgers began to wake, stir, and start leaving for their long day at work. Besides, she'd rather not run into folks in the pastor's rooming house—especially first thing in the morning. But one lodger surprised her.

The pastor himself.

"Hey there, sunshine." He greeted her with a sleepy smile and moved to the table.

She grinned up at him. "I thought you'd be gone." He was wearing overalls over a T-shirt plus work boots and a tool belt. "That's some serious gear. You're rebuilding a church?" She gave him a wink.

"It's honest work." He winked back. He was carrying a hard hat. "Any coffee?"

She poured him a cup, but suddenly stopped—feeling self-conscious. She'd never once spent time alone with Jack so early in the morning. And to pour him coffee? Like a wife? She swallowed. She had questions for him, but now all she could barely do was hand him a cup of Folger's with shaky hands. She sat down.

"Am I scaring you?" He looked down bemused.

"Not if you tell me what you're doing."

"I'm surprising you." He drank from the cup. "Trying to, anyway."

"You're helping the work crew? At the church site?" She squinted at him. "Is that the surprise?"

"Not just the church. I'm working on something else."

Annalee studied his eyes. "Your house? You're working on the parsonage?" His pastoral residence had also burned to ash in the awful fire.

Jack pulled out a chair. Sat opposite Annalee. "Actually, it's *our* house. That's what I'm working on—our home."

Annalee blinked, listening.

"Then," he said, "we can move in sooner than later."

Annalee blinked again. "What about the rebuilders? They're making progress, right?"

Jack looked confused. "You don't want me working on it?"

"I'm just surprised—"

"I want us to have our own place." He offered a laugh. "Even a detective needs somewhere to lay her weary head." She didn't laugh, so he grew serious. "A safe place, Annalee—where I can look after you. Well, where we can look after each other."

"But—"

"You already have your cabin? I know." He studied her eyes. "Well, your dad's cabin—so it's sentimental. But you're not safe there."

She looked away. Moving into a home with Jack meant, first, marrying Jack. It was their lovely, unspoken hope. Building a future together. Except nagging her, right now, was Prissy's murder and Melody's war photo, while Jack was dreaming of setting up their nuptial house.

Annalee felt confused, torn. Guilty? For feeling conflicted?

"I need to get back there—to the cabin."

"Let me drive you."

"I feel like walking. To clear my head."

"Did somebody confuse you yesterday?"

"Cooper Coates. He warned me, said I'd gotten too close to a dangerous secret."

"Concerning what?"

"Did you know him, Jack? In the war?"

"I've known Cooper barely a year—after he joined our church." Jack set down his cup. "Never mind Coates. I'm staying with you all day."

"No need. I'm going back to the cabin. I'll be fine." She pulled her chair closer. "Thanks for working on our place. I wish I could help you, but I wouldn't know where to pound the first nail."

"I'll come find you tonight."

"I'll be fine. Finish your coffee." More wife talk? She grinned to herself. "Off I go." She'd truly better get going.

In fact, the walk to her cabin was pleasant. The sky pink. The summer morning in her neighborhood hummed with birdsong, the flutter of butterflies, the scents and sights of daylilies, roses, columbines, and the sparkle of twirling lawn sprinklers.

Annalee savored every step, waving at early risers sweeping their sidewalks and children already outdoors playing. A few more blocks and she could unlock her cabin and shed her ridiculous high-heeled shoes for flats or oxfords or some other common-sense comfort. She'd be glad to get home.

She took the rocky path down to her cabin. But in the same moment she froze.

"God, no." Her whisper burned in her throat.

Her poor yard had been dug up and trashed—the new lilac

plants torn from the roots, her non-growing seedling patch stomped down to nothing, and worst of all, the little maple tree planted by her father axed to the ground.

Vandals.

She rushed to the tree, racing past upturned dirt clods, and knelt in the dust by the downed branches. The leaves were already wilting. Nothing would save them. Short of her father's murder some eighteen sad months ago, no hurt—not Prissy's murder nor Nellie Mae Burch's killing—had felt more personal. She looked up at her cabin, hating to discover what was inside.

"I can't." She said that to God in a prayer. How could she bear whatever she'd find? Like her two front steps, so carefully repaired and repainted recently by Jack, now chopped to splinters.

Her front door, smashed in, stood ajar.

Annalee could've clambered up the damaged steps to peek inside. But as she told God: "I can't."

Well, she could. But gaping at whatever insults were wrought on her tiny place would just distract her from her day's work. She didn't even bother to close the cabin door. She'd clean up whatever mess awaited her when she got back home. For now, she turned away—still in those godforsaken high-heeled shoes—and walked herself past her downed maple tree and torn-out lilacs for the several blocks it took to arrive at Valerie Valentine's place.

Valerie was outside her house, weeding her already-pristine garden. She wore a plain housedress and simple flats. Seeing Annalee walk up, she gave her a little smile and invited her inside. "Like some iced tea?"

Annalee told her yes. So they went inside the woman's beautiful home. Valerie, now looking more like the housekeeper than the homeowner, led Annalee to her kitchen in the back of the house. "Do you mind sitting in here?"

"This is fine." Annalee pulled out a chair and sat down. She sipped her iced tea and looked around Valerie's kitchen. The room was sunny, painted pale blue with white trim, and decorated with framed watercolor paintings of flowers. One large vase of fresh yellow roses sat on a kitchen counter. Altogether, it was a pleasant space.

Valerie brought over a tray holding the pitcher of iced tea, a second tall glass freshly poured, a small bowl of sugar cubes, lemon slices, and a plate of shortbread cookies. All so nice. But Annalee was here to talk about murder.

"I'm still investigating Prissy's death." She said that evenly. This wasn't a house call. She was wearing a borrowed dress, although Valerie didn't seem to notice or care as she had the first time they met.

"How can I help?" Valerie sat down at the table.

"Your father and Ol' Man Kane. Can you tell me about them again?"

"Pardon me for asking." Valerie searched Annalee's face. "But why?"

"I understand. I'm trying to clarify Prissy's Alabama connections."

"Okay." Valerie nodded. "But can you tell me why?"

"Because of this." Annalee opened her pocketbook and drew out Melody's war photo of her dad. "You know all these people, correct?"

Valerie looked hard at the photo. "All but two. The ones I know are Cooper Coates, Thaddeus Hammer, and Malcolm Kane." She squinted at the photo. "They were in the Army together? Who are the others?"

"Here's Sonny Dawkins. He owned the colored carnival that's in town now, but he came to a bad end too. The other soldier is a childhood friend who was probably a cousin of Prissy, on her father's side. That friend was Lil' Baby Mack. That's what he was called. He was lynched in Alabama after the war—a pregnant white woman said Lil' Baby raped her."

Valerie flinched, shook her head. "What does that have to do with Prissy?"

"That's the thing." Annalee frowned. "I'm not sure, but somehow it seems connected."

"But how?"

"All I know is that Sonny Dawkins came to town with his carnival. He calls Jack, says he's carrying a burden, wants to talk, to get a new start. Then the next thing you know, Dawkins is dead." Annalee wrinkled her brow. "Same thing happened to Prissy. She moves to Denver, looking to move up in life, get a good start. You try to help her. Then, next thing you know, *she's* dead."

Annalee squinted.

"The only connection I see is Saxton seminary. Dawkins knew Malcolm Kane, the president, in the war. As for Prissy, you told her to go there and visit the same man. She goes to meet Kane, but refuses to see him again, correct?"

"That's right." Valerie nodded.

"She doesn't say why?"

"She refused to talk to me about him—or anything else."

"But she gets involved with somebody at the seminary who's sending her flowers every five minutes and probably giving her money. She doesn't have a job, but she always has cash. Somebody's caring for her."

Valerie dropped her head. "I feel so responsible. I was so busy trying to make my name, climb the social ladder. But little Prissy ends up dead—and also this Dawkins fellow? His friend too?" She frowned. "Have you questioned Malcolm Kane about Prissy at least?"

"I tried. But the front desk at the seminary said he refused to see me. The crazy thing is I've never seen him in person, but when it comes to Prissy's death, the one person I think about most is him." Annalee looked at the photo again. "Anything in this photo that looks odd to you? Or somehow not right? Or something just curious?"

"Well, everybody's younger. That's the only thing." Valerie

looked again. "Well, maybe . . . I don't know." She shrugged. "I guess that's it."

"What are you thinking, Miss Valentine?" Annalee scooted forward in her chair.

"It's nothing." She pushed the tray over to Annalee. "Like more tea? A shortbread?"

Annalee declined. She sat back in her chair, let her eyes scan Valerie's kitchen again—the lovely decor, paintings of flowers, the fresh roses. "Who taught you to love flowers, Miss Valentine?"

"My father. God bless his soul. He ended up working at Kane's lumberyard, but he had a green thumb from the get-go. We had our little place in the country, but Daddy kept it up by growing flowers everywhere. My mother helped me to cook and cater. Daddy taught me to drop a seed in the ground and make it sprout and grow. Even if I lived in a shack, I'd have flowers growing." She took a breath. "Daddy's the one who taught young Malcolm Kane about gardening. Ol' Man Kane thought it was a silly hobby, but Malcolm Junior loved it. At least that's what my dad told me. I'd left home then and never met Malcolm Junior until I moved to Denver."

"Yes, I remember you saying that. Small world."

"He's got that Mississippi drawl. The ladies love it."

"Ladies like your friend Charlotte Furness."

"Right." But Valerie made a side eye.

"So Nathan's not happy about their matchup, I understand."

"Is that what he told you?" Valerie scoffed. "That Nathan Furness. I never know when to believe him. He lives in the shadow of his late father, Charlotte says. The man bullied Nathan. Makes him odd about things. Obsessive."

"In what way?"

"Well, there's his gambling, like I mentioned. He's also got a mean streak. At a seminary golf benefit last year, Nathan cheated, changed his scorecard—but also a rival player's. Then lied when he was caught. He'd had a bet on the outcome."

"He must hate losing."

"Not just that. He hates seeing somebody else win. He's got a fine inheritance, Charlotte says. But he's terrified of losing what she'd leave him—his daddy's big stash. Nathan says it belongs to him. He earned it."

Annalee wasn't sure what that all meant. Indeed, her talk with Valerie hadn't helped much. She stood to leave.

Valerie thanked her for helping at the coroner's the day before. "The worst day of my life." Her voice caught. "I didn't deserve the help you gave me—you and the church ladies. So, thank you for walking that mile with me. It was a tough one. Prissy's body leaves in the morning for Alabama. I'll go with her."

"You're going to Alabama tomorrow?"

"I'll stay with Amos if he lets me—which will be a trial. But for family, a person does hard things. All I can say is, God helps us when we need it."

"He indeed does." Annalee picked up the photo from Valerie's table. "But may I ask you a strange favor?"

"I owe you, Annalee. What do you want?"

"Would you take this war photo with you? Ask Amos to look at it, see what he says about it, if it stirs any memory or anything." She pushed the photo across the table to Valerie, who looked down at it—but didn't pick it up.

"You're a strange one, Miss Detective." Valerie didn't laugh. "Take this photo to Amos? See what he says?"

"If there's anything that stands out, could you send me a telegraph? Or even call me? It's long distance, but I'll accept the call and pay for it. The phone number is at Irene Cunningham's place. She lets me take calls there." Annalee pulled her card from her purse, set it atop the photo. "Your family will be in mourning, so I'm asking a lot."

"Perhaps. But you're working on behalf of Prissy." Valerie picked up the photo and Annalee's calling card. "I'll explain that to Amos—if he'll listen. If anything catches his eye, I'll let you know."

Annalee stood there a minute longer. Had she covered everything? She thought then of Sherlock. *"You see,"* the great detective said, *"but you do not observe."*

Annalee closed her purse. "Any idea why Prissy would be writing to Malcolm Kane Senior? In Mississippi?"

"She wrote him?" Valerie looked confused.

"I have some evidence but see no reason why."

"I can't say either." Valerie stood. "Is there anything else?"

Annalee studied a painting on Valerie's kitchen wall.

"One other thing. The white man whose mama's land was sold to Ol' Man Kane. What was his name?"

Valerie gave her an odd look. "Mercy, his name. I'm going to say Sam. That's what my daddy called him. Mr. Sam this, Mr. Sam that." Valerie squinted. "I never met Mr. Sam. Just heard Daddy mention him often."

Valerie allowed herself a sigh. "Mercy, Alabama. I hate going. But here we are. If I find out anything while I'm there, I'll let you know."

Annalee thanked her. Then she gave Valerie what everybody needs in the harder moments of life. Annalee hugged her.

Valerie accepted it. They were searching for a hard answer together. The warmth of human kindness was a strong way to seal that bond.

Annalee walked back to her cabin feeling better, even if her talk with Valerie hadn't yielded much. Not yet anyway. And even if she felt conflicted about Jack building their house. *Mercy.* And even if she had a tough cleanup job waiting for her at her cabin.

On her way home, she stopped to watch some girls playing jump rope on a sidewalk. They asked her to hold the rope while they took turns jumping and singing. *Cinderella, dressed in yellow* . . . They'd tied the other rope end to a fence post in the grass.

"Sure, I'll hold this end." Annalee twirled while the girls jumped, even sang with them—about curious Cinderella. *Went upstairs to kiss her fellow. Made a mistake and kissed a snake. How many doctors did it take? 1-2-3-4-5* . . .

Annalee had sung the same song as a child. She didn't get picked every time for neighborhood games. She wasn't great at jumping. But she enjoyed the distraction on this day and told the girls thanks. Time to go.

They begged her to stay longer, even to jump the rope with them.

"I'm wearing the wrong shoes."

"Take them off!" One girl giggled, and they all laughed—Annalee too. Her poor shoes had taken a beating the past two days. So she slipped them off, stood in the front yard's cool green grass, wiggled her toes. She'd stay a few more minutes. Besides, a mother of one of the girls, who was sitting on her porch, came down to the sidewalk.

"Hey, Miss Annalee."

"Hey, Mrs. Gardner," Annalee greeted her. The Gardners had lived in the neighborhood forever and a day.

"How's your case going? That dead girl in the garden." Mrs. Gardner was holding a broom, sweeping her sidewalk.

"You heard something, ma'am?" Annalee kept twirling the rope. She studied Mrs. Gardner's face. The woman practically lived on her front porch, sweeping her steps all the livelong day, watering her cans of petunias during summer, shoveling her sidewalk during winter, mostly chatting up folks passing along. Catching neighborhood gossip. A good woman, and nice. But nosey enough to know things.

"Not much yet." Mrs. Gardner kept sweeping. "But I'll keep my ears open."

"I appreciate that." Annalee gave her a sober look and told the girls it was time to go. She had to get back to her cabin and face the music. It would be a nightmare.

"Sorry I couldn't help you today." Mrs. Gardner took the rope from Annalee. "These girls just wasting your time."

"Maybe not," Annalee said. The girls had helped her in their own way. *Made a mistake and kissed a snake.* That's what Prissy had done. Annalee wouldn't rest until she figured out who that evildoer was.

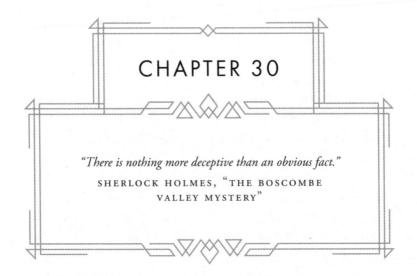

CHAPTER 30

"There is nothing more deceptive than an obvious fact."
SHERLOCK HOLMES, "THE BOSCOMBE
VALLEY MYSTERY"

WALKING HOME, AND TAKING HER TIME DOING IT, Annalee finally turned the corner onto her road, hating to see again what she'd left behind that morning—a ransacked wreck. She took in a hard breath, steeling herself for the worst. But as soon as she saw the black Model A Ford, with its government license plate, parked in the dirt by her cabin, she knew God sends help. Crazy help sometimes. But crazy help is better than none.

"Where've you been?"

It was Agent Robert Ames. Federal law enforcement man.

Annalee wanted to run to him, hold on to him even. But she held back. She couldn't rely on Ames every time she needed a rescue. Besides, Jack was determined to fill that role, and she longed for that too. Instead, she thanked Ames with her eyes for checking on her, but couldn't hold back a tear. He gave her his handkerchief. She wiped it away.

"How'd you know?" She handed back his handkerchief. She hadn't seen nor heard from him since her last case—a banking swindle involving two barnstorming pilots, one who'd tried to steal her heart. Her question now? How'd Ames know about her cabin?

"That's my job. To know." Agent Ames yanked off the dark fedora he always wore. "Glory, what a mess. Nobody lands in hot water quite like you."

"It just looks bad. I'm actually making progress."

"That's why your place is a torn-up mess?"

"Somebody's sending me a message. They're getting desperate. That's when guilty people start to make mistakes."

"You sound like one of my agents."

"Good. I hope so." But Annalee wasn't bragging. She wanted Ames to know the score. "I'm looking at big players—all connected to eminent Saxton seminary."

"You don't say. Curious coincidence. We're working on some serious fraud by somebody at Saxton. A respectable place, but one or two rotten eggs."

"So I hear. I'm working for a murdered colored woman who had curious ties there." Annalee pushed past Ames. "But first, I have to clean my little house."

"But why a ransack? What were they looking for?"

"A photo." Annalee gave him a quick summary about Coates, his war snapshot, and its ties to two Saxton men. She turned toward her cabin.

"Can you wait?" Ames reached for her. "My fingerprint guys are inside."

"Prints? The vandals didn't wear gloves? They're extra desperate."

"Trashed up your cabin pretty bad, but at least it's not befouled—"

"Just being in my humble place—which was my late father's

place first—is befouling it." She set her head. "Then there's the practical matter. I hate to ask, but what about my humble cash?"

"Where was it?"

"In my first aid kit on the shelf. Two hundred-dollar bills— money you paid me for working the last case."

"It's gone. The shelf was torn off the wall. If you had a first aid kit, they must've taken it."

"I'm getting it back—and everything else they took." Prissy's necklace too? She felt sick.

"How?"

"I don't know. First I have to clean up my cabin. Inside and out." Annalee walked around the outside of her property, kicking at dirt clods—while Ames grabbed a wilting lilac plant.

"Where are you staying tonight?"

"Right here." Annalee hiked a brow.

"Go somewhere else. You've got friends. Those ladies with rooming houses."

"Too dangerous. I won't have their homes destroyed because I'm staying there. I'll be fine here."

"You shouldn't be alone right now." He gave her a look. "When you going to marry that preacher?"

"Jack hasn't asked me."

"What's his problem?"

"We're not ready." Annalee studied Ames' eyes. "At least, I think that's the reason. We're tiptoeing up to the aisle, but I think we're both a little afraid."

Ames shook his head. "I'm going to join you on this case. Let's work together, wrap this up sooner. Plus, I can pay you. You need money."

"Jack's church will pay me. Well, they're supporting my investigation. I might get a little fee—"

Ames grabbed Annalee by the elbow. "Stop stomping around. Your boyfriend's church? Paying you? That's a conflict of interest."

Annalee sank down on a small boulder beside her axed maple tree. She looked up at Ames. "Folks want this murder solved. I know I'm getting close. I must be looking the answer straight in the face, but I can't see it."

Ames sat next to her. "That's how it works. But don't work alone. Let me help." He helped her stand. "Let's go clean your cabin."

"That's not necessary—"

"I still owe you, Annalee—for not helping solve your dad's murder. You had to solve it on your own. Now I know better. Besides, two are better than one."

"Ah, the Bible again." She gave Ames a look.

"Even I read it sometimes."

"Do you go to a church? You should come to Jack's service."

"I'll come to Jack's service on the day he's marrying you."

Annalee laughed. "It's a date."

Ames tilted his head. "Now, let's clean that cabin."

Inside, Annalee grabbed her father's worn cowboy hat off the trashed floor, shook it out, plopped it on her head, and helped while Ames nailed her shelf back on her wall. He cleaned up her little window. Patched up her steps as best he could. So most that was wrecked got corrected.

As she swept up, Annalee reflected on the ways of the folks trying to stop her from finding Prissy's killer. Attacking her modest home didn't discourage her. That made her more determined. But Prissy's life was forever stolen by someone trying to cover up a murderous truth. Annalee wouldn't rest until she learned who was working so intently to hide it.

"Now what?" Ames asked. His fingerprint people had done their work and gone, finding nothing. "You're still going to stay here by yourself tonight?"

"I am." Annalee set her jaw. "But first, I need to pick up something. Can you drop me off?"

"Only if you let me give you this." Ames pulled out a money clip and slipped out one fifty-dollar bill. Annalee accepted it, told him thank you.

"Now where do you need to go?"

"It's close by." She gave him a look and put down the cowboy hat. "Thanks in advance for the ride."

In ten minutes, Annalee was climbing out of Ames' Model A and marching up to Cooper Coates' front porch. She rang the doorbell. He answered, looking surprised.

She stepped to the door, spoke through the heavy screen. "I need your dog."

Coates blinked. "Where is Pastor Blake? Why are you alone?"

"He's busy. I need your dog."

"For what?"

"I need a watchdog. Just for a few days."

Bullet had run to the door. He stood next to Coates, looking out at Annalee.

"Hey there, Bullet." She stooped down and gave the dog a smile.

Bullet sat on his haunches, his eyes bright. He thumped his tail.

Coates studied her. "You are one confounding young woman."

"You were right. I'm not safe. I could use the dog for two days. Three at the most. I'll take good care of him—"

"Do you have any idea whatsoever the value of this dog?" Coates shook his head. "He's a purebred shepherd. Professionally trained. He's not just a pet. This dog is a war veteran—"

"I figured that."

"Bullet understands three languages, knows two hundred commands—"

"Why is he called Bullet?"

"His full name is Lutzen Von Braun Austenberg. Bullet is his nickname. He earned it in battle. And no, I won't tell you how. And no, you can't 'borrow' him for two or three days."

"May I care for Bullet then? Feed him the right food? Let him sleep by my bed, just for two nights." She blinked. "Maybe three?"

"He's too strong for you, Annalee. You couldn't control him, even on a leash."

"I don't want to control him. I've befriended him—"

"You never explained how that happened."

"One day I will." Annalee gave Coates a half smile.

"What do you want from me?"

"Somebody ransacked my house—my little cabin." Annalee moved closer to the screen in Coates' door. "They tore up my yard, axed down my maple tree, practically demolished my two front steps, and then tore things off the wall inside, knocked over furniture, and—"

"They're looking for that photo."

"They wanted to scare me too." Annalee pressed her mouth. "Well, they got my attention. I'm not dropping the case—because of Prissy. I'm doing this for her." She set her jaw. "Or maybe for all of us. But I need protection." She pointed to Bullet. "I'll take care of Bullet like he's my own child." She didn't say it out loud, but she prayed it. *Please.*

Coates sighed, pulled out his pocket watch, checked the time. "It's almost seven. Where are you going now?"

"Back to my cabin."

Coates opened his door, let Annalee step inside. Bullet licked her hand.

"I'll give you a ride to your place. Bullet can stay with you tonight."

"I'll never forget this." Annalee searched his face.

Coates fastened his gaze on her. "If you get out of this alive, it will be a miracle. You have no idea what you're up against."

Annalee knelt to Bullet, wrapped her arms around his muscular shoulders. The dog snuggled into her embrace.

Coates looked down at her with his dog. "You're something special, Miss Annalee. I can see why Pastor Blake has fallen for you, even though you're a handful." She didn't know how to respond to that, so she kept silent. He helped her stand. "When I look at you, I see Melody in a dozen years. I guess that's why I want to help you. I'd like to see you survive this."

"Then tell me what you know."

"I can't. I have to put my family first. That's all I can say now."

"Where is Melody?"

"She's spending the night with a neighbor friend—a little girl down the block."

"So tell me what I need to know. Then I can solve the case."

"I'm sorry, I can't do that. You'll have to figure it out for yourself. If you do and you come through this in one piece—"

"That's my only option. To find out who killed Prissy—and why. Then to see her killer face justice. Then I can move on with my little life." She stood tall. "My life with my Jack."

"That young man is crazy over you, I believe."

"And I'm crazy over him." She blinked. "I believe."

"Well, let's get Bullet's things." Coates pulled a leash off a hook on his foyer wall. "Looks like he gets to spend the night with a friend too."

CHAPTER 31

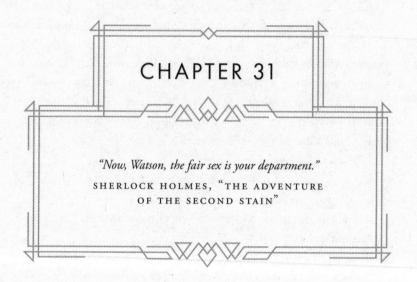

"Now, Watson, the fair sex is your department."
SHERLOCK HOLMES, "THE ADVENTURE
OF THE SECOND STAIN"

BULLET SNIFFED AROUND ANNALEE'S TORN-UP STEPS, then hopped to her front porch a different way. She didn't want the dog to get splinters, so she was glad he followed her path around the damage. Other debris around her place, inside and out, was picked up, but not all. Ames had done a bang-up job helping her with the cleanup. But the place still showed its ransacked ordeal. Tomorrow she'd offer to pay Mr. Mason to haul away the axed-down maple tree. For now it was time she and Bullet settled in for the night.

"It's a little cabin." Annalee talked to the dog, helping him check out her place after Coates left. The man had stayed longer than she'd expected. Coates had packed food for the dog, plus a water bowl. He'd also wrapped sandwiches for Annalee and himself. They ate at her little table, which she'd picked up off the floor, cleaned off, and washed down.

Neither talked much. Coates gave her some tips about the dog.

"He'll bark if he hears anything suspicious, which is what you want in a guard dog. I walked him around outside several times, so he shouldn't have to go out again tonight, or need any water to drink until daybreak. But if you do have to walk him, leash him before you open the door."

Annalee scratched Bullet under the chin. He was sitting at her feet. "What about his commands?"

"Four will take care of it. Sit. Stay. Heel. Down. Avoid telling him no. That's stressful for a dog. It's confusing. Well, one more command. Come. That'll take care of you for one night."

"Should I walk him home in the morning?"

"I'll pick him up no later than nine."

Annalee tried to think of other things she should ask. She'd never in life owned a dog, although she'd always wanted one. Now here she was preparing to share her cabin with one of the most impressive—if not fearsome—canines she'd ever seen.

"But I'm glad you're here," she told Bullet after Coates left.

She let him follow her around as she took a closer look at her place since she and Ames did their cleaning. That's when she noticed something curious. The damage outside her cabin was much more violent than what she'd encountered inside. It was as if two different people had been involved in the ransack.

She thought of the war photo and who was in it. Cooper Coates wasn't the vandal, she felt certain. He'd been trying to help her stay safe. Next came Sonny Dawkins, but he was dead. Lil' Baby was too. That left Thaddeus Hammer and Malcolm Kane.

What happened when they were in the war together? Annalee pondered a popular poster used by British recruiters. It asked, *Daddy, what did YOU do in the Great War?*

That was Annalee's question for the uniformed men in the

photo she'd given to Valerie Valentine, the one Valerie would show her half brother, Amos. Annalee knelt on the floor next to Bullet and looked the dog in the eye, asking him the same question. *What did you do in the war, Bullet?* And what in tarnation happened with those men in the photo?

Bullet licked her nose and didn't answer. She hoped to heaven that Jack could shine more light, even if secondhand—something he'd learned in his pastor duties.

Now, at almost 10 p.m., she told Bullet it was time they called it a night. She swept her floor one more time even though no trash or torn-up newspapers or other debris remained. The cabin still felt violated. She was angry at whoever had crashed through her humble home to make their awful point. *"Drop the case, Detective."* But Annalee refused to fold.

Instead, she told Bullet to lie down on a blanket pallet while she freshened up in her little bathroom and changed into her night-clothes. In the bathroom's tiny mirror, she gazed at her reflection—telling herself not giving up was the right choice. Besides, a dog was here to help. She clicked off the bathroom light.

Outside her cabin, the night sounded still except for the whirring buzz of the summer cicadas and katydids. Curling up in bed, Annalee reached down to stroke Bullet's noble head, told him thanks for standing guard over her tonight. The dog closed his eyes and let himself enjoy the attention. If anybody came around, Bullet's sharp ears would hear it—his bark fierce enough to scare away any trouble.

Still, she'd lit a candle to give a flicker of cozy light to the cabin while she fell asleep. Getting drowsy, she reflected on the day, the bad and the good, including jumping rope with Mrs. Gardner's carefree, bright-eyed girls. *"Cinderella dressed in yellow . . ."*

Whispering the rhyme in the fading candlelight made Annalee think of other little rhymes she'd sung as a child. She smiled to herself. So many seemed to be about kissing. *Johnny gave me apples.*

Johnny gave me pears. Johnny gave me fifty cents to kiss him on the stairs. How many kisses did he get? 1-2-3-4 . . .

She recalled another rhyme. *Janey and Johnny sitting in a tree. K-I-S-S-I-N-G.*

Mercy, she thought, that Johnny got around. *Down in the valley where the green grass grows. There sat Janey sweet as a rose. Along came Johnny and kissed her on the cheek. How many kisses did he get this week? 1-2-3-4 . . .*

Annalee opened her eyes in the dark. She'd sung those songs without thinking, while she was a little girl, about actually kissing. She just loved the rhyming, especially that long rhyme—the one about Miss Mary Mack.

All dressed in black. With silver buttons. All down her back. She jumped so high. She touched the sky. And she never came back.

Annalee threw back her covers, sat up straight. Bullet looked up sharply and growled low.

"It's okay, Bullet," she whispered in the dark, quieting the dog. But that line seized her thoughts like nothing had since Prissy was killed.

"And she never came back." That was true of Prissy. She'd jumped so high, all the way up to Denver—the infamous Mile High City—from Alabama, but she never came back. Not alive. Instead, she was getting carried home in a stupid casket.

So maybe, Annalee thought, there was someone else in this murder case who never came back. She thought of the war photo, of the five men—standing together so cozy in their uniforms, Black and white together in a war where Black and white together hardly ever happened. But they all came back. Annalee blinked in the dark. But who didn't? Cooper Coates wasn't saying. Sonny Dawkins was lately dead. Lil' Baby too. Thaddeus Hammer was a girl-chasing buffoon. And Malcolm Kane. No matter what Nathan Furness said about him, Annalee still hadn't met the man face-to-face to judge for herself.

She reached for Bullet, calming herself for sleep. "It's late, boy—"

But Bullet had leaped to his feet. A furious growl rumbled in his throat. He slouched low toward the door, angry and barking.

"Down, boy." Annalee tried that, then remembered what Coates said. If Bullet heard something outside, he'd react. He leaped at the door. Somebody was pounding on it, leaving Bullet raging to fairly tear it down.

"Bullet!" She didn't want to stop him. Danger. Then she heard her name.

"Annalee!" Jack's voice.

She ran to the door. "Bullet! It's okay." She grabbed the dog's leash, struggled to hook it, held on, but Bullet was pulling her across the floor.

"Annalee!" Jack called again. "You okay?"

"I'm coming!" She jerked the leash. "Down, Bullet!" She threw back the dead bolt, opened the door, and let Bullet see Jack. The dog sniffed him like crazy, paced around him, half growling, then whimpering, finally acknowledging that Jack wasn't a threat.

"What's Bullet doing here?" Jack grabbed the leash, dropped to his knees to calm the dog. She sank to her knees too—all three of them panting hard.

"Oh, Jack." She clung to him, the dog squeezed between them. Jack pulled her close.

"What happened to your yard? To your cabin?"

"You were right," she told him. "We should be together."

He pressed her close. "It's alright now. I'm here. I know."

Jack stayed the night. Mrs. Stallworth would've flipped over backward. But he did the right thing. He slept in his car, telling Annalee he was right outside.

Just after dawn, he knocked on her door, told her he'd check on her later. He did have an early meeting with Sammy Burch to sadly plan his wife Nellie Mae's funeral.

"Does God even know?" Annalee whispered to Jack in the dawn light. "Does God care?"

Jack surprised her with his answer.

"He'd better."

An hour later, Coates picked up Bullet, arriving early. He pulled his big Caddy onto the yard outside Annalee's cabin and knocked firmly on her door—ignoring that Annalee was still in her robe when she answered. Then he packed up his dog's belongings and left. Annalee barely had time to say thank you or to ask if Bullet could stay one more night. She blinked. Or maybe two.

Instead, she aired out her cabin, leaving the door open while she swept the floor under Bullet's pallet. She took the blankets outside to air on her porch, stepped into her bathroom to prepare for the day, walked out to find something to wear, and gripped the bathroom door.

A man was standing in her cabin.

"Get out—"

"Miss Spain!" He dropped his eyes and turned himself away since she was draped in her bathrobe. "It's Leroy here—from High Plains Floral." He touched his stained straw hat, still looking down. "I knocked, but you didn't answer."

"Mr. Leroy? I didn't hear you. I'm sorry." She pulled the robe around her shoulders. "Can you wait on the porch? I'll be right out."

Annalee stepped back into her bathroom, hiked a brow at her little mirror. Mr. Leroy? What in the world had he come to tell her?

But Mr. Leroy hadn't come to talk.

"I brought you a tree." He pushed back his hat. "A maple tree." He pointed to a long red truck emblazoned with High Plains Floral's logo on its side. "Some floral bushes too. Plus a couple perennials and things."

Annalee rushed to the truck. A twenty-foot maple tree sat in a huge root ball on the truck bed, surrounded by flats of other plants.

"But I didn't order a tree." Annalee ran to the truck's other side. "Or anything else. It must be a mistake." She grabbed Mr. Leroy's arm. "Please take it back. Mr. Leroy, I don't have the money for this."

"Don't matter." Leroy grabbed for a shovel. "It's paid for."

"By who?"

"Folks at my church. Other churches too. They heard your yard was tore up by somebody trying to scare you. You working on that murder case—that young girl found dead in a garden, of all places. Hurts my soul just to think about it. But anyway, pastor called a special neighborhood meeting last night at Zion Baptist— that's my church—and took up a collection for you. I donated too. Plus, I could use my store discount."

Annalee looked at the graying man in his worn overalls, at his grizzled face, his calloused hands, his stained hat, his muddy, dog-eared boots. She grabbed his precious hands, held them a grateful moment, stepped closer to him. Tears sprang to her eyes.

"How can I thank—?"

"Now, quit your crying." Mr. Leroy pulled out a frayed hand-kerchief and offered it. She wiped her face with it.

"Your help means everything. It's lonely some days being a detective, Mr. Leroy."

He nodded as if he understood. "Going it alone is hard. I been alone all my life. My mama got taken from me when I was a baby, so I got nobody. No sisters, no brothers. Never been married. Never could afford a wife."

"Why'd you come to Denver?"

"Heard it was a better life here. Better than Mississippi." He shrugged. "But it's been hard here too." He managed to wrangle the maple tree off the truck and dragged it to the yard. "I may need your help with this root ball. One of the other church men is coming by, but he's running late."

"I'll change my clothes."

Annalee came back out wearing her jeans, plain oxfords, and a simple white shirt. She'd grabbed her dad's garden gloves and his old cowboy hat, plunking it on her head. It was far too big for her, but she loved snuggling into it. She pulled it low on her head.

Outside, Mr. Leroy was digging up the trunk and roots of the damaged tree. He'd started sweating, and Annalee went back inside to bring out a pitcher of water and her one nice drinking glass on a small tray. Mr. Leroy emptied two glassfuls.

While he drank, Annalee moved three flats of plants and flowers off the truck. Every item looked especially lovely to her—and also loving—as if Mr. Leroy had kindly handpicked everything himself.

"Have you worked long at High Plains Floral?" She was curious.

"I came in 1901, the year they opened." He poured a third glass of water.

"You must practically own the place."

"Suppose I do." Leroy laughed a bit and adjusted his stained straw hat.

"You've seen a lot there probably." Annalee could hear herself probing, but she asked anyway. What did Mr. Leroy know?

"Tell you the truth, I try my darndest to see as little as possible. Folks buying pretty flowers for ugly reasons, to look good when they're bad, say sorry when they don't mean it."

He put down his drinking glass and started digging a hole in the ground for the maple tree's roots.

Annalee grabbed a hoe off the truck, started digging too. "Any people from Saxton seminary ever do business there?" A direct question.

"Saxton? That religious school? Sure, all the time. Their head man—the president—orders showy flowers, big displays for fancy shindigs." Mr. Leroy wiped his brow. "They're having something out there tonight. When I leave here, I'll go back to the store and pick up the Saxton order. A big truckload. Delivery by five. Their little party starts at seven."

"Tonight?" Annalee pulled on her hat. "Did you need anybody to help you?"

Mr. Leroy looked confused. "The store don't hire extra help on the spot."

"Not to hire me. I'd be an extra pair of hands, to show my thanks for your help here today."

Mr. Leroy dug in the ground some more and finally looked up. "Is this for your case, miss?"

"You have a sharp eye, Mr. Leroy. But you wouldn't be in danger. I just need to see Malcolm Kane, the president, up close." Annalee stepped closer. "Have you ever met him?"

"Sure, plenty of times."

"Can I ask—what's he like?" Annalee was pumping Mr. Leroy for information and scheming to get herself onto Saxton property undercover—which all felt underhanded to her, so partly wrong. Still, her questions helped her case.

Mr. Leroy seemed to understand. He stopped working to hold Annalee's gaze. "He's a tall man. Lots of wavy hair. Silver. He's somebody you notice when you see him."

That description fit with what Annalee had seen in Melody's war photo. Malcolm "Mal" Kane was much taller in stature than everyone else—not that this actually mattered. In the war photo, his hair was still mostly dark.

"So, he's tall?"

"Right. Talks with a Mississippi drawl. I'd recognize it a mile off." Mr. Leroy frowned. "But there's something about him—"

"Something wrong?" Annalee asked.

"Well, maybe not." He turned aside. "I better get back to work on your yard. I don't want to be late for tonight."

"May I go with you?"

"I'm not sure. Let me think on it more."

Mr. Leroy looked unsure too. Had he said too much? He got back to his work. As he did, another truck pulled up and the driver, a man in overalls, got out. She recognized him. One of Jack's church members.

"Sorry I'm late, Leroy." The man gave Annalee a nod. "Nice to see you, young lady."

She said hello. "Thanks for helping." The men were up in age, but they had known years of labor. That was clear. So they were hauling, planting, and potting before Annalee could get back inside her cabin.

She made her bed, swept her floor—for the umpteenth time. She studied her face in her little mirror, knowing no matter what Mr. Leroy decided, she was going to Saxton seminary tonight to look Malcolm Kane in his curious eyes.

Outside, Mr. Leroy and the other man were busy remaking her yard into something she wouldn't recognize. The new leafy maple tree got planted. Flowering bushes sat in nice semicircles, border plants lined her walkway, and perennial flowers stood guard behind them, placed just so. A neat layer of gravel covered any bare ground—and Mr. Leroy's friend repaired her steps. Her little yard looked like a new place.

Whoever had tried to destroy it was getting their comeuppance, and she was getting a lovely little garden.

About three thirty that afternoon, Jack's church member headed to his truck. Annalee had brought out egg sandwiches for both men around lunchtime and the other man now told her thanks.

"We're in your corner, young lady. I hope you solve that crime." He waved to Mr. Leroy. "Sorry I can't work that Saxton shindig tonight."

Mr. Leroy turned to Annalee. "You probably want to go."

"I won't get us in trouble, Mr. Leroy. I promise." She swallowed, her nerves firing. "These clothes alright? Simple work clothes?"

"That'll be fine. But stick with the hat. Keep it low. For a disguise."

"You sound like a detective." She grinned.

"I'm just a flower man. But if I help your case, call me Sherlock too."

Annalee laughed, not fretting over her nerves. "The game's afoot tonight. Let's go."

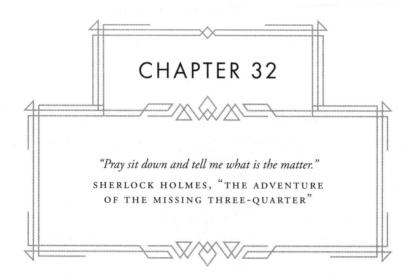

CHAPTER 32

"Pray sit down and tell me what is the matter."
SHERLOCK HOLMES, "THE ADVENTURE
OF THE MISSING THREE-QUARTER"

ANNALEE AND MR. LEROY ARRIVED AT SAXTON SEMINARY at five sharp. Workers had set up a raised stage on the lawn in front of the sprawling brick administration building. Portable steps were arranged on each end of the stage. A podium was positioned mid-stage with row after row of folding wood chairs arranged on the grass. Four oversize spotlights were being erected at each corner of the setup. Annalee scooted out of the High Plains Floral truck to help Mr. Leroy start loading floral displays on a rolling cart he'd brought along.

"What a setup. Look at your flowers." Annalee started counting displays.

"Each row of chairs gets a display. Set one at each end."

"Gracious, it'll look like a church wedding."

The displays were frilly white, in fact—big bunches of white roses prettied up with lacy sprays of baby's breath. "Lovely." Annalee gave the tiny flowers a touch.

"Their real name is gypsophila. Funny word." Mr. Leroy steered the cart. "Just means they grow great in gypsum soil. It's chalky."

"You know your plants, Mr. Leroy."

"I taught myself, I guess."

Sounds like me, Annalee thought. She'd fallen into being a detective with no plan whatsoever—learning on the fly. Even now, she was pushing a load of plants with Mr. Leroy while keeping one eye out for Malcolm Kane. But if they met, what would she say to him?

Mr. Leroy had his mind on the plants.

"They're curious things—little plants." He straightened the cart. "Half the time, they're not what they seem."

Annalee tilted her head. "Like little deceivers, you mean?" She studied his grizzled face.

"Well, like this here baby's breath. It's a pretty little thing, but if you got kitty cats, and they eat it, they'll be sick as a dog."

"What other plants are like that?" Annalee had started setting out the displays.

"Lots of them. Calla lily, day lily, lantana, azalea, oleander. Then there's rhubarb leaves, daffodil bulbs, rhododendron—that whole plant." He hiked a brow. "Mistletoe is for kissing, but don't eat it. That plant can kill you."

She thought of the death camas. "Looks like one thing, but it's something else."

"Like people. They can be the same way. Wait, look." Mr. Leroy gestured to the stage. "There's the president, Malcolm Kane."

Annalee set down a rose vase, turned toward the stage. A tall, silvery man wearing an impeccable white linen suit had stepped to the platform. He walked its perimeter, studying the setup. As he reached one end, another man climbed to the stage. Annalee squinted and held her breath. It was Nathan Furness.

Annalee yanked the brim down on her cowboy hat, picked up two more plants, and glanced again at the stage. Kane and Nathan had formed a huddle, talking intently, their heads just inches apart, appearing to Annalee not like a mistrusted president and his peeved trustee but like two conspirators. Nathan looked up, toward the lawn chairs. Annalee slowly turned herself the other direction. *Don't make a scene.*

"I'll start in the back, on the outside rows." She whispered to Mr. Leroy. "What kind of program is this? Did they tell you?"

"Some ambassadors' shindig."

"Welcome Ambassadors."

"That's it."

Annalee set the flower displays on the two back rows, moved to the High Plains Floral truck, walked to the opposite side to pick up two more vases, then froze.

Agent Ames was hiding in the shadow behind the truck.

"What are you doing here?" His voice was a whisper.

"I could ask you the same thing," she whispered back.

"We got a tip. Something's going down tonight. Not sure exactly, but we're here in case there's action."

"What kind?"

"A money deal. It's complicated. I don't want you in the middle of it."

"Something about Prissy?" Annalee's eyes searched his. "Her killer? You're making an arrest?"

"Not quite. We got a reliable tip on something else. But stay alert. Things could get ugly."

"I will, if you'll do me a favor. There's a receptionist—a worried-looking woman—at the front desk inside the administration building. Would you walk inside and tell her Annalee Spain is outside setting up flowers? If she's decided she'd like to talk to me, I'm outside, wearing jeans and a cowboy hat."

"I'm a messenger now?"

"I hate to ask, but we play our roles. Tonight I'm a gardener."

"Right, but what if she says no? Or looks confused?"

"Tell her you made a mistake. I'd better go."

"Watch yourself."

Annalee helped Mr. Leroy finish adorning each chair row.

"Next, the stage," he said. "Give me a hand." Annalee helped Mr. Leroy juggle two oversize yellow rose sprays atop his rolling handcart. Glorious showstoppers. Scents intoxicating.

Annalee closed her eyes a moment, breathing in the aroma of the precious oil of rose, understanding how Prissy could've been won over by a suitor bringing repeated bouquets of such heady glory. But why the extravagance? What exactly was the suitor scheming to extract from her? Or persuade her? And where'd he get so many flowers?

Mr. Leroy hurried Annalee and his cart toward the stage, sensing they needed to finish the setup and clear out. Guests were arriving, vying for the best seats. An all-white crowd, of course. Annalee recognized many. Top-tier politicians. Big-church pastors. Saxton trustees. Thaddeus Hammer was shaking hands right and left. Was he running for office? His wife kept pointing him to their seats. The program would start soon, and high rollers in the crowd appeared ready—both to see the goings on and be seen. News reporters were snapping photos.

Nathan Furness also was there, overseeing the placement of large, framed photos. Or maybe they were paintings—his own creations? Each was covered in a silky gold drape. At some point, Annalee presumed, the drape would be dramatically pulled away and the painting presented to its recipient.

"We're starting." Nathan pointed Mr. Leroy off the stage, ignoring Annalee, not recognizing her, apparently, as he rushed off the platform.

Annalee and Mr. Leroy settled the last floral spray onto its corner and made haste to descend the steps—Annalee pulling down her hat brim.

But at the exact same moment Malcolm Kane bounded back to the stage, and their eyes locked for a fraction of a millisecond, letting her see for one tiny moment a frisson of nervous fear so entrenched in the man's soul it almost snatched her breath away. If time itself could've stood still, she prayed it would stop right then so she could confront Kane face-to-face and demand he tell her what he was up to at Saxton seminary—and if Prissy Mack was dead because of it.

Kane seemed unnerved by her hat, looking back to stare at it an extra second. Then he turned from her and sauntered to the podium, throwing wide his arms to give the audience a presidential greeting thick and dripping with an extra serving of his Mississippi drawl. "Well, bless my soul!" Wild applause answered him. "Oh, my gracious!" He poured it on thick. "Welcome, my gallant sirs! My fair ladies! Aren't you beautiful tonight!" Wild applause again.

Annalee glanced back to watch him work the crowd, but stumbled on that last step, reached out to catch herself, and was caught, to her shock, by Kane's wide-eyed receptionist.

The woman gripped Annalee by both elbows, keeping her from falling, but whispered in her ear. "I'm afraid, Miss Spain." Her eyes flashed. "Something's all wrong."

Annalee jerked back, gave her a quick look, and whispered, "I'll be watching."

With that, Annalee matched her pace to Mr. Leroy's, turned from the stage, and rushed away from the applauding audience toward the floral truck still parked on the street.

"Are you staying?" She felt jittery and conflicted. She despaired of Mr. Leroy getting caught in the middle of a fray. But if he left, she'd be here alone with no way to flee.

"I can't leave now." Mr. Leroy pointed to the stage. "The

program's started. After it's over, I have to collect what's left and hustle it back to the store. Is something the matter?"

"I got word of trouble. Something bad is going down."

"At this program? With all these pretty flowers?" He shook his head. "I'm not surprised. That Malcolm Kane don't even like flowers, trouble or not."

"He doesn't? Well, flowers won't help here anyway." Annalee knelt down on the grass, looked beyond the crowd at the raised stage, then changed her mind. Because flowers perhaps had everything to do with her investigating trouble and how close she was to figuring it all out.

Malcolm Kane held the audience in the palms of his hands. He'd opened the program with a flamboyant but terse prayer. Short and sweet. Followed by a gushing thank-you to all in attendance—"from our donors to our doorkeepers"—for being on hand to honor one of the seminary's most respected programs, the Welcome Ambassadors.

He didn't make a speech. Instead, he invited four key donors to stand, one at a time, to receive applause. As he called their names, they stood—appearing humble but also, by the cut of their silk summer suits and gleam of their fancy watches and pocket chains, showing their wealth. The newspaper people flashed photos.

Malcolm Kane tilted his head. "And one more beautiful person to recognize." The crowd sat at attention. "The lovely Charlotte Furness! My bride-to-be! Darling, please say hello!"

Near the back, Charlotte Furness stood from her chair, waved with white-gloved hands.

"Sweetheart! How'd you end up back there! Come forward, my dear."

Kane turned to the receptionist, waiting near the stage apparently for this kind of abrupt instruction.

"Bring an extra chair!" Kane frowned. "Not that wooden chair. Find something substantial."

The receptionist stumbled from her seat, found assistance from a junior faculty member—the young man Annalee recalled meeting at Jack's church—and together the two managed to find and wrangle to the front row an impressive-looking armchair.

"Now to the lights!" Kane grumbled that they weren't turned on and his receptionist leaped up again, raced to the young faculty member for help.

The two sprinted the perimeter of the audience, she and the young man stopping at each corner just long enough to flip the switch on the spotlights.

Their blinding glare flashed across the lawn, onto the stage, onto Malcolm Kane. He stepped forward into the dazzle. His audience dazzled too—their expensive-looking clothing now properly lit and shining. "Now, how's that?" Kane saluted the crowd. More applause, laughter, approval.

The man was a showman. Watching him, Annalee thought suddenly of Sonny Dawkins of the colored circus. Not half the showman as Kane, he'd seemed determined to do his best, except poor Dawkins had died.

Kane, fully alive, leaned into the podium to pronounce his thoughts on "The Occasion."

On and on, he intoned raves about "our Welcome Ambassadors." Kane grinned, white teeth gleaming. "And they're all here tonight!" Applause.

Annalee watched the ovations. Nathan Furness had suggested strongly that opinions on the Welcome Ambassadors had turned sour. But not with this crowd.

They adored the occasion, it seemed, and Kane basked in their approval. He ran down protocol, explaining how each ambassador—introduced by her trustee mentor—would be presented with a one-of-a-kind gift, plus $100 in U.S. Liberty Bonds, an anonymous offering from one generous donor. More applause.

With dramatic flair, Kane called up each young woman to the stage, invited her trustee host to join her, then read off a glowing resume noting her history, accomplishments, chosen field of study, college or university, service record at Saxton, on and on. More news photos were snapped. Smiles all around. The girls looked nervous but proud. Annalee wasn't sitting close to the stage. Even from far away she could see hands wringing but wide smiles as the girls stepped onto the stage, each dressed in expensive-looking dresses of different pastel colors—many flapper style—but of varying designs, hem lengths, and silky fabrics. They also wore fancy black patent leather party shoes. Annalee squinted, noticing from afar the shoes looked the same style as Prissy's. Curious.

"Come closer," Kane said to the first girl. "I don't bite." Audience laughter.

Annalee watched the show, not finding anything actually wrong with it—although each young lady looked discomforted as her mentor trustee reached for the shiny golden drape and ripped it away, revealing a painted portrait of the young lady.

"Have you ever seen a more lovely girl?" Kane interrupted any response with "Not unless it's our next sweet ambassador. Come on up, beautiful!" And on it went.

He's building up to something, Annalee thought. She squinted across the lawn at his receptionist, standing back from the stage. Her stiff posture and clenched hands suggested something bad or dangerous in play. Annalee couldn't guess. Nathan Furness paced the perimeter beyond the audience, on the opposite end of the lawn.

Scanning the crowd, Annalee looked for Agent Robert Ames but didn't see him. Among the many parked cars, he probably was watching and waiting, prepared to dive into the fray—whatever it turned out to be.

He wouldn't have to wait long. Annalee sat up straighter, too, glancing at her friend Mr. Leroy, who was closely watching the goings-on himself. From their position on the lawn near the floral truck, Annalee pulled herself to stand. If she had to flee in the truck or even by running—for some reason—she wanted to be ready.

Her breathing quickened. Mr. Leroy's too, she noticed.

Kane had leaned in. "And now at last—but certainly not least—let us give a boundless round of Saxton applause for our final trustee friend and a dear leader. Drum roll, please! Ladies and gentlemen, Mr. Thaddeus Hammer!"

Hammer stood, basking in the adoration. Taking his time to kiss his wife's hand, leave his seat, saunter down the aisle, wave at admirers and friends, then step up importantly to the stage, he looked like a man never more sure of his hard-earned place in life.

Kane pumped the crowd. "Here he is! A veteran of our U.S. Army, esteemed executive director of the Western States Agricultural Association, faithful husband, Saxton friend, mentor extraordinaire, and yes, a devoted man of God."

Kane said that with a straight face. Hammer nodded modestly. *"It's all true,"* he seemed to agree. Then Hammer stepped to the podium. His summer attire luminous in the bright lights. He smiled with broad satisfaction.

"Your love for me this evening means the world to me. I'm saving most of it, however, for my mentee, Miss Elsie Louise Bell—who, sadly, couldn't be with us tonight."

The crowd responded with disappointment. They wanted to see in the flesh Hammer's young mentee.

"But it's my great and deep pleasure to display Miss Bell's painted portrait, which will hang, with the others, in the Saxton hallway gallery for all to see. Would you like to see her?"

The crowd sounded eager assent. Annalee realized she wanted to see her too—even though, if she were honest, she felt a cold disdain for Hammer, even if she didn't actually know him. Maybe some others felt the same way, and if they could, they'd rid the seminary of him. Was that the trouble that seemed to be brewing?

Because when Hammer lifted the shiny gold drape and pulled it slowly from the portrait, the young lady revealed wasn't pink-cheeked, young, and properly white.

She was Black.

Her face, her eyes, her hair.

The crowd gasped. One man leaped to his feet, yelling, "Idiot!"

Hammer dropped the shiny gold cloth like it was on fire, jerked his head at Kane. "What's this?"

"It's Prissy," Annalee whispered to herself.

It was a portrait of Prissy Mack.

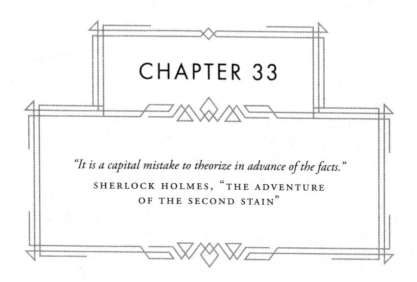

CHAPTER 33

"It is a capital mistake to theorize in advance of the facts."
SHERLOCK HOLMES, "THE ADVENTURE
OF THE SECOND STAIN"

SOME HARD THINGS, WHEN SEEN, provoke the true nature of a people. Or the true nature of their times. Jesus himself faced such certainty when he ate bread with riffraff. How dare he? "This man receiveth sinners," the fancy folks said. Worse, he "eateth with them."

This seminary crowd, most on their feet now, were sending Thaddeus Hammer the same appalled message. *A colored girl? With you? At Saxton?* They acted enraged, horrified, sounding sickened.

So Hammer called Prissy an ugly name now and kicked at the painting. But it refused to fall over, as if it was nailed to the stage, leaving Hammer to yell at it—his face mottled and ruddy, his voice carrying throughout the rows and rows of shocked guests.

"She isn't Elsie. This is Prissy!" His words shrieked and echoed.

Ames and his cohort of federal men were rushing the stage, showing their badges.

"But I didn't kill her!"

A collective gasp rose from the audience, but Kane didn't protest. He'd stepped back from the commotion, out of the bright lights.

Annalee looked for Nathan Furness, but he'd disappeared too.

Hammer, meantime, was still screeching into the night about Prissy.

"I didn't kill her! It's not my fault. But she was going to blackmail us all!"

He pivoted to point at Malcolm Kane, but Kane had removed himself.

Annalee stepped back herself to study the outraged crowd, wondering when they'd try to flee too. She would've expected not a stampede, but at least to see some guests stepping past their chairs to hurry away.

But most still stood, gaping at the stage, hardly moving, as if glued to the nicely clipped lawn underfoot. A beloved citizen was being reduced to shame and disgrace right before their blinking eyes—and all due to a colored girl, the worst association possible in their eyes.

Are we that frightening and awful, Lord? Annalee believed she knew what many here would say.

After all, look at Hammer. Handcuffs were going on his wrists despite his pitiful bawling. He stood exposed to the world, railing next to Prissy's portrait, then pushing against the federal men, trying to break free and run.

"You've got the wrong man! I tried to help Prissy! Ask Kane." Hammer jerked around. "Where'd he go? Malcolm Kane!" He dropped to his knees. "Oh, Lord!" Hammer bawled louder. "Tell them!"

Agent Ames pulled Hammer up, escorted him to a waiting

car surrounded by uniformed police, ignoring his pleading and crying.

At that, some Welcome Ambassadors did start rushing away—some alone, others with friends and shocked-looking family members. As they ran, Annalee could see up close the young ladies' shoes. She was right. They were the same as Prissy's. Black patent pump. Swirly gold design on the toe. But how did Prissy get hers? A gift from Malcolm Kane? A man she didn't want anything to do with? Not adding up.

Hammer's wife, meantime, helped by a flock of women, was rushed out too—her hands over her face. Charlotte Furness, her face stark white, was fleeing as well. All looked now as if they couldn't leave this nightmare fast enough.

That left Kane's receptionist to rush to the stage and urge calm.

"Apologies, everyone! We're so sorry. Please watch your step! No pushing, please." She jerked past Prissy's portrait.

Annalee watched it all, pursed her lips, still hearing Hammer's words: *"You've got the wrong man!"*

She nodded to herself, oddly thinking the same thing—that Agent Ames had hauled away the wrong man, carrying off Hammer in handcuffs. But arrested for what? The death of Prissy Mack? Some other fraud?

Agent Ames was shrewd. She didn't know his strategy. But she'd track him down soon, she told herself, to nail down exactly what had happened.

For now, she turned to Mr. Leroy. "We need to go."

"I can't." Mr. Leroy pointed to the multiple vases of roses still on the lawn. "I still have to pack up." He wiped his hands on his overalls. "Mercy, what a mess."

"C'mon, I'll help." Annalee reached for the moving cart, started pushing it. "We'll work fast."

"I'll drive you home, miss. You shouldn't go back alone."

It was nine now or later. Cars were pulling away from the

campus. News people were packing up, rushing away—probably on deadline. What a story!

Guests climbed in cars, squealing away, some folks flashing hateful looks at Annalee and Mr. Leroy. One man slammed on his brakes to yell, "You people did this!" He spat out of his window. "I hate every last one of you!"

Annalee didn't bother to look at him.

"Let's start in the front row," she said to Mr. Leroy, "and work back."

Pushing the cart together, they were surprised to find the receptionist waiting for them. "I can help." She grabbed a vase from a row, set it on the cart.

Mr. Leroy thanked her just as a junior faculty member—a young white man—rushed over to help too. He was the same young man who'd helped earlier, and who'd also visited Jack's church a couple of times to hear showcased national speakers. She recognized his wild thatch of ginger hair and round, thick eyeglasses.

He was studying different preaching styles, he'd told her, and added Negro orators to his academic survey, defying a dean who said there was nothing at all worth learning at a colored church.

Annalee longed to ask if the young professor had heard any good sermons lately. But it was late, they all looked bone weary after the evening's outburst, and as much as Annalee wanted to lob questions at the receptionist and this helpful young man about what had happened, neither looked prepared to jabber about a single thing.

About halfway up the aisle, Annalee did present one question to the receptionist.

"Did you know? About tonight? About that painting of Prissy?"

"The colored young lady? Is that her name?"

"You didn't know about her picture? Not beforehand?"

"I never know anything that happens here beforehand." The

woman bristled. "But I had a feeling something no good was brewing. Then when I found out you were here—with the garden store—I thought maybe you were here undercover, like those detectives in the stories."

"It's only by chance I'm here—helping Mr. Leroy from the garden center. But why'd you act eager to see me?" Annalee interrupted herself. "And what is your name?"

"I'm just Mary. Mary, the receptionist. Dyed hair and high-heeled shoes. I've been here since dirt. That's why I've been so tied in knots about what's happening here. I love Saxton seminary. But look what's happening." She grabbed another vase of roses, slammed it on the cart.

"Something's not right." Annalee understood that feeling for sure. "So tell me, Mary. What in the world is it?"

"I wish I could put my finger on it. But things haven't been right since Malcolm Kane came here as president."

"When exactly?" Annalee set another vase of flowers on the cart. They were making good progress, collecting leftover rose displays like they were born to it—but talking over Kane's upheaval at the same time. Mr. Leroy and the young professor were wrangling a flower spray off the stage. They headed to the truck to return for the second one.

Mary pushed a stray blonde curl off her forehead, then turned to Annalee. "Four years ago, the former president died suddenly. A big national search to replace him led to Malcolm Kane. He came highly recommended—U.S. Army veteran, ordained chaplain, college credentials, son of a Mississippi lumber baron, all the right stuff. A trustee traveled to Mississippi to meet him—"

"Which trustee?"

"Thaddeus Hammer."

"Why'd he go to meet him? They were Army friends in the war. I think." Annalee pondered the photo.

Mary looked confused. "Who told you that?"

"Nobody told me, but I have evidence."

"That's so curious." Mary narrowed her eyes. "Thaddeus Hammer was chief trustee—and led the search committee. He pushed for Malcolm Kane over all other candidates, said he was being courted by colleges all over the country. So the other trustees got on board, approved Trustee Hammer's request to take a train to Mississippi and talk Kane into coming here." She hiked a brow. "Trustee Hammer's a smooth talker, glad-hander, big man about town. If anybody could convince Kane to drop everything and come to Saxton as president, it would be him. That's exactly what happened. No other candidates were considered."

"But then—"

"Something changed, Miss Spain. No, not something. Everything changed. Kane showed up. Wowed everybody. Backslapping and hand-shaking all over the place. He wasn't anything like I expected. I'd hoped for a softhearted man—led by the Holy Spirit of God himself. But . . . well you've met him."

"No, I've just seen him once," Annalee said. "At tonight's program. He's quite a showman." Annalee helped Mary empty the cart and move flower vases onto the truck bed. Together, they pushed the cart to the opposite side of the lawn, started picking up the remaining floral displays.

"He's a Jekyll and Hyde. Have you read that story?"

"Two people in one person." Annalee squinted, reflecting on Kane.

"That sums him up. Kane's all pious and holy with older alumni and godly churchmen—the few still around in this town. But he's sly as a fox and syrupy with the donor crowd. Did you see how he disappeared when the trouble started? Him and Trustee Furness." Mary pursed her lips. "I'm gossiping now, I guess, but the things I've seen in him. Nervous and jumpy in private. Then, in public, turning on the charm. He has helped colored college girls but turns away when that Thaddeus Hammer is chasing after one of them." Mary looked embarrassed. "I don't mean to offend you, but when you came here that day, I thought you were one of them." She studied Annalee's eyes. "I apologize for how I acted— and what I thought. I didn't even know you."

Annalee acknowledged that, but Mary wasn't finished.

"Then, when you gave me your card and said you were a detective, I was actually glad. I hoped you were looking into all the underhanded goings-on, thanks to Hammer. Or Kane. Or both."

"I've been looking hard. All I've seen is a fuzzy, unclear picture, but I'm starting to make out pieces of it." Annalee picked up the last vase of flowers and set it on the cart. "Let's get the lights."

With Mary, she walked around the perimeter of the lawn, helping her cut the power on the spotlights. As they hit each switch, swarms of moths and other insects suddenly were left to flounder in the dark. The sky went black.

Shadows under the leafy trees on campus loomed long and dark. They looked to Annalee like all she had faced in this case, more darkness than light, more shadows than clarity. *So when will the blasted gloom lift?* She asked that more than all. The mystery couldn't go on forever.

Annalee headed toward Mr. Leroy's truck, but here came more gloom. Three cars of joyriders had driven their vehicles onto the campus, taking the main road. Seeing Mr. Leroy climbing into his truck, they cursed him with ugly names.

The young seminary professor stepped down from the truck, ran at them. "Get out of here!"

The joyriders responded with more ugly names hurled at him too. Annalee turned to stand beside the truck, peering at the hooligans. She'd expected they'd be kids. Teenagers. But these were grown men—Klan maybe—working themselves into a late-night froth. Seeing Annalee, they cursed at her too. But she didn't blink. Her shoulders back, showing not a trace of concern over their noise, she tamped down whatever deeper thing she was feeling.

The hooligans sped away.

Annalee turned back to Mary. "Do you have a ride home?"

"I was going to take the streetcar—"

"Not tonight, Mary. Mr. Leroy will drive you."

"There's room?" Mary asked.

Annalee opened the door to the truck. "Not really. But we'll find it."

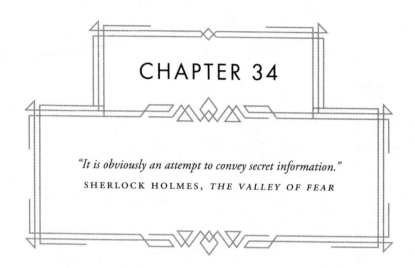

CHAPTER 34

"It is obviously an attempt to convey secret information."
SHERLOCK HOLMES, *THE VALLEY OF FEAR*

MARY LIVED IN A BRICK DUPLEX APARTMENT a few blocks south of downtown. But she asked Mr. Leroy to drop her off two blocks before. She'd walk the rest of the way, but they knew what she meant. She didn't dare be seen getting out of a truck late at night driven by a colored man. Not even an aging colored man like Mr. Leroy. They all knew the consequences. Trouble for her. Deadly for him.

So Mr. Leroy idled his truck to give Mary a hand. Instead, she swung back the handle on the truck door, scooted out in a flash, and headed toward her house.

The young Saxton professor had already told them goodnight at his campus apartment.

That left Mr. Leroy driving Annalee to her place before

returning to the garden store. On the way, he reminded her to water her new tree—every day—and her other new plants.

"I hope I don't kill them. God help me to keep them alive."

"He will." Mr. Leroy slowed his truck to let her out, gazed at his handiwork. "Look how nice they look." He wasn't staying, she understood. So she waved him a goodbye.

Her cabin was dark, and she was alone, but she'd just have to click on her lamp and try to calm her soul. She watched stoically as Mr. Leroy drove away, his truck lights fading as he turned a bend and disappeared into the night.

Annalee swallowed, feeling especially solitary. But a noise.

"Bullet?"

The dog, sitting on her little porch, panting softly, jumped to his feet.

"What are you doing here?" Annalee knelt and hugged the big dog around his neck. He whimpered at her touch and swished his tail. She laughed. "How'd you get here?"

"I brought him. You'll need him. Tonight."

Annalee jerked around. Cooper Coates stood in the shadows beside her cabin. "I heard about the trouble tonight at Saxton." He studied her reaction.

"At Saxton? What happened?" Annalee stroked Bullet.

"I heard you were there—"

"Just talk."

"Don't deny it. Doesn't matter who told me. But I brought Bullet for backup."

Annalee shook her head. "You're helping me? You're not helping me? You confuse me, Brother Coates."

"I understand. It's a confusing business. But I actually believe you're going to figure it out soon."

"Not because of you—"

"I'm sorry I said anything to you. But it's too dangerous for my family to say more." He set his jaw. "I'll pick Bullet up in the morning. Here's a bag with his things. I've got to run. Melody's with one of the college girls, and the girl needs to get home before midnight. I parked down the road. Good night."

He turned and was gone.

"Just me and you then, Bullet." Annalee sat down on a step and pulled Bullet to her. If Jack were here, she'd feel better, but Bullet was a great backup. The dog sat on his haunches, then lay down and rested his head in her lap. She stroked his fur and gazed up.

"Look at all that twinkling up there. Have you ever seen—?"

Annalee froze.

"Oh, Bullet. Of course." She shook her head. "Millions of stars, but what gets our attention? The one that's shooting by— the showy one. It makes us look, forgetting all the millions of hardworking stars shining faithfully without fanfare. That's what happened tonight."

She then told Bullet what happened at Saxton, described the disturbance with Hammer—the trustee finally yelling, *"You've got the wrong man."*

Annalee looked at Bullet. "Don't you see? Agent Ames did arrest the wrong man—on purpose. It was a charade. A masquerade. Malcolm Kane and Nathan Furness set up the painting of Prissy, turning attention on Hammer—and away from them, from whatever they're doing, together or apart." She wasn't sure. "But Hammer took the heat—and in fact, Agent Ames probably didn't know about the painting, but he used the commotion to rush in and haul off Hammer. For his own safety." She stroked Bullet's head. "That Agent Ames is shrewd."

Using the scheme of Kane and Furness against them, Agent Ames would make them think they were in the clear over some Saxton wrong because Hammer was the one hauled away.

"If only I knew what that wrong was." She pursed her lips. "It was in the war. I know that for sure. But what?"

Annalee opened her cabin door, led Bullet inside, turned on her little light, and got them settled for the night.

A few moments later, when she heard a light knock on the door—and Bullet sniffed but didn't bark—she figured Cooper Coates had returned for some reason. She opened the door, but look who stood there.

"Hi, Professor."

It was Eddie Brown Jr.

"Can I come in?"

"At almost midnight?" She pulled him inside. "What in the world—?"

"I have a telegram. For you."

Annalee closed the door tight behind them. "That's not funny."

"Hi, Bullet! What're you doing here?" Eddie patted the dog.

"Don't change the subject. What's going on?"

"Like I said—I have a telegram."

Annalee tapped her foot and glared at Eddie but regretted giving him such a harsh look. Still, she couldn't begin to weigh all the wrong in what he seemed to be doing—especially when they first met, back in Chicago, on a freezing night when he was doing the same thing: bringing her a telegram, which she hated. Telegrams always meant bad news.

She pressed her mouth, not saying a word, holding his gaze, waiting for Eddie to explain. He finally began.

"So—"

"Don't take all the livelong night." She crossed her arms, then uncrossed them.

"Okay, Professor, I came by to tell you that I might be moving in with Officer Watkins—you remember him?—and his family. His boys are great. His wife, too. She keeps saying she's sorry I live in a boys' home, and they could take me in if things work out, and—"

Eddie took in a deep breath. He gave her a wavering smile.

She studied his sad gray eyes, finally reached for his hand. She walked him to her table. "Let's sit down, Eddie."

She pulled up two chairs.

Eddie slumped into one of them, looking sheepish. "Are you angry at me?"

She didn't answer. Instead, she asked her question. "Is this what you want? To move in and join their family? And what does it have to do with a telegram?"

He searched her face. "What if I'm not sure? About the Watkinses, I mean."

She blinked hard. "With family, there's never a sure. You just trust and try."

She reached for him again, held his hands.

"Every one of us wants a loving family. I understand that—just as you do, Eddie—maybe better than most folks. But when you're out past midnight, breaking every single rule at the boys' home by being out alone, at half past everything, the Watkinses may find out about it and think twice—"

"I'll stop breaking the rules. I promise. But look what happened tonight. I ran into the Western Union man. He couldn't find your cabin—said he didn't like coming to colored neighborhoods anyway. You should've heard the stuff he was saying."

"I don't need to hear." Annalee shook her head.

"So I told him I knew where you lived and was heading there now. 'I'll take the telegram to her,' I said. He mumbled, 'Swell,' shoved it in my hand, and took off. Didn't even pay me. But I was coming here anyway, so here it is."

Eddie pushed the telegram across the table.

Annalee squinted at it. She'd only received two telegrams in her existence, but both had changed her life.

"Want me to open it for you?" Eddie reached for it.

"Actually I got it." She grabbed it, tore it open, told her shaking hands to cut it out.

"What's it say?" Eddie bounded up behind her, peered over her shoulder to read. "Who's Valerie Valentine?"

"She's a woman at Reverend Blake's church." Annalee read the telegram silently, but Eddie was already hunched over her, scanning it.

"Look, Professor, it says, 'I got it. Call me. Main 3403. Birmingham.'" Eddie wrinkled his brow. "What's she got?"

Annalee folded the telegram, laid it down with a firm gratitude. "She's got my breakthrough." She gave him a wink. "Getting me closer to solving my puzzle."

Eddie laughed. "Sounds like that game at the carnival."

"Right, the one with the pea under the shiny cups. How does it work?"

"Sleight of hand, Professor. Your mind thinks it's following one thing, while the other person is moving the pea somewhere else. You're looking at the wrong thing the whole time—"

"And you don't even know it." Annalee stood. That made her think of something. "It's like what George Washington Carver told me. He said, 'When we watch the world well, we see what needs to be seen.' I've been watching the world hard, but not well." She grabbed her little purse. "I need to talk to Valerie."

"When? Tonight?" Eddie stood back. "I'll help you find a phone."

"It's too late. I'll walk you to the streetcar. C'mon, Bullet."

The dog walked between them in the dark on her road, and Annalee was never so grateful to have a big, fierce canine by her side. Nobody would bother them, she felt certain. And nobody did.

Still, as she waved to Eddie on the streetcar—probably the last car of the night headed his way—she kept her eyes peeled. Something was about to break. For her case. Maybe for Eddie too.

With Bullet by her side tonight, she was staying alive so it would.

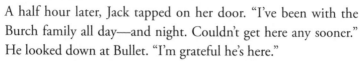

A half hour later, Jack tapped on her door. "I've been with the Burch family all day—and night. Couldn't get here any sooner." He looked down at Bullet. "I'm grateful he's here."

"Coates brought him."

"Did he tell you the secret? His war secret?" Jack wrinkled his brow. "No, I didn't think so. I wish he'd come clean so we'd all know. Except I've been thinking—"

"I have too," Annalee said. "Tell me."

"What if the secret goes back farther than the war?"

"If it does, I'm getting close." Her eyes widened.

"I'm proud of you."

She tilted her head at Jack. "Where are you sleeping tonight?"

"In my blasted car." He pursed his lips. "I'll be right outside. All night."

She smiled at him. "It won't always be like this."

He stroked her hair. Then he leaned close, kissed her ear, nuzzling. He gave her a little grin. "Trust me. It won't be."

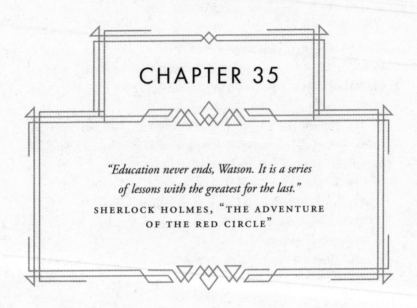

CHAPTER 35

"Education never ends, Watson. It is a series
of lessons with the greatest for the last."
SHERLOCK HOLMES, "THE ADVENTURE
OF THE RED CIRCLE"

COOPER COATES WAS TRUE TO HIS WORD. Well, this time anyway. Before eight the next morning, he knocked on Annalee's cabin door and retrieved his dog.

Jack had left in his car around dawn, waving when she opened her door but not stopping to talk. Same with Coates—he leashed Bullet and made haste. "Got to run. Be careful today."

Annalee swallowed. Why'd he have to say that?

Coates turned back. "Your yard looks great. Well done. Water everything good."

Water it good. That's what she was doing in this case. Watering every possible little seed, rumor, rumble, and detail until something sprouted. It felt to her as if a maze of different people each held a piece of the puzzle, but it was up to somebody like her to lay the pieces out on a table and snap them together.

It was Thursday, the week working its way down. But Annalee couldn't let down yet. Grabbing a watering can, she filled it, opened her cabin door, and then lugged the can outdoors. But hopping down from her little porch, she froze.

Her garden. It was a glory. On this fresh new morning on a summer's day, its transformation left her humbled, but also awestruck—even if she'd buried the worst of her fears in it, never to see the light of day. She hoped.

Mr. Leroy, meantime, was a plant magician, his own humble version of a George Washington Carver. Every plant, flowering bush, pretty flower, nub of rick, sand, or gravel—along with her beautiful new maple tree—was laid out in effortless harmony as if painted by a floral artist.

"Daddy, look," Annalee whispered. Her eyes tingled. She'd give anything for her late father to turn onto their humble path and see what Mr. Leroy and Jack's church member had rendered.

Sure, she needed to call Valerie Valentine. But first, after watering every growing thing in her yard, she'd walk the few blocks to Zion Baptist Church and personally tell the pastor thank you.

She dressed as if for a business meeting, wanting to appear proper to the Baptist pastor at the esteemed Five Points church. Zion Baptist was housed in a stately, stone-faced edifice on Ogden Street and led by a fiery preacher-orator named Frank Liggins. Annalee had heard him preach, and with his broad chest and booming voice, she thought he might blow the building right off its foundation. She felt intimidated to speak to a churchman like him.

Maybe he wouldn't be in his office and she could just leave a nice thank-you note.

When she arrived at the church, however, a prim female secretary invited her to sit in an outer office while the woman checked the availability of Pastor Liggins. Soon the door to his office swung open and Liggins thundered out, reaching for her hand.

"Young lady! Did you get your new tree?"

Tongue-tied for a moment, Annalee finally answered, "The tree's in the ground and rooting. I came to say thank you."

"So, those hooligans didn't get the last word?"

"Not yet. I actually think—"

"Think what? Speak up!"

Annalee studied his dramatic face, bushy eyebrows, piercing dark eyes, large head. The man was a force of nature. She couldn't compete. She let her voice drop to a humble whisper.

"I think I'm close. Close to solving the case."

Liggins dropped his voice too. "What else do you need? Are they helping you at Jack Blake's church? Mount Moriah? That's your church too, right?" He hiked a brow. "Well, I'm sure Blake is helping you. From what I hear."

"They're all in my corner, sir. They're also helping the Burch family."

Liggins nodded. "Right."

"I just need to make a phone call today," Annalee reflected out loud.

"Phone call to who?"

"Long distance. I can call from the stationer's—"

"You'll do no such thing. You'll call from here—where there's privacy. Where are you calling?"

"Birmingham. In Alabama."

Liggins looked conflicted. A long-distance call would cost the church a pretty penny, providing the phone operators involved— at least one in each city, and possibly others in between—were able to connect.

"Well, there's a phone in our extra office, second floor," Liggins finally said. "Long distance is fine. I'll cover the call myself."

Annalee was taken aback by Liggins' forceful, generous assistance.

"I shouldn't, Reverend Liggins. I came to thank you for the tree and flowers, but this is remarkable—"

"Don't think twice. You're doing great work." He laughed a big laugh. "Detective? That's what they call you? Well, I'm investigating things too. Big hoedown downtown for Five Points improvement! That's what I preach and teach. Get to work, people! We've got painters outside right now—painting every crook and cranny. We're a busy church!"

"I'm impressed." She meant that.

"Follow my secretary to that extra office. Don't come out until you've got some answers."

"Yes, sir." Annalee shook his giant paw of a hand. He saluted her, grabbed a briefcase from a desk, stormed out the front door, and was gone.

The secretary marched her upstairs, unlocked the small extra office located off a short hallway, and told Annalee to take as much time as needed.

The room was stuffy, as if rarely used—its only furnishings a small desk, a worn wooden chair, a wall calendar a couple of years old, and a dusty telephone. Not a perfect place, but Annalee felt grateful to use it to call Valerie Valentine and hear her story.

So Annalee unlatched the one window in the room and, with effort, pushed it open, letting in fresh summer air. A crew of colored painters was outside. Annalee watched them for a moment, picked up the phone, waited for the operator, glanced outside one more time.

Then she must've stopped breathing. She dropped the phone. It clanged against the floor.

Liggins' secretary, walking by, heard the noise and looked in the little room. "Are you okay, miss?"

Annalee tried to answer. But her voice caught.

"Miss? Are you okay? Mercy, have you seen a ghost?"

Annalee nodded. Because that's exactly what she'd seen.

The painter outside her window—standing up and breathing—should've been dead and gone, but wasn't.

That's because it was Sonny Dawkins.

Sonny dropped his paint can. His brush too. Paint spattered on the church sidewalk, onto his pants, shirt, hands, up onto his face. He didn't stop to clean it up.

Looking over his shoulder at Annalee, he swung hard and ran. Watching him, Annalee could see, from that second-floor window, the strangest thing—a man who was supposed to be dead sprinting in and around her neighborhood of Five Points, apparently trying to duck into somebody's house.

But she knew most of the people in most of the houses on most of the streets in Five Points. So when she saw him cut across a lawn, run up some front steps and into a yellow house, she just shook her head. He'd run to Prissy's old rooming house, where the landlord was none other than Sister Louise Barnes of Hearts and Hands.

Annalee glanced back at Liggins' secretary. "I just had a start. I'm fine now."

"You still need the phone?" The woman looked concerned.

"I may return to use it later. Will that be okay?"

"I'll be here all day. No problem at all."

Annalee gathered herself and left Zion Baptist Church. Walking down Ogden Street, she took herself straight to Louise Barnes' place, walked around the side of the yellow house, opened the little metal gate into the backyard, knocked on the back door, and waited for Louise Barnes to open it.

When she did, Annalee put a finger to her lips and whispered she needed to talk to one of her lodgers—the newest one.

"The painter?" Louise Barnes whispered back.

"That's the one."

"I'll get him. He just came in. I saw him run upstairs."

"I know," Annalee whispered to herself. She sat down on Mrs. Barnes' porch swing on her little backyard veranda and waited.

After a while, the door to Mrs. Barnes' back porch slowly opened.

Sonny Dawkins eased out—paint splashed all over himself.

He stood awhile, looking at Annalee. Then he sat down in a porch chair opposite her and put his head in his paint-splattered hands.

"It's not how it looks," he finally said. He gave her a sad glance. "I just got back in town. I needed a job. So I got hired. My dad was a painter. I know my way around the work. I've been here two days. One day in this rooming house."

Annalee studied his eyes. She'd never seen a young man look so conflicted and worn. She had a thousand questions, but she started with just one.

"What happened in the war?" An odd query. Why not ask how he'd come back from the dead? Instead, she spoke of war.

But Sonny didn't look surprised. "So you know about that." He sighed. "I knew we couldn't hide it forever. That we had to put it to rest. So here you are, asking me about it."

"What happened, Sonny?"

"You're Jack's girl, right? If you weren't, I wouldn't tell you a single thing. But he saved my life once over there. I might as well come clean."

"What happened?" Annalee asked a third time. "You were there with Thaddeus Hammer, Cooper Coates, and Malcolm Kane—"

"Lord, yes. Poor Malcolm—"

She sighed. "I sound like my own echo, Sonny. What happened?"

Sonny studied her eyes, closed them a long minute, opened

them again. "You're a detective, I hear. So I suppose you'll find out sooner or later. The thing is . . . somebody was killed."

Annalee narrowed her eyes. Not Lil' Baby. He didn't mean him. "It was a world war, Sonny. Millions were killed."

"Murdered, I mean." Sonny glanced down a moment. "Someone was murdered in France."

Annalee waited. She pressed her mouth, admonished herself yet again to just listen when folks finally talk.

Sonny straightened his chair. "I guess you want to know who?"

Annalee blinked.

"It was our Malcolm." Sonny winced. "It was Malcolm Kane."

Annalee listened. She cocked her head. She sadly nodded. Kept nodding. *Of course.* She sighed forever. Blast it all. She'd been looking at the truth—and looking at that photo—all the livelong day, but couldn't see it. Or simply couldn't believe it. Malcolm Kane of Saxton seminary? He wasn't Malcolm Kane at all.

He was a slick imposter. Some in that war photo knew it. They'd spent every day since the war trying to hide it. Or blackmailing the imposter for their silence.

"What happened?" Annalee asked for the umpteenth time.

"We were in France . . ."

Mercy, a long story. Annalee didn't roll her eyes. Some stories are long by necessity. She set a latch on the swing so it wouldn't rock, sat back to stay quiet and hear it all. She nodded at Sonny. "Tell me."

"France can be heaven. Curious but lovely people. Everything growing and green, even in war. Nobody rushing or working too hard. Folks don't do that over there. They're just sitting in the sun. Talking, laughing, singing, drinking. Nazis or no Nazis. Nobody wanted to fight—"

"Or to die?"

"Too much of that happened. I was sixteen. I lied and said I was eighteen. Some were younger. They'd talked themselves into the Army so they could eat. But colored soldiers were treated worse than dogs. Half starved at some training camps. Couldn't get a change of clothes for months at a time."

Sonny ran down the long list of indignities. Insult after insult. Annalee had heard much of it before—segregated units, white officers refusing to salute colored, labor detail not combat. Not even valor by Negro men, when it came, was acknowledged. One white colonel, a chief of staff, made his reputation slandering Negro achievement on the battlefield—calling verified battle reports hokum, not bravery.

"Still, I made my way," Sonny said. "I met some good people from Alabama, some from Mississippi—including white men like Malcolm Kane. A fine chaplain, but not really a soldier, not at heart. Mal was a flower man. Loved flowers. He didn't want to fight a war, but his old man had called him a sissy if he didn't. Once he signed up and got to France, he determined to give the war his best—"

"A decent man."

"Then things went sour. Another guy from Mississippi started hanging around. He made me skittish because he was white, and as colored guys, we weren't supposed to fraternize with white soldiers anyway. But there we were—three of them, three of us."

"What a curious circle of friends."

"Me and my buddy, named Lil' Baby, were dirt poor. The outcasts. We never fit—so we broke away. Cooper Coates was high rent. Fancy background. He kept trying to teach colored soldiers like us how to 'get rich.' Start your own business. Man, he preached that day and night." Dawkins frowned. "Then, that Thaddeus Hammer loved crossing the color line—loved the risk, I guess. Mal Kane preached to us all, trying to save our miserable souls—"

"Who was this third white man?"

"Sam Loman. That's his name. Smooth-talking Mississippi guy. A little older than the other white men, but not an officer. Bitter to the core. A backstabber too. Life had hurt him somehow. I never found out why, but I wouldn't turn my back on him. Finally, I broke away from all of them except Lil' Baby. We'd joined up together. But we stopped hanging around the others—"

"But you were in a photo. A war photo. I saw it. Five men, arms around each other—you, Cooper Coates, Thaddeus Hammer, your friend Lil' Baby, and someone described as Mal Kane, the same man presiding at Saxton seminary now."

"Whoever wrote down those names must've wanted it to look like he *was* Malcolm Kane. In fact, Malcolm Kane—the real one—was the one who took the stupid photo." Sonny frowned. "I remember that day. How'd you happen to see it?"

"Long story—"

"I won't ask then."

"But tell me about Malcolm. The real Malcolm."

"I searched for him after the war ended—because he was a decent man. I'd started with the carnival, trying to make something of my life. But I couldn't rest. I was carrying too much on my shoulders."

Annalee studied his face. "About Lil' Baby Mack?"

"You know about him?"

"Minnie told me. They lynched him for messing with a white girl." Annalee studied his eyes. "But Lil' Baby didn't even know that girl. You knew her."

Dawkins swallowed. "Nobody should be lynched, but especially not Lil' Baby. It was me courting that girl. I was working like crazy, saving to open a colored hardware. She admired my ambition. We got to flirting. She ended up pregnant, lied about Lil' Baby to protect me—and I guess I let her. When I came to Denver and heard Malcolm Kane was a preacher here—and running a seminary—I found my way to Saxton to find him." He winced. "I needed to confess my sins. Just spill it all. Oh, I know I could pray and tell God. But I wanted to look my confessor in the eye. But who do I find? 'Malcolm Kane' is that bitter backstabber Sam Loman. From the war."

"You didn't know."

"I saw him walking across the campus. A student said, 'Oh look. There's the president, Malcolm Kane.' He heard the name, turned and smiled at the world, but saw me. Time stopped. Or felt like it. Mercy, if you could've seen that look he gave me. It was a dare like I'd never seen. Sam is running a game on folks as 'Malcolm Kane'—and his look said he'd kill to keep it a secret. Kill me. Because he'd killed before—killed the real Malcolm. I don't know how he did it, but I bet my life he killed him, so I've been on the run ever since he saw me. I faked my death—paid off the colored ambulance workers—and not even Jack knew about it. Jack thought I was dead, my body shipped back to Mississippi or God knows where."

"Instead, you disappeared for a while, then show up back in Denver. Painting churches. So, how'd you do it? Fake your death?"

"A cheap carnival trick. My version of Houdini. You store air in your stomach. Slowly release it when you need to. I'd practiced it for fun, but I used it that night. Same thing with not blinking my eyes. A silly trick I'd already practiced for fun, so I used it. Nobody was watching me much anyway. All eyes were on Big Bruno the bear."

"Weren't you fearful of him?"

"He wouldn't hurt me. I raised that bear from a cub. Anyway, the Denver Zoo is taking him. I'd arranged that beforehand."

Annalee studied his face.

"Why'd you come back, Sonny?"

"To expose Sam Loman. I thought I'd go to Saxton. Alert the papers. *An imposter's running the seminary—and he killed a good man to do it.* But nobody would listen—not to a colored 'vagrant.'

That's what they called me, an Army veteran. *Get off our property.*"
Sonny winced. "Think of that, Miss Spain. I came to shine a light,
but nobody wanted to see it."

"Jack will listen to you."

Sonny nodded. "I'm grateful for him. He saved me from killing
a white officer one night in France the last week of the war. Came
out of a crowd and got me out of a bad fight and a nasty jam.
But I've got to get my own life on track. Maybe I'll catch up with
the carnival in Kansas City. They're heading there next week. But
maybe I'm ready for something else. Start my own blasted painting
business. Main thing, I've made my peace with God. What other
people do is their business."

"Did you know Prissy Mack?"

"Who's she?"

"Somebody killed her."

Sonny narrowed his eyes. "Because she knew the secret too?
About Malcolm?"

"That's what I think."

"So the war isn't over." Sonny shook his head. "Poor Malcolm.
Sam Loman killed him dead. I'm sure of it. Then Sam stole
Malcolm's military tags and disappeared during the fog of war.
You know that term?"

"It's Prussian. I know it, yes."

"Then that no-gooder Sam came back to the States as the
esteemed Malcolm Kane."

"Sounds good, Sonny. But the family of Malcolm Kane would
discover the ruse."

"Only if he went home to his family. But he didn't go home.
I'd bet my last breath on that. Malcolm despaired of his father, the
old man. Swore he'd never go back to Mississippi. His siblings and
mother were dead. Why go back? Instead, his imposter ended up
in Denver—"

"With the help of Thaddeus Hammer. Maybe Coates too?" Annalee stood. "I've got to make a phone call."

Sonny stood too. "Don't blow my cover. Those men will kill me dead—even if I deserve it for what happened to Lil' Baby."

"This isn't about you. It's about the truth. And I agree—it needs telling."

Annalee stepped off Louise Barnes' porch. "What time is it? I've got to run. Be careful, Sonny. Stay low."

"You too."

"Don't worry about me." She smiled. "It's the bad guys who've got something big to worry about."

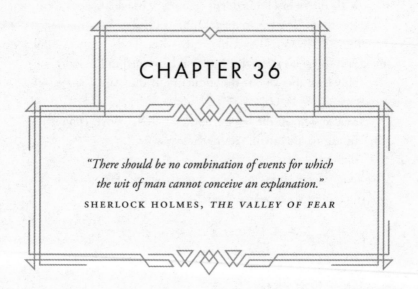

CHAPTER 36

*"There should be no combination of events for which
the wit of man cannot conceive an explanation."*
SHERLOCK HOLMES, *THE VALLEY OF FEAR*

AT THE ZION BAPTIST CHURCH, the pastor's secretary was locking
the front door. Her lunch break maybe. Annalee ran to stop her.
"Can I still make that call? I'm sorry I ran off."

The woman grinned at her. "You're a busy young lady. Pastor
Liggins likes that in a person. So yes. I'll unlock the door."

"I owe you."

"Take your time. I'll be at my desk."

Annalee pushed through the door and raced down the hall
beyond the secretary's desk. Liggins had already left for the afternoon. His office and other doors appeared locked up tight.

At the stairs, Annalee passed the church sanctuary, its double
doors locked too. But as she peered through two tiny glass windows, at the gold cross hanging in a shaft of early afternoon sun
behind the choir loft, she let herself breathe in peace.

I'm making a call, she said to herself, taking in a long breath. Then she whispered a prayer. "Let it make a difference."

She took the steps to the second-floor office. The phone was placed on the desk again. The secretary must've made order and picked it up off the floor.

Annalee grabbed the handset, knowing who to call first.

"Operator. Your number please?"

"Main 7678, please."

Annalee knew the number by heart. "Please be there, Agent Ames." Finally:

"Talk to me."

"Did you know?"

"Annalee, I know. Malcolm Kane is a fraud. He's paying blackmail to cover it. Putting trustees in compromising situations, then blackmailing them to pay his debt."

"So what are you going to do?" She crossed her arms.

"I've got even bigger fish to fry. Somebody involved with that seminary is a stone-cold killer."

"And killed Prissy Mack—"

"And the real Malcolm Kane."

"But not Thaddeus Hammer. Is that why you arrested him?"

"Not him. We hauled him in to root out the truth. Hammer is terrified of jail. He's slowly coming clean. He knew 'Malcolm Kane' was a fraud. He promoted him, however, because the so-called Kane would let Hammer indulge his worst lusts and habits. Hammer even paid off 'Kane' with his own bribes. Hush money."

"Mercy, there's no honor whatsoever among thieves." Annalee squinted. "Was Hammer the one courting Prissy like crazy? Sending flowers every five minutes, pretending they came from High Plains Floral?"

"Hammer? He says no and I believe him."

"So the fake Kane was her suitor? The one sending her flowers?"

"Roses and whatnot are growing all over the campus. He could send them easy. Is that what you think?"

Annalee shook her head. "But it doesn't add up. I heard Prissy visited Kane once but took one look at him and never went back." She paused, taking another tack. "Why was Hammer claiming Prissy was in the wrong?"

"Transferring guilt—to the victim. I see it all the time—"

"But what if there's more? What does everybody know of Hammer?"

"He's a rich womanizer."

"So what if he encountered Prissy and tried to sweet-talk her—as he's known to do. But she asked for money in exchange for her silence?" Annalee tested her questions on Ames.

"But would she do that? From what you've learned about her?"

"I'm not sure. Like what about Nathan Furness?"

"What about him?"

"He talks out of both sides of his mouth. Says one thing, then acts like another."

"Yep, it's a little hornet's nest. That seminary has a sterling reputation. But a couple of bad apples keep turning up. Several trustees are begging us to clean house."

"So that's my big question: who romanced Prissy, then probably killed her? Did Hammer tell?"

"Oh, he knows." Ames sounded certain. "But he's not saying because he's terrified. If whoever courted Prissy is the killer, he'd take Hammer down too. As for that commotion last night with the painting—why?"

Annalee swallowed. "I think I may know."

"Talk to me."

"First I have to make a phone call."

"To who? Where?"

"To Alabama. Birmingham."

"Who in the world do you know there?"

Annalee looked out the window at the setting sun. "The one with the answer."

Hanging up her call with Ames, Annalee stood in the tiny second-floor office and reflected on the call she now would make. Valerie Valentine had the answer—one of them, at least. *I got it,* Valerie's telegram declared.

Annalee prayed that she did, but not for herself. She thought, indeed, of Prissy. Of Nellie Mae Burch. Of Jack's mother. She blinked. Of her own mother. Mercy, nobody could count the untold other women—and girls too—who'd crossed paths with men's vices and villainy and ended up on the wrong end of their destiny.

How, and by whom, had that taken in poor Prissy?

From her little purse, Annalee pulled out Valerie Valentine's phone number and lifted the handset again.

"Operator. May I connect you, please?"

Annalee blinked hard and cleared her throat. "Long distance, please."

"What city, please?"

"Birmingham—Birmingham, Alabama."

As she said it, Annalee tried to imagine the place. She unfolded the telegram.

"Number, please." The operator sounded young, but efficient and professional.

"Main 3403," Annalee read from the Western Union message.

"Hold, please." The operator kept up her procedure.

Annalee waited with something she didn't have—endless patience. Outside the office window, the sun was taking its time arcing west toward the mountains. Wisps of summer clouds would later find their pink glow. The sky wouldn't be fully dark for hours—although Annalee had felt in the dark the entirety of this case.

Many shrouded minutes seemed to pass. Then finally, to her surprise, Annalee heard the marvel of a voice more than a thousand miles away.

"Hello?" Valerie's voice sounded distant and uncertain. "Main 3403? May I help you?"

"Miss Valentine?" Annalee spoke in her clearest loud voice. "Can you hear me?"

"Annalee? I know who it is." Valerie's voice sounded clear and loud now too. "In the war photo. That's not Malcolm Kane."

"Right—"

"That man is Sam."

"But who is he?"

"Remember I told you? Ol' Man Kane bought a poor man's land, underhanded. The young man he cheated was Sam Loman, who swore he'd get back at the Kanes. That's what Amos told me anyway."

"Simple revenge," Annalee whispered to herself.

"I can't hear you." Valerie broke in. "I have to go. These calls are expensive. Prissy's funeral is in the morning. We're laying her to rest. Goodbye—"

"Wait!"

"I have to go, Annalee—"

"One last question. Did Prissy know Sam?"

"I'll ask my brother."

Annalee heard muffled voices. Valerie finally returned.

"That's right. Prissy knew Sam. Maybe not by name. But she would've recognized him." Valerie paused. "Funny thing. He never looked to me like a Kane. Prissy must've seen that right away, surprised to see Sam out in Colorado."

Annalee nodded. A surprise. A deadly one too.

CHAPTER 37

To FIND OUT HOW DEADLY SAM LOMAN WAS—and when and how Prissy had encountered him at Saxton seminary—Annalee stopped on her way home at Cooper Coates' place. He was returning from taking Bullet for a walk.

Coates unleashed the dog, opened the gate to the lilac arbor, gestured Annalee inside. They sat on his ornate patio, fragrant potted plants surrounding them. Coates stroked his dog's gleaming fur. "I walk him the same time every day. Clockwork."

Annalee wasn't surprised. Whoever killed Prissy knew that.

"How long are you gone?"

"An hour. We walk thirty minutes. At the park on Twenty-Eighth Avenue, I let him chase balls for twenty minutes. Then we walk home. It takes sixty minutes."

"While you were walking Bullet, before your garden party, was anybody here?"

"Loads of people. Caterers. Waiters. The college girls practicing their music a million times. A tailor delivered a suit. He'd made alterations. Melody was here with her caretaker—her mother's elderly aunt. They probably were upstairs in the house. I put out snacks and iced tea, even sliced lemons, mint, cubes of sugar, the whole bit, for everybody."

"Did Malcolm Kane come by?"

Coates winced. "Kane avoids me."

"But did he stop by? While you were walking the dog?"

"I doubt it, but I wouldn't know."

"Do you know why I'm asking?"

Cooper Coates swallowed. "You know about him now?"

"I know he's a fraud, but more than that. I know he was paying hush money to you and maybe others. But he had to be tired of that—using seminary and ill-gotten funds—especially if Prissy wanted hush money too. Just my guess. So with Prissy's hand out, everybody's payout gets cut. Or stops. Including yours."

Coates shifted his eyes. "Clever theory."

Annalee nodded, then cut to the chase. "Did you kill Prissy, Mr. Coates?" It was a hard question, asked while sitting on the man's prettified patio—but she had to ask.

"I didn't even know her." Coates sounded truthful. "I never laid eyes on her before I saw her dead body in my potting shed."

"But why did she die there?"

"Obvious. Her killer wanted to frame me. Take the heat off himself." Coates wrinkled a brow. "Or to frame somebody else? I actually like that theory better. Your killer's slick."

"You seem to know a lot about murder. Is that why you drive around town at night, with your lights out—"

"Killing people?" He scoffed. "Late-night hours are my time

to think. I let my mind wander—about my life, work, family; my past, my present."

"Because of Melody?"

Coates pursed his mouth. "You are one smart young woman."

"Smart? I don't even know how to measure smart. But I know you have a daughter, Melody, born—"

"Conceived while I was still in France."

"Oh, Lord have mercy." Annalee shook her head. She studied the rosebushes planted around the garden. "And Sam found out?"

"Actually, the real Malcolm did. I let him read my mail one day. He was a good listener. A chaplain. So I told him that Melody's mother had died in childbirth. Her great-aunt, an old lady, wrote to tell me. I doubt she was trying to demoralize me. But in the letter, she placed a picture of little Melody, the child I didn't father."

"And Sam?"

"He had a field day with it. Told me Malcolm was making fun of me behind my back. The next time I saw Malcolm, I wanted to take his head off—until I could tell Malcolm didn't know how Sam discovered the letter. Finally I could see. Sam was doing all he could to get somebody in our 'gang' in France to have Malcolm's head. Finally one of us did."

"Who killed him, Mr. Coates? Was it Hammer? Sam himself?" She studied him. "Or did you even care?"

He shrugged. "When the war ended, over time, and we all ended up in Denver, I'm not ashamed to say I just saw an opportunity. I've been blackmailing two of them. Sam was defrauding the seminary, living as an imposter—plus, my money's on him as Malcolm's killer. Then Hammer was acting the fool with every other woman he met. So they could just send me money every month to keep me quiet. So that's what they've done. Both Sam and Hammer."

She searched his face.

"That's a crime, Mr. Coates. Blackmailing."

"Murder's worse. Besides, I used the money for good—to finance campaigns of good, solid candidates, help finance business opportunities for poor colored people trying to get a break in a cruel world, plus build a life for myself."

Coates squared his shoulders, patted his lap, gestured Bullet to lay his head on his knees. "Everything was going great, Miss Spain, until you showed up."

Annalee rolled her eyes. "Me? What on earth did I do?" But she already knew. Coates confirmed it.

"You called me out on neglecting Melody. It's not her fault how she came into this world. I'm the only parent she knows. Her aging aunt can't take care of her anymore. If I go to jail and my assets are seized, she'd be out on the street. I can't take that chance. So last week I contacted my two marks—Thaddeus and Sam—and told them the jig is up. Their money disgusts me and, confidentially, I'd started to disgust myself. I'm done with it. You can tell your Jack Blake what I've done if you'd like. He knows Melody's origins. He's helped me learn to forgive and move on."

Annalee held back a smile, but felt grateful for Jack's good pastoring. "Still, Mr. Coates, you're not home free. Blackmail truly is a crime."

He nodded. "But I don't expect to hear another word from either of them about it. It's time to put my energy into rearing Melody. I'm going to give her my best—"

"Father!" Melody ran out of the house. "You're back from walking Bullet." She noticed Annalee. "Are you staying for dinner, Miss Annalee?"

Annalee stood, accepted a hug from Melody. Bullet moved to lick Melody's hand, letting his tail swish.

"Another time, Melody. What can you cook?"

"Popcorn!" Melody laughed.

"Then we'll have that. Let me know when it's on the menu."

Annalee gave her an understanding smile, trying to stir a feeling that everything was wrapped up as far as Coates was concerned. He didn't kill Prissy or the real Malcolm Kane. Annalee felt sure of that.

But dangerous men still hadn't come to heel. She still had work to do.

Melody ran back into the house. Annalee watched her go. But she suddenly felt despair.

"Why a long face?" Coates asked.

"I'll have to tell the authorities what you've told me. About the blackmail."

Coates winced. "Even if the one person it hurts is Melody?"

"Truth will never hurt Melody. I'm sorry you didn't think of that before."

"You're preaching at me."

"That's for Jack to do—for all of us. For me too."

Coates studied her eyes. Then he stood. "Do you want to take Bullet with you tonight? A murderer is still at large."

"Maybe two murderers. I'm still not sure. But they won't be at large for long." She stroked the dog's head. "So Bullet gets a night off."

But Annalee wouldn't. Her final plan would take time—and more than some crazy luck—to pull off.

When she got home, it was after dark. Jack's car was parked outside her cabin—lit up on the front seat by a flashlight he was holding with his left hand. With his right, he was scribbling words in a small notebook, balanced on his knee. His hard hat lay on the floor.

"What are you working on?"

"I'm still a humble pastor. On Sundays, I give sermons."

"She smiled at him. He sounded weary. "May I ask your next topic?"

"It's percolating." He stifled a yawn. "But if I keep working on it . . ."

"Come inside. You're beat. I'll fix you a nice cup of—"

"Coffee. So I can stay awake and keep working."

Jack scooted out of the car, pulled Annalee behind him to the cabin door.

"Your yard looks nice," he mumbled.

She shook her head. He looked exhausted. He must've worked at the rebuilding site all day. He was still wearing jeans and a T-shirt, heavy work boots on his feet. Inside her cabin, she urged him to untie his boots and lie down on her little bed while she soaped a washcloth for him and washed her hands. She'd fix him a snack and that coffee.

"I had one crazy day," she said from her bathroom. "I've got so much to tell you—"

But before Annalee could run the water good, Jack was fast asleep. His head on her pillow, he'd curled across her summer quilt, closed his weary eyes, and was out like a light.

Annalee knelt by her bed, watching his breath rise and fall, reflecting that she'd never actually seen Jack simply asleep. Not like this. There was an intimacy to his slumber—to Jack lying across her bed, feeling so safe and secure in the little cabin with her that he'd stopped fighting his fatigue and surrendered. To her.

Love can do that, she realized.

Annalee tilted her head, surprised at her next odd thought.

Was that what happened to Prissy? With total surrender, she'd followed the person she thought loved her into Cooper Coates' potting shed, expecting a kind moment, and met instead her end?

Annalee stood up.

It was late, but she needed to honor her instincts and make a quick trip. Jack would have to understand. To answer any questions, Annalee wrote him a note and left it on her table. *I had a quick errand. Back soon.*

Then she closed and locked her cabin door, grabbed Jack's flashlight from his car, and stole away into the night.

She had urgent work to do.

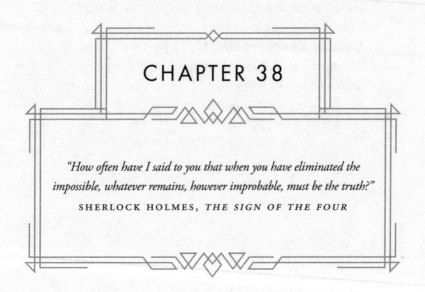

CHAPTER 38

"How often have I said to you that when you have eliminated the impossible, whatever remains, however improbable, must be the truth?"

SHERLOCK HOLMES, *THE SIGN OF THE FOUR*

TWO NIGHTS LATER, she was ready. Annalee just needed one other thing. "Change your dress," she said to Mrs. Stallworth.

"Why?" Mrs. Stallworth frowned at Annalee. It was Saturday afternoon and she had finally finished preparing the Sunday dinner for Mrs. Cunningham's rooming house lodgers.

"We're going to the carnival, Mrs. Stallworth. They're closing. Tonight's their last night."

"They can close without me."

"No, they can't. If all goes right, I'm nailing Prissy's killer there tonight, and I need a crowd for my final plan."

"I'm one little person. Not a crowd." Mrs. Stallworth turned her back, placed an apple pie in the kitchen's pie safe. At the stove, she stirred green beans and tasted one. "Not bad—"

"Mrs. Stallworth!"

Annalee's friend dropped her slotted spoon. "What in the world are you saying?"

"I'm saying that this one little person—" Annalee pointed to herself—"won't be the only one left who cares about justice for Prissy Mack."

"Well, I hear you. Mercy alive—"

"She wasn't perfect, Mrs. Stallworth. In fact, she was playing with fire—hanging around with dangerous people, including probably that no-good Thaddeus Hammer, letting him wine and dine her in private, convincing her to try blackmailing a killer." Annalee glared. "Hammer would've wanted that more than anything—Prissy blackmailing the man whose lie was a poison bringing out the worst, it seems, in so many of them."

Mrs. Stallworth stiffened and crossed her arms. "How do you know all this, Annalee?"

"Because Denver's a small town and I spent half Thursday night and all day Friday talking to the people who could help me put this case to bed."

The phone rang. Mrs. Cunningham walked into the kitchen. "It's for you, Annalee. Somebody named Mary?"

"Mary at Saxton. She must've found what I'm looking for."

"What's that?" Mrs. Cunningham looked intrigued.

"Your evidence?" Mrs. Stallworth added, suddenly sounding like Annalee.

Annalee gave them her best look. "Now you're talking. That reminds me. Mrs. Cunningham, can you ask your Hearts and Hands telephone board to call your members? Ask all available to meet at the carnival tonight? It's the last night—"

"And she needs a crowd," Mrs. Stallworth said. "For her final plan." She blinked. "We're nailing Prissy's killer."

"What time?" Mrs. Cunningham pulled a telephone list from a kitchen drawer.

"Six p.m. By seven, the place should be packed. Just what I

need." Annalee rushed to the phone. "Mary? Sorry to keep you waiting."

"I have it." Mary's whisper sounded tense.

"Did anybody see you?"

"I pray not. The campus is dead as a tomb. There's nobody in sight. The president's office was locked, but I have—"

"I hear you." Annalee broke in. "This is a party line. You've said enough. I understand."

"What time tonight?"

"Six o'clock."

"I've never been to a colored carnival before."

"Well." Annalee blinked. "First time for everything."

Annalee drove Jack's car. He'd walked earlier to see the Burch family. The children had questions for him.

"I'll see you Sunday morning," he'd told Annalee. "Bright and early." He'd searched her eyes. "And no streetcar tonight. Take my car." With a close hug, she'd agreed.

Now at the Masons', she watched Mr. Mason back Jack's Buick out of the garage and wipe it down with his special auto shine before Annalee and six people piled inside. Her passengers were Mrs. Stallworth, Mrs. Cunningham, Mr. Cunningham, Mrs. Mason, Mr. Mason, and Mrs. Louise Barnes.

"What a treat." Mr. Cunningham leaned back in the Buick's back seat, put his arm around his wife's shoulder, looking content and joyful to let somebody else drive him around. "Even on a Saturday night. I'll make up my fares another time. Hit the gas, Annalee."

She nodded, steeled herself, drove with intense attention. Her passengers seemed to be talking all at once, enjoying each other's company, not worried when Annalee once missed the clutch. Her mind, indeed, was on other things—taking care of her business at the carnival grounds.

Everything had to work like clockwork, which meant it probably wouldn't. She blinked. *Guide my feet, Jesus. And help me drive this car.*

At the carnival grounds, other packed cars were unloading passengers when they arrived.

"Park in the back," Mr. Cunningham told her. "When it's time to leave, you won't be blocked."

"Good advice." Mrs. Cunningham's voice sounded excited. The others' did too. The carnival lights did that. Twinkling and blinking in the evening sky, they teased, beckoning folks inside.

"Lock it up, Annalee." Mr. Cunningham kept giving instructions. "Ladies, hold on to your purses." Everybody laughed, but Annalee was grateful for the reminder. She grabbed her purse—her big one—and slung it over her shoulder.

At the ticket counter, they got in a long line. But it moved fast. Zimba manned the gate.

"Hey, Miss Annalee. You brought me a crowd."

"It's packed. What a night."

Her telephone call to Hearts and Hands must've set Five Points abuzz.

"We're with you!" a man called out to her, and others were giving her their thumbs-up.

Annalee answered with thanks, paid for her ticket, and bought two more for Mrs. Stallworth and Louise Barnes. "Knock 'em dead, Zimba."

"I always do. Look for my act."

But Annalee looked first for Minnie Sawyer. The wire walker wasn't on the high wire yet. Annalee pointed her friends in another direction in the meantime. They nodded, headed to the attractions, gaping at the flashing lights and greeting friends and neighbors.

Annalee headed for Minnie's little trailer, praying the sky walker was there—and ready.

At Minnie's door, Annalee knocked and whispered, "It's me." She didn't have to wait.

Minnie threw open the door. "I thought you'd never get here—"

"Wow. Look at you." Annalee could've hugged Minnie. "You look just like Milly." Annalee took in Minnie, head to toe, but saw instead her younger sister. "You're wearing her bronze. If I didn't know you, I'd think it was her."

"It's the hair. Milly loves a side ponytail. So here you have it." Minnie flipped her curly ponytail. "That's what you wanted, right?" She stepped aside. "Come on in."

"It's more than that." Annalee slipped in the trailer. "Minnie, you look altogether new—"

Annalee wanted to say more, but she froze. Minnie's trailer took her breath away. It was clean as a whistle—stem to stern. Bed made. Clothes picked up. Trunks packed. No piles of clothes, tangles of costume jewelry, nor shoes scattered about. The only thing on Minnie's corkboard was a calendar with today's date circled with two penciled words: *Final night*.

"Truly, you look made over." Annalee turned to Minnie. "Everything does."

"Well, this is a new day." Minnie sat on the armrest of a chair. "Besides, I'm ready to quit this town, Annalee. To quit the life I've been living. I need a new path. If I don't transform myself now, I might not get another chance." She studied Annalee's eyes. "So let's get on with it."

"What changed your mind?" Annalee seriously wanted to know.

"Two things. First you came out here by yourself—late on a streetcar, even after what happened to that poor colored woman last Saturday night. You pleaded for my help—flat out said you couldn't solve your case without me, no matter the cost. After you left, I sat myself down, looked myself in the mirror and asked if I'd put myself in harm's way for somebody else."

Minnie hugged herself. "Then I thought about my sister. Milly's been chasing all over town with that Malcolm Kane, trying to milk him for money—letting him use her to entrap others. That's my guess anyway. But if he's the one who killed Prissy Mack—and you think you can prove that tonight—then what would stop him from killing Milly? I couldn't live with myself if that happened."

"Did you talk to your mother?"

"I didn't have to talk to her. This is about me. That man needs to be stopped dead in his tracks. I just pray we can do it."

"I'm praying with you," Annalee whispered.

"I'm ready." Minnie stood.

"When does your act start?"

"It starts when I start it."

Annalee opened her purse. "Is it a problem for you to hold this while you're on the wire?" She held out a white business envelope with a large rose drawn in red lipstick.

"No problem. I'm not using the balance bar tonight. I'll just hold it in my shaky little hands." Minnie accepted it from Annalee. "Anything else?"

"You'll be great. Just make sure the rose is visible. Turn it toward the crowd." Annalee headed toward the door of the trailer. "Keep doing that." She set her jaw. "Then we'll catch us a killer."

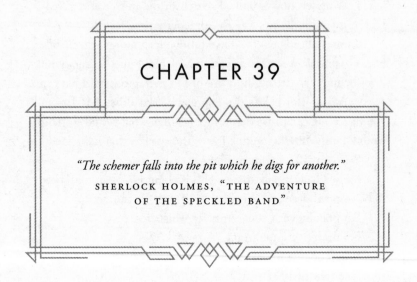

CHAPTER 39

"The schemer falls into the pit which he digs for another."
SHERLOCK HOLMES, "THE ADVENTURE
OF THE SPECKLED BAND"

ANNALEE HAD NEVER SEEN SO MANY PEOPLE pressed together in one place. Elbow to elbow, arm in arm, laughing and strolling, munching on popcorn, eating cotton candy, playing the carny games that couldn't be won.

Searching faces in the crowd, Annalee prayed like crazy to see the one man she needed in the mix—the one coming to see the closing act of the pretty acrobat he'd lured to his campus, probably one of many girls over time.

First, however, she saw Mary from Saxton. Mary had brought along the young professor from Saxton, apparently so she wouldn't be at the carnival alone. He gave Annalee a kind smile and hello.

Seeing Annalee, Mary's eyes grew wide. "I have it." She opened her purse, let Annalee peek inside.

"Perfect." Annalee gave Mary a quick hug, then grew sober. "Can you do this?"

"On my own, I can't. But I'm asking the good Lord to help me."

"I'm praying that for me, too."

They exchanged serious smiles and hugged each other again. They needed that mutual warmth when, out of the press of people, they found themselves face-to-face with the chill of the last person on earth Annalee had expected to see tonight. It was Nathan Furness.

"Ladies." He gave them each a cold nod, turned to Mary. "What a surprise to see you here. Not at work? Sorting the mail?"

Mary blinked at Annalee. "Good evening, sir."

Annalee's heart took a funny jump. What in the world was this? She'd spent the last hard day and a half orchestrating the setup of Sam Loman—to be arrested for the killing of Prissy Mack, figuring he'd believe she'd blow his cover as Malcolm Kane. But here instead in the crowd was Nathan Furness. No smiles. Slick as a cat.

He'd followed her here? Gotten wind that she was tying up the case tonight? That wasn't far-fetched. Hearts and Hands gossip could've reached him easily if he'd been out skulking around for her in the neighborhood—thinking tonight was the night she'd try to finally nail him.

Now he stood inches away, glaring at her.

The look in his eye said he'd played hide and seek with Annalee long enough. But all of it had been a charade. Making surprise visits to her cabin. Begging to hire her. Confessing his sins. Planting her lilacs. All in an attempt to keep tabs on her investigation while making himself look like a hero. Now he was ready to pounce in a deadly way. And never mind "Malcolm Kane," who tonight was nowhere in sight.

Annalee stiffened. A sick feeling gripped her stomach.

"You feeling okay, Miss Spain?" Nathan studied her eyes. He

was dressed in his elegant way, his summer whites dazzling in the midway lights.

"I've never been better." Annalee lied straight through her teeth, as her late father, Joe Spain, would've described it. "In fact, I'm going to grab a little snack. Anybody want anything?" Her voice sounded silly even to herself. A little snack? In the middle of a deadly takedown? But she needed to put distance between herself and Nathan and find her partner in crime. She whispered a grateful prayer when she saw him standing in the shadows behind the popcorn shack: Agent Ames.

"I'll go with you." Mary excused herself too, her eyes showing panic.

"Nope, stay right here with me." Nathan grabbed Mary's wrist. "It's been a while since we've talked. How are things on campus?"

Mary struggled to pull away, but Nathan held tight.

"Hey!" The young professor frowned at Nathan. "They'll be right back. You know how women are. They like consorting together." He disentangled Mary from Nathan. "I'll be waiting here when you get back, ladies." The professor gave them a strong smile.

Annalee nodded a stronger thank-you.

Mary then stuck to Annalee like glue as they pushed together through the press of people. "What's happening, Annalee? Where is Kane?"

Annalee studied the crowd. "Something tells me he isn't coming." Or going anywhere else in this life, she thought. The imposter Malcolm Kane? She felt sure he was already dead.

Ames confirmed it. He waited for Annalee to reach him.

"Talk to me." His eyes scanned the crowd.

"I blew it. I fingered the wrong man."

Agent Ames set his mouth. "I know. Our mark—'Malcolm Kane'—is stone dead. An agent just informed me. Looks like poison." He pursed his lips. "Nasty business. But don't lose focus."

"Can we play it out the same way?"

"Same thing." Agent Ames squinted at the high-wire lights. "And look. The show's about to start. Take your places."

Annalee purchased a quick popcorn, returned with Mary to find the young professor alone. Nathan had moved toward the base of the high wire. Annalee loathed that. What was he planning—and why?

Meantime, Minnie had stepped from her trailer—looking fetching and strong in her sister Milly's bronze performance outfit. At her appearance, the crowd cheered. Zimba announced her with his megaphone and followed her with his spotlight as she climbed the ladder to the high wire.

Every head at the carnival looked up. Minnie started her act, twirled on the platform, stretched a toe onto the wire, sliding herself forward—not using a balance bar, her arms out to each side, her head held high like a queen.

Minnie skipped. The crowd gasped. But the wire barely moved.

Zimba grabbed the megaphone and pumped the crowd. "What poise! No foibles or fear! Show her your love!" Wild applause.

Annalee steeled her eyes on Minnie, looked down at Nathan, looked over at Mary, and prayed that their little plan would still somehow work, even if she didn't see how. Then, it started.

Halfway across the wire, Minnie reached into her bodice and pulled out the white envelope, shifting it from hand to hand, the lushly drawn rose visible in the spotlight.

"What's that?" In the crowd, people began to question, not understanding.

But Nathan's face went white.

Annalee understood. Nathan's look revealed what she was beginning to see was true.

Nathan had drawn the rose on the envelope, sent it to Malcolm's office, placed a letter inside demanding hush money, and signed it as Prissy. Knowing the Kane family in Mississippi, Prissy knew Sam wasn't Malcolm—the idea was preposterous.

She would've revealed that to Nathan after he encountered her at the seminary. Walking across campus, she would've caught his ever-sharp eye. Who was this dainty young thing? Admiring the flowers. Tiptoeing up to rosebushes to smell them. Touching the pretty petals. Not put off when a sleek, rich-looking young man whispered a question. *"May I take you to tea?"* Flattered, she'd go with him, loving his high-class style, adoring his effusive attention.

So, Nathan courted Prissy. No, not Thaddeus Hammer, Annalee realized now. Nathan showered her with the flowers— some from gifted bouquets for his paintings, some boldly stolen from seminary gardens. Some probably from Thaddeus Hammer's fancy backyard. Then Nathan wrote her sweet notes, painted her portrait, listened amazed when she whispered to him the truth about the fake Malcolm Kane—providing a scheming Nathan the perfect motivation for cutting Malcolm out of his mother's bounty and protecting his inheritance.

But Prissy wouldn't cooperate. Sure, he was an imposter. But blackmail? Prissy wouldn't lower herself. An ugly scheme. Too common, she probably said. Too unseemly and low-rent. She'd explained her logic to Nathan, probably—smiling at him, letting him kiss her soft hands, her lovely neck, her pretty mouth, never guessing Nathan would then decide to frame Kane by getting rid of her.

Thus, Nathan lured Prissy to Cooper Coates' fancy potting shed—promising to show her the most beautiful rose in the world. *"Let's have tea in this beautiful shed,"* he would've said. He'd open a handkerchief, show her the stunning rosebud, hand her a cup of tea—tainted probably with the vile death camas weed. Then, after a moment, as she gripped at her throat, grasping vainly for air, clawing at her necklace and bruising her neck in the process—but still grasping her pretty rose—he watched her die. Her "killer," Malcolm, framed.

But Malcolm was a no-show at the party.

So Nathan must've been frantic, pointing anywhere else—at Kane, at Hammer, even at Cooper Coates—to keep anyone from seeing him for who he truly was: Prissy's killer.

Annalee glared at Nathan. What a sad, selfish monster. And what a monstrous plan.

He didn't just hate losing, as Valerie Valentine said. "He hated seeing somebody else win."

Now he'd turn on Annalee? His next mark?

But Nathan's eyes were on the high wire. A colored girl who would've looked to him like Milly Sawyer was sliding her toes across the wire in leather slippers—waving the white envelope holding Prissy's forged blackmail letter, adorned with a lushly drawn rose in a style close enough to be Nathan's.

Or so he thought. Thus, he needed that letter and envelope—now.

Annalee could see the resolve in Nathan's face. Turning into the crowd, he elbowed forward but was blocked. Almost all of Negro Denver seemed to be attending the carnival's closing tonight, including Annalee's church friends, their Hearts and Hands buddies, all their husbands, neighbors, and countless more. The crush of humanity wouldn't yield. But Nathan looked crazed with intent.

By sheer determination, he plowed his way finally to the high-wire ladder. Then, while all eyes were trained up at the cable, Nathan grabbed the ladder to the platform and shook it. Hard.

The platform shook. The wire, too. Minnie must've felt it. But she never looked down. She used the give, instead, to execute a little jump. The crowd gasped and cheered.

Frustrated, Nathan grabbed the ladder one more time, shook it again. Hard.

Minnie must've known something was wrong. But as Annalee marveled, watching Minnie with heart in throat, Minnie never looked down. She made an even higher jump, landing with one foot back on the wire, to the crowd's wild astonishment.

"Can you believe it?" Zimba was in heaven. "Look at our girl! She's best in the West!"

Not for Nathan. His fear and frustration had contorted his face, making him look almost deranged. Around him, people noticed.

"He's trying to kill her!" yelled a man in the packed crowd.

Eyes turned to Nathan—the only white man in the throng under the wire—and the crowd reacted. Angry shouts cut the air. "Stop him!"

"Oh, no." Annalee whispered, watching hands from every direction grasping for Nathan, clawing at him, determined to stop the crazed-looking white man from shaking the platform again and endangering "our girl."

"Agent Ames!" Annalee screamed. She scanned the crowd, praying to find the federal bureau man. Ames had seen the threat and was pushing his way toward the platform.

"Federal agent! Comin' through!" He held his badge above the jam of people, signaled his men for backup.

But two colored patrolmen were already plowing their way toward Nathan. Seeing them ahead, Ames yielded to their lead, following them toward Nathan—ready to help save him from himself, but arrest him too.

Annalee reached for Mary. "You okay? Stay close."

Mary looked terrified at first. Tension in the crowd was high. Racial tension. Call it what it was, Annalee said to herself. But Mary suddenly looked resolved. "I drew that rose on the envelope—like you told me. So no more shying away for me. I'll be fine."

In fact, the crowd had gone silent because Nathan had started climbing the ladder to the high wire.

"He's going up!" a woman yelled.

Zimba aimed the spotlight on Nathan, who didn't seem to notice. He just kept climbing higher and higher, finally reached the platform three stories up, and stepped one foot onto the wire.

"Give it to me!" Nathan yelled at Minnie. She reacted a split second but didn't turn. Head still high, she kept toeing the wire, waving the white envelope, taking herself with haste across the cable—moving toward the red painted dot on the opposite side.

Nathan knelt and grabbed the wire, started shaking it.

One of Ames' men blew a shrieking whistle. "Stop! We're the law!"

The colored patrolmen blew their whistles too.

Nathan ignored it all, yelled louder at Minnie, slid his foot farther on the cable, pushing down to make it bounce and knock her off. He yelled again.

Minnie surely felt the wire's movement, but she never looked down. Instead, as Nathan threw his body fully onto the wire—making some mad attempt to reach Minnie while also escaping the cops and crowd below—Minnie trained her eyes on a red painted circle on the opposite end of the platform and moved to it without once turning back or stopping.

"Give it to me!" Nathan screeched.

But doing a final twirl, Minnie reached the opposite platform, waved the envelope at the audience, made a deep bow, and stood upright with a triumphant smile, her head still high, her bronze outfit gleaming in Zimba's spotlight. She yanked at her ponytail ribbon, letting her hair go free. The crowd cheered.

Just as quickly, however, they gasped.

Nathan Furness was falling.

Annalee would've expected a three-story fall off a high wire to look like a scene from a moving picture, where time is slowed to a crawl and a body takes forever and a day to drop.

Instead, Nathan Furness fell in a wild, ireful flash. He hit the ground like a rock.

Agent Ames and the patrolmen raced to where he fell, standing around him. One of the men turned back, urged the crowd to please back up.

"Do you have a stretcher?" the patrolman yelled to Zimba.

Zimba nodded. They had a stretcher, indeed.

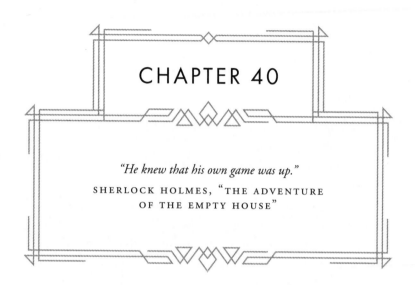

CHAPTER 40

"He knew that his own game was up."
SHERLOCK HOLMES, "THE ADVENTURE
OF THE EMPTY HOUSE"

NATHAN FURNESS WASN'T DEAD. Perhaps in this curious case, Annalee thought, enough dying had happened. Instead, he was a broken mess. Guilty as sin, too. Sprawled on the ground—his body crushed in countless places—he looked Ames in the eye and whispered, "I did it. I killed Prissy Mack."

He would later blame the fake Malcolm for starting the trouble. Everyone's. "That's why I killed him, too," Nathan said. "Why should he live when my darling Prissy couldn't?" Then he shuddered a sigh and cried.

Ames told Annalee this after the ambulance raced Nathan away.

The accident hadn't closed the carnival early. Instead, to Annalee's surprise—or maybe not—the throng of people remained on the carnival grounds 'til all hours, still riding rides, still buying popcorn, still marveling at Zimba "eating" fire, still playing carny games they couldn't win.

Annalee, however, went home. She first made Minnie promise to send an update on her new life. "You're done with the high wire?" she asked her.

Minnie offered an odd smile. "Crazy thing is, maybe not. I'm actually good on a cable."

Annalee smiled and gave her a hug. "So true, Minnie. I'll look for you in the papers."

After urging her friends to stay and enjoy the evening, Annalee drove Mary and the young professor to their homes. Mary had given Agent Ames the real envelope holding Nathan's forged blackmail letter "from Prissy." Ames grabbed it with a handkerchief and placed it in a brown folder. Its fingerprints would show who had touched it—Sam, Mary Brown, and Nathan Furness. The lipstick used to draw the rose would turn out to belong to Nathan's ex-Welcome Ambassador, Stella.

Same for the black patent shoes that Nathan had given to Prissy, further tying him to Valerie Valentine's precious murdered niece. The soles were worn because poor Prissy must've walked all over town, meeting Nathan at secret rendezvous places—him not willing to pick her up in his car and risk being seen.

All this was too much to juggle in her amazed and still jittery mind, Annalee told herself. Despite some wrong steps, she'd helped solve Prissy's murder and nab the killer. She'd get back Prissy's locket now, understanding it would be at dead Malcolm's—that he was the one who'd ransacked her cabin inside and stolen it, looking for the photo—warned about it by a panicky Cooper Coates. Nathan, on that same night, would've violently trashed her yard outside, trying to frighten her off the case.

But that yard was a haven now. She was ready to sit by herself on her tiny porch in the moonlight, watch the shooting stars, quiet her heart, reflect on the discovery of truth in every human's life, and its urgency to be told.

Thus, back on her little porch, Annalee was surprised by a humble metal box waiting beside her door. It was rusty and dirty—like the box she'd buried in her garden—because that's what it was. The same box. A message under it said *High Plains Floral*. Annalee frowned, confused.

She read over the message. *This box got dug up when I did your yard work. Then it got put on the truck for three days under my tools. Sorry I'm just returning it. May God bless you always. Mr. Leroy.*

Annalee looked up at a cloudless sky. *Tonight, Lord?*

On this night, when she'd pulled the veil off another colored girl's hard truth, here was destiny demanding she look again at her own. To her surprise, she wanted Jack here with her now. That's what he'd tried to tell her. They needed each other, being together for all that life tried to throw at them. She had secretly longed, instead, for her mother to be the one who would be her all. Now here was her poor mother in a torn-up letter, awaiting her in a rusty box that wouldn't stay buried—telling her not good mothering things, but that she didn't know what being a mother meant.

I wish I knew how, but I never had nobody mother me. Maybe you can fix that broken line.

Annalee's hands shook as she picked up the bits of paper to piece them together, like the puzzle of a mystery, so she could read it all again.

Underneath the besieged note was a tarnished locket on a cheap, silver-colored chain.

Annalee held it in her hands a long time. Something finally helped her open it.

Inside was a tiny, faded photo showing the face of a young colored woman—big, luminous dark eyes—glancing coy over her slim shoulder, wild curls askew, trying her best not to smile. Looking at it seemed, to Annalee, like looking in a mirror. Her

breathing stopped. The torn-up letter awaited. She bent over it in
the dark, let the moon shine on the paper so that she could read it.

*My name is Jane. I guess you been looking for me. I suppose
I'm your mother—*

A sob tried to destroy Annalee. She didn't indulge it for long.
Finally she held it back. Then she kept reading.

*I took a train up to Denver. That's what folks been doing. I
couldn't last down there in Carolina or Alabama. Mississippi
neither. So I came out west to Colorado. Awful pretty up here.*

Annalee swallowed. Jane was still in Colorado? But that seemed
unlikely. The letter looked decades old.

*Didn't know I was having no baby. Riding all over these
mountains. Joking with the miners. Teasing with the
wranglers. Then next thing I knows, my tummy swells up
big and, in the dead of winter, here you comes. Pretty little
thing. But what I do with a baby? Or being a mother. I wish
I knew how, but I never had nobody mother me. Maybe you
can fix that broken line.*

*Some peoples say they knowed a family that would take
you. But when they seen you they didn't want no colored child.
They left you in the hills I guess, but a colored man named Joe
found you. That's what I was told. I'm glad he took you in.
Must be a good man. I'm sending this letter to him. But no
need to look for me. I'm going further west. California maybe.*

*I'm sorry I wasn't right by you. Forgive me anyway. I know
you making me proud.*

Signed, Jane

No last name.

Annalee sat on her porch, in the dark, for the longest of long times. She bit her stupid trembling lip. In her Sherlock stories, when truth comes, it's at the end of a long, clever, dramatic search. But in real life, truth can fall on your head in half a minute, ready or not. As Holmes had said, "Any truth is better than indefinite doubt."

Annalee had wanted to discover this in a different way, maybe with Jack at her side—watching a veil pulled away from her beginnings, revealing a sweet and beautiful story.

Instead, here was this rusty box. There, inside, was the truth of her mother. Her Jane. No last name.

So Annalee spoke to her Jane.

"It's getting chilly, Mother. Let's go inside."

On her little shelf, Annalee dusted the spot where her stolen first-aid kit had sat and set down the rusted metal box so it wouldn't fall off. Next to it, she lit a candle. She watched it burn to its end.

The tears on her face got wiped away. Then Annalee made Jane a promise.

"I will make you proud." She set her shoulders, thinking of Prissy Mack and Nellie Mae Burch and Naomi Day and countless others like them—in the brutal past and perhaps still to come— who might need her humble help. She'd try to be in their corner. That was her truth. To herself. And to Jane. So she closed her eyes and thanked God for watching over her all these years—anyway. She curled up under her summer quilt. A scent of Jack lingered on her pillow. She inhaled him in. Then she told herself good night.

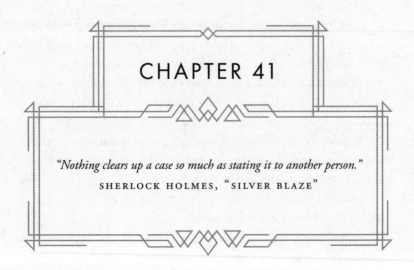

CHAPTER 41

"Nothing clears up a case so much as stating it to another person."
SHERLOCK HOLMES, "SILVER BLAZE"

JACK'S MORNING SERVICE WAS PACKED, even though many there had probably been out late at the carnival the night before. But it was a sparkling Sunday morning, or trying to be. So they were in church.

Annalee saw Jack notice her on her pew, in her usual place on the aisle. While the choir sang before he preached, he held her gaze. She gave him her best look back. Jack smiled. Annalee didn't know what that meant. He rarely acknowledged her from the pulpit. But she didn't worry. She just knew she couldn't wait to talk to him after service.

For now, however, she listened to his brave, lovely Scripture for the morning, his deep, young man's voice barely a whisper.

The LORD is my light and my salvation; whom shall I fear? the LORD is the strength of my life; of whom shall I be afraid?

He looked over his congregation, held their attention.

When the wicked, even mine enemies and my foes, came upon me to eat up my flesh, they stumbled and fell.

Though an host should encamp against me, my heart shall not fear: though war should rise against me, in this will I be confident.

Jack read the entire psalm. Annalee closed her eyes to listen. When she opened them to hear Jack preach, she was surprised to see an usher standing by her pew. With a gloved hand, he pointed her one seat over to make room for a latecomer. She stood to move; then her knees sank.

George Washington Carver was standing there, beaming at her. He scooted onto the pew.

"You're back, sir?" she whispered.

"Just for a moment," he whispered. "I'm on my way to Chicago. I stopped by to find you, asked for you by name."

She looked up at Jack, hoping he'd see this special guest, stop his sermon to acknowledge the humble scientist. But Jack was preaching now as with thunder—deep in his message that, with God, we should never be afraid. "We're always on his heart and mind. Don't ever doubt it!"

"Amen!" Professor Carver cried out. He closed his eyes a moment, then leaned to Annalee. "You solved your mystery, Miss Detective? I feel sure of it." He smiled at her. "Your garden too?"

He sounded so certain. So Annalee whispered, "Actually, it's solved, yes." She searched his kind eyes, thinking of Prissy, but also

Jack's mother, Naomi, and her mother, Jane. "With godly help," she added.

Carver pulled the pink posey from his buttonhole and placed it in her hand. She whispered a grateful thanks and then threaded the lovely little flower in her hair.

He nodded approval.

"I must go," Carver whispered lower. "But if you're ever in Alabama, stop by and say hello."

He squeezed her hand. Then he turned up the aisle and melted away.

Jack spoke the last two verses of the Twenty-Seventh Psalm to end his sermon:

"'I had fainted,' dear church." He looked across his congregation. "'Unless I had believed to see the goodness of the Lord in the land of the living.' So, 'wait on the Lord: be of good courage, and he shall strengthen thine heart: wait, I say, on the Lord.'"

In the pews, the congregation was affirming him—many moaning, crying, declaring, even shouting, "Amen."

Annalee stood and joined the choir and people around her as they sang the closing hymn, "Ride On, King Jesus." Jack's benediction sounded more confident than she could recently recall. She tilted her head, watching him as he stepped from the pulpit and walked with assurance up the middle aisle.

But on this Sunday, he stopped at Annalee's pew. He reached out his hand to seek hers, held it as he led her from her pew and continued walking.

The warmth and strength of his hand assured her that this gesture was right and good. It told everyone in the sanctuary how much the two trusted one another, especially in an often cruel world. So Annalee held on tight, accepting this declaration of her, but also of them—as people fighting in the world, each in their own way, and being in love in the world, together.

Watching them, the congregation released whispers from pew

to pew. Then a church trustee suddenly shouted, "That's alright, pastor!"

Others then joined him. "Alright! Go ahead now, Blake! Amen! Amen!"

Annalee departed from the sanctuary with Jack, surprised that, at the end of the aisle—in the narthex—she let him embrace her.

"Your case is closed," he said in her ear. "That's well-done."

"Both cases." She stepped back. "Jack, I found my Naomi Day."

He searched her eyes, ignoring the bustle of departing church members, some now giving them both their warm regards, showing their approval.

"Your mother?" he whispered to Annalee. "You found her?"

"She found me. I promise to tell you how." Annalee blinked. "Her name is Jane."

He touched the posey in her hair. "'God is gracious.' A perfect name for a garden."

"May I grow one with you?"

He hiked a brow, held her gaze a long time. "That sounds like a proposal," he finally said. "May I ask you the same?"

"Will it mean another case? For the two of us?"

"I'm still ready. Are you?"

She nodded at him, smiled as he held her face in his hands, then whispered to herself the same brave, conquering words. "Amen. Amen."

A NOTE FROM THE AUTHOR

WONDERFUL READERS! Thank you so much for following Annalee into this third installment of her mystery adventures in *Truth Be Told*. It offered me much truth to explore—including even the meaning of Annalee's middle name, Jane. It means "God is gracious." Derived from the old French name Jehanne, it was further derived from the Hebrew name Yochanan, which means "Yahweh is merciful."

It's a compelling concept to consider, especially regarding God's handiwork in this mystery—including the beautiful rose that played an enthralling role. Wildly beautiful and deeply fragrant, the flower acknowledged the roses of my youth—when "a rose, by any other word," as Shakespeare wrote in the play *Romeo and Juliet* (and which often is misquoted), "would smell as sweet."

In today's era, fragrant roses seem rare because commercial flowers are bred for disease resistance, but the durability gene and fragrance gene in roses aren't compatible, and fragrance loses out. Floral experts predict another ten years could pass before commercial roses offering both disease resistance and lovely fragrance make it to market.

My story's gardening themes were deployed, meantime, to sweeten the travail of social circumstances reflected in the story, including what's known as the Great Migration—when some six million African Americans, between 1915 and 1970, fled the Jim Crow South for kinder horizons up North but met equally harsh attitudes and dangers.

Driving the white backlash was a supremacy preached from even the White House. In President Andrew Johnson's 1867 annual message to Congress, he claimed that Black Americans had "less capacity for government than any other race of people" and would "relapse into barbarism" unless controlled by their white superiors. Giving Blacks the vote, he stressed, would result in "such a tyranny as this continent has never yet witnessed."

Black citizens were portrayed as inhuman, lowly, and criminal—enemies of civility, if not of God himself, worthy of only the worst treatment. The goal? To keep Black citizens "in their place," a practice of racial and social segregation ordained by the Supreme Court itself in the *Plessy vs. Ferguson* ruling of 1896. (Growing up and seeing *Whites Only* signs as a child is an experience seared into my own memory.) Harsh constraints were also economic. Denied bank loans to acquire farms after the Civil War, many Blacks were trapped in the Southern system of sharecropping, renting land while "owing back" for seeds, fertilizer, and food—never earning enough to get free.

The resulting poverty was crushing, leaving millions of Black families trapped in debt for generations—threatened with violence and even murder if they considered fleeing.

For deeper understanding of this time, I studied migration narratives compiled by journalist Isabel Wilkerson in her riveting book *The Warmth of Other Suns: The Epic Story of America's Great Migration.*

Her story felt personal because both my parents joined the migratory millions—my father (a decorated U.S. Army veteran) leaving Mississippi and also Missouri, and my mother (a physical education teacher) heading to Colorado with him from North Carolina after World War II.

To advance such Black "uplift," the Negro women's club movement burgeoned during the migration years—as did civic club life for African American men. In *Truth Be Told*, my fictional Hearts and Hands club is modeled after my late mother's beloved church women's group in Denver, the Ever Ready Club at Cleaves Memorial CME Church, my childhood church. (Mama also was a proud member of the Denver chapters of two notable Negro women's clubs—the Links, Incorporated and Jack and Jill of America, Inc., and in college joined Alpha Kappa Alpha Sorority, Incorporated, founded at Howard University.)

One's social status was often defined, in fact, by club membership, a phenomenon I took a risk to explore in *Truth Be Told*. A kind of Black elitism had developed among some successful Black professionals and entrepreneurs—with certain clubs and even certain churches holding higher status as aspirational, struggle defined Black civic life as much as a fervent fight for racial justice.

What were other truths I dared to explore in *Truth Be Told*? They included:

- The sadly commonplace sexual exploitation of vulnerable young women by powerful men—and the pushback on such behavior, known today as the Me Too Movement as revealed in books such as *She Said: Breaking the Sexual Harassment Story That Helped Ignite a Movement* by journalists Jodi Kantor and Megan Twohey.

- The bigotry of Denver's 1920s police department, which, by 1924, was infiltrated by the Klan, whose members included Denver Police Chief William Candlish—a Grand Dragon of the KKK. During his tenure, which ended in 1925, ledgers show that at least fifty-three Denver police officers were members of the Klan. A fierce contingent, some were known to carry hardwood billy clubs with leather-covered lead weights attached to the top—a contraption so potentially deadly and damaging that they're no longer used by most police departments in America.

- The scourge of lynching—which took the lives of thousands of Americans, most of them Black, without due process of law. In the South, an estimated two to three Black citizens were lynched in mob violence each week in the late nineteenth and early twentieth centuries, cheered on by crowds that even included children. In Mississippi alone, five hundred Blacks were lynched from the 1800s to 1950, according to the Equal Justice Initiative, and some argue lynchings in that state have not stopped.

  Nationwide, the figure climbed to nearly five thousand, reported the PBS resource American Experience, targeting Blacks "deemed 'uppity' or 'insolent,'" or for "activism" such as trying to register Black voters or support Black business growth, or just hooligan menace.

  Violating white womanhood, however, provoked especially horrifying terror.

  In Colorado, on November 16, 1900, a fifteen-year-old Black teenager named Preston "John" Porter Jr. was burned alive while chained to a railroad stake in the town of Limon, after being accused without evidence of killing a white girl. When his body fell partially from the stake, kerosene oil was poured on him again to reignite the fire. A mob of more than three hundred cheered the spectacle.

  Lynching provoked fierce opponents, including Black journalist Ida B. Wells, who was forced to abandon her newspaper office in Memphis when it was torched.

For relief from such terror in *Truth Be Told*, I offered inspiration from the enthralling life of agricultural scientist and inventor George Washington Carver. Born into slavery, he evolved into a charming, homespun, pioneering botanist whose self-effacing personality was as legendary as his work with the peanut—just one of hundreds of plants, trees, and flowers whose traits and characteristics he studied, painted, and shared over a remarkable lifetime of international renown.

Time magazine, in 1941, declared him a "Black Leonardo"— a stark contrast to his birth, about 1864, to an enslaved young woman in Diamond Grove, Missouri. Roving slave raiders kidnapped both of them when he was a weeks-old infant. They'd failed to extort money from Carver's enslaver—a German immigrant named Moses Carver. So the raiders abducted the infant George and his mother, selling them in Kentucky. Moses Carver persuaded a neighbor to travel South and return them, but the neighbor could only find the child, trading him for one of Moses Carver's best horses valued at three hundred dollars. From that day, George Washington Carver never saw his mother again.

Back in Missouri, the child and his older brother were raised by Moses Carver and his wife on their homestead, letting the often sickly younger boy, George, pursue his passion for growing, studying, and painting flowers.

Carver would become the first Black student at Iowa State Agricultural College (now Iowa State University) in Ames, and later its first Black faculty member. A conservationist intent on helping "the man farthest down," Carver finally took a teaching position at Tuskegee University in Alabama, where he traveled back roads to teach impoverished Southern farmers to rotate their crops—growing soil-enhancing, protein-rich plants such as soybeans and peanuts, breaking their dependence on single-crop cotton farming. On another front, Carver testified before Congress in 1921 to support a proposed tariff on imported peanuts, among other extensive speaking and lecturing (although I found no record of him speaking in Denver).

Less known is Carver's impassioned love for the humble Christ, his practice of daily Bible study and prayer, and his dependence on God's direction for all his horticultural research.

With Annalee's story involving a murder in a garden, I took a risk to weave Carver into this third novel. Many of the quotes I attribute to him are from the plethora of biographies, articles, essays, and other material published about and by him, though in some cases I stretched the timing of when those materials were published for the sake of story.

All these various elements found their way into *Truth Be Told*. As the protagonist of the series, Annalee Spain continues to press through the challenges of being a young Black woman in an adverse environment while also trying to fight and solve crime. Softening that hard road is her ongoing relationship with her beloved close friends and of course, her deepening romance with the Rev. Jack Blake. Thank you for joining them on their valiant journey!

ACKNOWLEDGMENTS

WHEN IT COMES TO BRINGING A BOOK INTO THE WORLD, scores of amazing people deserve thanks. But where to start? For *Truth Be Told*, my acknowledgments start with readers. From book clubs to library patrons to bookstore customers, readers of the Annalee Spain Mysteries have lifted, cheered, and inspired this book and its series in countless and remarkable ways. In particular, my warmest thanks and regards to these inspiring book club hosts in Colorado and beyond:

Yvonne Parker and Debbie Verhoeff at Affinity at Copperleaf, Jennifer Ford Keel and Joslyn Ford Keel with Denver Alumnae Chapter of Delta Sigma Theta Sorority Inc., Faye Rison with Delta Dears of Delta Sigma Theta Sorority Inc. (Denver Deltas), Kathy Jackson with Theta Zeta Sigma Chapter (Rhoers Colorado) of Sigma Gamma Rho Sorority Inc., Lynn Zeller of Arno Book Club (Pinehurst Country Club), Lee Everding and Jessica Jones with Denver Eclectics, Helen Gray, Georgia Tatum, Rhonda Marshall, Donna Fahrenkrug, Harriet Hogue and Linda Murray with the Pauline Robinson Book Club, Velveta Golightly-Howell and John Howell, and Bobbie Harbert with Sister-to-Sister: International Network of Professional African American Women, Inc., Wherda Utsey with Campbell A.M.E. Church (Denver), Master Gardener

Betty Jacobs, Linda Gibson, Constance Williams, Sandra Fish, the Rev. Stephanie Price, Claudia Holland, Sandra Kelly, and Meghan Gagliano.

Speaking of book friends, my kindest thanks also to every subscriber of my email Readers' Circle, whose members range from readers across the U.S., Canada, Australia, and Iceland. Special book friends in that group include Lisa Kewish and Lauren Wilhoite-Willis.

Among librarians, a special shout-out to Jamal Rahming of Wilmington Public Library in Delaware; Brittany Robinson, James "Mr. Jim" Ramsey, and Shelly Stash of Denver Public Library; Jen Degen of Douglas County Libraries; Brian Matthews of Pikes Peak Library District; and Emma Hunter of the Mission Viejo branch of Aurora Public Library.

Church friends to the Annalee Spain Mysteries include Shorter Community A.M.E. Church, Highlands United Methodist Church, Lowry Community Christian Church, and Campbell A.M.E. Church and its "Coffee with Authors" program.

My kindest thanks also to these amazing podcasters, broadcasters, and bloggers: Steve Chavis; Jim Walker (Dr. Daddio); Anna Randell, Joy Groblebe, and Becky Keife of (in)courage; Judith Briles; Laura Padgett; Amy Julia Becker; Terri Gillespie; Emily Humphries; Chautona Havig; Natasha Sistrunk Robinson; KyLee Woodley and Darcy Fornier; Dorina Lazo Gilmore-Young; Rebecca Maney; Lisa Q. Mathews and Chicks on the Case; Carly Stevens; and Katherine Scott Jones.

Educators and community leaders who've supported my Annalee Spain journey include the Rev. Dr. Teresa Fry Brown, Janice Satchell, Dewayne Robinson, Michelle Warren, Joanna Meyer, Midian Holmes, Scott Lundeen, and Robert Gelinas.

Major thanks also to wonderful bookstore friends of Annalee Spain, including Baker Book House and Chris Jager, West Side Books, and the amazing Barnes and Noble book family in Colorado including Janice, Milinda, Milan, Randall, Diana, Joe, Mike (who made his store's *Double the Lies* display), Lauren, and Zuzana.

My greatest thanks, as well, to these author friends, film directors, photographers, and writer advocates including: Jermain Julien, Kia Stephens, Joyce Dinkins, Katara Patton, Jenny Errlingson, Kerrie Anderson, Rebecca Maney, Sandra Dallas, Povy Kendal Atchison, Jeff Crosby, Cindy Carter, Sandra Byrd, Jennifer L. Wright, Anna Lee Huber, Robin W. Pearson, Piper Huguley, Amy Julia Becker, Xochitl Dixon, Susie Finkbeiner, Kate Holbein Rademacher, Brian Allain, Angela January, Marty Meitus, Patti Thorn, Toni Shiloh, Jamie Lapeyrolerie, Elisa Morgan, Carla Foote, Tim Gustafson, Stephanie Landsem, Leslie Leyland Fields, Mary Taylor Young, Michele Cushatt, Traci L. Jones, Dorena Williamson, Janet Singleton, Gina Dalfonzo, Lesa Engelthaler, and the entire INK family.

In a special category are two people who have helped bring Annalee Spain to life: Ford model Wanaki Shores-Navata, who portrays Annalee Spain on the cover of the Annalee books, and audiobook narrator Zakiya Young, the actress extraordinaire who gives voice to the Annalee stories. Beautiful women, I give you my warmest thanks.

To my Tyndale publishing team, please know you bless me every step on the book journey, especially my acquisitions editor Stephanie Broene, story editor Sarah Mason Rische, and our publisher Karen Watson, along with Lindsey Bergsma, designer of the gorgeous Annalee Spain book covers, marketing guru Andrea Garcia, publicity manager Isabella Graunke, author advocates Andrea Martin and Wendie Conner, and supporters in editorial, sales, and marketing, including Elizabeth Jackson, Shelley Bacote, and Cassidy Gage.

In my beloved church family, my kindest thanks to every single "Shorter Church member" along with our pastor, the Rev. Dr. Timothy E. Tyler, First Lady Dr. Dwinita Mosby Tyler, the

Rev. Naomi Harris, the Rev. Alan Pettis, the Rev. Greg Miller, the Rev. Dr. Carolyn Smith, the Rev. Michael Gallant, the Rev. Andrew Midgyett, and the Rev. Tanya Davis Ezidinma.

My immediate family, of course, helps me beyond measure. I owe particular thanks for their early support of *Truth Be Told*—especially for early readings and input from my biggest cheerleader, my husband Dan Raybon, and my ever-ready sister Dr. Lauretta Lyle and sister-in-law Diana Rochon. Wonderful thanks to everyone in my family, from the youngest to the oldest, for your enthusiastic support—providing everything from tweets and shares to posts and likes, kindness and help—including to my amazing daughters Joi and Alana and their families, my always affirming son-in-law Paul, brothers-in-law, nephews, nieces, cousins, and every loving kin-circle friend.

For each of you named here throughout these acknowledgments, and for the joy Annalee and her story give me, I thank my God.

DISCUSSION QUESTIONS

1. At the beginning of *Truth Be Told*, Annalee finds something potentially life-changing in her garden but, unable to face it yet, reburies it. Has there ever been a time when you've avoided facing a hard truth, even for a little while?

2. How much did you know about historical figure George Washington Carver? What does his presence in the story mean to Annalee?

3. Themes of truth and illusion run throughout *Truth Be Told*. Where do you see these at play at Cooper Coates' garden party? At Sonny Dawkins' carnival? At Saxton seminary?

4. Still reeling from witnessing the murder of a young Black woman, Annalee questions whether God is truly with her, and with her community. How would you respond to her doubts?

5. Jack preaches a sermon to his congregation about hope, concluding, "We hope with our boots on." How would you describe what it means to hope with boots on?

6. When Nathan Furness brings a lilac plant to Annalee, claiming he wanted to do something after the death of Nellie Mae Burch, she challenges him by saying, "You want to help colored people in Denver? To help me? Then help run the Klan out of town. Tell the mayor to cancel his membership. Campaign against the KKK candidate for governor. . . . Nathan, hire some colored people." Do you agree with her suggestions? In today's world, how can those in a position of privilege best use their influence to improve conditions for others?

7. Annalee's young orphaned friend Eddie Brown longs for a family. Is the Watkins family a good solution? Would Jack and Annalee be better, if the law allowed them to adopt Eddie?

8. Valerie Valentine looks back on everything she's done to rise above her past and break into high society, ultimately wondering what the point of it all was. Jack responds, "The point? . . . To God, you were always enough. We all are. The lie is that we aren't." Do you believe that you are enough in God's eyes, just as you are? Have there been times in your life when you believed otherwise?

9. Throughout the story, Annalee is introduced to several young Black women in danger of falling through the cracks of society—Prissy Mack, Minnie Sawyer, Nellie Mae Burch, Jack's mother, even her own mother. How does she work to keep each of them from being lost or forgotten?

10. Which twists and turns in Annalee's investigation came as the biggest surprise to you? Were you surprised by the identity of Prissy's killer? What were your feelings about what Annalee learns from the letter buried in her garden?

ABOUT THE AUTHOR

PATRICIA RAYBON is a Christy Award–winning author, essayist, and novelist who writes at the daring intersection of faith and race. A former Sunday magazine editor at the *Denver Post*, Patricia's personal essays have been published in the *New York Times Magazine*, *Newsweek*, *USA Today*, *USA Weekend*, *Guideposts*, *In Touch* magazine, *Christianity Today*, the *Washington Post*, and for National Public Radio's *Weekend Edition*. She's also a regular contributor to the global ministry *Our Daily Bread*.

Her first fiction, the Annalee Spain Mysteries, features a young Black theologian—a fan of Sherlock Holmes—solving crime in Colorado's dangerous 1920s Ku Klux Klan era. The series' debut title, *All That Is Secret*, won a Christy Award for first novel and was picked by NBA All-Star Stephen Curry as his Literati Book Club selection for Women's History Month in March 2022.

Her nonfiction books include two notable memoirs: *My First White Friend: Confessions on Race, Love, and Forgiveness*, a winner of the Christopher Award, and *I Told the Mountain to Move: Learning to Pray So Things Change*, a 2006 Book of the Year finalist in the *Christianity Today* magazine annual book competition.

An award-winning feature writer during her years at the *Denver Post* and the Scripps Howard newspaper *Rocky Mountain News*,

Patricia joined the journalism faculty at the University of Colorado at Boulder midcareer as an associate professor where she taught undergraduate and graduate students for fifteen years before her promotion to professor emerita. Now writing full-time, she also teaches at writing conferences and workshops nationwide.

A lifelong Colorado resident, Patricia and her husband, Dan, a retired educator, are longtime members of the historic Shorter Community A.M.E. Church in Denver. Their extended family includes two grown daughters, a son-in-law, and five grandchildren who share their passion for movies, popcorn, college hoops, and historical dramas and mysteries on Masterpiece on PBS. Join her Readers' Circle at patriciaraybon.com and get a free copy of her prayer download, "The Busy Person's Guide to Hearing God."

Connect with Patricia online at
PATRICIARAYBON.COM